The

Sinners

~ ~

Elizabeth Flaherty

ISBN: 0615609678
ISBN-13: 978-0615609676

www.flahertybooks.com

From Little B's Briefcase

DEDICATION

To the "team." Your comments, criticisms and patience
made this possible. I am truly blessed to be surrounded by
people who make me better at what I love to do.

And in a special way, I need to thank
MLR, MFM, MFB, MFA/P, and MFCs.
Your love and support have made me the person I am today.

When God, in the beginning, created man, he made him subject to his own free choice....

Before man are life and death, whichever he chooses shall be given him.

SIRACH, 15:14, 17

~ ~

Like a spire, a solitary woman rose from the barren desert landscape. Icy ocean waters seeped from her pores, dripping from her fingertips onto the parched land. Her appearance defied nature, just as her presence defied the natural order.

She was the first to set foot on the spot in centuries. The scorching heat and relentless drought made existence there intolerable. In a world where millions of people crammed into cities and surrounding suburbs, this remote section of land was a uniquely perfect choice.

The nearest town to the south lay fifty miles away. Thirty miles to the north was a small Navajo reservation. The roadway between the two was traveled most frequently by coyotes, deer, and fleeing jackrabbits.

She stood in the vast emptiness, waiting in silence for its coming. At first there was only a rumble, like thunder from the earth itself, but it grew into a vibration that she could feel at her very core.

Several miles away, on the shoulder of the deserted highway, a billboard materialized on command. Images promised beauty and tranquility, advising drivers they could find all they were looking for just up ahead.

Five hundred yards from there, a smaller sign emerged from the ground, pointing to a gravel road that was slowly rising to the surface.

The narrow but distinct drive wound away from civilization, rising and falling sharply with the landscape, gradually leading to a point lower than the main road – a barren spot of land, a few miles to the east, tucked in an abnormal little valley.

At the woman's feet, grass began to sprout, covering almost an acre on either side. The green seedlings rose and merged into a lush carpet of grass, unnatural amid the desert landscape. The picturesque surroundings provided the ideal setting for the final piece.

Beneath the grass, with a final shudder and a predatory growl, the ground broke away and an enormous structure arose – a southern style mansion, with imposing columns and ornate entryways.

Peccavi, as the hotel would be called, was designed with every imaginable amenity, catering to the specific needs of its very specific clientele. The décor, colors, furniture, and paintings in each of its seven suites were carefully chosen for its predetermined guest.

The sodden woman stood in the drive and admired the creation. The only telltale sign of the hotel's origin was a crusty coat of dust and clay from the depths that had formed it, but it took her only a moment to remedy that. A violent storm swirled in the valley, all but invisible to the highway above. Gusts of wind and teeming rain cleansed the building, grass, and drive. When the storm passed, Peccavi stood ready – a gleaming new hotel, beckoning visitors to come, and stay for a very long time.

She had promised seven guests. Seven worthy inhabitants. For her, the guest list was obvious, as were the methods to lure her prey. She was confident they would come, knew they would be challenged, and certain they would fail. There was no way for them to see the danger. No way for them to know their checkered pasts were about to collide with their futures. No way for them to know they finally would be getting what they deserved.

~ 1 ~

They could dress it up any way they wanted, but Katherine Lincoln knew what they were really doing. This wasn't a getaway to a luxurious vacation destination. It was an exile. No longer worthy of the Hollywood glamour, no longer trusted among the vast temptations, she was being banished to the desert.

She knew they had their reasons – even the most casual glance at the tabloids reminded her of that. But that didn't make it better. Not so long ago they would have catered to her, sent her anywhere she wanted. Now, in what was a not so subtle hint, the mini-bar was completely empty.

The limo had the standard DVD player with an assortment of movies – all of them her own. A reminder of what she had been. She'd never liked watching herself on screen. After everything that had happened, it seemed unimaginable to even try.

As if knowing what she was thinking, her cell phone began to ring – her agent.

"Donnie," she said in greeting, her voice sweet and completely false.

If he noticed the fabrication, Donnie's own tone concealed it. "Kat, angel, are you on your way?"

Reminding herself she was a good enough actress to fake this, she replied, "Sitting in traffic actually."

"It's L.A., of course you're in traffic. Arizona is going to be a breath of fresh air."

Dry, parched, lifeless air, Kat considered adding, but instead she asked, "How'd you find this place?"

"Former client owns it. Actually, she had a supporting role in your last movie."

From the tone of his voice, Kat could tell he didn't mean the last movie she'd finished.

Still on some shaky ground, she continued, "Would I have known her?"

"Katherine," he asked, "do you even remember the plot of the movie?"

His soft tone did nothing to blunt the force of the truth. They'd been shooting for a couple weeks when she'd collapsed on the set. She'd looked at some of the unedited film in rehab. It had been so unfamiliar she found it astonishing she'd even known her lines at the time.

"So, I guess I wouldn't know her." Kat hoped the humor didn't sound as flat as she felt.

Donnie sighed deeply. "Honey, look, I like you. Honestly. That's why this all pisses me off. But you're doing the right things. We'll get through this."

"Tell me about the hotel," Kat said, trying to sound accommodating. Donnie was an okay guy. She knew he looked out for her. She also knew she hadn't repaid him in kind.

"The place sounds fantastic. They're going with an oasis-in-the-desert sort of thing. Very remote. Very private. The owner's got big plans for the place. Though I gotta say, she's not helping her cause with the name she chose."

"I noticed. Weird name. What was it? Pecking? Peckvini?"

"Peccavi. She tells me it's Latin. Some important meaning to her or something. I don't know. Latin's not my thing."

Kat chuckled. "Mine either. I guess we'll have to take her word for it."

There was a pause on the other end of the line and Kat took a moment to appreciate the smile on her face. This is what it used to be like. It'd been fun, originally.

"Donnie, I'm going to make this work. I promise."

"Good girl. That's what I like to hear." His voice took on a softer tone before he continued, "The production team is sending somebody out to meet with you at the hotel."

Kat's chest grew tight with anxiety. She knew what was coming. Part of her had known it was inevitable. Instead of waiting for Donnie to break the news, she asked directly, "Peyton?"

She could hear Donnie chewing on his cigar on the other end of the line. "Look, I know what you're thinking," he began.

She was thinking Peyton O'Neil had been out to ruin her since the day they'd met. She'd been thinking he was more assassin than producer. But she asked only, "When is he coming?"

She knew Donnie heard the fear in her voice, but his reassuring tone did nothing to put her at ease. "The producers just want to see you in person, talk to you, make sure you're doing okay. It's understandable."

Of course it was understandable. Peyton always made it seem that way.

"When is he coming?" she repeated.

"He's flying out tonight," Donnie admitted.

There would be no reprieve. No chance to prepare for the assault.

"It has to be Peyton?" It was pointless to ask, but she had to try.

"The doctors say he saved your life, Kat," Donnie replied.

It was true. Awful, but true. She should never have taken this part. She should have backed out the moment she'd heard that Peyton was on the production team. She wasn't ready. Seeing Peyton was only going to prove that.

"Kat, are you okay?" Donnie asked, his voice worried, a little desperate.

There was only one answer to that question. She really had no other choice. This was who she was. She didn't know how to be anyone else.

"I'll be fine," she assured him.

Of course, she wouldn't be. And part of her wondered if Peyton had saved her life just to remind her of that.

~ 2 ~

Biff Winn was headed north on Route 23, smiling at just how isolated the terrain was becoming. The scorched earth was a stark contrast to Malibu's sandy beaches and sparkling ocean. This was the perfect place to lay low. No one would come looking for him out here. No one would want to.

A billboard on the side of the highway gave him his first glimpse of the hotel. A full-color photo revealed a huge building adorned with marble columns, thick green lawns, and a beautiful circular drive. Though it sparkled with newness, the place looked like something from an era long past.

The hotel looked classy. That meant rich guests. And rich guests in an isolated place were bound to pay top dollar for the cache of drugs he'd brought along with him. This place was going to be a gold mine.

Biff was so busy mentally counting his money he almost missed the turn. A narrow gravel road wound away from the highway for a couple of miles before it dipped into an oddly shaped valley. After another half a mile, Biff could no longer see the highway. The hotel was so isolated it was almost as if it didn't exist.

He pulled his convertible next to a battered Toyota in the small parking area. A sexy blonde was staring at herself in the rearview mirror. Her lips were puckered as she carefully applied a striking shade of red lipstick. She was either completely oblivious to his presence, or she was coming on to him.

She blotted her lipstick and smiled seductively. She knew he was there.

He hopped out of his car and stretched his five-six frame as much as he could. Shoulders back, stomach in. He smiled broadly in greeting.

She smiled back through slightly crooked teeth, flipping her long hair as she got out of the car. "Howdy," she replied in a sexy drawl.

"Texas?" he asked.

She giggled. "How'd you know?"

"Lucky guess?"

She walked around her car to stand closer to him. She was at least four inches taller than him, but with the view he had of her sizable breasts, eye level was rarely this pleasurable. With long legs, tiny waist, and even a pretty face, she was amazingly sultry, and it was immediately obvious that she was not afraid to use sex to get what she wanted.

"Trista," she said, clearly aware of and comfortable with his attention.

"Biff," he replied, grudgingly raising his eyes.

"You a guest or an employee?"

He could tell she was hoping he was a guest, a guest with money. He knew the look. He practically invented the look.

"I'm the hotel manager," he said, adopting his most authoritative tone.

"Then I guess that makes you my boss. I'm housekeeping."

"The whole housekeeping staff?" His eyes darted up to the large building in front of him. It looked awfully big for one person.

Trista raised one eyebrow. "Shouldn't you already know the answer to that?"

"If you're going to assume I know things, you're going to be awfully disappointed."

She smiled at that and Biff grinned in return. Now he was getting somewhere.

"Tami said she just had the cash for me at first. She's hiring a bigger staff once the place gets up and running," Trista explained.

Tami Ghyl. The owner. It still bothered him that he couldn't place her. A name like that, Biff would have thought he'd remember it. Hoping to catch a clue, he said casually, "Ah yes, Tami. How is it you know her?"

"I don't actually. It's kind of a long story," Trista replied absently, reaching back into the car to grab her suitcase. "So, what's this place like inside?"

Biff fished the keys out of his pocket. "Wanna come with me and check it out?"

~ 3 ~

On the excuse of going to find some water, Trista slipped away from Biff. He was harmless so far, flirty, nothing too heavy-handed. Despite that, she could tell he was looking for a way in. He was the type of guy who wasn't above using his position to convince a girl to expand the scope of her job description. Until Trista was sure she didn't have a better way to approach the situation, she needed to keep a little distance from the California boy.

She took her time wandering through the lobby, which looked like one gigantic, beautiful antique. There was an enormous mahogany double staircase opposite the entryway that led up to what Trista assumed were the guest rooms. Paintings of serene desert landscapes covered deep rose walls. The furniture was the same wood as the staircase, upholstered in a soft rose and white fabric. It would have looked like an old-fashioned sitting room if not for the huge front desk.

She was admiring the view when an even more impressive sight moseyed through the door. He had the look of a guy who'd just brought in a herd. Tall and lean, with thick sandy hair curling up from under a ten-gallon hat. He was sexy with a capital S.

The beautiful cowboy smiled and, shutting the doors behind him, said, "Leaving these open is an invitation to coyotes and God knows what else."

Trista nodded amiably and offered one of her most inviting smiles. "Well, then I guess it's awful good you showed up to help us out."

He took a slight step back, obviously just a little shy, and said, "I'm Steve Rich."

She closed the space between them. "You must be the cook that Biff said was joining us."

Since it was very clear he had no idea who Biff was, Trista took his arm and she wondered what one did with all those fabulous muscles in a kitchen. "I'm Trista," she said sweetly. "You just follow me and I'll introduce you to the manager."

She was disappointed to see a certain hesitation in his eyes – the type of hesitation that had nothing to do with meeting your boss and everything to do with not being interested in the girl flirting with you. Obviously, her cowboy was going to require a little persuasion.

He managed to disentangle himself, but he followed her behind the front desk to the door of the office. Inside they found Biff settled behind a massive old desk, his short stocky frame all but swallowed by the grandness of his surroundings. He was studying a book, brow furrowed, doing a rather poor imitation of the studious boss. He glanced up, obviously expecting to see Trista. His eyes narrowed at the sight of what he undoubtedly saw as his very tall competition.

"I'm guessing you're the cook?" Biff made no effort to stand. He merely nodded in Steve's direction and attempted to look aloof. Unfortunately, the act only drew attention to how artificial Biff's bleached hair looked next to Steve's sun-kissed golden locks.

"Biff and I were just trying to figure out what we're supposed to do to run a hotel. You have any experience?" Trista asked, batting her eyes at both men.

"I'm just a kitchen guy," Steve explained, keeping his eyes on Biff, his body language screaming that he couldn't be less interested in Trista.

"Looks like you aren't just the kitchen guy," Biff said in a superior tone, "looks like you're the whole kitchen staff. Actually, it's just you two helping me run the place for a while," Biff said, his eyes back in the book.

"Well, I'm thinking Steve here is going to be mighty helpful with whatever anybody'd need," Trista said with a wink.

Biff rapped on the desktop to get their attention. "I'm glad to see Steve's finally decided to join us, but we've got guests coming and we need to get up to speed. According to this book, we're expecting five today."

"The first guests are arriving today?" Trista asked. It didn't give them a whole lot of time to get prepared.

The look Biff gave her told Trista that he was far too important to deal with her stupid questions. "Tami left this book. It explains everything. She says we can expect that everything is ready to go. There's no set up that we'll have to do."

"You said there were five guests arriving," Steve prompted.

"Yeah, right. Five guests. There's a couple – the Lichtenhoffs – and another guest named Amy Lichtenhoff."

Trista laughed. "Really? Funny, I knew an Amy Lichtenhoff in high school."

"Think it's her?" Steve asked, finally looking her way.

"Not a chance. Her family was dirt poor. They wouldn't have the cash for a place like this," Trista admitted, before she remembered that she was trying to pretend she didn't come from the type of town where Wal-Mart was high-end.

She wasn't sure if she was relieved or annoyed that neither Biff nor Steve noticed her slip.

Biff continued with his orders. "And there are two other guests. Katherine Lincoln and Peyton O'Neil."

"Kat Lincoln?" Steve asked, too quickly for Trista's taste.

"Didn't she just get out of rehab?" Trista hissed.

Though she'd intended her remark for Steve's benefit, there was something in Biff's eyes that caught her attention. It looked like Biff might have the sort of side business that made him interested in a person's drug preferences.

"So, what else does the book say?" she asked, leaning suggestively over the desk, trying to get the stars out of Steve's eyes.

"Check-in is at three, so that gives us a couple hours to get ready. The Lichtenhoffs are in Suite Three. Amy's in number one. O'Neil is in five and Lincoln is in seven, which are in the wing over the rooms that are normally ours."

"Normally ours?" Steve asked.

"Yeah, that's the cool part. Until the place fills up, we're allowed to use the guest suites."

"Really?" Trista gushed, forgetting Steve's behavior for the moment. "We can just wander through and pick whatever we want?"

"Unfortunately, no. She's specific with our rooms too. I'm in number two, by the Lichtenhoffs. Trista, you're in four. And Steve, you're in six."

Next to Kat, Trista almost added, but thought better of it. That damn actress was already causing trouble.

Instead of whining, Trista batted her eyelashes. "Could one of y'all help me get my bags? I'd like to check out my room."

To Trista's delight, both men jumped at her request, holding her jealousy at bay – for the moment.

~ 4 ~

Steve followed Trista and Biff to the girl's suite at the top of the staircase. He supposed the grandness of the lobby should have prepared him for the room, but it was still astounding. The walls were a deep green, which might have been dark if not for the wall of floor-to-ceiling windows overlooking the crystal pool below.

The room had distinct sections to it. The entrance opened into a large sitting room with overstuffed furniture. Beyond that was a door leading to a massive sparkling bathroom. And to the left, curtained glass doors stood open, revealing a canopy bed, big enough to comfortably sleep five.

Paintings of dogs were scattered throughout the room. A team of hounds on a hunt. A floppy-eared Labrador sleeping on a deep green couch. Puppies frolicking on a suburban lawn.

"Wow," Biff said, dropping Trista's bags. "This place is awesome. Fucking awesome." He tossed a key at Steve as he retreated. "Here, Stevie. I'm gonna go check out my new digs."

Anxious to slip away, but not wanting to be rude, Steve asked if Trista needed anything else.

He immediately regretted the gesture. Trista smiled broadly, her accent thicker than usual, and her head cocked alluringly. "I'm just fine, honey. But be sure to stop in later. I'd love to help you with dinner. It'll give us a chance to get to know each other a little better."

Steve knew the drawl was for effect, and the offer was not about helping, but he smiled politely in agreement as he escaped.

The hall was surprisingly dark, with the only illumination coming from small fixtures placed high on the walls. The dim bulbs barely cast enough light for Steve to find his way.

If the owner had been going for romantic and serene, she missed her mark by about a hundred watts. Instead, it felt like something dark was hidden in the shadows, something secret, maybe even something evil.

These haunting thoughts were chased from Steve's mind by the bright afternoon sun that poured through the windows in his room. It was identical to Trista's except for the deep blue walls and folksy country paintings. Cows. All kinds of cows. Dogs in Trista's room. Cows in his. Tami was starting to seem like a pretty odd woman. Maybe that explained her decision to hire him.

~ 5 ~

The long drive to the hotel was not improving Waylan Lichtenhoff's mood. He glanced at his wife in the seat opposite him, staring out the window, eyes squinting against the desert sun.

"Find me a decent radio station," he growled.

She jumped at the sound of his voice, hands shaking slightly as she silently turned her attention to the radio. It was good to see her listen. Good to see someone listen. Stupid Amy. She should have known better than all of this.

He wasn't the type of man who came running just because his daughter called. It was Amy who should be coming to him. If she wanted to come back home, she should crawl. Crawl on her hands and knees back to Texas. He wasn't her damn chauffer.

But it wasn't kindness or sympathy that had him loading his bags into the truck and heading to Arizona. It was something darker, stronger. Yes, he wanted her to crawl, he just wanted to be there to see it.

It'd been six years since Amy had left. Six years since she'd slipped out in the dark of night and hadn't returned.

About a month after she'd left, she'd sent a note – a ridiculous tirade about her mother, about her childhood. Stupid girl. Her mother'd been dead for years. Dead because she'd deserved it. Dead because she didn't know what was good for her. Like mother, like daughter.

Even after all this time he'd never doubted that she'd return. She'd never be able to survive alone. Never be able to survive without him. He'd known she'd beg him to let her return. Beg her daddy to let her come home. And he would. Of course he would. She was his only child. It was a father's duty to care for his own. To teach them what was right and what was wrong. And that girl had a hell of a lot to learn.

Gloria's small voice brought him out of his thoughts. "There aren't any stations. Just static. Can I get you something else?"

That was his Gloria. Always accommodating. That's what marriage was all about. Yes, it was time to bring the girl back. Maybe Gloria could show her a thing or two.

~ 6 ~

The trip had taken hours, but Kat had to admit the hotel was beautiful. The combination of antebellum style and barren desert provided a strange tranquility. Just standing in the lobby, she began to relax. No press to avoid, no scripts to memorize, no costars to appease. Just her and the desert. She could breathe for the first time in months, maybe years. Maybe this wasn't going to be as bad as she'd expected.

The limo driver again tapped the small bell on the counter and glanced at his watch. Kat was about to tell him he could leave the bags when a stocky man in an obnoxious Hawaiian shirt came careening down the broad staircase.

"Sorry," he said, catching his breath. "You're our first guest."

He slid behind the front desk, and continued with more charm than Kat would have expected, "Ms. Lincoln, right?"

Kat smiled politely. "Yes."

He grabbed a key off the rack behind him. "I'm Biff Winn, the manager. I imagine you're exhausted from your trip. You'll be in Suite Seven." To the driver he said, "If you leave her bags here by the desk, I'll make sure they're brought up."

The driver was out the door faster than Kat could blink, leaving her alone with the manager, who grabbed a couple of her bags and started up the sweeping staircase. She recognized his look – the hair, the clothes. He was from L.A. He was exactly what she'd been hoping to escape.

At the top of the stairs, he slowed his stride so he was next to her. "If you need anything at all during your stay, I'm your man," he said with the confident tone of an unscrupulous salesman.

Kat recognized his tone, but it didn't make sense. She'd been here for less than five minutes, far from the temptations that had gotten her into trouble. No way the hotel manager was offering her drugs.

He continued, "We're a full-service establishment. I assure you, I can get anything you need."

Thankfully they arrived at her suite quickly, and Kat continued to ignore his unnerving remarks. The room itself was sufficient distraction. The cheerful pastel orange walls were worlds away from white sterile hospitals and rehab centers. It was good to be free, even if it meant sharing a hotel with this strange little man.

Biff laid her bags on the chair in the sitting room and turned to face her. He smiled broadly and extended an open hand in her direction. "On the house."

She instantly recognized the cylinder and the beautiful white powder it contained, and she could feel her hand begin to reach for it before a smarter, stronger part of her broke the trance.

"Mr. Winn, I think you have the wrong idea," she said, taking a step back.

"I'm just here to help." Biff assured her, stepping closer. "We can do this very quietly, if that's what you're worried about."

She was surprised to discover that her thoughts were of her own mortality, and not Biff's discretion, though a small tremor in her voice revealed the depths of her desire. "No, it's not that…"

Clearly, Biff heard only the longing. The predatory gleam in his eyes was becoming more obvious. "I'm sure you're accustomed to only the best, but you won't be disappointed."

Glancing away, she stuttered, "No…. No…. You don't understand. I don't do that."

"That's not what I've heard."

His mocking tone was a mistake, since it brought out only stubborn determination. "Well, you heard wrong," she snapped, meeting his eyes more sharply than she'd expected. "Please have the rest of my bags sent up."

Biff shrugged. "Whatever you say."

Slipping his hands and his destructive gift into his pockets, he grinned at her in a way that was clearly designed to look charming, but only looked menacing. "You need anything at all, you just let me know."

And with that he left her completely alone.

For a moment Kat stared at the closed door, trying to digest the unexpected offer. Donnie tried to warn her about this sort of thing. People were going to act differently with her now, because they saw her differently. Amazingly, life had just gotten worse. She hadn't thought it possible.

She'd been a Hollywood darling. Everything the studios wanted: girl-next-door looks with striking sex appeal, and enough talent to succeed in a small dramatic film, carry a blockbuster, or blend into an ensemble. Even with all that, much of her celebrity status came from her innocent image. As much as the tabloids searched, there were never stories of wild parties or even the most platonic dates.

But two months ago, when she'd been taken from the set by ambulance, the lid had been blown off her big secret. Any suggestion of innocence was wiped away. All-American girls did not have heavy cocaine habits.

Once the blood was in the water, the sharks began to circle. Every jerk she'd ever had a drink with came forward with absurd lies about her character and her battles with addiction. Former costars suggested she was half in the bag when she shot many of her movies. Anonymous studio sources claimed they'd known she was headed for trouble. Likely some of the same jackasses had gone to the press before, but her actions had given them instant credibility.

The hotel manager was nothing different really. New. But not different.

Kat sighed and reached into her purse. At the bottom she found the small, laminated yellow card she'd brought from rehab. In her own slightly unsteady print was a quote that had gotten her through the past few weeks and reminded her just how close she'd come to death. It was an obscure Bible verse she'd found after a particularly frustrating counseling session:

> WHEN GOD, IN THE BEGINNING, CREATED MAN, HE MADE HIM SUBJECT TO HIS OWN FREE CHOICE.... BEFORE MAN ARE LIFE AND DEATH, WHICHEVER HE CHOOSES SHALL BE GIVEN HIM.

The card was a reminder. A welcome friend. She couldn't take the easy way out. She owed her family more than that. She owed herself more than that.

She stared out the panoramic windows at the dry, cracked earth that looked distressingly symbolic. The lush garden she'd lived in was gone. Years of building a life, a reputation – gone – destroyed by her own hand. There were a thousand Biffs hoping to profit from her weaknesses, and a thousand Peytons waiting to profit from her successes.

Without the cocaine, she was alone. Alone in a world a hundred times worse than the world she'd feared before. She wasn't sure she could handle it. Actually, she was almost certain she couldn't.

She was surprised by the warm tear that slid down her cheek. How the hell was she going to do this?

A soft knock on her door forced her to gather herself. She cleared her throat and hoped her voice wouldn't fail her. "It's open."

A tall, broad shouldered and absolutely beautiful man entered her room, her bags under his arms. He had sun-bleached blonde hair and the most beautiful deep blue eyes she'd ever seen. All topped off with a big cowboy hat that was sexy as hell. Looking at him was almost distracting enough to take her mind off her troubles.

He was speaking. She forced herself to pay attention. "Where would you like your bags?"

It was a miracle she got any words out, but she managed, "The bedroom, please."

Kat watched intently as he carried her suitcase and small carry-on into the other room. He had a fantastic body, the type of guy who was physically fit because he was active, not because he spent seven days a week with a trainer.

As he came out of the bedroom, he took off his hat and ran a hand through his hair. "I just want to say, it's a real pleasure to have you here at the hotel. If there's anything you might need while you're here, I'd be happy to oblige. I'm Steve Rich. I run the kitchen."

She smiled instinctively. The Kat-Lincoln-million-dollar-smile was so automatic in these situations she hardly knew she did it anymore. He was a fan. Good to know she still had a couple of those.

"Thanks so much for the offer. I expect I'll be keeping a pretty low profile on this trip, but I'll be sure to find you if I need anything."

There was something in his reaction that surprised her. Embarrassment? No, it seemed like something more. For an instant he seemed like he was going to explain, but then it passed. He smiled at her amiably and turned to leave. He was halfway to the door when he turned back.

She almost laughed at how stupidly happy she was that he wanted to talk to her more.

"Just so you know, the owner of the hotel passed along your special diet," he offered. "I won't have any problem adjusting the menu for you."

Kat cringed. Special accommodations made her feel like such a diva. There was no way this adorable man was the kind of guy who thought well of people who had special diets.

Fretting she was already alienating the first person to be sincerely nice to her in ages, she thanked him quickly and wished she was as good at talking as she was at reciting lines.

Steve offered a kind smile. "Are you sure there's nothing I can get you?" he asked.

His voice was deep and sincere. And she almost believed he would get her anything, even things she hadn't realized she'd needed. She took a small step toward him before she could stop herself.

She felt so immersed that words were difficult, and she almost stuttered. "I don't think so…. Um, what time is dinner?"

"Between six and eight, but if there's something you need now…"

Kat immediately thought of several things she needed from Steve at that moment, but none were related to food. "No, really, I'm fine. I, um, I guess I'll see you at dinner then."

She cursed her inability to formulate a sentence.

Steve smiled easily, seeming to both sense her discomfort and push it away. "I'll be taking the orders and cooking the food. So you can bet you'll see me later." He put his hat back on and tilted it slightly to say good-bye.

"Thanks again." She smiled broadly. Conversation was not her strength, but smiling was part of the reason she got paid millions.

The smile he returned was a little crooked and very sweet, and left Kat wondering how she could spend more time with the cook.

~ 7 ~

The hotel was even more fabulous than Trista could have hoped. With luxurious rooms, gorgeous views, and full access to the rich and famous, this was her way in. She was finally going to get everything she deserved.

She dug through her suitcase and fondled the fifteen hundred in cash at the bottom. Tami Ghyl, her new boss, assured her there would be more where that came from. The money, and the chance to escape her tiny little hometown, had made her decision to take the job an easy one.

As she'd expected, the high-priced salary meant a high-priced hotel. High-priced hotel meant high-priced guests. If she played her cards right, she figured she could score herself a rich husband – preferably someone else's – then she could get the cash without losing her freedom.

Soon enough she would never look at another person's life and covet what they had. Jealousy was obliterated when you had more than anyone could ever dream of.

Who would have thought it would all have been set in motion by a stranger's phone call? Tami said she'd seen

Trista working in the diner, and been impressed with her ability to charm the customers while deftly handling the orders. Though Trista had no housekeeping experience, Tami was confident she would pick up the job in no time.

Trista suppressed a giggle as she wiggled into a tight skirt. She chose a deep green one matching the striking walls of her hotel room. The color was so overwhelming, it felt only natural to work with it.

She was again digging through her suitcase, looking for a pair of sandals, when she noticed the picture on the wall opposite her bed. Trista smiled at the sight – a long-haired spaniel that looked just like Princess, the dog she'd had growing up.

Princess was the sweetest animal that ever lived, but she would always wander off. One night, the dog didn't come home for dinner. Concern grew into alarm when darkness fell and Princess still hadn't returned. The next morning, Trista and her best friend, Amy, had gone looking for the dog. They'd found her lying by the roadside, hit by a car.

Amy had been so supportive, offering a shoulder to cry on and doing everything she could to make Trista laugh. It was funny to think of Amy now, since a woman with her name was a guest at the hotel. What were the odds of that? Two Amy Lichtenhoffs in the world? She wouldn't have thought it possible.

~ 8 ~

In disgust, Biff returned the cocaine to the bottom of his suitcase. The day had started out with such promise, but things had taken a bad turn very quickly. He considered himself a very persuasive man. In his life he'd convinced a lot of people to do a lot of things they never thought they would. That's what it took to be a great salesman. Product was important, but pitch was everything. Yet he was standing in his room, alone, having struck out with the actress and already losing the attention of the hot maid to some idiot in a cowboy hat.

One look around his room only made him more depressed. In a hotel filled with gorgeous rooms with magnificent views, he was standing in the middle of the ugliest room he'd even seen.

The room was weird. Just plain weird.

It had a nice view of the driveway, which was good he supposed. He could be in his room and see when guests arrived. That had to be worth something. But when the high point of a room is the parking lot view, it's hard to be optimistic.

Why the hell would anyone paint a room yellow? Not even a pastel yellow, which would have been a little girly, but reasonable. The room was a horrible sunflower yellow. Deep and robust, like a gigantic '70s-style smiley face had vomited everywhere.

And the color wasn't the worst of it; the paintings were the real problem. Frogs as far as the eye could see. Fancy-colored frogs. Fat frogs. Little frogs. Regular old toads. Their beady little eyes followed him around the room.

Maybe he should have been more suspicious when he'd gotten this job offer. He'd screwed a lot of people in his life. His mysterious caller could have been one of them. The call really had been out of the blue. And no matter how hard he tried, he couldn't remember having ever met the woman before. But she'd clearly known him.

She'd known about his drug connections, known about his side business in pornography. Hell, she'd even known that his little turf war with the Bosco brothers had left him in no position to decline her offer. She'd even teased him when he'd negotiated salary.

Yeah, she'd known him. But he was beginning to realize that might not be the best thing.

Biff flung the suitcase on the floor and tried to focus on the positives. The bed was bigger than anything he'd ever seen. When he flopped down in the middle of it, he was pleased to find a firm mattress. Just like he liked them. Soft but firm. He grinned up at the ceiling, relieved to see only stark white, without a hint of the terrible yellow.

Laying there, he tried to forget about the color; forget about the creepy little frogs ogling him. He needed to keep stupid thoughts like that out of his head and pay attention to the work at hand.

He had a hot maid working for him and a know-it-all cowboy cooking the meals. The maid would be willing to join up with a guy if the price was right. The problem was he didn't have the cash to wow her.

And of course there was the actress. It was disappointing that she didn't bite on his first offer, but that wasn't the end of the negotiation. Frankly, it was barely the beginning. He just needed to finesse things a bit. Maybe he'd gone too cheap with his offer. Handouts probably wouldn't impress someone like her. And besides, he'd sort of cornered her. As far as she knew, he was working for the tabloids or something, trying to scoop a story on her relapse. He needed to build some trust.

Even as Biff considered how to win her over, he realized he'd just put his finger on an even better plan. The tabloids. He could get pictures. How much money could a "Kat Lincoln on vacation" photo bring in? A picture or two of the chaste actress and starstruck Stevie would probably bring in even more.

The million-dollar question – and God, did Biff hope it was worth that much – was what was the better value: sell the pictures to the press or to the woman who wanted to keep them from the press? And if he could also get some evidence she was still using cocaine, Biff suspected he might be in for quite a windfall.

He tried to focus on the question, but he could only think about the tiny frog eyes that were surrounding him. Watching him. Stupid room.

He turned quickly, almost expecting the frog would look away. Instead, eyes stared fixedly. They would watch him as he slept. If he could manage to sleep.

~ 9 ~

Focusing on the evening's menu was proving next to impossible for Steve, who simply could not chase thoughts of Kat Lincoln from his mind. Preparations needed to be made. Tables needed to be set. Menus needed to be checked. But no matter what he did, the images kept returning.

She was gorgeous. But there was more. She was magnetic. Of course, she made millions because half the world felt drawn to her.

But his feelings were hard to dismiss so quickly. It had been years since he'd fallen for someone. And there were good reasons for that. In fact, it was best he stay far away from the fairer sex. He was nothing but trouble for them, especially someone as fragile as Kat.

Maybe that was what he was drawn to. Thinking about it now, he found himself mostly pulled in by her eyes. Chestnut brown, soft, sweet, and terribly sad. The sweetness he had expected; the sadness had been a surprise. He wanted to know what was going on behind them, needed to know more about their haunted look.

He'd heard the stories about her overdose. It was one of the biggest stories of the year. America's sweetheart had a serious problem with cocaine.

Steve hadn't wanted to believe it, but now that he'd seen her, he thought it might be true. The woman on the billboards appeared charming and carefree, but the woman he'd just met seemed broken and alone. Kat Lincoln looked like a person in desperate need of a friend. Steve was beginning to wonder if he might oblige. It was insane, but her pull was already too strong.

He was so focused on his thoughts that the voice from the doorway startled him. "Hey, cowboy, you promised you'd come get me before you wandered down here. You avoiding me already?"

Trista leaned slyly against the doorframe, eyeing both him and his kitchen. Her long, blonde hair was perfectly in place, her makeup striking, mostly because of the vivid red lipstick that Steve was beginning to recognize as her trademark. Under the flashy red was a broad smile that was a little too contrived. Her blue eyes sparkled with mischief. By many standards, she was sexier and more beautiful than Kat, but the wicked look in her eyes gave Steve chills – and not the good kind.

"I figured you'd want some more time to get settled in up there," he said as casually as possible, mindlessly opening and closing cabinets, trying to look busy.

She ignored the comment and let her eyes wander over the kitchen. "Nice place. Is there a menu?"

"I think I saw some in the dining room."

"What'cha got over there?" she asked, approaching with a coy smile, glancing at the menu on the counter in front of him.

Not tall enough to peer over his shoulder, Trista slipped under his arm to get a better look.

"What do you think?" he asked, extricating himself and heading to the pantry for supplies.

Trista hopped up on the counter and stared at him intently. He could feel her eyes boring a hole in his back. "Am I making you uncomfortable, Stevie?"

He cringed at the question. No way could this conversation be anything but ugly. As he turned to reply, a commotion outside spared him.

Trista's eyes lit up. "Is that a helicopter?"

Steve smiled in relief. "Sounds like it. What do you think – O'Neil or the Lichtenhoffs?"

The gleam in Trista's eyes was obvious, completely confirming Steve's belief that she was a gold digger.

"I'm gonna go check that out," she said absently as she fled the kitchen.

~ 10 ~

Trista watched in awe as the helicopter arrived in a flourish, kicking up loose sand and scattering small plants. A single man emerged from the copter with a confident stride. His black and silver hair looked divinely tousled by the tumult, but his perfectly tailored double-breasted suit was still crisp. His whole being screamed self-assurance, power, superiority.

He had an unmistakable look of Hollywood, which meant he probably had some connection to the stupid actress. But Trista refused to focus on that now. This was exactly what she'd spent her whole life waiting for.

He was alone, so Trista assumed that meant he was Peyton O'Neil. And she immediately decided she would make certain he wasn't alone for long.

Biff looked as impressed as she felt. Fortunately for her, Biff chose to play the role of manager, quickly dispensing his employees to make his high-end guests comfortable. A task that Trista was more than happy to perform. Without taking his eyes off the helicopter, Biff handed Trista the key to Peyton's room.

"Why don't you go and open Mr. O'Neil's room? So he can go right up."

Trista snatched the key out of his hand. "With pleasure."

Pleasure was, in fact, the operative word for Trista, who wasn't about to let an opportunity to properly welcome Peyton O'Neil pass her by.

~ 11 ~

Kat heard the helicopter also, and knew it had to be Peyton. She was sure he was behind this scheme to ship her off to the desert. He'd probably intended to follow her all along. Get her alone. And back her into the proverbial corner. Maybe even a literal corner.

Of course, she hadn't shared that theory with her agent or anyone else connected to the movie. She knew how it sounded. And she knew that a recovering cocaine addict didn't want to run around spouting paranoid theories.

But, unfortunately, she also knew Petyon. It wasn't paranoia when someone really was out to get you. If only the rest of them understood that.

It was one of life's terrible ironies that had it been Peyton who'd found her lying unconscious in her dressing room. Peyton, who had been out to destroy her life since the moment he met her, was the reason she was still breathing. Though she should have been grateful, having Peyton as her savior was almost worse than having no savior at all.

It was like being back at the beginning – he in the position of power, she in the position of weakness. He'd exploited it then; there was every reason to think he would again.

She'd met Peyton ten years earlier, on her first movie. She'd had a supporting role in an independent film with renowned writer/director Marcus Lett. Peyton had made it clear what he was after from the moment he'd appeared on the set.

Kat had read hundreds of biographies and autobiographies of Hollywood starlets. She'd always looked down on those who'd had affairs with directors or producers. But, a twenty-three year old version of herself had been completely unprepared for the full-court press.

She'd been tempted. He'd offered all the advantages a young actress could want. When that hadn't worked, the veiled threats had almost pressured her into compliance. The truth was, he wasn't a bad looking guy. It wasn't like it would have been a terrible experience.

Looking back now, Kat had to wonder if the worst thing she'd ever done was deny him. Peyton was the ultimate narcissist. One night, maybe two, and that would have been the end of it. It was the conquest he was after. The power. Turning him down was the real problem.

He must have loved finding her on the floor of her trailer with blood trickling from her nose. The broken mirror and telling white powder next to her. It proved she couldn't do it without him. He was still on top. She was no more than the amateur he'd always said she was.

Kat was certain this was all about returning to the beginning. Returning to their first meeting. Alone. Promises would be made. Offers to help. He knew more about her now. There was more of a history. There'd be comments about her virginal image, suggestions she wasn't as sweet as she looked, remarks about her addiction. Jabs that would make her feel even more unsteady in her new life.

What was she supposed to do if he asked again? Maybe, not fucking him the first time had been a mistake, but now it was different. This was her new start. Could she allow one of her first acts as a recovering drug addict to be sleeping with her producer? If she did that, she might as well kiss the last bits of her tattered self-respect good-bye.

And that, she realized, was exactly what Peyton was hoping for.

~ 12 ~

Half an hour later, Gloria Lichtenhoff's husband pulled his dusty pickup into the hotel's small parking area. The place was enormous and beautiful. And the sight of it filled Gloria with dread. She sat silently, waiting for Waylan to make the first move. She allowed herself a sidelong glance, careful not to let him see.

It was even worse than she had feared. He was frozen at the wheel of the truck, staring at the hotel, rage radiating off him.

What had Amy been thinking asking them to meet her here? Any idiot would know that a place like this would make Waylan angry. And Waylan always made sure that the people around him felt worse than him. The girl was a fool. Always had been. Never learned that fighting back was the quickest way to a black eye.

Waylan swung the truck door open with fury. "Don't just sit there," he growled at her. "We're meeting the girl inside. The sooner we get her, the sooner we get the hell out of here. Godforsaken desert," he added under his breath.

Years of experience had Gloria out of the truck and padding half a step behind her husband in an instant. One thing about Waylan, he was always looking for a more convenient target. If she wasn't quick, Amy's mistake would be her problem too.

Inside the lobby there was a short man behind the front desk. The condescending look he sent their way was going to make things so much worse. Gloria took a small step back, out of the line of fire.

"I'm supposed to meet my daughter here," Waylan barked, before the twerp could say anything.

The little blond man looked between the two of them, his disgust obvious. Gloria smoothed her threadbare housedress and glanced sheepishly at Waylan's faded denim jeans and dingy T-shirt.

Fortunately for all three of them, there was a flicker of fear in the man's eyes.

"Your name?" he asked.

"Waylan Lichtenhoff. My daughter's meeting me here," he snapped, laying a heavy hand on the front desk.

Gloria allowed herself a small smile at the sight of the faint tremble in the manager's hands as he flipped open the guest register. "Mr. Lichtenhoff. We've been expecting you. Your room's ready."

"My room? I don't need a room. I need my daughter, that's it." Waylan pounded the desk with his beefy fist, sending a pen flying.

Waylan's eyes blackened with wrath, and Gloria couldn't help but smile at the manager's obvious panic.

"Sir, I believe Miss Lichtenhoff is expected later this evening. We have a room for you and your wife and a second room for her. It's already been paid for."

"Paid for? Who paid for it?"

"Honestly sir, I have no idea, but it's taken care of." Biff offered the key. "You're in Suite Three. Miss Lichtenhoff is in number one."

"Suite?" he asked.

Gloria was pleased to see that Waylan was slowly becoming intrigued by the prospect of a free room, and a good one at that. She knew it bothered him that the little brat was paying for it. But the girl would pay plenty later.

"Yes sir, it's a suite. Shall I take you up?"

Waylan snatched the key out of his hand. "We can find it ourselves. There are two bags in the bed of my truck – Texas plates. Bring them up."

Gloria followed her husband up the stairs, enjoying the sight of others cowering in his presence. It was nice for him to have the opportunity to focus his rage on someone other than her for a change. Amy's return was long overdue.

~ 13 ~

Kat considered taking dinner in her room. Avoiding Peyton was certainly the safest plan, but it was also the coward's way out. She hated that running and hiding was becoming an instinctive reaction.

Summoning all her courage, she took the seemingly endless journey downstairs, calming herself with thoughts of Steve. At least he would provide a happy distraction while she ate. If she was lucky, he might even throw her one of those adorable smiles.

The hallway leading to the dining room was tucked behind the sweeping staircase in the lobby. It was lined with large, bright windows offering a fantastic view of the sparkling pool. Maybe she'd catch some laps later. The exercise might clear her head.

At the end of the hall was a cozy dining room with about ten empty tables. Two large doors opened to a covered patio and the sound of voices. She was craning her neck to see who was lurking outside when Steve came through a swinging door carrying a large tray with two covered plates.

As he delivered the tray to the patio, he flashed a smile and told her he'd be right with her.

The moment Kat was alone again, that horribly familiar feeling began to settle back in. She told herself it was the fear Peyton was nearby waiting to pounce, but there was more to it. She felt like she was being watched.

It was silly, really. She'd been watched almost constantly for years. Paparazzi. Fans. Others with more illicit objectives. It was probably the reason she hardly ever dated, or even casually went out in public. It had always made her nervous, but it had never been this intense.

Maybe the recent wave of sensationalistic stories was upsetting her more than she'd thought. Or maybe, and this was the more frightening possibility, it had always felt like this. Was it possible she'd always felt this exposed, but had just been too high to notice?

It felt like hours before Steve came back from the patio, tray tucked under his arm. He walked with his head high and back straight, much more confidently than earlier. He looked like a chef and restaurateur, even with the cowboy hat still firmly on top of his head.

"Welcome," he said. "Would you like to sit inside or on the patio?"

There was no one inside and at least two people on the patio. Kat longed for the fresh air, but the answer was obvious. "Inside. Could I have that table in the corner?"

It was the farthest point from the patio and the entrance. She prayed she would blend in with the walls, but knew it wasn't likely.

Steve again seemed to read her mind. "I'm happy to bring something up to your room if you'd rather."

She smiled in response, as much at herself as at his kindness. With a deep breath, she committed to the table. This was the first day of the rest of her life. She would not spend it hiding in her room.

~ 14 ~

Kat needn't have worried about Peyton. He was still in his room. His bed, to be precise. He was feeling relaxed and invigorated. He hadn't intended for this trip to be a vacation, but, with the services this hotel had to offer, he was quickly realizing he was going to be able to combine business and pleasure with relative ease.

The new dimension to the trip was welcome. He was annoyed he had to waste so much time chasing Kat Lincoln halfway across the country. There were hands to be held, deals to be made, and production schedules to attend to. In fact, he'd only been able to leave after assuring the studio he'd be in touch on a daily basis and would return whenever they sent the helicopter.

Despite the difficulties with scheduling, everyone understood the personal interest he took in Kat. She was a celebrity, a superstar. America loved her. They always had. She was one of those unique actresses men fantasized about having and women fantasized about being. She was money.

It was time she understood just how much he could help her. How much she needed him. He would build her back into the success she once was, and take her beyond. That's what he did – he built success, and he was very, very good at it.

He would never forget the sight of her lying on the floor of her trailer. She'd knocked everything off her dressing table in the fall and was lying face down among the shattered mess. He'd seen the razor blade first and immediately assumed suicide. Before he could look at her wrists, Peyton saw the mirror and the powder and realized the truth.

He was about to call security in disgust when he realized the opportunity. He checked for a pulse. It felt steady. Too fast, but strong. She was down, but not done. Get her to the hospital. Get her into rehab. It would bring her down a peg, something Kat had always needed, and then he would bring her back. Bigger and better than ever. She would be a superstar again. A superstar who owed her life to Peyton O'Neil.

Peyton looked back on the moment with fondness, but he reminded himself that the plan was not yet done. Kat was not with him. At least not yet. There was, however, a young woman who was dying to show him a good time. And, for the time being, she was more than suitable entertainment.

Trista was standing in front of one of the large windows. Her perfect, naked body was silhouetted by the setting sun. She was all curves, without an ounce of fat in any of the wrong places – rare for someone who hadn't been surgically enhanced. But, in Peyton's expert opinion, Trista was the real deal.

"What are you looking at, beautiful?" he asked coyly, shifting in the bed to get a better look at the curve of her firm butt.

She didn't turn around, but she shifted her weight in a way that assured him she knew where he was staring. "You've got a super view of the pool from here. I love pools."

"I have a nice view from right here. I hadn't noticed the pool."

She turned and gave a broad smile that he hardly noticed.

"The view from here's awful good, too," she replied.

Peyton wasn't at all uncomfortable with the way she assessed his body. He was older than her by a good twenty years, maybe even thirty, but it didn't matter. He took excellent care of himself and he had the sort of chiseled good looks that only got better with age. In fact, he had a very well paid doctor who made sure that was going to be the case for many years to come.

And Peyton knew he had something else that women desired more than good looks – power and wealth. This pretty thing had never in her whole little life been with anyone as important as him. He saw it in her eyes. It was a look that was even more arousing than her perfect breasts.

Peyton smiled and motioned for her to join him back in bed. He leaned back into the purple sheets like the modern-day royalty that he was, and let her worship him in the best way she could.

~ 15 ~

As Kat was finishing her dinner, she saw Steve and the manager exit the kitchen together. Steve was heading toward her and Biff was heading toward the lobby with a tray. She prayed it was room service for Peyton. The thought only had a moment to flit through her mind before Steve was standing at her table, asking if he could get her anything else.

She couldn't stop staring at his eyes; they were so peaceful. So calm. So the opposite of how she usually felt.

But that wasn't all of it. Not really. There was no judgment in his expression. He looked as if he saw something special in her, something she no longer saw in herself.

It took conscious effort to break the trance and answer coherently. "It was fantastic. I couldn't eat another thing." The second part wasn't entirely true.

"If you don't mind me saying, you don't need to lose weight," he said, shaking his head.

Kat smiled. No one understood. She would never be thin enough for the people who handled her wardrobe. "Thank you," she said simply. Talking too much usually got her into trouble, but she didn't want their conversation to end so quickly. "You make this rabbit food taste so good, it's a waste not to sell your skills in L.A. You could make a fortune. The anorexics would love you."

He chuckled at her response. "The anorexics are big in food in L.A.?"

"Oh, they control the food," she joked.

"Good to know."

They exchanged silence again for a moment, but it was much more comfortable.

"Was the manager taking room service upstairs?" She hated to bring Peyton into a perfectly good conversation, but if he was taking dinner in his room, it might be safe to take that swim she'd been thinking about.

Steve paused a minute, clearly wanting to say something, but even more clearly uncertain he should. He cautiously volunteered, "He's taking it up to Mr. O'Neil's room. Do you two know each other?"

Kat bit back a bitter laugh. "We've worked together a few times. He's a producer. Actually, he's working on my next movie."

Steve still seemed cautious as he continued, "I only caught a glimpse of him when he arrived, but he looked like a shark. Though I imagine a lot of people in Hollywood look like him."

Many that look like him, but few as vicious, Kat thought. But she steered the conversation away from Peyton. "Have you ever been to L.A.?"

"Nope. I've gone east a couple of times for vacations, but I've never been that far west."

"You should get out there sometime. It's something to see."

"Really?" The look on his face told Kat that Steve was pretty sure he didn't want anything to do with Hollywood and the people in it.

She smirked at his response. "Well, I can't say it's the greatest place I've ever been, but it is something to see. The beaches are stunning – the sun sets into the ocean there. I know it's kind of a dumb thing to get excited about, but I grew up on the East Coast, and we only get sunrises over the ocean."

The smile that she received in response told Kat he was beginning to loosen up a little. And the way it made her heart beat faster told her something even more interesting. "I've never seen the sun rise or set over the ocean. It must be beautiful."

Kat nodded.

"I imagine the studios are impressive. Do they still do tours? I think a friend of mine visited one of the big studios on a trip out there one winter."

"I'm not sure actually. Security is pretty tight these days. But if you can get into the studios, they're amazing. The ultimate imagination playground. Huge warehouse-sized spaces are transformed into living rooms, bedrooms, space stations, beaches. It's like a tiny little universe on a big lot."

"A place where illusion rules."

Kat laughed. "Yes, illusion is king. Fun if you're an illusionist."

"Really?" he asked seriously.

The change of tone caught Kat off guard. She'd been kidding. *Was it really fun?* "Sometimes it's fun," she admitted.

Steve nodded, seeming to appreciate her honesty, showing more interest in her thoughts than anyone had in months, maybe longer.

Though she had brought the topic up in the first place, Kat was beginning to feel uncomfortable with Steve's questions, not because he was prying, but because she felt like she wanted to tell him everything. "I should probably head back up to my room," she said with a little hesitation.

"Yeah, I have a million things to take care of in the kitchen," he agreed.

She heard reluctance in his voice, but it might have been wishful thinking. Either way, she was determined to find out more about him, even if the more sensible side of her brain was insisting that she should keep her head down and her nose clean – literally and figuratively.

~ 16 ~

Trista sighed deeply as she rolled off Peyton and nestled in next to him. She'd been with a lot of men in her life, probably more than most women her age. But it had never been like this. This was a man who knew what he was doing.

"With moves like that, you must own Hollywood," she murmured.

He ran a hand over her hair, smoothing it back into place. "Not all of Hollywood. Most of it, though."

Trista stretched contentedly and tried to focus. As super as this was, she needed to be sharp. "So, you said you're a producer? What brings a guy like you to the desert?"

Though Peyton continued to stroke her hair absently, Trista sensed a subtle change as he considered her question. They were clearly entering what she believed would be the working portion of their encounter. "I'm here on business, actually."

"Business? Really?" Trista was suspected that the actress was going to play in here somehow. It was essential to know her competition early in the game.

"Have you heard of Kat Lincoln?"

It was a loaded question. She was smart enough to see that. She was also savvy enough to know that it was in her best interest to keep her feelings to herself, until she knew what "feelings" would serve her best. She merely nodded in response, keeping her face as blank as she could.

"You must have heard of her troubles lately."

"I saw things in the tabloids. Are they true?" she asked, widening her eyes with feigned innocence.

Peyton shook his head sadly and pulled Trista closer. "Unfortunately, yes. Poor girl almost threw everything away. But she's been through rehab, and I'm part of the production team hoping to bring her back in a new movie. We think it'll be great for her and us. The problem is, of course, we don't know if she can do it. You see, she's very good at covering up her addiction."

"I see," Trista murmured cautiously, absorbing the information and calculating its usefulness.

"Kat will be spending some time here at the hotel, trying to get back on her feet. You must know that."

Trista nodded, but remained silent.

"I'm here to see how things are going. None of us have seen her in person since that horrible afternoon," Peyton added. His voice oozed with what was supposed to sound like paternal sincerity. Trista wondered if it was a tone he used with all of his actresses or one he specially reserved for Kat.

"That's nice of you, coming all the way out here to help her," Trista replied, sitting up slightly and trying to get a better look at his face to gauge his interest.

"Kat and I have worked together a number of times. It's important for me to take care of my actresses."

His tone was more possessive than Trista would have liked, but she was still feeling more confident. "Anything I can do to help?"

Peyton smiled. The predatory gleam in his eyes told Trista that he thought he had her right where he wanted her. "Since you mention it, I think there is."

Trista smiled. This was going to be easier than she'd hoped.

~ 17 ~

It was close to nine-thirty when Steve finished cleaning the kitchen and preparing for breakfast. He considered putting his feet up and watching something mindless on TV, but thought better of it. He needed to burn off some energy. It was too dark to go for a run, so the best option was the pool. Maybe some laps would get the beautiful actress out of his head.

He was so distracted when he got to the pool that he was standing only a few feet away before he realized someone was already swimming. The fleet figure gliding through the water was unmistakable. He was transfixed, not only by her perfect body, but by the power of her stroke. Her urgency was as impressive as it was distressing. What was she running from?

He was trying to convince himself to turn around and go back upstairs when Kat stopped abruptly at his end of the pool. She grabbed the side with one hand and quickly wiped the water out of her eyes with the other.

Realizing he'd startled her, he said quickly, "I'm sorry. I was just going."

She seemed to relax at the sound of his voice, leaving Steve to wonder who she expected to be prowling around the pool.

She smiled sheepishly. "No, I'm sorry. I'm just a little jumpy these days. You don't need to go. It'd be nice to have the company."

The last sentence sounded like a lie, so he gave her an opportunity to change her mind. "I figured it would just be me out here at this hour. I didn't mean to disturb you."

Before he could retreat, Kat stopped him. "I really would like the company," she said. "My trainer is always saying I get lazy when I swim alone. I could use a little competition. You know, if you were planning on swimming anyway."

Steve saw more optimism and openness in her than he had before. It took only a moment for him to join her.

The workout was tougher than he'd expected. She was an excellent swimmer. Though he was stronger, she had more grace and skill. Her efficient strokes made it difficult to keep up. He was relieved and a little breathless when they finished. So much so that he was comforted to see her cheeks were flushed as well.

"I'm thinking you swim often," he said, as he caught his breath.

"At least once a day. I used to run, but it kills my knees now. I guess I'm getting old." Kat grinned at the last statement and, for the moment, the sadness vanished from her eyes. She looked different. Her shoulders not as stiff. Her back not quite as straight. Before he could respond to her joke, she was out of the pool, as if to prove she was still spry despite her alleged old age and bad knees.

Steve found himself staring again. A sarcastic voice in his head laughed at his previous thought that he wasn't falling for her. He couldn't take his eyes off of her. Her long toned legs, her full hips and breasts pressing alluringly against the fabric of her one-piece suit. Her washboard stomach reassured him he was right when he'd told her earlier she didn't need to lose weight. She was perfect already.

Even as the thought crossed his mind, he shook it off. This was a terrible idea. Terrible. He only needed to think of Lucy to know that.

If Kat noticed his gawking, she didn't give any indication. She grabbed a towel off one of the chairs and ran it over her wet hair, squeezing out the water, as she settled onto the lounge chair.

Steve joined her on the patio and toweled off his own dripping hair, hoping to wipe the thoughts from his mind as well. It was a moment before he realized she was staring at him in much the same way he'd ogled her. He smiled at her more in reaction than response.

She quickly looked away, her already flushed cheeks growing a shade darker.

"Well, Ms. Lincoln, you certainly don't swim like a woman with bad knees," Steve said amiably, taking a seat next to her, hoping to ease her embarrassment.

Kat laughed. "Ms. Lincoln? The only people who call me that are trying to sell me something. Are you trying to sell me something?"

A slow smirk spread across Steve's face as he shrugged. "I don't know, are you looking to buy something?"

Kat's eyes glittered with humor. "You are trying to sell something, aren't you? Tell me what it is before I get so sucked in by your pitch I'll buy anything."

"Ah, but isn't that the point of a pitch? I'll have you eating out of the palm of my hand before you even realize you should be watching out for me."

Kat casually crossed her legs and leaned back in the chair. "I guess that's what all this has been about, huh? The great meal. The workout. You're just buttering me up. You're not a nice guy. You just want something."

Steve laughed a deep, hearty laugh. "Hell, everybody wants something, don't you think?"

Though the comment carried the same flirtatious tone as his previous remarks, Steve saw a dark shadow cross Kat's face. She sat up a little straighter in the chair and slowly crossed her arms.

"That's the way of the world, right? Every man for himself," she replied, anger and frustration edging into her voice.

"Ouch," he said quickly, trying to repair the damage. "Spoken like a woman who's had a pretty rough time of it lately."

"You and the rest of the world certainly had a chance to read all about it." Even as she said the words, Kat's head dropped in what should have been frustration, but looked more like shame.

She muttered something under her breath, and then gently pushed her hair out of her eyes and faced him, gathering herself and sliding on a mask that Steve could see she was very used to wearing, even if she wasn't very comfortable with it. "I'm sorry. That was out of line."

He leaned a little closer and placed a gentle hand on her arm. "I'm made of tougher stuff than that, Ms. Lincoln. You won't scare me off so easily."

Her mask slipped a little. "It's been a rough couple months." She sighed and added, more to herself than to him, "I can't believe it's been less than three months."

"Rehab?" he asked cautiously.

"I just got out a couple days ago."

Steve wondered why he felt she was waiting for him to condemn her. "It must be awful to have your mistakes splattered all over magazines, newspapers, and television."

"Do you always know the perfect thing to say, or am I just catching you on a good night?"

He laughed. "Any idiot could see that would be tough. Nobody'd want the world to know their deep, dark secrets."

Kat only shook her head. Steve thought of the pompous ass who'd arrived earlier in that ridiculous helicopter. He imagined people like him would eat Kat alive for mistakes like the ones she'd made.

Before he could say anything more, she smiled and teased, "How about you, then? What secrets would you want to keep from the tabloids?"

Though Steve thought of one thing immediately, he hoped the look of decades-old regret didn't show on his face. "That's why I'm just a cook – too many deep, dark secrets."

"Just a cook?" Kat snorted. "There is no *just* in my description of tonight's meal, trust me. How many years does it take to polish your skills like that?"

Steve chuckled. "I guess cooking on the ranch prepared me pretty well."

Kat gaped. "Do you mean this was your first night in a commercial kitchen?"

"It didn't show?"

"Not even a little," Kat replied, the admiration written all over her face. "What were you doing before this?"

"I ran the kitchen on a ranch in Montana, not too far from where I lived as a teenager."

"You're a natural."

"Must be in the blood," Steve replied without a thought.

"A family of chefs?" Kat asked.

Steve cringed involuntarily at the question. Before he could respond more appropriately, Kat was scrambling to apologize. "I didn't mean to pry."

He grinned at her apology. Half the world knew every dirty little secret she'd ever had and she was apologizing for asking a reasonable and obvious question.

"No," he insisted. "I'm sorry. There's no secret about it. My parents ran a diner. A little local place. That's probably where I caught the cooking bug."

"Near the ranch?"

Again, it was a simple question. She couldn't possibly know the complicated answer it would require. Normally, he would try to end conversations like this with dismissive responses, but Kat's sincerity was obvious, as was her understanding.

"I moved to the ranch when I was a teenager. I went to live with my uncle after my parents were killed."

The sympathy was plain on Kat's face, as she looked even more apologetic. "My God, both of them?"

"The tornado hit during the lunch rush. They had some warning, but there wasn't enough time." Steve lowered his eyes. "They were trying to get people to safety when it hit. Ten people were hurt. My parents and three others were killed. The people that survived said it would've been a lot worse if my folks hadn't acted as quickly as they did."

It'd been years since he'd talked about it. Though almost two decades had passed, the memory was sharp as ever. He remembered the look on the principal's face when he broke the news. He remembered the sheriff, leading him to the emergency room where both of his parents were laying on metal gurneys, white sheets concealing their faces.

"I'm so sorry," she said sincerely, laying a hand over his. "They sound like they were amazing people. So brave. You were very lucky to have had them."

He'd never thought of himself as lucky, but when she said it, he realized she was right. He was lucky to have had them, if only for a short time. "What an optimistic way to look at it."

"If you're looking to me for optimism, you obviously have a very dark life."

Steve laughed at the reply, even as he considered the implications. The woman he had met earlier had seemed broken in the way she now suggested, but he could see more in her now. And the longer they talked, the more he could see a light glowing inside of her. And, unless he was seriously misjudging her, Kat was as surprised as he was.

~ 18 ~

Twenty feet above Steve and Kat, Trista was standing in the darkness of Peyton's room staring down at the pool. She was fixated on Kat's perfect legs and the casual way she leaned back in the chair. How could Steve be falling for that? She wouldn't have thought he'd get sucked in by the California flash. Yet there he sat.

The fire was burning in her eyes when Peyton came back from the bathroom and wrapped his arms around her. "Staring out at the moonlight?" he asked, without looking out the window.

"Actually, I was just watching your favorite actress."

Peyton's body immediately became rigid. The playfulness disappeared and he stepped closer to the glass. They both watched now. Kat was facing them, but she was completely unaware of their gaze. She was laughing and looking more relaxed than Trista felt she had any right to look.

"Who the hell is she talking to?" Peyton snapped.

"Steve Rich. The guy who runs the kitchen."

"She's flirting with the cook?" he practically shouted.

It was suddenly quite obvious that Peyton's feelings for Kat were more than professional. "Looks that way. I thought you were just worried about her doing drugs. Are you worried about who she's flirting with too?"

Trista watched as he willed himself to calm down, to look professional. "It's a complicated business. My first priority is to make sure she doesn't do anything to hurt herself. But entanglements with the wrong people could be as hard on her career as the drugs."

Trista nodded, as if the lame excuse covered his overreaction.

"What do you know about this cook?" he asked, turning his full attention to Trista, finally.

"Not much. I think he's from the Midwest, but his accent's hard to place."

"That's all?"

She merely shrugged. Entirely sick of talking about Kat, Trista asked, "Is this another one of her vices?"

Peyton's attention was back at the window, staring down, body rigid. "What?" he asked, as if he'd barely heard her question.

"Is she in the habit of sleeping with the help?"

Peyton recoiled at the question, confirming all of Trista's concerns. "I'm beginning to think Kat has a few more vices than we realized," he replied.

~ 19 ~

Kat couldn't believe how easy it was to laugh with Steve. Actually, what was really surprising was just how easy it was to talk to him. She couldn't remember the last time that someone had treated her so normally.

She didn't feel a flicker of concern when he asked, "Can I ask you a personal question?"

She laughed. "More personal than what we've already been talking about?"

"What's your relationship with Peyton O'Neil?"

"Peyton? Why would you ask about him?" she asked, trying to keep her voice even.

Steve smiled that adorable smile of his. "Your head just about explodes every time his name comes up. I'm figuring there's a story there."

She'd never talked to anyone about what had happened with Peyton. It wasn't that she thought she'd done anything wrong, but she was sure it would somehow sound like she had. Yet she didn't hesitate now.

"Peyton is known in the business for his hands-on approach," Kat explained. "At the start of my first movie, he made a pass at me and I said no. He made it clear that things would be very difficult for me if I didn't play along."

"Slimeball," Steve muttered.

Kat smiled at the insult. "About a week later, he stopped by my dressing room again and we went through the same song and dance. That time I was ready for it. I was more firm. And he was even more angry."

Kat stared up into the night sky. This was the part she dreaded telling. She had no verification; it was all innuendo, rumors. "A few minutes after he left, the lead actress came into my dressing room. We talked for a bit, but things were awkward. She was suddenly very distant. I can't prove it, but I'm sure Peyton must have told her there was something going on with us."

Steve nodded, but as she'd feared, she saw doubt in his eyes.

"A couple days later, the director called me in on one of our non-shooting days. He said there were rumors that I was having a lot of trouble adjusting to life in California. People told him I was going through some kind of depression. That I'd been drinking on the set." Kat realized that, after all she'd done, it didn't sound that far from the truth. "I swear. I didn't start using drugs until years later. I never drank on set," she added, as if that was somehow worse.

Steve didn't say a word, but his eyes willed her to continue.

"Anyway, things spun out of control pretty quickly. My shooting times kept getting reshuffled. The other actors started avoiding me. After about a week, Peyton showed up in my dressing room again, looking incredibly smug. He had shown me what he was capable of. It was time for me to give up. To beg. But I didn't crumble. Quite the opposite, actually. I totally freaked out. Screamed at him. Accused him of everything I'm telling you now. I even blamed him for the flat tire I'd gotten the day before. I told him – and this I remember vividly, because it was so cocky and ridiculous – that I'd rather crawl back to New York over broken glass and do dinner theater for the rest of my life than sleep with him."

Kat chuckled at the memory. She'd been a spunky kid, once upon a time. She wondered if she still had a little of that in her.

Steve laughed along with her. "So what happened after that?"

"Oh, nothing really. Peyton hates me. I hate him. I'm just paranoid enough to worry he's still out to get me."

"No, what happened with the rest of the movie shoot? Did things improve?"

Kat had never really thought about that part of the story. "Actually, yeah, things kind of went back to the way they were before all the nonsense started."

"Did people overhear the fight?"

"They must have. It was a crappy dressing room. Those walls wouldn't have kept any sound in."

"Maybe it made people realize you were the victim in all of this and not…"

"The drunk slut Peyton was telling them I was," Kat finished the sentence for him.

"I'm not sure I would have said slut," Steve smirked.

Kat slowly shook her head, considering the years she'd wasted worrying about this. "I can't believe I never thought of it that way." She placed a hand on his knee. "Thank you. Between the food and the talking, I'm beginning to think you may be my guardian angel."

"I'm just happy to return the favor," Steve said absently, putting a hand over hers.

Kat immediately tensed and pulled her arm away. "What favor is that?"

"What?" Steve replied, obviously just realizing what he'd said.

"You said you're returning a favor. What favor?" she persisted.

He hesitated and, as he did, her heart raced.

"You did something for a friend of mine once. I guess she's really the one who owes you, but since she's not here, I thought I could stand in her stead."

Kat relaxed a little, intrigued by the statement. "Really? Who?"

"There was this girl on the ranch," he continued, sheepishly. "She must have been ten, maybe twelve. Great kid. Quiet. Always reading. Always writing. She wrote a screenplay. And one night, when she got back from one of your movies, she was all fired up. Determined she was going to get you to read it. I don't know how she found your information, but she sent it to you."

"Holly Trailor?"

He grinned in relief. "Yup."

"Donnie, my agent, passed it along to me. She wrote the cutest note; I just had to read the script," Kat gushed. It was one of the rare times in recent years she'd enjoyed something related to work. It was fun to read the story. So innocent. So purely entertaining. And so fantastic to know this little girl thought enough of her to track her down. The memory was only dampened by the realization that Holly Trailor might have a significantly reduced opinion of her these days.

"I can't believe you know her. The screenplay was really good. I was happy to read it. Hell, it was better than a lot of the crap I get."

"That's what you said in the letter. You told her she should keep at it, and send you more once she got a little older. Your letter meant the world to her."

Kat blushed deeply. It had been nothing. The writing had been good, very good. "It was no big deal."

"It was totally a big deal. I can't explain how big of a deal it was. Here she was, this brainy little kid living in the middle of nowhere. Her mom had died in childbirth and her dad tried his best with her, but he never understood her writing. Never understood why somebody would sit under a tree and read a book all day. I used to try to talk to her. Try and convince her she should keep at it, even though people didn't understand. But your letter was a turning point for her."

The story brought an unexpected warmth to her heart. It was wonderful to see, if only for a second, that there was something she'd done in the past few years that wasn't completely destructive. "Really, honestly, I was flattered she sent it to me."

"Well, anyway, that's why I feel I owe you one, why I've been so uncomfortable around you. I've always admired what you did. You must have thought I was a stupid fan. I'm not."

"So, you don't like my movies?" Kat joked.

He snickered at her response. "You know, you really don't know how to take a compliment. Isn't that a problem in your industry?"

"Not being able to take criticism is a problem. The compliments are few and far between, and typically they're a sure sign somebody wants something." Yet, as Kat looked into his eyes, she was fairly certain the man sitting before her didn't want anything. It was strange. It was nice.

"Sounds like a pretty rotten situation."

Kat shrugged. "I'm not complaining. I get paid a ton of money to go to work every day and pretend I'm someone else. I'd be an ass if I sat here feeling sorry for myself."

The way he looked at her made Kat believe that he could see it all. The loneliness, the pressure, the isolation. He seemed to see the sadness and want to fix it. And she almost believed he could. He reached out and brushed a stray hair away from her face, his finger lingering on her cheek longer than was necessary.

It was bizarre. Things just didn't happen this way.

The voices of innumerable counselors echoed in her mind. *Now is not the time to get involved with someone. Now is not the time to give in to over-zealous consumption.* Drugs. Drinking. Sex. These were all addictive. She had to be careful not to transfer her addiction. She was supposed to avoid temptation. Avoid exposure to these forbidden fruits. That was exactly why she'd been sent into seclusion.

The only thing distressing her more than the counselors' warnings were Donnie's —*They're all waiting for you to fail. The press is dying for the scoop. They want to know the details, the more sordid the better. They'll dig. They'll fabricate. And they'll entrap you, if you give them the chance.*

But she couldn't run away from this. And the longer she sat there, the more distant the voices became. She didn't feel afraid. She just felt the warmth of his hand on her cheek, the energy radiating off his body. She leaned closer to him almost as a reflex. She needed to kiss him. Needed to be near him. Her heart was pounding so hard as she felt his tongue on her lips that she almost didn't hear the thunder.

He pulled away and they both looked up in time to see a second flash of lightning.

"We should get inside," he said, looking as dazed as she felt. "Storms move quickly out here."

Thunder boomed in agreement. Kat took the hand he offered and they ran into the hotel as the rain began to fall. They stood hand-in-hand in the doorway for a long time, uncertain how to proceed.

"There's something you need to know," Kat said suddenly.

She didn't know if it was the kiss, the storm, or just the effect of standing so close to him, but the words were pouring out of her mouth. She wasn't sure she could stop talking even if she wanted to. "I am an inept conversationalist. My agent even writes what I'm going to say in interviews. I was born to have people write lines for me."

He smiled. "You're doing just fine."

His quick dismissal was almost unbearable. He had to know the truth. He had to understand. The hype was too much; she could never live up to it. "People expect me to be the characters I play in the movies. I'm not that woman."

Steve's smile broadened as he spoke. "I've never seen any of your movies."

Her eyes grew wide. "None?"

"I'm sorry, I feel really bad about that. I just don't get to a lot of movies. I'll run out tomorrow and rent them all if you want."

In a second, she had him in a tight embrace. This was the greatest news ever. No overblown expectations. No living up to her characters. For the first time in a long time, just being herself wasn't the fast track to certain disappointment.

~ 20 ~

Biff was sitting behind the front desk flipping through Tami's book when he heard laughter coming from the dining room. It sounded like the actress, which was odd. Kat Lincoln seemed serious and brooding, not the type of person who would be giggling in the hotel dining room. Yet the laughter was unmistakable. Biff had heard it in all of her movies. The only thing more distinctive than her laugh was that trademark smile the execs loved to paste all over billboards.

Actually, she was really nothing like he would have expected. There was no sign of the million-dollar smile and, until now, no indication she even knew how to laugh. Biff was wondering what might have caused the change when Kat and Steve appeared from around the corner. Their flirtatious smiles were unmistakable. Biff groaned inwardly.

Steve, hatless for the first time since Biff had met him, smiled and waved as they walked by, leaving Biff to simmer in fury. Damn it if Steve and Trista hadn't already managed to weasel into the lives of the two wealthiest people in the hotel. Though Biff would have expected this sort of thing from Trista, he was astonished at Steve's ability to maneuver so quickly. Obviously Biff had underestimated him. A mistake he would not make again.

He slowly chewed on the end of his pencil, trying to calculate how to make this bad turn work for him. And after a moment, the image of Kat and Steve brought a smile to his face. He'd forgotten his recent idea – the pictures. The only thing better than Kat Lincoln vacation photos were Kat Lincoln and her secret lover photos. This had huge money potential.

Biff was grinning at his entrepreneurial venture when he heard Waylan thundering down the stairs, loud enough to drown out the sounds of the storm and vehement enough to wipe the smile off Biff's face. The monster was ranting before he reached the bottom of the steps.

"Can I help you?" he choked.

Lichtenhoff stood at the edge of the front desk. The difference in their heights was more intimidating than ever. "What time are you expecting Amy?" he snarled.

"I don't have a specific time," Biff stuttered.

"What time is check-in?"

"Anytime after three and before ten."

"It's after ten." Waylan managed to make the statement sound like an accusation.

Biff wasn't sure exactly what he was supposed to say to that. So he stood silent, hoping he didn't look as afraid as he felt. This was a nice hotel. He wasn't supposed to be threatened by the guests.

The giant man pounded his fist on the desk. "I want the key to my daughter's room."

Despite his fear, Biff thought it might be wrong to hand the key over. Not because he gave a shit about Amy, but because it seemed like very bad business.

"I can't just give you the key to her room," he protested, wishing his voice sounded more assertive.

The thunder muted Waylan's response, but Biff could tell there were a lot of expletives. He was seriously considering taking the key by force; Biff could see it in his eyes. Suddenly the right business decision was seeming less important. Besides, the girl had technically missed check-in. He'd warn her when she finally showed up. Then it was her problem, not his.

Waylan snatched the key from Biff with a grunt. As he began to climb the stairs, a bright flash of lightning sent the lights flickering. *Crazy storm*, Biff thought, *it sounds like it's pouring outside.*

~ 21 ~

Waylan didn't notice the rain or the thunder. He was a man with a single-minded determination. He'd be ready for Amy the moment she arrived. Did she really think she could make him wait like this? That was not the way this game was played.

The door to Amy's suite was at the end of the hall to the right was his room, where Gloria was undoubtedly planted in front of the television.

The old key fit perfectly in the lock. He bullied open the door and flicked the nearby light switch. But the room remained dark.

Damn hotel, he thought, *didn't even have enough sense to make sure the light was working.*

He could see the outline of a lamp on a table in the sitting area. Waylan grumbled and felt his way toward the lamp, the faint light from the hall guiding him. As his fingers closed around the switch, the door slammed shut.

He spun around in the blackness. There was a crash behind him, which could only have been the lamp he'd just been reaching for.

"Who's there?" he snapped.

A laugh met his question. It was soft at first, but as it grew in volume and mirth, he recognized it.

"Amy! Goddamn it, have you been here all along? What are you doing? Turn on the fucking light!"

"I don't think so, Daddy." Her voice came from the vicinity of the now closed door.

"When did you get here?" he demanded.

"It feels like I've always been here," she replied, her voice airy and vague.

The voice came from behind him this time, causing Waylan to spin in the blackness toward the sound. How did she move without him knowing? The damn dark. He was so disoriented. His eyes should have been adjusting, but he found that the longer he was in the room the less he could see.

Even as he wondered what could cause that, he began to cough. Smoke. The room was filling with smoke. He looked around desperately. Fire!

He couldn't see any, but the smoke was getting thicker by the minute. He could feel it assaulting his lungs, burning his eyes. He fumbled toward the door, searching for an escape.

She was laughing again. It was deeper this time, throatier.

Finally, his hand closed around the doorknob. Though he tried to turn it, the knob wouldn't budge. His mind was racing. How could he be locked *inside* a room?

"Daddy." Amy's voice was right behind him, not more than a foot away.

He spun around to grab her, but caught only air.

"It's not that simple anymore," she taunted. Now her voice sounded as though it came from above him. "This time we play by my rules. It was easy to beat the shit out of someone less than half your size. It's time to even things up."

"By setting fire to the room and locking us both in here? That's insane!"

He was getting scared. Never in his life had he known fear like this. He'd always been bigger and stronger than anyone he'd ever met. Never failed to elicit fear with just a threat. Now he was trapped.

"Do you see a fire?" Amy asked calmly. She sounded further away again.

"What? A fire? No, I don't see a fire, but this smoke…" He started to cough again. Breathing was becoming difficult. Window. He needed to get to a window.

"There's no fire. Just smoke."

His eyes burned terribly. It was all he could do to keep them open. "What the hell are you talking about?" he shouted.

"Exactly, Daddy. Hell. Welcome to Hell."

~ 22 ~

Steve found himself sitting on the couch in Kat's suite before he even realized the mistake he was making. He told himself he was just there to talk. Just there to offer his friendship. Wasn't that the plan?

Yeah, kissing her by the pool, was that part of the plan, too? He snarled at himself.

But as much as he didn't trust himself to stay, Steve couldn't bring himself to leave. She would think he was avoiding her, that she'd done something wrong. How could he do that to her?

He was wondering if his excuses could sound any more lame, when Kat emerged from the bathroom. She was wearing a plush robe that she'd undoubtedly chosen as more appropriate attire than the bathing suit she'd been wearing moments before. He wondered if she knew it only served to reinforce just how much he wanted to remove what little she was wearing.

It had been a long time since he'd felt this intoxicated by anyone. He simply did not allow himself to get into situations like this.

"Would you like some water?" she asked, holding up two glasses. "I'd offer you something stronger, but my agent was pretty careful about making sure the mini-bar was empty."

"Water's great," Steve replied, wondering if it would be inappropriate to pour it over his head in an attempt to gain a little clarity.

As Kat handed Steve the glass of water, he saw a perfect, neutral topic of conversation. Something innocent – something that had nothing at all to do with how gorgeous she looked.

It was a small ring. Noticeable because it seemed to be the only jewelry she wore. On a thin, white-gold band, five tiny pearls surrounded a small yellow diamond, creating a jeweled daisy.

"That's a beautiful ring," he said. "Was it a gift?"

"I had a ring just like this made for my mom the Christmas after my first big paycheck. The next year, she gave me this one," Kat paused, and it seemed to Steve she was about to end the story there. To his surprise, she continued, "I think she could already see the strain I felt from work. She gave me the ring and told me that whenever I wore it I would know she was there. I'd never be alone."

She sighed. "I never take it off. There are times I want to, times it feels like I should. Like I'm just not worthy of it. That doesn't even make sense, I'm sorry."

Steve was looking at Kat now, not the ring. He could see the guilt. The fear. The love for her family. The shame for her failings. "It sounds like you have a wonderful family."

She slid her hand away, obviously feeling self-conscious from the admission. "I feel like you know an awful lot about me. Why don't you tell me more about you?"

He shrugged and looked away. "There really isn't all that much to tell."

"Now come on, that's not fair. You know what a lunatic I am. Now it's your turn. Tell me about life on a ranch. That must have been cool."

"Cool? Not really."

Kat smiled at his hesitancy. "Come on," she encouraged, "horses, cows, wide-open spaces...."

Steve couldn't help but smile back. "Yeah. There were a lot of cattle. A lot of horses. But trust me, when you're cleaning up after them, the spaces don't seem all that open."

She laughed. "Yeah, I imagine the smells can be a little overwhelming."

"That's how I ended up in the kitchen. Running away from the manure."

"It must have made you feel closer to your parents, being in a kitchen." He could see that Kat regretted the statement the instant she saw his reaction. She took his hand. "I'm so sorry. I shouldn't have brought that up."

He hated talking about his parents, but her gentleness and determination not to pry made it easier. "I was never very good at ranch work, but I was good in the kitchen. And yes, it always made me think of my parents. I can still see my dad working at the griddle. My mom waiting tables. They both had an amazing flair for it. They made that little diner a second home for a lot of people."

Steve absently picked up the yellow card from the table, trying to avoid eye contact, and trying even harder to come up with a new topic. The card was laminated, the words written with determination. It was a Bible verse about choice. BEFORE MAN ARE LIFE AND DEATH, WHICHEVER HE CHOOSES SHALL BE GIVEN HIM. The words were chilling.

Kat blushed and took the card from him. "Just a little reminder from rehab."

He sat back on the couch, the full effect of the words settling over him. He was slowly realizing just how serious things were for her. "Heavy stuff."

Kat seemed to shrug off his concern. "I had a problem. By the time I started that last movie, a crash was inevitable. It was a matter of when, not if. I was lucky to come close enough to scare the crap out of myself but not actually kill myself."

Steve's eyes darkened with anxiety. The overdose. The hospitalization. The stories really were true.

She continued to explain and, as she did, he caught a glimpse of her strength. "I just felt so helpless. Ending up in the hospital the way I did made me feel even worse. When I found the Bible verse it opened my eyes to something I'd forgotten. Win or lose. Live or die. It was on me. My choice. I'd chosen the path I'd taken. I have the same power to choose the right one now."

"Aren't you supposed to be acknowledging a higher power, admitting you can't do it by yourself? Seems like you're taking on a lot."

Kat smiled slyly. "You sound like one of the counselors. Think about it; I am acknowledging a higher power. God gave us free will, right? So by reminding myself not to squander it with stupid choices, aren't I acknowledging a higher power?"

He didn't know if she was right or wrong, but he liked her determination.

"I've got another confession," Kat said, clearly trying to change the subject. "I've never been to Kansas or to Montana. Tell me, which is the most beautiful?"

Images of flat, fertile farmlands immediately filled Steve's mind. "That's easy. Kansas."

She grinned. "Why?"

"It's home," he admitted.

Kat smiled wistfully at the notion. "Home? Yeah, I can relate to that. For me it's busy streets. Cabs. Buses. Subways. Aloof New Yorkers. Pretty different than Kansas, I guess, but in some ways home's the same for everyone."

~ 23 ~

Home was something Waylan Lichtenhoff was missing very much as well. At home he was never caught off guard like this. At home he had the upper hand; he could control his problems. And his problems could never have locked him in a burning room.

He stumbled toward the windows. He could still see the faint trace of what should have been the window frame behind the blinds, but the smoke was quickly becoming overwhelming, the darkness disorienting.

Somehow, Amy moved about freely. His voice was growing scratchy from the smoke, but hers only grew stronger.

"I came here like you asked me. I don't know why you're doing this," he coughed. "You've made your point. You're going to kill us both."

She laughed. A hearty, scary laugh. "Nope. Just you."

And then Waylan heard another sound. A low growling. The sound a guard dog makes as you approach. He froze in place, trying to identify the source of the sound. Damn smoke, he couldn't even see the windows anymore.

The growling continued, and began to grow louder. It came from all sides. Twenty dogs. At least. It had to be. He strained to see, but the harder he looked the more the dense smoke burned his eyes.

He was virtually blind. He desperately spun around, trying to find the source of the sounds. His coughing choked him. Each time Waylan tried to catch his breath he swallowed more smoke. The poisoned air filled his lungs. The coughing racked his body, driving him to his knees.

He collapsed to the floor. This was it. He was going to die of smoke inhalation. While his daughter stood by and watched.

"Oh, no, Daddy. You aren't getting off that easy," she spoke in his ear, seeming to read his mind.

As she spoke, the growling grew louder. Loud enough that he could hear the animals over his own deep coughs.

"Do you remember my sixth birthday?" she whispered. "Do you remember? I came home a little early from school. I had run all the way because Mom had promised me a gift. I was so excited. I ran up to the house. I saw your truck in the driveway. I was so happy you were going to be there too."

Waylan could feel something touch his shoe. It butted his foot like a dog or a wolf might. He tried to pull his leg away, but he lacked the strength. As his daughter spoke, the animal began to slowly gnaw on his boot.

The anger in her voice was more obvious now. It was almost like the growl of the dogs that were closing in. "I walked in the house, expecting to see a cake or something, but I heard you yelling. Yelling at Mom. You were always yelling at her. Yelling and hitting. I decided I needed to put an end to it. As I marched into the kitchen, I saw you punch her right in the face. Her nose was bleeding. You'd broken it again. I ran up and grabbed you around the leg. I had to make you stop. Do you remember what you did? Do you?" she demanded.

He tried to speak, but he couldn't. He was choking to death. The animal was probably still chewing on his boot, but he couldn't be sure. He couldn't feel his feet anymore. Most of his body was numb.

Her voice was calm again, chilling. "I'll tell you what you did. You kicked me across the room. You broke my arm. For my sixth birthday, you broke my arm. That wasn't the last time you broke my arm. Or my leg. Or my nose. Or a rib. Do you know how many of my bones you broke?"

She paused in her story and, as she did, he could feel more animals close in around him. He could hear their low growls, sense them circling, and though he thought they might be touching him, he couldn't be sure. It seemed he no longer had any feeling at all.

"Well, Daddy, I have a gift for you. One dog for every bone you broke. I hope you enjoy them as much as I will."

At her command, the animals attacked.

He'd been wrong.

He still had feeling in his extremities.

~ 24 ~

Biff awoke with a start. He was disoriented; his neck was stiff; his legs were asleep. He was in a chair, at a desk, in a bright room. An office? It looked like an office. A boom of thunder reminded him where he was – the hotel. He was working. Waiting for a guest who might never come.

The thought of the missing guest reminded him of his dream. A weird dream really. He couldn't remember when he'd last thought about her, never mind dreamt about her. It'd been almost a month since the Coast Guard had found his empty boat. Empty, that is, except for the note of resignation. The ultimate surrender.

Such a waste. That was what made him so mad. The girl had potential. She could have been successful. *They* could have been successful, together.

Funny she came to mind now in such an odd dream. He didn't really see her in it, but he heard her. Heard her very clearly. Actually, he could still hear her voice echoing in his mind.

She'd spoken in a lover's whisper. Promising their time together wasn't over. That there was more to come.

He shivered at the memory.

He stood for a moment, stretching his back. His watch told him it was three A.M., which meant a couple of things. Amy Lichtenhoff was probably not coming. And, unless the rain had stopped and then started again while he'd slept, it had been raining for almost five hours.

It was the rain that made Biff sit back down. Maybe the unexpected weather had delayed his missing guest. If so, she'd be tired when she arrived. No reason to make matters worse by being unavailable. Amy was clearly the woman with the money in the Lichtenhoff family. Which meant Biff had an interest in being as nice as possible.

He smoothed his shirt and folded his hands across his stomach, hoping she would arrive soon so he could finish the night in the overstuffed bed that had looked so inviting earlier.

~ 25 ~

Kat awoke the next morning with a broad smile. She'd fallen asleep in Steve's arms. They were sitting on her couch, her legs stretched the length, his propped on the coffee table. Her head resting on his shoulder; his head resting on hers. It was remarkable they'd been able to sleep that way. Yet she'd awoken without even a stiff neck. They just fit together somehow, like pieces in a jigsaw puzzle, matching but completely different.

They'd slept intertwined, but there'd been no more kissing. In fact, Steve hadn't even tried anything. Of course, that was good, she knew. It was best if they took this slow. Whatever this was.

It had been a night for stories. Her childhood in New York. His in Kansas. His time in Montana. Jobs. Hollywood. But she couldn't remember when she'd fallen asleep. She wondered if it had been while he was talking.

As she was fretting about her potential rudeness, Steve blinked awake. Looking down at her and seeing her eyes open also, he grinned.

"Good morning," he said. "I guess I was so boring I put us both to sleep."

Kat laughed. "I'm sorry. I was so wiped out from the trip."

"It was about four in the morning. I fell asleep right after you."

"I don't remember the last time I stayed up so late just talking," she admitted.

"Me either." Steve seemed about to say something more, when he noticed the time. He practically shouted with surprise. "It's after seven! I'm sorry, I have to go. I've a ton to do before breakfast."

Kat sat up quickly. "How can it be seven? It's still dark out."

A low rumble of thunder answered her question.

"It's still raining?" he asked.

Kat joined Steve at the window. The rain was coming down in buckets. The ground below was soaked. Small streams of water had formed overnight, eroding the desert sand and creating a world that looked unnatural.

"Steve, is this normal? Does it rain like this in the desert?"

"I don't know. Maybe?" His tone of voice did nothing to put her mind at ease.

They stood staring at the strange weather until Kat finally spoke. "You should go. Do you need any help getting things together for breakfast?"

Steve turned to face her, taking her hand as he did. "I'm betting that forcing a guest to work in the kitchen is frowned upon."

"It's not like that," Kat insisted.

"It's exactly like that, but it's okay. I promise. I'd like to see you later though," he said, giving her hand a squeeze.

She smiled. "You know where I'm staying. Besides, I'll be down for breakfast in a bit."

Steve kissed her forehead. "I look forward to it."

~ 26 ~

"So we have a deal?" Peyton asked.

Trista climbed out of bed and gathered her clothes. "I'll keep an eye on her. Drugs. Erratic behavior. Don't worry."

He smiled and added, "I promise I'll make it worth your while."

Trista allowed Peyton one long last look as she retrieved her shirt from the floor. "I don't doubt you will."

Peyton paused before he added his final request. "And let me know what's going on with her and the cook."

The hesitation bothered Trista even more than the statement. It confirmed his interest was more than professional. "I'll see what I can find out."

She finished getting dressed before she asked, "Are you concerned with what they're doing behind closed doors, or with what they're doing in public?"

Peyton's eyes narrowed, seeming to sense what she was thinking. "I need to know everything. Superstars have to be careful with their private lives. Superstars just out of rehab have to be even more careful."

Trista promised she'd take care of it, and gave Peyton a long kiss good-bye before she headed downstairs. He needed to remember who was on his side and who was ignoring him.

She'd be damned if she'd let the likes of Kat Lincoln steal the attention of the only two attractive men in the hotel.

It didn't take her long to get showered and ready for her first full day of work. It was still fairly early when Trista wandered down to the office, looking for her cleaning supplies.

She was amused to find Biff behind the big desk. His feet were up, his head was tilted back, and his arms slack. He was either dead or dead asleep. His deafening snoring indicated the latter.

"You have a beautiful room upstairs and you sleep down here?" she teased, poking his shoulder.

He sputtered awake and Trista held back a laugh. "Wake up, Sleeping Beauty. Time for work."

Biff blinked repeatedly, as if he was trying to clear the fog from his contact lenses. "It's still dark," he grunted.

"It's eight o'clock, baby. It's just a rainy day," Trista explained.

He squinted at her and then out the window at the downpour.

Trista dutifully began to gather her supplies to clean the downstairs level before the guests got in her way.

Biff stretched and rubbed his eyes. "Before you get started, do me a favor. Go up to Suite One, check if Amy Lichtenhoff arrived last night."

"How'd she get in if you didn't give her the key?"

"I gave the key to Waylan."

The name made Trista forget about cleaning. "Waylan?"

"Waylan Lichtenhoff. Her father," Biff snipped. "Huge guy. I didn't want to start any trouble."

Trista's heart was starting to pound. "Waylan Lichtenhoff? How huge?"

"Enormous. Come on, run up there, knock on the door. You can pretend you didn't know anyone had arrived."

Trista wavered between the desire to tease Biff and her confusion about the Lichtenhoff situation. Mocking Biff won out. "You're just afraid of pissing off this 'enormous' guy."

Biff smiled. "Bet your ass I am. You're a girl. He won't hit you."

"That, my little friend, is not always true." A man named Waylan Lichtenhoff had taught her that. Unwilling to seem afraid, she agreed to the request. "I'll do it, but don't think you don't owe me."

Biff shrugged at the notion.

She left her supplies and headed upstairs. Maybe it was her fear, but the halls seemed darker than they had the day before.

She knocked lightly at first. Receiving no response, she rapped two more times.

"Housekeeping," she called into the room.

Again nothing. Stupid Biff. There was no one there. Just to be cautious, she knocked one more time before she put her master key in the lock. She even listened at the door for signs of life. Nothing.

When she opened the door, she was almost overcome by dense, black smoke. She stumbled backward, intending to cry out for the others, but as she opened her mouth to shout, her lungs filled with the stifling fog. She ran back down the hall.

She found her voice as she reached the stairs. "Fire! Come quick!"

Biff crashed out of his office. "Fire?"

"Quick!" was all she could spit out.

Biff ran toward her, grabbing a fire extinguisher. Steve, who had heard the commotion, already had the extinguisher from the kitchen. They both raced up the stairs, past Trista, and down the hall. She hurried behind them.

The cloud of smoke was still hovering, but oddly it looked less dense. Trista hung back as Steve charged into the suite with Biff close at his heels. In seconds, Biff was running back out of the room, his hand over his mouth, eyes wide with terror. He rushed past her, turned, and vomited in the corner.

Steve slowly exited the room and leaned weakly against the doorway.

"What the hell is going on?" Trista asked.

Steve shook his head slowly. "Call the police. There's a dead body in there."

Trista looked between Biff and Steve, questions filling her mind.

"I'll go," Biff volunteered, scurrying away.

Steve dropped the extinguisher. "Go with him," he said. "He may need some help."

Trista shook her head in confusion, but followed Biff. When she caught up, he was standing behind the front desk shaking the telephone.

"What are you doing?" she asked.

With trembling hands, he gave her the phone. "No dial tone."

Her eyes grew wide. "Check your office."

She tested the phone again, but the line was dead. In his office, Biff was completely melting down. He looked like he was muttering to himself as he roughly ran his fingers through his short hair.

"Biff!" she shouted. "Pick up the fucking phone!"

He didn't even seem to hear her, so Trista pushed past him and tried the phone herself. The sound of another dead line greeted her.

She shook Biff's shoulder. "Do you have a cell?"

He let out a high-pitched, hysterical laugh. "No signal. I tried it yesterday."

A chill of panic was threatening to overwhelm her, but Trista held it together. "Come on. We need to check the other phones."

She tried to pull Biff with her, but he refused.

"You have to check the phone in your room!" she insisted.

His eyes grew wide. "No fucking way. You have the master key," he snarled. "Use that if you're so desperate to go back there."

"Goddamn it, Biff!" she growled, but she left him behind.

In her own room, only the now familiar silence greeted her. The panic was growing worse, and Trista would have sunk to her knees at the phone if she hadn't remembered just how foolish Biff had looked downstairs. She would not allow herself to break down. The adrenaline drove her back down the hall where Steve was still leaning against the doorframe.

"What did the police say?" he asked.

"No phones. I'm checking Biff's room."

Again, there was only silence on Biff's phone. Her expression when she returned to the hall seemed to be all Steve needed to know. He shut the door to Suite One.

"It's the rain," he said. His tone was even and calm, but his eyes were anything but. "The flooding must've knocked lines down. I'll check my room to be sure. Do you have a cell?"

"I checked. No signal."

"Okay," he said with a stiff evenness in his voice. "You stay here. Don't go in there."

He walked down the hall toward his room, his shoulders slack, no urgency in his step. Trista looked between him and the closed door. What could possibly be so awful?

Fear pulled at her heart, but curiosity even more. She couldn't just stand here. Trista Collins was not a woman who just stood around.

~ 27 ~

Steve fought the images flashing in his mind. So much blood. Soaking through the carpet. Pooling on the floor. Splattered on the walls. The ceiling.

He forced himself to sort through the grim reality of the scene and focus on anything important. It had been a person on the floor. It had looked like a person. But it should have been an animal. An animal carcass in the woods. Not a person. Couldn't be a person.

Steve wasn't surprised to discover the phone in his room was dead. Damn rain. He didn't have a cell phone, but Kat would. As he knocked on her door, he couldn't help noticing she had the same room as the dead man, but on the opposite side of the hotel.

She greeted him with a broad, flirty smile. "Back so soon?" But as she looked at him, her smile vanished. "What's the matter?"

"Do you have a cell phone?"

She nodded and grabbed the phone out of her purse. "What's happened?" she asked, handing it to him.

"We had some trouble down the hall. We need the police. Could you check your room phone? Make sure it's not working."

"Why wouldn't it be working?" Kat asked, checking the phone without waiting for his answer.

Fully expecting that her room phone would be as dead as the body down the hall, Steve turned his attention to the cell phone readout, which was insistently informing him that it did not get service at this desert oasis. He was tilting the phone against the windowpane and considering if it would help to stick it outside when Kat spoke again.

Her voice shook a little as she spoke. Steve wondered if it was fear or dread of her own suggestion. "Peyton will have a cell. You should check his too. Just to be sure. Do you know what room he's in?"

"He's next door to you," Steve replied as kindly as he could.

Though he saw the pain in her eyes, he gave Kat credit for her resolve. She followed him to Peyton's door, a mask of confidence now concealing the trepidation he'd seen.

Peyton answered their knock, looking perfectly pressed, yet comfortably casual in khakis and a button-down shirt. His collar was strategically open. His smile was smug and his voice condescending.

"Can I help you?" he asked Steve. Then, seeing Kat, he immediately disregarded someone so obviously below him. "Kat. I was going to stop by later this afternoon, but you've beaten me to it."

"Peyton, we need your cell phone. Do you get a signal here?" Kat asked, her voice surprisingly strong.

He shook his head. "I tried last night. There was nothing. Why?"

As if to answer his question, a shrill scream came from the other side of the hotel. Steve spun on his heel and sprinted toward it, cursing under his breath. Kat ran after him with Peyton following close behind.

As Steve rounded the corner, he saw that the door at the end of the hall was open wide. Deep red blood spatters covered the maroon walls and pooled on the hardwood floor. What might once have been a leg was tangled near Trista's feet, her white sneakers perilously close to several pools of blood.

The carnage was overwhelming, even on his second visit to the room. He could barely tear his eyes from the tattered remains and the shreds of clothing that were stained such a deep red they looked almost black. The scene was so horrible that he was no longer aware of Trista's screaming.

But Trista was still screaming. And if he didn't do something soon she'd probably drop to the floor right next to the mutilated corpse.

Steve slapped her to get her attention. "Trista! Look at me!" he shouted. "Step away. Now!"

The slap stopped her screaming and left only roaring silence. Trista allowed Steve to lead her back into the hallway.

"Why the hell did you go in there?" he growled.

Trista shook her head. "I'm sorry," she said softly.

Steve suspected that she'd never been so sincerely sorry in her life. Letting it go, he turned to Peyton. "Do you have that phone?"

"I'll get it," he replied, clearly straining against the urge to run all the way back to his room.

Putting a gentle arm around her waist, Steve turned Trista towards Biff's room. Conscious of the open door behind him, he asked Kat to help Trista, while he took care of matters in Suite One.

As he spoke, a tiny woman poked her head out of the room across the hall from Biff's. "Is something wrong out here?"

Steve was dumbfounded. Trista's scream had brought all of them running from the other side of the hotel. Yet Gloria Lichtenhoff was just now peering out to see what was happening? He turned to Kat. Understanding, she helped Trista into Biff's room, leaving him with the woman.

"Mrs. Lichtenhoff," he began slowly. "Is Mr. Lichtenhoff in there with you?" He feared he already knew the answer.

She opened the door more completely, seeming to understand things weren't okay. "He was in Amy's room. Has he done something?"

The look in her eyes told Steve that Waylan had a habit of doing things that got him in trouble. This time though, it looked like something had been done to Waylan. Unless it was Amy Lichtenhoff in a heap on the floor.

"When did you last see him?" he asked, trying not to jump to any conclusions.

"Last night, before bed." Gloria shrunk away from the questions.

"Can you tell me what he was wearing?"

Gloria's eyes narrowed with suspicion. "Beats me. What's going on?"

"It's really too early to tell," Steve replied, glancing toward Suite One. "Could you wait here, just a second?"

He needed to close the door. He also needed to take a closer look and see if there was anything that might help identify the body.

He reluctantly examined the room. The only fabric he could see was stained so badly it was impossible to identify the original color. But there was one heavy black boot with the toe completely gone. Almost as if it had been chewed off.

The boot was enormous. One that would have been worn by a man that stood well over six feet tall. A man like Waylan Lichtenhoff.

~ 28 ~

Kat led Trista into Biff's room and sat her on the couch. The poor girl didn't even seem able to speak. Uncertain what else to do, Kat ran cool water over a cloth in the bathroom.

She could understand how Trista felt. By the time her mind even processed the horror in that room, it was too late. She couldn't help but stare at the crumpled heap on the floor and the haze of blood and tissue that surrounded it.

In one of Kat's early movies there'd been a scene where a body was torn up by a lawn mower. She'd always thought it had been overdone, ridiculously gory. She realized now that she owed the effects guys an apology. They'd actually understated it.

She placed the cloth on Trista's head, wondering what she should do if the girl couldn't manage to pull herself out of this. Almost instantly it was apparent that Kat need not have worried.

Trista jumped to her feet, pushing Kat aside.

"I'm okay," she snapped.

"Are you sure?" Though Kat had to admit the color was returning to her face. Through an act of sheer will, she was gathering herself.

Trista shook her head in an apparent attempt to clear the cobwebs. "I'm fine. I was just startled. What the hell happened in there?"

The mangled body sprung to mind, making Kat wonder if she'd ever close her eyes again without seeing it. "I don't know. I don't think anyone knows."

As Trista's eyes cleared, her invasive stare became more disturbing. Now that the shock was fading, it was obvious she wasn't a girl at all. She was calculating and, oddly, she seemed to consider Kat competition. When Peyton walked into the room, Kat saw why.

"Trista, are you okay?" he asked.

Peyton's mask was back up. He was the suave, in-control gentleman the world knew. The look he exchanged with Trista told Kat that the young woman had wasted no time staking her claim. But Kat dared not hope the dalliance would distract Peyton from the real reason he was there.

Trista immediately played her part as well. Her drawl was more obvious than ever, as was her calculating nature. "Did you see it? My Lord!"

Peyton embraced her dramatically and whispered something in her ear, leaving Kat to wonder what was worse – the mess in the other room or the drama playing out before her.

When Steve joined them a few minutes later, the small woman from the other suite was close at his heels. She immediately caught Trista's attention.

"Gloria Lichtenhoff? What the hell are you doing here?"

The woman squinted at her. "Do I know you?"

"I went to high school with Amy. What're you doing here?"

"We were supposed to meet Amy, but she never showed up."

The words were still hanging in the air when Biff barged into the room, his wet hair plastered to his forehead, his clothes dripping on the floor.

Peyton was the first to get the obvious question out. "What happened to you?"

"We need the police. I went to get the police," he sputtered.

Gloria's eyes grew wide.

Steve put a hand on her shoulder. "We don't know anything yet." Then he turned to Biff. "What happened?"

"The road to the highway's washed out. The water has to be ten feet wide. It looks like a river."

"And the rain's still coming," Steve added, looking out the window.

"Are we trapped here?" Kat asked, the fear seeping deeper.

"Unless you know some other way out," Biff snarled.

"Now, let's stay calm," Peyton said. "Do either of you have a truck? Maybe you could get through. We need to get the authorities. This is a dire situation. There's a dead man in that room."

Kat noticed Gloria was looking a little unsteady on her feet. "Why don't you sit? This must be very upsetting for you."

She allowed Kat to lead her to a chair. "It's just so peculiar."

Kat ignored the men and focused on Gloria, who had an odd look on her face. It was either grief or relief, and Kat wasn't sure which was worse.

"Did he say there's a dead *man* in that room?" Gloria asked.

It was a trickier question to answer than Gloria realized. Kat thought back. She'd assumed it was a man. "I don't think anyone's sure what the situation is."

Gloria looked at Kat skeptically. "Do they think my husband's dead?"

"There's a body in Suite One. That's all we know right now."

"I want to see it," she replied, with a surprising bite in her voice.

Kat knelt on the floor next to her, placing a gentle hand on Gloria's shoulder. "I'm not sure how to put this, but you really don't want to do that. I can promise it won't help with an identification."

"She got him good, huh?" she asked with a small smile, her eyes black and distant.

Kat pulled her hand away. "I'm sorry, I don't understand."

Trista's voice came from behind them. "Let's just say he got what he deserved."

Kat looked between Trista and Gloria. *Was it possible anyone deserved that?*

Gloria nodded. "I won't believe the bastard's dead until I see the body myself."

"I helped Amy hide the bruises for years. I bet he didn't treat his wife any better," Trista explained, glancing at Gloria.

There was a fire in Gloria's eyes when she spoke. "He treated me just fine until that tramp ran off."

Kat was relieved when Steve interrupted the conversation. "I think maybe we should all go downstairs. I locked up the suite. Biff and I are going to see if we can get through to the highway with my truck."

Peyton was standing next to Steve, doing his best impression of a knight in shining armor. "I'll take care of you ladies while the boys see about getting the police."

As he spoke, thunder crashed outside.

"Why don't we go downstairs and wait in the dining room?" Peyton suggested, placing a reassuring hand on Trista's shoulder. "Hopefully they'll be back quickly with some help."

Everyone agreed, but Kat suspected the others weren't all that happy about having Peyton as their only defense either.

She just couldn't shake the fear that there might be a killer after them all.

~ 29 ~

As the others headed into the dining room, Steve pulled Kat aside.

"Don't trust any of them," he said in a sharp whisper. "I don't know how the hell someone mauled that huge man, but don't assume one of them isn't involved."

"Don't worry. I've never been able to trust Peyton. And hell if I'll trust the woman he's sleeping with." Kat laughed at the confusion that flooded Steve's face. "That would be Trista."

"Really?" was all he managed to get out.

"As for the lady who's glad her husband was torn to shreds, I don't plan on developing a long-term relationship with her either," Kat added.

Steve nodded slowly, either surprised or impressed by her observational skills.

"Honey, I swim with the sharks every day. Generally I don't deal with dead bodies, but people with agendas are the heart and soul of Hollywood." Casting a wary glance at Biff, she added, "You watch your back with him, too."

"Biff? He's harmless."

"He's a dealer. They're shady. Trust me. I've got some experience in this area, too."

Steve chuckled. "Now you're being paranoid."

"He offered me a free sample when I arrived."

Steve looked at Biff, who was impatiently tapping his foot. Kat liked the protective look that spread over his face. She suspected he was seriously considering how best to keep Biff away from her in the future. Despite all the anger he directed at the drug dealer, when he turned his attention back to her, his eyes softened. He gave her a kiss on the cheek and made her promise to stay safe. Grinning at his innocent display of affection, Kat made him promise to do the same.

Steve straightened his cowboy hat and went out into the storm with Biff. A flash of lightning and a rumble of thunder made Kat wonder again if any of this was a good idea. But then she thought of the body upstairs. Whatever steps were necessary, they had to get the police.

She wandered into the dining room to join the others. There was coffee prepared already. Kat hoped it would help clear her head a little. Something had to.

Trista handed her a cup when she approached. "You move pretty quick," she hissed.

Kat felt her heart race. Even with all she'd seen, she was surprised that Trista would be so direct. And she couldn't see any reason at all why she'd care if there was something going on with Steve. But, Kat knew how to hide her emotions, perhaps better than any of them.

As calmly as she could, she accepted the coffee. In an even voice, she replied, "Not as fast as you, I'm betting."

The look she received in retort could have burned through steel. Out of the corner of her eye, Kat saw Peyton watching the exchange with a half-smile. He couldn't have cared less about Trista, but it was clear she was an ally. Just one more person to take Kat down.

~ 30 ~

Steve and Biff had found nothing but more bad news outside. It was with heavy hearts and sodden clothes that they rejoined the others. In the instant before anyone became aware of their return, Steve observed the group.

It looked like Kat had been right about Trista and Peyton. The girl was practically sitting on his lap. But more disturbing was the way Trista was watching Kat, who was standing by herself, sipping her coffee and staring out at the unceasing rain. Biff seemed to notice Trista's focus as well, and he cast his own predatory watch over Kat. She was nothing more than a jackrabbit in a room of wolves.

Gloria, on the other hand, seemed carefree, as she was animatedly discussing something with Peyton. They could have been attending a society tea party.

It was Peyton who noticed their return first. Reading their expressions, he asked, "No luck with the truck?"

Steve couldn't help but wonder if he'd been working on the rhyming quip since they'd left.

Biff sloshed into a chair at the table with the others. "I told you, the road's washed out."

Peyton cast Biff a dismissive glance. "Then we have to deal with this ourselves. You saw the body," he said, pointing to Steve. "Is it this woman's husband?"

Steve had known from the moment Peyton had arrived on his helicopter that he was going to hate him, but until that moment he hadn't realized just how much. The son of a bitch had seen the same body Steve had. He knew how this conversation was going to go, which was clearly why he was passing it off. "It's going to be hard to identify the body. You see, Mrs. Lichtenhoff…"

"Oh, please, call me Gloria," she cooed.

Not only did the recent widow look unfazed by their conversation, she looked as if she was enjoying the attention. Avoiding her name entirely, Steve got right to the point, "There was a size thirteen boot next to the body. Does that sound right?"

Gloria cocked her head in curiosity. "That's right, but I don't understand. Just a boot? What happened?"

That's what we'd all like to know, Steve thought. "I have no idea. I saw a sheep once that'd been mauled by coyotes. Ma'am, that sheep looked very much like the body we found upstairs."

Gloria's eyes grew wide with excitement. "There're coyotes in the hotel?"

Biff snorted cruelly at the question. "Do you think they're just roaming around upstairs? I don't think coyotes know how to open and close doors."

Steve stepped in hoping to avoid a conflict. "I was just trying to explain the state of the body. I'm sorry if I gave the wrong impression."

Biff seemed about to say something more, but Kat interrupted. Her voice sounded distant, as if she was oblivious to the conversation going on around her. She didn't even turn to face them. Her eyes remained locked on the unrelenting storm. "Do you think whoever did this is still in the hotel? It's been raining like this for hours. The road's flooded out. Could someone really have gotten away?"

It was a shame Kat didn't see the panic spread over Biff's face. Steve suspected that under other circumstances she would have been amused by her ability to scare the pants off the man who'd been trying to manipulate her from the moment she'd arrived.

Biff wiped a stray bead of water from his face, his eyes wide. "We have to search the hotel. Make sure we're alone."

With all the finesse of the gamesman that Steve suspected he was, Peyton moved fast. "Good idea. I think we need three groups. One to remain in the lobby to watch the exits, be certain no one slips out. One group can take the east wing, the other the west. Gloria should remain in the lobby; it'll be less strenuous for her. I'll keep her company."

Trista shot him a cold look.

Kat was apparently paying more attention than Steve thought. She quickly suggested that she and Steve search the east side of the hotel, where their rooms were. She met Trista's furious stare without blinking, leaving Steve to wonder if she felt that confident or if she was a better actress than he would have expected.

Biff, however, was still focused on his own worries. "What do we do if we find someone?"

Steve shrugged, enjoying his suffering. "Yell, I guess. Hopefully we'll be able to overpower him."

Biff didn't appear particularly satisfied with the response. But before he could say anything more, Peyton stood and ended all further conversation. "Gloria, shall we proceed to the lobby?" He offered her his hand and led her gracefully into the front room.

Steve couldn't help but stare in wonder. It was like they were going to a black tie dinner, not waiting in the lobby for a killer.

~ 31 ~

Biff insisted they begin their search downstairs. He figured the longer they put off searching the upstairs rooms, the more likely something miraculous would happen so they wouldn't have to go into the room with the body. In fact, he was so upset by the prospect of going back there, he was almost hoping they'd find the killer before then.

Since they were already in the dining room, Biff and Trista began their search there. Trista grabbed another cup of coffee while Biff began searching.

"Are you going to help or what?" he grumbled, peering from behind one of the tables.

Trista shrugged and leaned back against the wall. "I find it very hard to believe the person who mauled the body upstairs would be cowering under a dining room table. This is all incredibly silly."

Biff stood and stretched before he crawled under another table. "How are you going to sleep tonight if you aren't sure we checked every inch of this place?"

He grinned as he watched Trista's smug smile fade. Though she tried to maintain a casual air as she joined him, his observation obviously scared her as much as it did him. He considered mocking the fear he saw in her eyes, but he decided there were other ways to elbow his blonde friend. "So, are you having fun with Daddy Warbucks?"

"Actually, I am," Trista snipped, the smug confidence returning to her eyes.

"He's a little old for you, don't you think?" he asked, straightening up after looking under the last table.

"He's sophisticated." Glancing under a table she added, "And experienced."

"And at least twice your age."

Leaning against the glass door, Trista peered out at the covered porch. "Probably. So?"

"I'm betting the sophisticated and experienced lack a bit in the stamina category," Biff chuckled. "I will never understand women. The last girl I was dating, she was always going on about this old guy she worked with. I didn't understand it then, and I sure don't now."

Trista only shook her head, focusing her attention more closely through the glass. "Do you think we need to go out there?"

"I've just started to dry off, no way am I going back out there. Just make sure the door is locked."

Leaving Trista to the task, Biff wandered into the attached kitchen. The sight of the gleaming pots made him think of the cowboy chef and wonder if he was taking advantage of the additional time alone with the actress.

~ 32 ~

Bracing herself for the search, Kat hadn't given any thought to the fact she was alone with Steve. They were looking for a murderer who had slaughtered a man so violently he was smeared across the floor. How could that not be terrifying?

What was surprising was the reality once the search got started. It wasn't as simple as she'd expected. Yes, she was petrified a knife-wielding lunatic was lurking in every dark corner. But there was more.

She was in Peyton O'Neil's bathroom and, for the first time in her life, she was glimpsing another side of him. A hairbrush was placed neatly on the bathroom counter, a meticulously organized shaving kit next to it. A bottle of imported cologne next to the mirror. Everything matching silver and gold, perfectly placed on the counter at rigid right angles. It was odd to think of Peyton shaving, combing his hair, applying cologne, using the travel-sized pack of dental floss.

"Jesus, this man is anal," Steve noted, joining her in the bathroom.

Kat tore her eyes from the toiletries, embarrassed to be caught staring. "He's very tidy," she agreed. "I don't think there's anyone hiding in the bathroom," she pointed out, trying to suggest she'd actually been looking.

"It's strange, isn't it, to see inside a person's life? To see the stupid things – toothbrush, mouthwash. You don't think about people doing stuff like that. But I guess that's exactly what makes us human."

"It's mostly just weird to think of Peyton as human." Changing the subject, she added, "Was there any sign of anyone in the other room?"

"No. You were right about Trista and Peyton, though. Based on a few items in his trash can, I'd say he had sex with somebody last night. Since I'm pretty sure it wasn't you, and I'm betting it wasn't Gloria, I'm gonna have to go with Trista."

Kat nodded with a certain resignation. It wasn't something she'd wanted to be right about. "She's absolutely his type."

"His type?"

"Very young. Very pretty. Very pliable."

"I'm not sure how pliable Trista is."

"I'm guessing, if there is something in it for her, Trista will do just about anything," Kat said.

"That may be true," he agreed, following her out of the bathroom.

Kat looked at the royal purple walls in disgust. So pretentious. So Peyton. It was like the room had been designed for him.

Steve scanned the suite once more. "These rooms really don't provide many places to hide."

"No. They don't," Kat replied absently. She rubbed her eyes, hoping to clear her head a little. "This whole thing is surreal. I don't know if I'm in shock or if the trauma of all this hasn't set in yet, but honestly, it's like I'm acting. Like I'm just playing a role. I'm speaking the lines and conveying the emotions, but not completely embracing the whole thing.

I'm half a step away from it. It's like I'm waiting for someone to yell, 'Cut!'"

Steve let out a long breath. It looked like he'd been thinking the same thing.

"I guess that makes two of us," she said.

His eyes lit up a little, and the sight of them made her heart do an unfamiliar little dance. "I don't think we've known each other long enough for you to be reading my mind."

Kat tried to push the rushing fantasies out of her head. As casually as she could, she said, "It's been quite a morning. That's bound to speed up a friendship. Don't you think?"

Steve's agreement was equally casual and Kat wondered if there'd really been anything special in his voice to begin with, but she pushed the thought from her mind. That left only one thing to think about. The isolation of the situation. The lingering dread. It was entirely possible that her mind was fabricating an elaborate fantasy with Steve because the rest of it was simply too much to take. They were in a hotel in the desert with a dead body and possibly a murderer. Alone and trapped by rain that wasn't showing any sign of stopping.

~ 33 ~

Trista was certain that it was entirely Kat Lincoln's fault that she was trapped searching the worst half of the hotel. It was crap. Kat was avoiding the dirty work, which Trista suspected was most likely her typical M.O. Celebrities. Nothing but spoiled, self-absorbed babies. Fortunately for Trista, the situation provided a unique opportunity. And she wasn't going to feel at all bad about taking advantage of it.

The silver lining didn't do much to improve her mood, and seeing the mess Biff had left in the hallway earlier only made things worse. "Don't think I'm cleaning that up," she snapped, pointing at the vomit soaking into the rug.

"Isn't that your job?" he replied, walking past without a glance.

"It's my job if one of the guests does it. Not if you do. And besides, I don't think searching rooms for a killer is my job, either."

Biff threw up his hands and turned to face her. "You say that as if any of this is in my job description."

Trista only shook her head. "You're cleaning that mess up."

Biff just rolled his eyes. Then looking between the Lichtenhoffs' suite and his own he asked, "Where should we start?"

The answer was an easy one. "Let's start in your room. I've been dying for an excuse to dig through your bags."

When Biff opened the door, Trista skipped past him, trying to aggravate him and make it impossible for him to control what part of the room she searched.

He called after her as he headed toward the bathroom, "Seriously, keep your hands off my stuff."

She waited until she was sure Biff was safely out of eyesight and then she discreetly dug one hand into his open suitcase. At the bottom, she could feel cylinders and tiny plastic baggies. Exactly what she'd hoped. She'd seen the glint in Biff's eyes when Kat's drug problem had been mentioned. She'd suspected it was a seller's interest.

Wanting to be thorough, she did a complete search of the bedroom before joining Biff in the sitting room.

"All clear?" he asked absently as he peered behind the curtains.

Trista grabbed his arm, hoping to get his full attention and distract him at the same time. "Before we go, I have a question for you. It's really just my gossiping nature getting the best of me, but I was wondering..." Trista paused, pretending she was embarrassed to be so curious. Lowering her voice she asked, "Is she still using?"

Biff's eyes grew wide at the question – the look of a guilty man who was cornered. "Who? Using what?"

Trista smirked, resisting the urge to laugh at his poor performance. "Oh, come on. Don't play dumb."

"I'm not playing," he said stubbornly, the shock beginning to fade from his face.

Trista placed her hands on her hips and stood determinedly between Biff and the door to the hall, which he was now eyeing as his only escape. "Kat. Is Kat still using?"

Biff stood his ground, arms crossed. "Using drugs? How the hell would I know?"

"Drug dealers tend to make it their business to know who is and who is not using."

"Drug dealers? What makes you think I'm a drug dealer?"

Trista put a hand on Biff's shoulder. "A great number of things made me *think* you are a drug dealer. The stash in your suitcase confirmed it."

Biff shook off her hand. "You went through my suitcase? Where the hell do you get off digging through my stuff?"

"Calm down. I didn't take anything. And I'm not going to do anything about it. Hey, I'm happy to help you out. If people ask me where they should go to get hooked up, I'll send them your way."

Biff stared at her, seeming to try to figure out her game. "Referrals can be important," he replied cautiously.

"I'd want a small finder's fee, of course."

As she'd expected, the monetary demand seemed to immediately put Biff at ease. Blackmail was clearly something he understood. "How about the producer?"

"Peyton?" Trista laughed. "No, he's clean as a whistle. What about Kat?"

"I don't pass around information about my clients."

His indignation was too overblown to be believed. Clearly, he'd been turned down. "Did she bring her own?"

Biff shrugged. "Possible, I guess. She's got a hunger in her eyes. It's just a matter of time."

That was good news. "Do you think you could give me a heads up if she starts buying?"

Biff still seemed suspicious of the questions. "Why would I do that?"

Trista hoped that the money would bring it back into something that made sense to him. "I'll give you a few free referrals."

"I haven't agreed to pay you for the referrals."

Trista smirked. "You will. Do we have a deal?"

Biff shrugged and seemed to give up on the idea of figuring out what was going on. "Sure, I'm in."

~ 34 ~

For the first time in a long time, Kat wasn't giving any thought to the plots against her. There were far more sinister things that required her immediate attention.

Steve had explained that no one was using the first floor of the east wing because it was reserved for staff quarters, but that didn't explain how isolated the space felt. As they walked down the cavernous hallway, with its stark wood floors and naked white walls, Kat felt like she was back in the hospital. Trapped. Alone. Each footfall echoed off the walls with an almost deafening clap.

There were five doors, presumably leading to the employees' rooms. Anxiety only rose when she realized the first door was unlocked. This was exactly the kind of place that a killer might hide.

"Stay behind me," Steve whispered. "If anything happens, scream. Okay?"

Kat nodded and obeyed. Screaming would be easy; getting her to stop would be far more difficult.

Steve swung the door open, revealing something worse than her fears. The room was empty. Completely empty. No furniture. Bright white walls. Bare wooden floor.

A million unanswerable questions swarmed Kat's mind as she peered over Steve's shoulder. *What if there had been other guests? What happened when there were other guests?*

"I guess the owner didn't want us staying down here." Steve gave her a look that she knew was supposed to exude confidence and humor. It failed.

It took no more than a minute to check the empty room and the small attached bathroom. They moved on to the next door and then the next, only to find the same empty room. The same absurdly vacant space.

Standing in the center of the last room, Steve pulled Kat close. She could almost feel the same fear coursing through him.

Kat buried her head in his chest and asked the question that had been haunting her since they'd set out to search the hotel. "What are the chances someone killed Lichtenhoff and ran off?"

"In this weather?" Steve asked.

It was enough of an answer for her. "That would leave the six of us."

He tilted her head up to look at him. "Actually, it would leave the four of them. I was with you all night."

Kat nodded. That was better. She hadn't really thought of it, but they'd seen Lichtenhoff alive yelling at Biff when they went upstairs. At least there was someone she knew she could trust.

But there was still something that was bothering her, a fear that she knew his words couldn't ease. "Could any of them really have done that to him?"

Steve stiffened and looked away. "I gotta tell you," he admitted, "I don't know how anything human could have done that. About three inches of the toe of his boot were chewed off; I swear it looked gnawed on. Like a dog would do to a bone."

Kat looked more closely at his face, which was shadowed by his hat. She couldn't tell for certain, but he looked serious. "Are we back to the coyote theory?"

He refused to look at her. "I don't know," he said quietly.

Seeming to feel her dissatisfaction with his answer, he continued, "I don't think coyotes wandered up to the second floor. I also don't think a person is capable of that kind of damage."

Kat sighed deeply. "Where does that leave us?"

"Nowhere good," Steve replied, pulling her closer.

~ 35 ~

Still uncomfortable with Trista's meddling, Biff hurried her out of his room and over to the Lichtenhoffs' suite. Taking the opportunity to get some space, he took responsibility for the bathroom, leaving her to attack the bedroom. To his aggravation, she was sitting on the bed when he finished up.

"Jesus, are you digging through their stuff, too? This is not a treasure hunt," he growled.

Trista didn't seem to hear him. Staring at the frame in her hand, she said absently, "I guess Daddy really did hate her."

Standing over her, Biff snapped, "What are you talking about?"

She held up a picture frame. The glass was broken and the frame was twisted, as if it had been thrown up against the wall. "This is Amy," she explained, handing him the picture.

Biff's heart raced at the sight. He snatched the picture out of Trista's hands and shook out the broken glass to get a better look. She was younger. Much less makeup. Terrible hair cut. But Christ, it was her.

"You look like you've seen a ghost. What's the problem?"

"This is Amy Light," he replied, not taking his eyes off the picture.

"No, it's Amy Lichtenhoff. I went to school with her. We were friends for years."

Finally looking up from the photo, Biff grabbed Trista's arm. "When was the last time you saw her?"

"The day after high school graduation," she replied, trying to pull away.

He only tightened his grip. "When was that?"

"About six years ago. Why?" she whined, finally extracting her arm.

"I met this woman three years ago. We were living together until about a month ago. Her name was Amy Light."

"Amy was headed to Hollywood," Trista said, rubbing her arm. "I guess she took a stage name when she got there. So?"

How could she not understand the problem? "Don't you think it's strange that her picture ends up at my hotel?"

"Kinda. But whatever."

"Don't you think it's even more odd that you know her too?"

Biff saw the alarms go off in Trista's head. She wasn't quite ready to admit it yet, but she saw his point. "I guess it's odd. So what?"

"Amy's dead."

Trista's jaw dropped. "Why would you think that?"

He threw the picture to the floor. "I don't think it. I know it. She's dead. Been dead a month. But she has a reservation in my hotel. A hotel where her old friend works. Where her parents were supposed to meet her. Where her father ends up murdered."

As the panic washed over Trista's face, Biff wondered what it all meant. But every way he looked at it he came back to the same thing – they were in trouble. All of them.

~ 36 ~

Gloria hardly noticed when Kat and Steve returned. She was enjoying channel surfing on the flat screen television in the hotel's large sitting room. Peyton was a gentleman, quietly leafing through a magazine, respecting her space, not insisting on ridiculous conversations. She suspected that the return of the others was only going to signal the end of this small reprieve.

After a moment, Steve cleared his throat. At the sound, Peyton looked up expectantly and Gloria reluctantly turned off the television.

"Did you find anyone?" Peyton asked, laying his magazine on the end table.

Though Steve said they hadn't found anyone in the hotel, Gloria could see he was hiding something. She'd been with Waylan long enough to know half-truths when she saw them. The stupid actress looked just as cagey when she asked about the others.

Peyton seemed oblivious, but Gloria thought it was possible he just didn't care. "They went upstairs a while ago, but haven't come back yet."

The actress looked anxiously up the broad staircase. "Do you think we should go find them?"

Gloria wondered if she was playing up her concern for the others just to make herself look good.

Peyton rolled his eyes, clearly agreeing. "They had an extra suite to search. They're fine. Sit. Relax."

Their resident cowboy peered up the staircase and seemed to try to look down the dark hallway, but eventually he gave up, taking a seat in an overstuffed chair facing the staircase. Though there was a chair near Peyton, Kat ignored it and wandered over to a window.

Gloria was about to turn the television back on when Trista bounded down the stairs. Biff walked behind her, heavy footed. Annoyingly, but not at all unexpectedly, Trista quickly wiggled onto the couch between Gloria and Peyton. Like Kat, Biff refused a seat. Instead he paced around the remaining empty chair, wringing his hands.

It was looking like these two had something to share with the group too. The obvious discomfort in the room made things a lot more interesting than Gloria had expected. She almost didn't mind the interruption of her shows. Almost.

"You didn't find anyone?" Biff asked. He seemed to be stalling for time, trying to gather himself.

The actress seemed to notice the tension too. She joined the group, leaning against the arm of Steve's chair. She looked to him for what appeared to be much-needed support. The weakness made Gloria smile.

Kat asked the cowboy, "Do you want to tell them?"

He nodded and told a fairly dull story about finding some empty rooms. Though Trista seemed interested at the revelation, Peyton looked as bored as Gloria felt. Biff, on the other hand, didn't even seem to be listening. When Steve asked him and Trista what they had found, Biff tensed even more. He looked to Trista, obviously praying for a reprieve.

"Why don't you tell them?" she said amiably, but with a certain viciousness in her eyes.

Biff returned to his pacing. "I don't know how to say this. I knew Amy, the girl who's supposed to be staying in Suite One."

Gloria jumped to attention. This was a story worth listening to.

"You're just realizing this now?" Peyton snapped.

Biff lowered his head even further. "The woman I knew was named Amy Light. She was an actress. We lived together for a few years."

Gloria couldn't help but notice a change in Peyton's face. It sure as hell looked like he knew an Amy Light, also.

Biff continued, "There was a picture of Amy in the Lichtenhoffs' room," he explained. "It was her."

Waylan had clung to that picture when Amy wasn't around. People who didn't really know him thought it was sweet.

Focusing on the more interesting matter at hand, she volunteered, "Amy was an actress. She could've changed her name."

Biff didn't even seem to hear her. He just continued talking, pacing, his eyes downcast. He stumbled over his words before finally taking a deep breath and stating flatly, "Amy's dead. She killed herself."

A smug smile filled Gloria's face. "Coward," she muttered, more to herself than anyone else.

Steve shot her a confused and slightly suspicious look. The goody-two-shoes seemed to think Gloria should pity her stepdaughter. A stupid thought.

He looked back to Biff and asked, "When did this happen?"

Biff fell into the chair, seemingly relieved at being done with the story. "A month ago."

Gloria's interest quickly changed to suspicion. "That's not true. She called us a couple of days ago. Told us to come here."

Biff shook off the comment and leaned his head back. "She was upset. A movie she'd been working on closed up.

She'd hoped it'd be her big break. The producer promised her plenty of exposure."

Gloria was about to protest again, when she saw Kat shift. It was almost as if her knees had gone out from under her. She was suddenly very pale. Her eyes were locked on Peyton when she asked, "What was the name of the movie?"

Biff didn't notice the glare that Kat got from Peyton, but Gloria sure did. Biff was too busy staring at the ceiling, too stupid to know he should be paying attention. "Some romantic comedy. 'A Week After…' something…"

"*A Week From Tuesday*," Kat said; it was a statement, not a question.

Trista's glance swung from Biff to Kat, her teeth bared. "That was your movie!" she cried. "The one that closed down because you were too smashed to remember your lines."

All eyes turned to Kat now. Her hand was clenching the arm of the chair, as if she couldn't even stand, never mind run. What was even more interesting was the look in her eyes. The woman didn't want to run. It was like she felt she deserved the accusations; she almost welcomed them. Gloria was pretty sure that a drug addict with a guilty conscience was a tragedy waiting to happen.

Ever the hero, Steve seemed to notice the same thing. He placed a gentle hand over hers, and gripped it tightly when she tried to pull it away. It seemed he already knew this story. Obviously Kat had wasted no time cozying up.

He turned a protective and nasty eye toward Peyton. "You were a producer on that movie, weren't you?"

Gloria hoped for an angry response to further escalate matters, but Peyton was a disappointment. His face was unreadable and his voice dramatically solemn. "I knew Amy well."

Biff's eyes grew wide. "That was you? She told me about you. Told me you were taking a special interest in her." Looking between Peyton and Trista, he added, "Now

I understand what kind of special interest she was talking about."

Peyton pretended not to hear the suggestion. "Amy was very talented. Her scenes were fantastic. Don't you remember, Kat? She played your best friend."

Gloria marveled at the way he played the fragile actress. It was no wonder she had such a complex. She seemed lost in the memory, and didn't reply, but Peyton let the moment hang, giving her plenty of time to blame herself.

"She was going to be heavily involved in promotion," he explained to the others, plainly trying to paint himself as a mentor, not a predator. "It would've given her a real boost. How could I have known the movie would never make it to the screen?"

Kat seemed to wither even more with the last comment. Steve was holding her hand more tightly now. Pretty soon he was going to have to hold her up.

Trista, possessive as always, didn't like the attention that the actress was getting. She took the opportunity to shift the focus. "Steve, you're the only one who hasn't explained how you knew Amy. Want to confess?"

Unlike everyone else in the room, Steve seemed completely unfazed by the revelations. He answered without any hesitation. "I have no idea who she is. I've never met anyone named Amy Light or Amy Lichtenhoff. I can't even think of anyone named Amy that I've ever known."

Gloria believed most of what he said, but there was something at the end. It seemed like he might have just remembered something – or perhaps someone. He'd known an Amy. And something very bad had happened with her.

Peyton rolled his eyes at Steve's response. "It'd be easier if we were all honest."

Still the only calm voice in the room, Steve asked, "How would it change anything? What does Amy have to do with any of this?"

"We all know the same girl. This is a lead. Don't you think that's important?" Peyton snarled.

"It's odd, but so what? We should be focused on Waylan. He's the one who was murdered. Besides, according to Biff, Amy's dead," Steve replied.

Gloria sat up a little straighter at his comment. It was a lie. With all the fun going on around her, she'd forgotten to push the point. "I talked to her two days ago. Waylan did, too. We drove here to meet her. She's alive."

Biff started pacing again. "All I know is what the Coast Guard told me. Amy took my boat out. There was a suicide note. I suppose it's possible she's alive. But hell, that's a pretty dramatic way to disappear. The boat was worth some cash. Why not steal it and sell it? She's dead. Nothing else makes sense."

Gloria waved her hand dismissively. "I don't care what makes sense. I know I talked to her."

Steve sighed, glancing nervously at Kat, who looked like hell. "It doesn't matter. Amy isn't here. This has nothing to do with her."

"So it's just a coincidence that we all knew her?" Peyton snapped, unable to keep the tension out of his voice.

Steve threw up his hands. "I don't know her. I swear."

Gloria suddenly realized what the others were missing. Maybe you had to really know Amy to understand. Fortunately, Gloria knew her stepdaughter very well. She looked at each of the guilty souls in the room. "You know, Amy had a good reason to be angry with every one of you."

The comment brought a roar from everyone in the room but Kat, who probably didn't even hear her.

Gloria ignored their denials. She looked at Steve first. "I don't know what you did, but it's so bad you won't even admit you knew her."

Steve started to argue, but Gloria waved a finger to silence him, and she moved on to Kat. "I don't see many movies. Don't like 'em. But I've seen ads for your pictures. You're pretty big shit. I don't doubt for a second that she'd kill you for blowing her chance. The girl has to have a little of her father's temper."

Kat couldn't even look up. Gloria knew she was just too easy; it wasn't worth spending any more time berating her.

She leaned across Trista to glare at Peyton. "Don't look so smug. No one believes you're the good guy here. You were using her."

Peyton gaped. "Using her? Using her? How? I was trying to help her...."

Gloria shook her head. "I'm bettin' you were helping her right into your bed."

Peyton clenched his teeth at the allegation. He looked at the others, clearly about to protest again, when Trista placed a hand on his knee. "Don't bother, baby."

Disregarding Peyton's fury, Gloria turned to Biff. "What'd you do to her?"

Biff's pacing stopped short. "I've got no idea what you're talking about."

"Drugs," Steve accused.

Biff's dark eyes flashed at Steve and then at Kat, telling Gloria exactly who'd sold Biff out.

"I didn't give her anything she didn't ask for," Biff explained. "Besides, if it wasn't for me, she wouldn't have been able to afford to go to all those auditions."

"And why was that?" Gloria asked, sensing she'd stumbled onto the real story.

Biff shuffled his feet uncomfortably. "I made sure she had work."

Peyton sat forward. "What kind of work?"

Biff met his eyes defiantly. "The kind that pays well."

"The kind that'll put her on the cover of *Hustler* if she makes it big?" Peyton sneered.

Biff shrugged. "It paid the bills. She was hot. And she was good at it. Probably better than she was in your movie."

Feeling she'd made her point, Gloria turned to Trista. "And you," she said simply. "You, worst of all."

"What the hell are you talking about?" Trista growled.

"Other than Biff here, was there ever a man Amy wanted that you didn't fuck first?"

Trista stared in disbelief. She opened her mouth twice to protest, but both times she was at a loss for the words.

Gloria continued, "I could hear you two talking. I saw what happened. Why do you think she left town?"

"She left town to get away from the man who beat her for fun!" she exclaimed, but the pain in Trista's eyes and quiver in her voice confirmed Gloria wasn't wrong.

"Tell them whatever you want," Gloria replied, gesturing dismissively at the others. "Waylan got what he deserved. Aren't y'all just a little worried you're next?"

Trista's eyes were afire with hatred. "Aren't you? How many years did you stand by and watch him hit her? The doctors. The school. How many others offered you help? You were just too fucking lazy to do anything about it."

"It was between her and her father. It wasn't my fight," Gloria snapped back.

"Has anything ever been your fight? I met you twelve years ago and I'll be damned if I ever saw you raise a finger to do anything for anyone. Aren't you worried she's going to come after you?"

Before the weight of Trista's words could sink in, Steve thundered to his feet. "Enough! Amy isn't here. We just finished searching the hotel. There's no one here but the six of us."

Placing an arm around Kat's shoulders, he said, "I think this conversation is over."

Peyton rose also, his anxiety just below the surface. "He's right. Whoever killed Waylan is long gone. We should try to go about our business for now. Soon enough, the phones will be working and we'll be able to call the police."

Gloria suspected they all knew Peyton was wrong. She could see the fear in their eyes. Despite the shouting, the accusing, they were all in a panic. They weren't sure Waylan's killer was gone; they really couldn't be certain there was no one else in the hotel. But they needed to run away;

they needed to hide; they needed to pretend that everything was normal. Life as a widow just got more interesting.

~ 37 ~

Steve escorted Kat to the kitchen, offering her a chair at the small table. He really wanted a beer, but he thought better of it with Kat there. Instead, he poured them both glasses of ice water.

"Drink that," he ordered.

"I killed that girl," Kat said.

"That's crap," he argued, joining her at the table. "Gloria talked to her two days ago. She's still alive. She probably just wanted to get away from Biff, so she faked the whole thing."

Her hands were clenched so tightly in front of her that he wondered how they could still be shaking.

"I don't even want to think what she had to do for Peyton to get those promises."

"She made her choices in life. She has to live with them. Just like you do."

Kat refused to meet his eyes. Instead, she stared at her clenched hands. "She couldn't have known I was going to self-destruct."

"She couldn't have known the movie would be successful, even if everything had gone as planned."

"Without me, she would have had a chance," Kat replied, her shoulders sinking even further.

Steve ran a hand over his face in frustration. "Please drink your water."

Seeming to lack the strength to argue, Kat took a sip.

"You feel guilty about this." It was a statement, not a question, but Steve still waited for Kat to look up before he continued. She met his eyes for an instant before looking away. "You're a drug addict. You're supposed to admit that your addiction hurt others, right? Isn't that one of the steps?"

Kat nodded, and focused her attention on the condensation that was beading up on her glass.

"I don't know much about this, but I can't imagine that's all there is to it. It'd be a pretty bad program if you were supposed to admit that you hurt others just so you can beat yourself up over it."

"She killed herself because of me." Kat's voice was pleading, not for forgiveness, but for condemnation.

"If she killed herself at all – and that's a really big if – it wasn't because of you. Maybe the movie closing up was a factor, but it certainly wasn't the reason. People lose jobs every day. They don't kill themselves. It's like your Bible verse says – everybody has the choice between life and death. It was her choice. Not yours."

Kat sat silently, but Steve continued, hoping she was listening. "From what I heard out there, this Amy girl had a crappy life. Your actions may not have helped, but she was on the edge already."

"So I'm just the straw that broke the camel's back?" Kat asked.

"You can't pretend the rest of it never happened."

The two of them sat in silence for a while. Steve watched carefully. Kat seemed calmer. Her hands weren't clasped as tightly. She'd stopped clenching and unclenching her teeth. But she stubbornly continued to avoid his eyes.

Hoping to shift her focus, Steve slid his hand over hers. "Why did you start using?"

Kat's head snapped up. "What does that have to do with anything?"

"I'm curious," he replied, gently rubbing her rigid hands.

"I don't want to talk about it." Kat couldn't hold his gaze. The guilt that Steve could see on her face was almost too much for him to bear. It looked like it was taking all her will not to run out of the room and hide. And they both knew that Biff was ready with the escape if she asked.

"Tell me the quick version if you want, but tell me how it happened," Steve insisted. He needed to keep her talking. Obviously she only slipped further away when she got this far into her head.

Kat began reluctantly. "I got more attention in my first movie than the studio expected. So my second movie, they went heavy on promotion. They had me on this worldwide schedule. It was a couple of months of interviews, parties, and red carpets. They had me up all night, running from one city to the next. What little free time I had, I tried to sleep, which meant I went for months without talking to my family or friends."

Kat shook her head. "Just the memory of it makes me tired. It was so not me, you know? I kept telling myself I'd get used to it. The 'glare of the lights' as they call it. But that was a mistake. I didn't get used to it. I don't think I ever will."

Steve nodded, wanting to tell her it was going to be all right. But they would have been empty words. Her eyes cleared a little as she told the story. Talking did seem to be helping.

"I started drinking to deal with it. The alcohol knocked me out on flights, helped me loosen up at parties. It worked for a while. But new movie offers came in fast. Before I knew it, I was on another project and the whole process was starting again. I was either shooting or promoting, or both, all the time. I started to drink more to cut through the stress. The hangovers were killing me."

Kat lowered her eyes, the shame apparent. She hated herself for this, anyone could have seen it. "I don't remember exactly when, but somebody offered me a line at a party. She said I looked tired. Said it would help. It did. And great side effects too. None of the calories of alcohol. I wasn't hungry as often. I used it for the occasional party when I needed a little boost. It went from there."

Steve lifted her chin and forced her to meet his eyes. "I respect you for realizing your addiction hurt more than just yourself. But it's an addiction. An illness. By the time you started that last movie, you probably didn't have much control over where this was going to end up."

Kat pulled away. She didn't want the excuses. He could see that. But he could also see that she was being much too hard on herself.

"Sometimes bad things happen," he insisted. "Sometimes we can prevent those bad things from happening. Sometimes bad things happen no matter what we do."

Kat shook her head. "I could've stopped. I could've never started."

Steve squeezed her hand. "You can't change what's past. All you can do is do better in the future."

"That's a cop-out."

"That's reality."

Kat stared back at him with what she undoubtedly intended to be anger, but all he saw was pain. "Stop being so nice," she demanded.

Steve smiled. "Honey, that's not going to happen."

There were tears in her eyes when she looked away. She brushed one aside as she stared out the window. "I should be the one who's dead. Don't you see? It should have been me. Not her. She just got hit by the shrapnel of my disastrous life. How was it fair that Peyton rescued me and nobody helped that girl?"

The weight of her pain bore down on Steve. He understood how she felt, better than Kat would imagine. "Life isn't always about what's fair. You have to accept what's happened and move on. Questioning it will make you crazy."

Kat wiped another tear away. "I was given so much and I ruined it all. If I'd known, I would have done it differently. Or I wish I would have."

The words echoed in Steve's mind, words that he'd said to himself so many times. Before, he'd thought he and Kat were different people from different worlds. Now, it looked like they had a lot in common.

~ 38 ~

From Peyton's room, Trista watched through the peephole as Biff slipped into Kat's suite. His right fist was balled up, concealing something small. Trista didn't have to use much imagination to know what it was. She turned from the doorway and smiled slyly at Peyton, who was sitting on his couch.

"Biff just left a little package for Ms. Lincoln."

"Already? Did you see her ask him?"

Trista considered lying, but thought the truth might be more useful. "I suspect this might have been a free sample. But something must have made Biff think she was looking."

Peyton nodded pensively. "We'll have to watch for signs that she took him up on his offer."

Trista smiled. Biff's move was encouraging. He was a professional. It was his job to know when someone was looking. Trista remembered the devastation on Kat's face earlier and she had to agree with him. Kat just needed an opportunity. The rest would take care of itself.

~ 39 ~

Biff slipped back into his room feeling accomplished. He knew a customer when he saw one. There was no reason to approach her again. The simple solution was best. Just leave the free sample. Once it was in her room, there was no way she'd be able to resist. She knew where to go if she needed more. And they both knew she'd need more.

Even though it was only noon, Biff was exhausted. It had already been a hell of a day. And he hadn't gotten much sleep waiting up for Amy.

He shook his head at the thought. He'd had no idea who he'd been waiting for. Pretty little Amy. Strange to think it'd been her all along.

He'd really thought things were going to work out for them. Thought he'd be able to get her out of the mainstream movie industry. She had a camera presence you rarely encountered in adult movies. He'd hoped to capitalize on that. At least he'd managed to make some cash after her death by selling some amateur video of the two of them.

He was still pissed that she'd packed it all in over some stupid movie. Even more pissed now that he'd met Kat and

Peyton.   Assholes like that weren't worth killing yourself over.

Biff pushed the memories aside and, focusing on his need for sleep, he closed the blinds. With them shut, the room was perfectly black. There was barely enough light to make out the doorway to the bedroom. In the darkness, he could almost pretend the morning had never happened. He was simply going to bed at the end of a long day.

He was sitting on the bed taking his shoes off when he heard it the first time. A whisper. So soft that he wasn't even sure he'd really heard it. His name. He stopped for a second and then laughed at himself. There was no one there but him. He was sure. Obviously he was exhausted. Needed sleep.

He snuggled into the enveloping softness of the bed. Warm. Cozy. He closed his eyes. Sleep.

Just as his mind started to drift away, he heard it again. Louder this time. His name. A voice saying his name. He sat straight up in bed and looked around. This time he was fairly certain he'd heard something.

He was shaking his head in disbelief when it happened again. Even louder. Definitely his name. The voice was familiar, though he couldn't quite place it. Someone was in the sitting room.

There it was again. He was certain. The sitting room.

He jumped out of bed.

"Who's there?" he growled.

He squinted in the dark. There might have been someone on the couch, but he couldn't be sure. The light switch was by the door. He moved toward it.

"It won't work," the voice said calmly.

"Amy?" It didn't quite sound like her, but it sounded similar.

She laughed at his discomfort. "The light won't work, Biff."

He reached the switch and, though he clicked it on, nothing happened.

"You're as trusting as ever, I see," Amy said.

"What'd you do to my lights? How'd you get in here? We searched the hotel. I searched this room myself. How are you here at all?"

"That's a lot of questions, Biff. Which one should I answer first?"

Squinting in the darkness, Biff tried to decide if she was really sitting on the couch. "Where did you come from?"

"Hell."

Biff shook his head in aggravation and started to walk toward her. Melodramatic as always. "Come on, Amy. Seriously, where were you hiding?"

His foot caught on the rug, and he looked down to regain his balance. When he looked back up, the silhouette from the couch was gone.

Biff's eyes darted around the room, hoping to catch a glimpse of her. "What are you up to?"

Her voice still came from the area around the couch. "You aren't quite as easy as Daddy, but you're pretty easy."

Barely listening as he scanned the darkness, Biff asked, "What?"

"You're predictable, Biff. I knew you'd come to work here. Knew you'd come back up here alone to score a new customer. Easy."

"What the hell are you talking about?"

Amy laughed. "Come on over here and I'll show you."

With his next step, his toe caught again on the rug. This time it caught him off guard. Before he realized what was happening, he was falling face first towards the floor. He fell so fast that his nose hit before he could stop himself. He could feel the blood flowing down his face immediately.

When he tried to straighten up, he felt a weight on top of him, like knees digging into the small of his back, hands pushing his head towards the ground. If this was Amy, she weighed a lot more than she used to. He could feel his arms being drawn behind him.

Oddly, her voice didn't come from behind him. Instead, it sounded like she was still sitting on the couch.

"Do you know what you did to me?" she asked. "What you took from me?"

Biff discovered his voice was weak. The weight on top of him was making it difficult to get air. "I don't know what you're talking about."

"You took my body and you sold it," she stated without anger.

"What?" he sputtered. "What are you talking about? I didn't take anything. I paid you. Fair and square."

"You got me so fucked up I didn't know what I was doing and you filmed me. I knew you'd sell the films whether I agreed or not. The only question was if I'd get paid."

The weight was getting heavier. Breathing was getting harder. But Biff tried to keep his voice cool, persuasive, "Baby, that was just for the first couple of films. After that, it was your decision."

The anger radiated from Amy, practically hitting him with physical force. "By the time I had a decision, there was nothing left to decide."

Biff tried to protest further, but couldn't get enough air. He was sure he was going to pass out, maybe even die. Was she going to kill him?

Amy let out a long, deep laugh, clearly savoring the moment. "It's not going to be that easy. I have a little gift for you first." The anger in her voice was gone again. Her tone was teasing, even flirtatious. "Listen carefully, Biff. Do you hear that?"

Biff forced himself to focus. At first there was nothing, but then he heard it. A hiss. Then another. To his right. To his left. He thought he could feel something on his leg, but until he felt it slither under his pants he wasn't sure. Snakes!

"Amy?" he whimpered, finding his voice. He desperately fought the urge to struggle.

One snake was sliding up his pant leg. Another slinking over his neck. One slithering up his shirt. A forked tongue hissing in his ear. He was surrounded.

Maybe if he didn't move they wouldn't hurt him. He could lay perfectly still. Take only shallow breaths. He closed his eyes so he wouldn't blink. He willed his heart to stop pounding.

"Lie among the snakes, my love," Amy said, her voice thick with mockery. "Maybe they'll welcome you as one of their own. You have a lot in common."

Sheer terror caused his cheek to twitch. Just a tiny twitch. But the movement drew their attention. Biff could feel a tongue slide across the spot. Followed by another. Though he tried to stop it, the sensation caused an involuntary muscle reaction, and the sudden movement was all the incentive the creatures needed.

The first bite was on his cheek. Quickly followed by his leg. His arm. His ankle. His neck. Once the biting began, it felt like it would never end. He wanted to scream, but the weight on his back turned the screams to yelps.

As he lay there helpless, all he could hear was Amy's laughter echoing. Echoing. Echoing. And then fading into nothing.

~ 40 ~

Mid-afternoon, Trista and Peyton appeared in the dining room, hungry and more than a little curious about Kat and Steve. Peyton selected a table while Trista skulked towards the kitchen, hoping to eavesdrop on any conversations that might be occurring. Unfortunately, an ear to the door yielded only whispers. As quietly as she could, she slipped inside.

Kat was sitting on the counter facing Trista, but Steve was standing directly in front of her, obstructing her view. He was very close. One hand rested on her thigh. The other looked like it was on her cheek or in her hair. Trista couldn't tell which. Though they were clearly talking, their voices were inaudible.

Trista cleared her throat. "I don't mean to interrupt y'all," she began with false charm. "But do you think we can get some food out here?"

Kat jumped at the sound of her voice. A good sign. The more off-balance Kat was, the more likely Trista was going to find the right information for Peyton.

Steve didn't even turn around. "I'll be out in a minute. You know where the menus are."

Trista was annoyed that he didn't even glance her way but, not knowing what else to do, she rejoined Peyton.

Once they were alone again, Steve took a deep breath and whispered to Kat, "I'm going to have to take care of them. You sure you're okay?"

She smiled that famous Hollywood smile of hers. "I'll be fine."

He shook his head. "Does that work on most people?"

"What?"

"The smile. Are people so taken in by it they forget the question they asked?"

The fabulous smile faded and Kat laughed. "Actually, yeah. I can't think of anyone it doesn't work on."

"Now *that* laugh is much more believable. I'm going to find out what those two pains in my ass want to eat. Are you going to go out and join them?"

"I'd rather stay in here with you, if I won't be in the way."

The suggestion was fairly ridiculous as far as Steve was concerned. She was a guest – and not just any guest. He was the staff. Even with all that was going on, blurring those lines was a mistake.

Kat hopped down off the counter and defiantly took a seat at the table. "There's a body upstairs. We're trapped here and we can't get the police. Rules of etiquette are out the window."

He only shook his head in response. "I'll be back."

Trista and Peyton were whispering conspiratorially in the corner when Steve walked in. The topic of their whispers was evident from the quick end to the conversation.

"Did you find the menus?" Steve asked when he reached the table.

Peyton offered Steve his own version of the Hollywood smile – just as broad, but filled with conceit. "Sorry we interrupted your mid-afternoon tryst."

Steve wanted to punch him and, if he hadn't known Peyton would take it out on Kat, he would have. "I don't know what Trista told you, but we were talking. And, by the way, I don't see how it's any of your business."

Peyton's smile became more of a sneer. "I know you don't know my business, but here's the thing, cowboy. I have a lot of money invested in that woman, and I'm not the only one who does. Until she proves she can stay on her feet long enough to bring in some profits, keeping an eye on her *is* my business."

Steve bit his tongue so hard he could taste blood. "Have you two decided what you want?"

The looks Steve got in response gave him more of an answer than he'd really wanted. They'd decided what they wanted and they were not at all happy that she'd chosen to hide in the kitchen to avoid them.

~ 41 ~

Kat watched Steve's temper rise as he served lunch. She considered offering to help again, but he'd made his feelings on that very clear.

She wished she had the courage to ask what was going on in the other room, but she knew it was a stupid question. It was obvious why Steve was getting angry, and though she appreciated his protectiveness, she felt bad about being the cause of the strain.

When he returned from a trip into the dining room, plates in hand, Kat figured that the others had left. The way he tossed the plates into the sink confirmed it.

"I'm guessing they left a big tip?"

Steve shook his head. Though he still seemed determined to keep his opinions to himself, he finally cracked. "They have no right to stalk you like that," he declared, flinging a stray fork on top of the dishes.

"Careful. You'll be even more pissed off if you break those." Her voice was calm, but her heart was pounding. It hurt to know her friends were suffering because of her enemies. It was yet another part of her life she'd been sweeping under the rug. Pretending it didn't bother her was the only way she knew to handle it.

"It has nothing to do with you," she added.

"I know it's not about me. It's about you," he snapped, turning to her. "But I'm sure as hell not going to stand here and let them treat you like that! What did you ever do to them?"

Kat smiled at the simple way he looked at things. His blue eyes were glowing with anger. It was an unfamiliar comfort to have someone who was ready to go to battle for her. "Peyton is angry because I won't let him control me. He controls everyone – that's the way he does business. He's hoping to use my mistakes to back me into a corner and force me to reconsider his original proposition."

Describing Peyton's agenda made it sound silly. It was about power and control. That's all it had ever been about. The fact that he couldn't control an addict he'd found unconscious on the floor was completely unacceptable to him. Kat could feel her inner tension begin to dissipate, as she realized that, in an odd way, she was winning.

She hopped up on the counter and ran her hand over Steve's face. "It's very sweet of you to look out for me. Thank you. But please don't let them make you crazy."

She gave him a kiss. Soft. Gentle. She felt strengthened and almost confident when he was around. It was a wonderful feeling. Wonderful enough to make her forget all the rules, all the promises she'd made to herself. At least for now.

"Well, that was sufficiently distracting." He grinned.

She smiled back. "Yeah, it was."

"You're okay?" he asked.

"Don't I look okay?"

"You look fantastic. But you always look fantastic. I just want to make sure what's underneath is all right."

The observation was unnerving, but freeing. There was no point in playing games with him. He was going to see through them anyway. It was both a good thing and a bad thing.

"You were the one out there fighting with them. I was safely tucked in here the whole time. I'm fine."

"What about the Amy situation?"

Kat sighed deeply. The Amy situation was another thing entirely. "I'll be okay. But I may require some significant attention from the likes of you to make sure," she teased.

Steve smiled a little at her joke, but seemed to mostly ignore it. He was looking deeply into her eyes in a way that made her feel that he was peering inside her, trying to find what was broken. Silly as it was, she wondered if he might actually be able to find it and fix it.

Seemingly satisfied, Steve laid a gentle hand on her shoulder. "I think we both need to eat something."

"Lunch sounds good," she lied. She couldn't have had less interest in lunch, but an end to this conversation was welcome. "Is there anything I can do to help?"

"Actually, while I get lunch ready, would you mind running up to Gloria's room to see if she wants anything?"

"But then I won't be able to watch and find out all your cooking secrets. How am I supposed to eat when I have to go back to L.A.?"

"I'm obviously controlling you with food. If I let you know all my secrets, I'd have no leverage."

Kat looked deeply into his sparkling eyes and she again felt his strength. It warmed her inside, made her heart beat a little faster, and clouded her mind a little, but in a good way for a change. He had leverage, and it had nothing to do with food.

"What are you staring at?" he asked uncomfortably after a moment.

She smiled at his discomfort and gave him another quick kiss. "You just keep thinking it's all about your cooking."

She hopped down off the counter before he could say anything else. "I'll go see if Gloria wants anything."

Without the sun pouring through the windows, the lobby was riddled with long, lurking shadows. The pictures, so cheery the day before, seemed dark and foreboding. Again, Kat was reminded of her first horror movie – the heroine wandering off alone, danger hiding in the shadows. She'd ended up on the bad end of an ice pick in that movie. She hoped real life would turn out better.

Though her anxious mind pleaded with her to run back to Steve, she refused to be a baby. They'd searched the hotel. There was no one else there. Besides, one scream would bring the others running.

She took a deep breath and ascended the stairs towards the dimly lit second floor, where a whole new set of horrors awaited: the pushy drug dealer, her sadistic boss, and his latest pawn. Though there seemed to be a new enemy around every corner, Kat knew she couldn't cower behind Steve forever.

The stench in the upstairs hallway only made matters worse. Kat wasn't sure if it was the body or Biff's deposit in the corner, but this wing was quickly becoming unlivable. She tried to keep her head down as she approached the suites. She didn't think she could even look at the door to Suite One. In her mind's eye, she could still see the body, smell the blood, taste the fear.

Yet in spite of her best efforts, her eyes were drawn to the door. Below the number, she noticed a scratch. A big one. But in the dimly lit hall it was hard to tell what had happened. Had someone been in there? Had their search not been as thorough as they'd thought? Had one of the others done this?

Kat took cautious steps toward the door. It was closed. Probably locked, but she didn't want to get close enough to try the knob. It was more than a scratch. Deep scars had been left in the rich, dark wood. Writing? It looked like writing.

It was writing, scrawled writing. Big block letters, all capitals. W-R-A-T-H. As the letters became more clear, she realized two things. Based on everything she'd heard earlier, anger had been a serious problem for Waylan. Also, she immediately thought of Amy. Was this her retribution?

Fear began to rise, but Kat tried to swallow it. One of the others had to have done this. Maybe Gloria? Her feelings towards Waylan were obvious.

Yet Kat's dread only deepened. The carving was jagged. Slashed in anger. She found herself unable to look away from the letters. As she stared, she heard a noise to her left. A scratching. The door next to her. Biff's door.

Dread quickly became panic as the scratching continued, and then intensified. Actually, it was more of a slashing noise. A knife against wood. Scraping. Tearing.

When Kat found the strength to look, there was no one there. But the defacement of Biff's door continued. No knife was visible. There was nothing there at all.

Yet a G had been scrawled in the door. An R was just completed. And, as some invisible force formed an E, Kat began to scream.

~ 42 ~

Kat's screams pealed through the hallways with a
terror that almost stopped Steve's heart. He was out of the
kitchen and up the stairs before his conscious mind began to
process what was happening. She was alone. Alone because
he'd sent her away. He took the steps two at a time and
almost ran down Peyton and Trista along the way.

He turned the corner ready for a fight, but he wasn't
ready for what he saw. The hallway was empty. Every door
closed. And Kat was cowering against the door to Gloria's
suite. She was screaming uncontrollably and tears were
running down her cheeks. It looked as if the devil himself
was standing before her, but she was entirely alone.

It wasn't until Steve laid a gentle hand on her shoulder
that she even seemed to realize they were there. It was like
the contact broke some sort of spell. Still she only stared
helplessly at him. Though she'd stopped screaming, she
didn't look like she could get her voice to do anything else.

He pulled her close, smoothed her hair and whispered
soothing words, incredibly relieved that she was physically in

one piece. But her behavior was disturbing. She was shaking terribly, and tears were still streaming down her face.

"What the hell is going on?" Peyton asked, looking much less sympathetic.

Steve glared at him. "Kat, honey, what happened?"

Kat's eyes were still wide with fear, her breathing uneven. Slowly, she raised a shaking hand and pointed at the door in front of her. Biff's room. There was something scratched in the door. A single word – GREED.

Trista looked between Kat and the door. A smirk of superiority on her face. "You're screaming over some marks on his door?"

Steve squinted at the scratched wood. "Greed? What's that supposed to mean?"

Kat pointed to the other suite.

"Greed and Wrath? What is that about? Kat, who did this?"

Her voice was raspy from the screaming. "The word just appeared."

Steve wondered if she realized just how crazy she sounded. Taking Kat's hand, he knocked on Gloria's door. Kat needed to sit down, gather herself.

"It's open," Gloria called from inside.

Steve opened the door, furious that she was in there and had done nothing. He wondered if Biff was in his room ignoring her, too. He'd kill the bastard for that.

Gloria was stretched out on her couch. Cheers were resounding from a game show. "Didn't you hear the screaming?" Steve asked.

"I assumed you fellas would handle that. I'm a very slight woman. What'd you expect me to do?"

Steve led Kat to an overstuffed chair near Gloria. She was so pale. Eyes so wide, yet almost vacant. He'd have to let Gloria's stupidity go. There were more pressing issues.

Trista was also looking closely at Kat, but there was no concern in her eyes, only suspicion. "What do you mean 'the word just appeared'?"

Kat looked away from them all and seemed to focus on her breathing, trying to get the shallow gasping breaths under control. When Steve put a gentle hand on her shoulder, she managed to look up.

Her eyes met his; the deep, sweet brown was now edged with desperation, fear. Something terrible had happened in that hallway and he was going to have to figure out how to convince her she could, and should, trust him enough to tell the truth.

When she finally spoke, she locked her eyes on Steve, seeming to need him for the courage to speak at all. "As I was walking down the hall, I saw the writing on Suite One first. I couldn't tell what it was initially. It just looked like scratches. When I got closer, I realized it was writing. There was nothing on Biff's door when I walked by originally. I would've noticed."

"Why do you think you would have noticed?" Peyton challenged.

"I would have noticed," Kat repeated. Steve tried to keep the doubts out of his eyes, but he feared his skepticism was already showing.

"The scraping started as I was standing there. I could hear it happen. A knife, or something like that, against the wood. When I turned there was no one there, no knife, but the scraping continued. There were letters being formed on the door. It was as if some invisible hand was scratching them as I stood there. The G and R were there before I turned. But I swear to you, the last three letters appeared as I watched."

Steve looked more closely at her eyes. There was no sign that she was unfocused, medicated. But he wondered if that was something he'd be able to see. As much as he hated to admit it, there was only one person in the room who might know the answer to that question. Reluctantly, he looked to Peyton. Immediately, Steve realized his mistake. His smug smile told Steve all he needed to know.

"You expect us to believe the letters just appeared?" Peyton was enjoying this. A lot.

Kat shook her head. "Honestly, no. I don't expect you to believe me. But I swear that's how it happened."

Trista laughed loudly. "Exactly how much coke does a person have to snort before they start seeing things? I'm curious. Maybe I'll try it."

Kat turned on Trista like an injured dog. "What the hell is your problem? You don't know me. Don't pretend that you do. I'm not high!" The shrillness of her voice was shocking. And unless Steve missed his guess, the tone surprised Kat more than anyone. In little more than a whisper, she pleaded, "I swear, I'm not using anymore."

Before Kat could say anything, he dropped to his knees and grabbed her chin roughly.

"Look at me," he ordered.

Kat met his eyes with focus and determination. "Steve, I…"

He held up a hand for her to stop. He had to try to see for himself. Her eyes were focused. Her pupils were a normal size. He couldn't see anything that told him there was something wrong. Certainly it wasn't a foolproof test, but the more he thought about it, he couldn't figure how she'd had time to do anything. She'd only left him a few minutes ago. He gave her a small smile and squeezed her hand. He could see Kat relax with the offer of support.

Peyton snickered at Steve's reaction. "Do you really think you can tell just by looking at her? She shot entire movies and no one knew. That's with make-up people, costume designers, and costars standing just as close as you are now. Please. Where'd you get it, Kat? Did you bring it with you?"

Kat reluctantly looked up at Peyton. "I know there's nothing I can say that'll convince you. But I know what I saw. And I know I haven't used since that day you found me. I'm willing to take whatever drug test you want when I leave here."

Steve watched as the smugness faded from Peyton's face. Despite his desire to mock, he was seeing the same thing that Steve was. Kat was clear-headed. It was almost impossible to believe that what she was telling them was the truth, but clearly Peyton saw that she wasn't high.

Trista wasn't so easily persuaded. "Kat, I saw Biff drop the package in your room. Lie all you want. Hell, as far as I'm concerned, use whatever you want. But please, don't bring us into your delusions."

The remark was disturbing. Steve looked between Trista and Kat. Had she accepted Biff's offer?

Kat shook her head, appearing as confused as Steve. "Biff offered me a sample when I arrived. I didn't take it."

A sly smile curled on Trista's lips. "Whatever you say, sweetheart."

Steve recognized the game she was playing. There was only one way to end it. "Why don't we bring Biff in here and ask him?"

Gloria looked away from the television for the first time since they'd arrived. "Why don't you have your little conversation over in his room? You're interrupting my shows."

Steve glared at her. "I'm sorry if we're bothering you, but there are some serious things happening here, in case you hadn't noticed."

"I've noticed that with all your yapping I completely missed the doctor's diagnosis."

"The doctor?"

"On my show, you idiot. I didn't mind the talking so much when you first came in. That was just a game show. But this is prime soap time now, and Tia is about to confront her twin about the baby. I'll be furious if I miss that."

It was all Steve could do not to hurl the television against the wall.

Trista only shook her head in disgust. "We should just go talk to Biff."

They were all heading towards the door when Gloria spoke again. "Hey, Steve, I'm awful hungry. Why don't you send a sandwich up? Maybe a steak sandwich. You have those, right?"

Steve stopped short, but refused to face her. "You're really ordering lunch? Now?"

"I could call downstairs, but you're obviously not there. I'd like to eat before the next show comes on. That one's better than this one. More fast-paced. Tough to eat and watch at the same time."

Knowing nothing he could say would change the situation, Steve bit his tongue and agreed to take care of it.

~ 43 ~

Kat followed the others to Biff's door. She wasn't sure what Steve really expected to accomplish by confronting him. Either he would refuse to admit he'd ever offered Kat drugs, or he'd lie and say he'd been filling her orders since she'd arrived. But it seemed Steve believed her, so she was happy to do whatever he asked.

She really hadn't expected any of them to believe her story. It was insane. It was just the sort of hallucination one might see if they were way too high on something. Too bad she didn't have any of the drug buzz to cut the fear.

Steve pounded on Biff's door. "Biff, if you don't open this door, we're coming in!"

He waited a beat before using the master key, and then opened the door slowly. "Biff?" he said again.

Much like Suite One, the room was undisturbed. It was dark; the blinds were drawn, the only light coming from the hallway. Nothing looked out of place – that is, except for the man lying in the middle of the floor. It was Biff. Kat could tell that for sure. He was face down. His body was puffy, bloated, and completely covered with red welts. Even as she peered closer to try to figure out what had happened, Steve pushed them all back.

He seemed to know something that the rest of them didn't. He was looking around the room. Searching desperately for a predator that Kat couldn't begin to guess.

Before Kat could ask, Trista pulled Peyton away from the door. "Snakes!" she said in a high-pitched whisper.

Peyton shook off her grip. "What about snakes?"

Steve looked at him in a mixture of shock and disgust. Kat felt herself take a small step farther from the doorway on instinct. Puffy, blotchy welts. Snakebites? That didn't sound wrong. Even though the idea of snakes in someone's hotel room sure did.

"There have to be hundreds of them," Trista said in the same sharp whisper. Her back was now against Gloria's door, as far from Biff's room as she could get.

Kat looked from Trista to Steve. She could see the look in his eyes. He was thinking the same thing. That's what he was searching the room for.

"Ladies," Steve said as calmly as possible. "Step away from the door. Go back to Gloria's room and close that door. Peyton, I'm going to need you to stand in the doorway and watch for snakes. I have to get Biff out of there. See if we can help him."

Peyton seemed to consider if there was a debonair way to escape, but finding none, he grudgingly agreed.

Steve looked back at Trista and Kat. "Go," he ordered.

Trista nodded and quickly retreated.

Kat, however, shook her head. "I'm staying here. You may need help. Peyton and I will both watch."

Steve glared at her.

"Go," she ordered, using the same tone he'd just used. "Biff needs help."

The room was shadowy and dark. Steve tried the switch by the door, but Kat wasn't surprised at all that it didn't work. There was something strange going on in this hotel, something bigger than all of them. And it seemed pretty clear that it was something evil.

Steve edged forward in the semi-dark, scanning the room as he walked. He headed straight for Biff, his head darting with every step. Each instant that passed, Kat's pulse rate rose. It was all that she could do not to call him back, beg him to leave Biff for dead and lock the door behind him. But even Biff deserved better than that.

"Do you see anything?" Steve called back to Kat and Peyton.

"Nothing," Peyton said. "Are you sure those are snakebites? There aren't any snakes. Really, it's much too dark to tell anything, don't you think?"

Steve didn't react to the question. He approached the body cautiously, grabbing one arm and plainly trying to keep a safe distance in case a snake remained intertwined.

Kat was so fixed on the sight that she didn't even notice that Peyton had taken matters into his own hands. In three long strides he was in the room and peering over Steve's shoulder.

"He looks pretty dead, I'd say," Peyton said without an ounce of compassion.

The sound of his voice caused Steve to jump and drop Biff's body. Kat suspected the sound of the body hitting the floor was probably all the confirmation they needed about Biff's well-being.

"What the hell are you doing?" Steve snapped.

Peyton switched on the table lamp and scanned the room one final time. "There are no snakes." He turned to Kat, who was still in the doorway. "You don't need to stand there."

But Kat only saw the fear in Steve's eyes. "I'm going to keep looking."

Peyton shrugged. "Is he dead?"

The muscles in Steve's jaw tightened before he spoke. "It seems that way."

Gently, Steve leaned down and turned Biff on his back. In the lamplight, Kat could tell she was looking at another dead body. Blood covered his face and the neck of his shirt. His nose was oddly bent, as if it was broken. His eyes were wide and staring at the ceiling. A large, inflamed bite stood out starkly on one cheek. She didn't know snakebites, but she thought it looked like she'd have expected a snakebite to look.

"Well, he certainly looks dead," Peyton agreed. "You sure those aren't hives or something?"

Kat was amazed at Peyton's calm. Not only was it upsetting to see the dead man lying before him, it was even worse to realize another of them was gone. One dead man might be a murder, but two felt more like a trend.

Seeing that he wasn't going to get an answer, Peyton continued, "Where are the snakes? Or is this like your coyote analogy?"

Steve looked cautiously around the room, under chairs and couches. He checked the bathroom. The bedroom.

"I think it's an allergic reaction," Peyton declared. "That would make more sense."

"It looks like he hit his nose. How did he fall face first into the ground? Why didn't he put his arms out?" Kat asked from the doorway.

Peyton shook his head. "Maybe he passed out and fell face first. That'd explain the nose."

Steve shook his head in exasperation. "These are snakebites. See the two dots in each of the welts? Fang marks. I don't know what else to say. I'd like Trista to look at them, too. It looked like she'd seen snakebites before." Steve looked up at Kat. "Could you ask her to come in here?"

Kat was reluctant to leave her post, but she nodded and went across the hall to get Trista. She found her pacing nervously just inside the doorway.

"What happened?" Trista asked the moment Kat opened the door.

"There are no snakes."

"Then how is he covered with snakebites?"

"That's the million-dollar question," Kat replied. "Steve wants you to come and look at the body. Just to make sure you agree."

A shadow crossed Trista's face; Kat was surprised to realize it was sadness. "He's dead?"

"Yeah."

"Dead, huh?" Gloria called from her perch on the couch. "You better watch your back, girls. Amy's coming to get you."

Trista rolled her eyes, and, for a moment, she and Kat were allies. "Let's go."

Peyton was standing in the hallway, looking closely at the carvings in the door to Biff's room. Steve was standing next to him, cautiously glancing back into the room.

"His sin?" Peyton wondered.

"What do you mean?" Trista asked.

"The word – Greed – do you think it's written on the door because someone perceived it to be his sin?"

"You mean the killer wrote why he killed Biff?" Steve looked between the carving and Peyton.

"It would make sense," Kat noted. "And Wrath would make sense for Lichtenhoff, if you believe Gloria."

Trista nodded. "This is one time I can agree with that worthless woman."

"Somebody killed the two of them and then wrote the reason they killed them on the door to their room?" *With an invisible hand?* Kat wanted to add, but thought better of it.

"It looks that way," Peyton agreed.

Trista was peering into the room. "Are you sure there are no snakes in there?"

"I searched everywhere. Nothing," Steve insisted. "I'd like you to look at the welts. Tell me what you think the marks look like."

Trista skulked into the room, her body tense. She spoke as she looked at the body, seeming desperate for any way to relieve the strain she was feeling. "Red welts. Swollen. Most of them have two marks, with slight tears. They've gotta be snakebites. But Jesus, there are so many. How the hell could there be this many? Did you see the ones on his stomach? My god, did they crawl up his shirt?" She stepped away on reflex, her eyes darting about the room.

Steve offered the only answer they had, "I don't know where they could have gone. Or how they could have gotten in here. But there's nothing here now."

Trista turned to Peyton. "Those are snakebites. Couldn't be anything else."

"What do we do now?" Kat asked. "We were assuming the person who killed Lichtenhoff was gone. It doesn't look like he is."

"It could just be a coincidence," Peyton suggested.

"I see like fifty bites. There have to be more under his clothes. No way can this be some freak accident," Trista replied.

Peyton rolled his eyes. "Are you suggesting that someone killed him by putting snakes in his room? That's insane."

"Are you suggesting that a ton of snakes just happened to get into Biff's room, through his locked door, killed him, and then left the way they got in?" Trista retorted.

Peyton scowled. And for once, Kat had to agree. The whole situation didn't make any sense. None of it did.

~ 44 ~

Though furious about Gloria's order, Steve found himself standing over a griddle frying steak. Since he was determined not to let her out of his sight, Kat was sitting at the table sipping a glass of water and staring at the falling rain.

"Can you tell me again what you saw in the hallway?" he asked over the snapping grease.

Kat continued to stare at the rain as she spoke. He could tell she wanted to drop the whole thing. That was a good sign. Didn't they say that the truly crazy have no idea what they're saying is crazy? He wondered if that applied to drug-induced hallucinations as well.

"The letters just appeared. It was like they were being carved right before my eyes, but there was nothing carving them."

He couldn't bring himself to really look at her as she spoke. The truth was, he believed her. Things were just strange enough in this hotel that the prospect of phantoms didn't seem that far off. But that didn't mean he was ready to admit it. "So, we're looking for an invisible man?"

"That would explain why we didn't find anyone when we searched the hotel." Though she clearly intended a joke, the comment carried no humor.

"We're looking for an invisible man, murderous snakes, and…" his voice trailed off. It felt too ridiculous to continue, even in jest.

"And mauling coyotes," Kat added for him. Finally looking in his direction, she added, "None of this makes any sense."

Steve agreed, but he didn't answer. Instead, he focused on cutting the roll and preparing Gloria's plate.

Ignoring his evasion, Kat plowed on. "Unless Waylan and Biff were connected in some way we don't know, Amy is the only thing they have in common."

He did not like the direction of this conversation. Discussions with Kat about Amy could only be disastrous. "Unless Amy is invisible, I don't see how she carved up those doors."

"Maybe Biff was right and Amy is dead."

Steve turned and gave Kat his full attention. "Are you really suggesting that Amy's haunting the hotel?"

She shrugged. "It's no more ridiculous than your coyote theory."

"The coyote comment was an analogy. It was never a theory," he grumbled, running a greasy hand over his tired eyes.

Undaunted, Kat continued, "Do you have a theory on how something human did that to Waylan? You said yourself someone or something gnawed on his boot."

"I said it *looked* like something gnawed on his boot. I'm not saying that's what really happened," Steve replied, as he flipped the steak one final time.

"To be clear," Kat said, "I think the ghost thing sounds dumb, too. As does the coyote theory. It also seems pretty unbelievable that a whole bunch of snakes attacked Biff. I'm dying for a logical theory if you have one."

Steve tossed Gloria's plate on a tray. He didn't look at Kat when he spoke. "I'll give you a theory: A crazy, violent lunatic murdered Waylan last night. The storm caused some snakes to seek shelter inside. They ended up in Biff's room."

"On the second floor?" Kat countered.

"Let me finish. Biff was overcome by the snakes. They killed him."

"And the broken nose?"

"Like Peyton said, he probably broke it when he fell."

"And what I saw in the hallway?"

"You're mistaken."

"Do you think you could actually look at me when you give that explanation, or do you prefer to avoid eye contact when tossing out viable theories?" Kat quipped.

Steve sighed and met her eyes. "I don't know. But talk of ghosts will only cause panic."

~ 45 ~

Gloria's thoughts were filled with ghosts of a different kind. Little Anna Maria had died on the show last week. After her funeral, she'd returned as a ghost. The story was that the heavens were allowing her to set things right – to hand out a little justice for herself and her family. Gloria thought it was a stupid storyline. A childish notion. If there was a heaven, they sure as hell weren't letting people come back to set things right.

Her disinterest gave her the opportunity to consider the goings on in the real world. She was having fun messing with the girl and the actress. She'd watched Waylan use mental manipulation for years. And she was quickly discovering she was a natural. A snide remark here. A sarcastic retort there. And poof! They were bugs at your feet.

Though Gloria's suggestion that Amy was on a rampage had originally been little more than gamesmanship, the more she thought about it, the more the theory appealed to her. Waylan was certainly a jackass, but who other than Amy would have hated him so much? As for the little man from

California, well, Gloria was going to have to find out more information about that situation.

A knock at the door brought the answer she was looking for.

"It's open," she called.

Steve came into the room, tray in hand, the nervous actress trailing behind him.

"You really shouldn't leave this unlocked. Until we know more, we can't be sure it's safe," Steve said.

Gloria snorted at the comment. "I'm not getting up to let you fools in and out every five minutes. If it's not one thing, it's another."

"With all that's happening, I think it's best if we're more careful," Steve remarked.

"What exactly is going on? Did I hear Trista talking about snakes? Did someone put a copperhead in Biff's bed?" she asked, practically grinning at the prospect.

Always cautious to a point of annoyance, Steve seemed to consider his answer carefully. "We don't really know what happened. But he died from a number of snakebites."

Gloria resisted the urge to roll her eyes at the plainly edited answer. "Did you find the snake?"

"No. We didn't."

Gloria nodded as she calculated. Amy slaughtered her father. Then she planted a snake in the room of her former lover? It actually made sense. Few men were more vicious than Waylan, making a vicious murder appropriate. And Gloria had little doubt that few men were bigger snakes than Biff Winn.

Again overreacting, Steve added, "There's no reason to worry, but keeping your door locked is a good idea."

Gloria laughed at his warning. "There's every reason to worry. At least for you people. This is Amy's doing. I'm sure of it."

"We don't know that," Steve insisted.

"You're deluding yourself. If I was in your position I would too, but happily I'm only here because I came with my husband."

"If this is Amy, why aren't you worried?" Kat snapped.

Gloria's lips curled into a smile. "Honey, Amy and I had an unspoken agreement. I stayed out of her life. She stayed out of mine. It worked for us. She's got no cause to fight with me."

~ 46 ~

Trista was pacing the room, trying not to obsess about Amy. She couldn't get Gloria's warnings out of her head. Could Amy really be after them all? The girl had always been too much of a doormat to stand up to anyone. Could a person change that dramatically?

They'd been best friends since kindergarten. Or they had been. Trista hadn't heard a word from Amy, not since the day she'd run away. Now that she thought about it, she realized it had been years since she'd gone. Not a letter, or a call, nothing. Was that really what a friend should have expected?

They'd had their differences. Particularly at the end. Amy had gotten so distant toward the end of senior year. But that had really been about Waylan, hadn't it?

Trista was consumed by the question when Peyton's growl invaded her thoughts. "You need to sit down."

She turned to find him sitting on the couch, feet propped on the coffee table, an open magazine on his lap. He looked completely unruffled, even if a little annoyed by her pacing.

She glared at him. "How are you this calm? We're trapped here!"

Peyton kicked his feet to the floor in frustration, but his voice was calm. "You're being dramatic. We're not trapped. We're just stuck until the rain stops."

Trista looked out the window at the constant stream of water. "I don't think this rain is ever going to stop."

"It's rain. Rain stops, eventually. And when it does we'll be on our way." Peyton ran a hand over his face. "It'll stop overnight. We'll be out of here first thing tomorrow."

Trista stepped closer to the couch, standing directly over him. "We could all be dead by then."

Throwing back his head, Peyton guffawed at the prospect. "And how exactly are we all going to die?"

"Two people have died in less than twenty-four hours. That doesn't concern you?"

"Why would it concern me?" he asked, pulling her onto the couch with him. "Waylan obviously pissed somebody off and they killed him. The kind of person that would chop him up like that wouldn't hide and wait for another chance. And it's you who keeps saying Biff was attacked by snakes. Nobody killed him. No problem. You're just panicking."

"You bet your ass I'm panicking," Trista replied, wiggling from his grasp. "What about the fact we all knew Amy?"

Peyton shrugged. "It's peculiar, but so what? Do you think tiny little Amy was capable of doing that to her father?"

"Well…" Trista hated to acknowledge the good point.

Peyton swung an arm over the back of the couch, letting his fingers tangle in her hair. Trista knew he was trying to distract her. She actually didn't want to fight him; she wanted to be distracted. The questions in her head were driving her crazy.

"And what about Biff?" Peyton pointed out. "Do you think Amy killed him by throwing snakes at him?"

Again, Trista saw the good point. But, as much as she wanted to, she couldn't quite let it go. "What about what Kat saw?"

Peyton smirked. "Please. For all we know, Kat carved those letters herself."

Trista sat back, enjoying the gentle feel of his fingers. Even as her body relaxed, her mind remained tense. She needed more than Peyton's vague assertions about their safety. She needed something to convince her to ignore Gloria's theories about Amy wanting revenge.

"Were you and Amy spending a lot of time together before the movie closed up?" she asked.

Peyton's hands stiffened and his face darkened in response.

Trista laughed. "I'm not judging. I'm just wondering how she was doing."

"She was fine, excited about the movie. Unfortunately, she was very naïve. With more time in the industry, that would have bitten her in the ass."

Trista sat forward a little. "What do you mean?"

"She was completely taken in by Kat. Bought her whole act. You see, Kat's very warm during her movies. Always throwing around compliments. Bringing gourmet coffee for the cast and crew. Nonsense like that."

"That sounds nice." Trista was surprised by the description. She would have expected Kat to be more of a diva. She was certainly famous enough.

"Please. Who's actually that nice? Kat just wanted to make sure all the stories in the tabloids were good. Now we know what she was trying to hide."

Whatever the truth, Trista was sick of talking about Kat. "Tell me more about Amy. Was she enjoying Hollywood?"

Peyton shrugged. "I guess. I only knew her during the movie. It was a hectic time."

"Was she happy with Biff?"

"She was sleeping with me. She didn't really talk about her boyfriend."

The questions were getting her nowhere. Yet Trista wanted to keep asking more. She wanted to know Amy was happier in L.A. That her desperate flight from Texas had been for the best.

Trista tried to shake off the paranoia, assuring herself that Amy had no reason to be mad, one way or the other. Gloria didn't know what she was talking about. Amy understood that men wanted Trista. She couldn't help it if it sometimes happened to be guys Amy liked. Things just happened. She couldn't be held accountable for that.

But even as Trista defended herself, names kept coming to her. Instances where Amy had lost her chance. Times when Trista had to admit she'd encouraged the boy's interest. Five. Ten. Fifteen. Could there have been that many? Were there more?

Logically, Peyton was right – this had nothing to do with Amy. Yet Trista couldn't ignore the gut feeling she had. And suddenly, it was very important that Amy was not angry about all those men from long ago.

~ 47 ~

Kat and Steve retreated to Kat's suite, hoping to avoid the other guests and try to forget all that had already happened. But the illusion of normalcy was impossible while Kat urgently checked each of the phones and watched while Steve searched the room for snakes. Lost in the desperate isolation of their situation, Kat was drawn to the window and the seemingly endless rain.

Steve came up behind her and wrapped an arm around her waist. He rested his chin on top of her head. She leaned into his embrace. It felt good not to have to stand on her own.

"I have to ask this, please don't take it the wrong way," he said after a minute.

She turned to face him. His jaw was set and his face serious. It was a second before she realized what he held between his fingers. A cylinder filled with a simple escape from it all. The sight of the powder struck a chord, and it wasn't just anger.

"Where the hell did that come from?" she asked.

"Your bedroom," he replied.

Kat searched his face for accusation, but amazingly found none. He'd just finished listening to her story of phantom ghost writing on doors and he actually believed that it was possible she knew nothing about the drugs in her bedroom. Kat wondered how she'd gotten so lucky. She was certain she didn't deserve it.

"That's what Trista was talking about?" she wondered. "One last gift from Biff?"

Steve appeared completely satisfied with the explanation. "Do you want it?"

Kat sighed. "Of course. But I'm going to dump it."

Steve nodded and handed her the vial.

Holding it in her hands was worse than she'd expected. Her mind immediately turned to the buzz. She'd gotten through so much with this crutch. So much that she could almost forget the bad that went with the good.

As she walked to the bathroom, drugs in hand, she felt a dull pain in her sinus passages. A throbbing of desire. Even as she poured the powder into the toilet, part of her begged for a hit. Just one. What harm could one do? The desperate tone resounding in her mind scared her enough that she even dumped the empty vial.

Steve put a supportive hand on her shoulder. The look in his eyes told her he understood.

"What do we do now?" she asked as she followed him into the sitting room.

He shrugged and sat down on the couch. "I wish I knew."

"How is it that no one heard either of them screaming for help?" Kat asked, sitting down next to him. "Don't you think Gloria would have mentioned it if she'd heard a commotion in one of the other rooms?"

"No one asked her about it explicitly. And I really don't think Gloria's about volunteering information."

Neither of them even considered walking back down the hall to ask her. The woman was not helpful. In fact, she seemed manipulative and cruel. It should have been easy to pity a woman who had been trapped with a violent and abusive husband. Yet it seemed Waylan's violence had never reached her. A veil of disinterest separated Gloria completely from the world.

Listening to the incessant tap of rain on the roof, Kat and Steve sat in silence. Even in chaos, Kat was surprised at the sense of peace Steve's presence brought. It was the type of companionship she'd been missing for a long time.

It seemed he was reading her mind when he spoke. "Tell me more about life in L.A. What's it really like to be a celebrity?"

The words were out of her mouth before she could stop them. "It's lonely."

Kat searched his face, trying to gauge his reaction to her admission. Again, she found no judgment, only understanding.

"Why do you do it?" he asked.

"I love the work. I keep telling myself I'll adjust to the rest."

Steve leaned his head on hers and tightly gripped her hand. "Do you think you ever will?"

Kat considered the question, just like she had in rehab. She'd even told Donnie that he should be prepared to cancel her next project. She'd thought about going home. She had enough money to give it all up. Maybe she could do some off-Broadway work.

But as the haze of the drugs cleared and her body recovered from the overdose, she realized she could never go back home. She just wasn't that person anymore. The problem was, she had no idea what person she was. All she knew was she was an actress, a Hollywood actress. So, she'd signed on to the next project. She hadn't known what else to do.

Now, sitting here with Steve, she considered his question – would she ever get used to it? She was still certain she didn't know the answer. But he made her feel strong enough to try.

~ 48 ~

Peyton sat with Trista as she anxiously watched the local news. She stared at the television, snapping her gum, constantly questioning the radar maps, asking questions about storm fronts, clouds and other things that Peyton knew nothing about.

"Could you please stop that?" he growled. Not only was the girl incapable of sitting still, he was beginning to think that gum might have to be banned.

"Stop what?"

"The gum. Please stop with the gum. I will do anything if you'll stop chewing that gum."

Trista smiled sheepishly and tossed the gum in the trash. "Sorry. Nervous habit. It's just this whole thing is creepy. Like horror movie creepy."

"You're being dramatic."

"I am not! Look at that weather map. Nothing. Now look out the window."

"Is the rain part of some conspiracy? That'd be a neat trick. Please."

Trista gestured vehemently at the window. "Did you see anything on the weather map that explains this?"

"No. But so what? Do you think every tiny storm shows up?"

"It's been raining for more than twelve hours. That's not a tiny storm."

Peyton shook his head. "Are you a meteorologist?"

"No, but…"

Peyton put a hand on her knee, hoping to focus her attention. "And neither am I. Obviously it's raining. Obviously there's nothing on the weather map. So, this must be a small storm. It's preposterous to think anything else."

Unfortunately for Peyton, Trista was not ready to be pacified. "We're completely cut off from the world. No phones. Nothing. We're trapped with two dead bodies! Completely trapped."

"Are you done?" he replied calmly.

"Don't be sarcastic," she snapped.

Peyton wrapped a protective arm around her and pulled her close. "I'll take care of you. I promise. You have nothing to worry about."

Trista buried her head in his chest. "Are you going to wave a magic wand and get us out of here?"

Tilting his head to hers, he whispered in her ear, "How about I have my helicopter come pick us up?"

Trista pulled back to get a look at his face. And Peyton watched the awe in her eyes. Now that's what he'd been missing. The adoration. The respect. It was in short supply in this hotel from hell.

Breathless, Trista asked, "How?"

"Do you really think they'll allow me to be out of touch for days? One day, maybe two. They'll be clamoring to talk to me. They'll call. They'll leave messages. They'll get frustrated when they can't get through. Soon enough they'll send the helicopter."

"Really?"   Trista's eyes were glowing with the possibilities.

Peyton was happy to keep feeding the dream. "The studio made me agree to come back the second they needed me.   And they'll need me.   The movies don't make themselves."

Trista grabbed him in a gleeful embrace. "That's the best news I've heard all day!"

Peyton laughed at her reaction. "I'm glad you're happy. Now that we've handled that, what do you say to checking on dinner? I'm starving."

Refreshed with a new confidence that they'd all be saved sooner or later, Trista bounded up from the couch. Buzzing from the power, Peyton was ready to face off with Kat again. It was time to remind her who worked for whom.

~ 49 ~

Steve was in the kitchen chopping and dicing, preparing food for the remaining guests. He wasn't sure if he was supposed to behave as if things were perfectly normal, but for the time being he didn't know what else to do.

"Are you sure there's nothing I can do?" Kat asked again.

"You can go upstairs and relax. You don't need to hang out here."

"I think I'm going to avoid being alone until I figure out what the hell I saw in that hallway, if that's alright with you."

Steve couldn't disagree. "Do you cook?"

Kat laughed. "I can make grilled cheese. And spaghetti. Though neither are allowed on my diet, so I haven't made them in years. I guess I don't have much to offer you, huh?"

"I'm thinking no. But the company is nice anyway."

Before Kat responded, Trista and Peyton barged through the swinging doors and into the kitchen.

"Excellent. You are preparing dinner," Peyton said in lieu of a greeting.

"Hello to you, too," Steve replied, without looking up from the onion he was slicing. "The menus are by the entryway. Why don't you grab a couple and pick a table? I'll be out in a few minutes to take your order."

Steve saw no indication that Peyton even heard the suggestion. In fact, he had already moved on to his favorite punching bag. "Kat, why don't you join us for dinner? It can't be any fun to sit in here and watch him cook."

"You'd be surprised," Kat replied, her voice neutral and unreadable. "I'm fine here, actually. Thanks for the invitation."

Steve was impressed by Kat's response. Though he knew she must be dying inside, there was no obvious outward indication. In fact, if he didn't know better he would have been sure that she was declining a perfectly reasonable offer from a perfectly reasonable person.

"How rude of me," Peyton continued, just as superficially unflappable, "you probably want to have dinner with Steve here. Why don't the four of us eat together?"

That suggestion did seem to catch Kat off guard. Steve saw her eyes dart to his before she seemed to gather herself again.

Seemingly calm now, Kat turned her full attention to Peyton. "Steve has to prepare dinner for Gloria, too. We're not eating until later."

Peyton flashed his most charming grin. "Has Gloria sent down a dinner order yet?"

"No," Kat replied, her eyes narrowing. Steve knew she saw that the question was a trap, but he couldn't figure out where the producer was going with it either.

"Perfect then. Trista, why don't you run up to Gloria's room and get her order. Once Steve gets that out of the way, we can all enjoy a nice dinner." Appearing confident that he had successfully forced Kat into his plan, Peyton turned to Steve, the slightest smirk curling on his lips. "Don't you think that works?"

"It'll delay your dinner." Though Steve had hoped for a better way to get out of this horrible plan, he couldn't think of anything else.

"The delay is no problem. Right, Trista?"

Trista didn't look at all pleased with the plan either. But she smiled broadly and agreed, her flirtatious accent in full effect. Steve figured it was supposed to convey just how cool and casual she was feeling, even though it did the opposite.

Peyton slid into a seat next to Kat, and grinned. "Perfect. I'll sit in here with Kat until Trista returns."

There were a lot of words that described this situation, but Steve was sure that "perfect" wasn't one of them.

~ 50 ~

Gloria was the only person in the hotel who had enjoyed the rain-soaked afternoon. Ever since the whole unpleasant mess with the manager, things were quiet, which was a nice change.

She already loved life as a widow. There was no one to order her around. No need to exert any effort to avoid the beatings or the constant nagging.

She wondered if she was entitled to some kind of death benefit. Maybe Waylan had the good sense to buy life insurance. Or maybe she could sue the hotel. Improper security. Bad telephones. Two people had died in twenty-four hours. Obviously, the place was unsafe.

Really, she was the kind of woman that deserved some cash to take care of her. Maybe she could even hire a maid.

A little after six o'clock, Trista appeared in her doorway holding a menu.

"Steve thought you might like something to eat," Trista said, in a tone that made it clear she didn't care what Gloria wanted.

"Nice of you to think of me." Gloria offered a patronizing smile as she took the menu.

Trista stood over her and glared. "You have them snowed, but I know what you're really like."

Gloria didn't even look up. The girl's silly accusations meant nothing. "I'd like the turkey club with some fries. Think you can remember that?" she asked, handing the menu back with barely a glance.

Through gritted teeth, Trista said, "Somebody will bring it up to you. I assume you won't be joining us?"

Resisting the urge to laugh right in her face, Gloria waved her away dismissively. "No. I'll take my meal up here."

Trista snatched the menu from her hands and stormed off like a spoiled three-year-old, leaving Gloria to revel in the newfound joy of being a bully.

~ 51 ~

Even with their history, Kat was stunned by the web that Peyton wove so deftly. He was leaning back in his chair, his legs casually crossed, as if the kitchen was the most natural place in the world to be socializing.

"Are you enjoying the hotel so far?" he asked Kat.

She could barely do more than stare in bewilderment. "Other than the two murders and the constant rain? Sure, it's fine."

"Today has certainly been a rough day, but you were here yesterday. You were able to enjoy the amenities. What did you think?"

Kat shifted in her chair, wishing she was talking to anyone else. "It's fine. A little remote, but fine."

From the corner of her eye, she watched Steve. She wondered if he always diced vegetables that fast, or if he was just trying to rush through this charade as quickly as possible. She had no problem with the latter, but she hoped he didn't lose a finger in the process.

"Donnie was the one who found the place," Peyton continued. "He recommended it to the production staff. I would have preferred something closer to L.A., but with the problems you've had lately, it seemed prudent to get you out of the city."

Kat felt her whole body tense at the insult. She was willing herself to come up with some reasonable reply, when Trista stormed into the kitchen and flung the menu on the table.

"I refuse to speak to that woman again. Ever. She's unbelievable."

Steve completely ignored the girl's tantrum. "What does she want?"

Trista quickly relayed the order and joined Kat and Peyton at the table. In an instant she was a completely different person. The Texas drawl was back, as was her charming smile. "So, what did I miss?"

Peyton seemed buoyed by her faux good humor. "We were discussing what we think of the hotel."

"Well, I don't know about anyone else, but I just adore the place. It's beautiful. I can't believe I got this lucky," Trista volunteered.

Kat wondered if it was possible to go into sugar shock sitting this close to Trista.

Peyton, of course, lapped it up. "I completely agree. Beautiful building. Beautiful grounds."

"The name could use a little work," Trista pointed out.

"The name?" Peyton asked. "Come to think of it, I'm not sure I ever heard the name. My assistant made the arrangements. What is it?"

"Peccavi," Trista replied.

Peyton straightened in his chair, both feet now firmly on the floor. "I'm sorry. What was that?"

"Peccavi."

Peyton stared for a moment. "That's a terrible name."

"Totally rotten marketing." Trista nodded agreeably.

"No, no," Peyton said, shaking his head. "That's not it. The name itself. The word. I don't know what the owner intended, but that name has a bad translation."

For the first time since his arrival, Peyton had Kat's full attention. "Donnie said the name was Latin."

Peyton sat back in his chair. "The owner intended to use the Latin?"

"What does it mean in Latin?" Trista asked. The artificial sweetness was gone. She almost looked human.

Peyton spoke slowly, seeming to calculate as he went. "It means 'I have sinned.'"

"What?" All three of them asked in unison.

Peyton ran a hand across the back of his neck, as if to shake off tightness. "'I have sinned.' It means 'I have sinned.'"

Steve put down the knife and joined them at the table. "You've gotta be wrong."

"I'm certain."

"That doesn't make any sense," Kat insisted, though it made more sense than she wanted to admit.

"How can you be so sure?" Trista asked.

"I went to Catholic school. For our Confirmation, we had a nun who thought it would be fun for us to memorize this one sentence in Latin. We repeated it over and over for months so it would be perfect when we went to confession."

Trista tilted her head to one side. "You did your confession in Latin?"

"No. No. She thought it would be special if we could begin our confessions with a Latin phrase. You know, something to make the confession significant for us. The phrase was – Bless me, Father, for I have sinned. The translation – Mihi benedicas, Pater, qui peccavi. Peccavi is 'I have sinned.'"

For a moment, they simply sat in silence. The phrase echoed through Kat's mind. Over and over. Part of her mind tried to comprehend; another part screamed for her to run for her life.

"Maybe you're remembering wrong. I'm betting Confirmation was more than a couple of years ago," Steve noted.

"I'm sure. I used the phrase in confession for years afterward. I thought it sounded kind of cool."

"Maybe we're pronouncing it wrong?" Kat suggested. "Do either of you know how to spell the name?"

Steve grabbed a pad and pen from near the phone. He scribbled down the word and placed it on the table.

Trista nodded. "I stared at the letter about the job for hours. I'm sure that's right."

Peyton picked up the paper and held it at a slight distance so he could see it better. "Our memorization of the phrase was oral. So I can't be sure. But that looks right to me."

"Does that mean someone named their hotel 'I have sinned'? That's insane," Trista snapped.

"Maybe the owner intended a different name, but screwed up the translation," Steve said. "Or maybe Peccavi means more than one thing in Latin. Like the words windy and windy – one means curving; the other refers to weather – yet the spelling is identical."

Peyton smiled broadly, in what Kat suspected was relief, though he never would have admitted it. "That makes perfect sense. Steve, you'll have to tell the owner about the double meaning. I'm sure he'll want to change it."

Though Kat smiled and chuckled at Peyton's response, she didn't find Steve's explanation comforting. There were too many reasons why Peyton's original translation made sense.

~ 52 ~

Gloria smiled broadly when Steve entered her room, dinner in hand. She had successfully scared Trista off. It was surprisingly enjoyable to intimidate a person like that, especially when you were exerting so little energy to do it. And having the sexy cowboy bring her dinner was just icing on the cake.

He set the tray on the coffee table and even asked if there was anything else she wanted before he left. He was cute, but she quickly dismissed him. He was interrupting her shows. She'd just discovered they had a whole channel dedicated to soap operas. This was some good cable.

The current program was not one of her usual shows. She nibbled absently on her fries as she watched. The sandwich would have to wait for a commercial.

Trinity was going to confront Channing about his affair when the channel changed.

Auto Racing. Cars flew by on the screen. One took a corner too wide and clipped the tail of the car next to him. A spinout ensued. Eight cars went off in various directions.

The car that was hit initially got the worst of it. Flipping over. Straight into the wall. It burst into flames.

Gloria muttered to herself. *How the hell did the channel change?* She flipped back to the soap channel. Two new characters were on now. She hadn't seen them before. It was hard to tell if they had a father-daughter relationship or a May-December romance. As the young woman ran a seductive finger down the man's chest, that question was quickly answered. The woman was leaning in to kiss him when the channel changed again.

An action film. A man with bulging biceps firing a machine gun. Men dressed in fatigues dropped one by one in bloody heaps, their bodies convulsing from the force of the bullets.

Gloria was disgusted. This was not her type of movie. What the hell was wrong with the television? She snatched up the remote again and entered the number for the soap channel.

The screen flashed to reveal a new image. A teenage girl in a warehouse filled with dusty antiques. Her eyes widened as she inched back. The music in the background was building to a climax. This was another new character. And it seemed a little intense for a soap, any soap.

As she retreated, she collided with a full-length mirror. Over her shoulder was the reflection of what she was backing away from. A gigantic man, wearing a black cape and a red vinyl mask. He raised his arm and revealed a machete.

There was no way this was a soap. Gloria tried to change the channel, but nothing happened. No matter what she did the image of the slasher kept reappearing.

Much to her horror, she watched the bloody scene as the masked man disemboweled his victim. Then he turned to chase the young man who'd tried to save the dead girl.

Gloria hit the channel-up button. The image flashed, but the movie reappeared. The young man was screaming for help as he ran down a decaying hallway.

Gloria entered a random channel number. Flash. The young man was cowering in a corner. She turned the television off and then back on again. Flash. The blade of the machete was raised, the face of the latest victim reflected in its amazingly shiny surface.

In desperation, Gloria turned the television off and kept it off. She looked down at her sandwich and realized she wasn't hungry anymore.

She was about to force herself to take a bite when the television snapped on. The dull squish of the blade piercing flesh told her she hadn't missed the death scene.

She hit the power button repeatedly, but the savage murder continued. She hurried over to the television and shut it off by hand. Blood continued to spatter all over the fictional room.

The plug. She had to find the plug. Next to the television stand was an outlet with two plugs. She yanked them both out of the wall. One lamp snapped off, but the carnage on the screen continued.

She cursed and reached behind the television. She found the cord running from the back of the TV. Slowly she began to pull it, trying to trace it to the power source. She hardly noticed that the cord felt oddly loose.

As she drew the cord toward her, the masked man began to laugh – an evil, menacing cackle. The volume rose until she found the end of the cord.

It was already disconnected from the wall.

When she touched the prongs in confusion, a spark of electricity pulsed through her body. In that instant, the television snapped off.

~ 53 ~

The shock was so disorienting it took Gloria a moment to realize that, though the television image had disappeared, the sound continued. The evil laugh echoed through her room, a frightening cackle rising from the lifeless television. Suddenly, the drug addict's ramblings about invisible hands writing on doors seemed more plausible.

Gloria stared at the television that was inches from her face, the cord lying lifelessly on top of it. The sound, she realized, didn't seem to be coming from the speakers, but from behind her.

Before she could turn, the laughter stopped and a voice spoke. "Did you really think the television was laughing at you?"

Amy? Gloria turned with some relief. The girl was standing in the entryway to the bedroom, wearing a soaking sundress, water cascading off her body.

"What are you doing here?" Gloria asked, rising to face her.

"Don't be embarrassed, Mom." Amy addressed her bitterly by the title Waylan had demanded she use.

Gloria took a step closer, but Amy remained fixed to the same spot. "Please, neither of us ever wanted you to call me that. Why do it now?"

"Now you're taking a stand on it? I think it's a little late for that, don't you?" Amy asked with no anger in her voice, but blackness in her eyes.

Gloria shook her head. *Such a dramatic temper. It was never a big deal.* As the thought crossed Gloria's mind, she could see Amy's anger flare.

Trying to change the subject, Gloria said, "You killed him?"

"I had some help, but yes."

"Coyotes?" Gloria was excited. She'd been right. Stupid Biff shouldn't have mocked her.

Amy smiled. "Just dogs. Big ones, though."

Gloria returned the smile, relishing in the victory. "He is dead? They wouldn't let me see the body."

Apparently disinclined to share her success, Amy's smile quickly faded. "Yeah, he's dead."

Undaunted, Gloria took another step closer. "Do you know those fools from California think you're dead?"

"I am."

Gloria scowled at her. The girl wasn't dead. She was standing right there in front of her, dripping on the floor. Though, Gloria realized, the water coming off her smelled oddly salty. Like the ocean. Nothing like rainwater.

She tried to dismiss the observation as ridiculous, but part of Gloria's mind was quick to point out that it was probably no more ridiculous than a television that worked when it wasn't plugged in.

"If you're dead," Gloria challenged, "then how are you standing here?"

Amy's smile now returned, but with a more menacing quality. "Revenge."

Gloria shuddered against a cold breeze that blew through the room. Amy's threatening explanation hung in the air.

An explanation that sounded uncomfortably like the theory Gloria had used earlier to harass Trista and Kat.

Still, Gloria wouldn't believe the implication. "Well, you got your revenge, didn't you? Your father's dead. That bonehead you were shacking up with is dead. You know, he told us what you were doing to make money. Money for sex from a drug dealer. You should be ashamed."

"Are you finished?" Amy asked calmly.

Gloria was appalled. "You must be kidding. Am I finished? I have half a mind to slap that smirk off your face."

"If you decided to do that, it would be the first time in your life you stood up to do anything."

"Wh-What?" she sputtered. "You did not... Of all the ungrateful..." The fiery hatred in Amy's eyes stopped Gloria's reprimand mid-sentence.

Amy's voice was still calm when she spoke, but there was a new ripple to it. A new anger. Though still not overt, the undercurrent was becoming more obvious. "Grateful? That's an interesting concept. Let's focus on that word – grateful. You're right, you know. I'm not grateful for anything you or that loathsome man did for me. Anything you did to me."

"I never did nothing to you."

Amy smiled a little at the retort. "Never did nothing *for* me either."

"A roof over your head. How about that?"

"He murdered my mother in front of me. You knew that. Hell, he told you himself so he could keep you in line."

Gloria took a small step back. She was beginning to think she was standing much too close to the girl. "I wasn't there. I had nothing to do with that."

In response, Amy took a step closer. "How many times did the police come to the house about the beatings?"

"How am I supposed to know?"

Though Gloria looked away, she could feel that Amy had again moved closer. They were only a few feet apart now.

"How many times did the school counselors beg you to admit what was happening? Beg you to take me to the police?"

Gloria looked up defiantly. "I didn't see any of your school counselors."

Amy's smile returned, more broadly this time. "Why, no, you didn't. How many letters did I bring home asking you to come in?"

"Those damn counselors. They don't know what the hell they're talking about."

Amy took one final step; they were now only inches apart. Gloria wondered if she had always been so tall. It felt like Amy was glaring down at her from a height more like Waylan's than her own.

"How many times did I have to get myself to the hospital because you couldn't be bothered?"

Swallowing her fear, Gloria refused to back down. "Hell, child, I've got no idea. You were such a whiney kid. Always complaining about something. If I'd taken you to the hospital every time you bitched, we would've lived there. You needed to toughen up."

"Broken arms. Broken ribs. A broken leg. I have two fingers on my right hand that will always be crooked. Even still," she said, holding up the hand.

"What do you want me to do about it? You got out. You left us. You left me with him. You left me alone to take his beatings," Gloria accused. "Never hit me a day in his life before you left. Not once. You aren't the victim here. I am!"

Amy let the desperate, angry words hang in the air a moment before she continued. "Actually, I wondered if you'd been punished enough already. He did take to hitting you an awful lot after I left. I know that now. But it doesn't change anything, really. If you had it to do all over again you still wouldn't get off your lazy ass and help a soul. In fact, you were tested. Just to make sure. Given a chance to do something good."

"Tested? What the hell are you talking about?"

Gloria watched with dismay as Amy's mouth curled into a grin. Her eyes mocked as she continued. "Last night. You were sitting on that couch. Watching television. Around midnight you turned up the volume. Why'd you do that?"

Gloria glared at the accusation, fear filling her heart. "I heard your father thundering around next door. I had no idea what was happening."

"You assumed he'd gotten a hold of me. Was taking his frustrations out on me. You could have helped. Easy as pie. Call down to the front desk, complain about the noise. Simple. But, you didn't call. You turned up the television," Amy declared, jamming a finger into Gloria's chest.

Gloria stumbled backwards, her voice wavering with the lies. "I had no idea what was happening. I just thought he was angry you weren't here yet."

"How about this morning when Trista screamed bloody murder next door? Weren't you concerned about her?"

Gloria tried to retreat further, but the couch was at her back. There was nowhere left to go. "That girl sounded like she'd seen a ghost. I wasn't going to run into danger."

Amy kept coming closer. "And Kat. What about when Kat was screaming just outside your door?"

"You don't open the door to that kind of terror. Besides, that woman is a messed up druggie. You know that."

Amy's face darkened with anger. "Three chances, Stepmother. Not a finger lifted. I can't say I wasn't pleased by your failure. I always thought you were deserving. But the rules have to be followed. Some things have to be proven."

Gloria eyed Amy cautiously. The girl's eyes were black with hate. Despite her calm voice, her cheeks were flushed, showing her true anger. Gloria wondered if she could run for the door without Amy stopping her.

Amy began to laugh, softly at first, but it grew in volume and hysteria.

"You're crazy," Gloria muttered.

Amy's laughter gave way to a broad smile. "Probably. It's funny you mention running away, though."

"I didn't say anything about running."

"No, but you were thinking about running. You see, that's what's funny. The running. I'm going to let you run. I encourage it actually. But first, I need you to sit," Amy explained, pushing Gloria to the couch. "I have some friends I want you to meet. Fire ants. Several thousand of them. They're crawling up your leg right now."

As she spoke, Gloria felt a tickle on her ankle. Then the other. Before she could react, the tickle was moving up her calf. She looked down and saw a swarm of red ants at her feet. Hundreds already halfway up her leg. Thousands rushing in a mass from under the couch. Gloria wanted desperately to brush them off, but found she couldn't move.

"No, no. No rushing off yet. In a second or two, they're going to start biting. Sharp little stings. I hear it's like tiny hot pokers attacking you. Once the biting starts, I'm going to let you move. There's only one thing that'll save you. Mud. Kills the sting, you know. Great stuff. Lucky for you the weather is just right for a little mud."

Gloria's eyes were wide with terror. Her heart pounded. The ants had almost covered her legs. They were working their way up her torso. She willed herself to move, but no matter what she did, there was nothing. She was frozen in place.

The first prick was on her upper thigh, followed by another on her stomach. One behind her knee. Two in rapid-fire succession on her hamstring. Each bite was painful, but bearable. However, the horror of the cumulative effect was quickly becoming clear. One after another, after another.

"Okay," Amy cried with glee, "don't forget about the mud."

She snapped her fingers and, instantly, Gloria found she could move. She sprinted for the door. With each step the biting became worse. Her knee. Her calf. Her ankle. Her shoulder. Her neck. God, they were moving up her body. She had to get outside. Fast.

A rush of bites crashed over her like a wave and she began to scream in terror and agony. Yet even over her own screams she could still hear Amy's laughter.

~ 54 ~

Kat was relieved when Peyton and Trista finally headed upstairs, leaving her and Steve alone to enjoy what she hoped would be a peaceful cup of coffee. Peace, however, was hard to obtain while the rain pounded on the roof, clawed at the windows. It sounded unnatural and surreal in the dark, desert landscape.

She was slowly sipping the coffee, trying to clear her mind of monsters both real and imagined, when a howl pierced the night, blocking even the sound of the attacking rain. Kat's coffee cup crashed to the floor.

It was a cry like a wounded animal might make. And it was coming from inside the hotel.

Together she and Steve rushed toward the sound, reaching the lobby in time to see a blur run through the main doors and into the rain. It was a person. A small person. That was all she could tell. The appearance of Trista and Peyton at the top of the stairs confirmed it was neither of them.

"What the hell was that?" Peyton shouted, showing more strain than usual.

"It could have been Gloria," Steve replied. "Can you check her room?"

Peyton nodded, obviously happy to be going in the opposite direction. Kat cautiously followed Steve outside and they both cowered under the small overhang, which spared them the full force of the rain, at least for the moment.

The driveway and parking lot were dimly lit by small lanterns, each less than a foot from the ground, all giving off a weak yellow light that was quickly swallowed by the rain and the black night.

She could still hear the screaming. It seemed to be coming from farther up the driveway, closer to the highway. There might have been some movement in the distance, but it was impossible to tell. An unconscious chill slithered down Kat's spine. The howls were sounding less and less human. If they hadn't seen a person run from the hotel, she would have been certain it was an animal.

Kat wondered if this was the type of sound you ran from or ran to help.

"We need a flashlight," Steve observed, though it didn't look like he was any more certain of what to do than she was. "I think there's one in Biff's office."

Happy to let Steve consider the tough questions, Kat slipped away and grabbed the high intensity flashlight from behind Biff's desk. When she returned, she could see the determined look on his face. He was going out to help.

Without a word, she snapped on the light and headed out first. She didn't want to risk being left behind under Peyton's protection.

The rain attacked immediately with a full body assault. Despite the brightness of the flashlight, the beam seemed to falter in the dense blackness. The saturated earth grabbed at her feet as if it wanted to claim her for its own. Kat wondered if she'd chosen wrong – maybe remaining with Peyton would have been a relatively benign choice.

The howling echoed in the night, making its origin unclear. It seemed to grow louder and then it would fade into nothing. It sounded almost muffled, like it was drowning in the rainy night.

They tried to follow the sounds, but the screaming faded away too quickly. Eventually, no real sounds came forth. There was only an inexplicable and disturbing splashing sound that floated through the black night.

They were left standing in the driveway surrounded by the sound of the teeming rain cascading into the puddles at their feet. The repetitious patter was maddening as they strained to hear any sign of life.

Kat didn't know how long they wandered in the rain. Virtual blindness limited how much ground they could cover. Without the cries to follow, their wandering was aimless, pointless. They conceded defeat and slowly walked back to the hotel, hoping the person they were searching for was not Gloria but some creature they were better off not finding.

When they walked into the lobby and found only Trista and Peyton waiting, they knew Gloria was gone. Kat couldn't help but think of the movie *Ten Little Indians*. As Agatha Christie would have pointed out, *and then there were four*. She shuddered at the thought.

They stood dripping in the lobby while Peyton and Trista relayed what they'd discovered. Peyton looked more ruffled than Kat had ever seen him. She could hardly believe the strain and fear in his cold, distant voice. "Her door was wide open. No one inside. Her dinner was half-eaten on the table. The television and the lamp next to it were unplugged."

"That's it?" Steve asked.

Trista shook her head. "The door. There were carvings on her door."

"What did it say?" But Kat didn't want to know. She just wanted to hide under her bed until this nightmare ended.

"Sloth." Trista's voice caught; her fear apparent.

"Wrath. Greed. Sloth," Steve said, more to himself than anyone else.

"The Seven Deadly Sins," Kat whispered. She'd seen enough movies to know the Seven Deadly Sins when she heard them. "Seven sins. Seven of us. What's left?"

Peyton scowled at her observation.

"It's been a long time since Sunday school, but I think you're right. What's left?" Steve asked himself. "Lust? Pride? Anger?"

"Anger and Wrath are the same, I think," Trista pointed out.

"Gluttony," Kat continued the list, thinking very much of herself.

"Okay, that's six, what else? Maybe I'm wrong about Anger and Wrath?" Trista asked.

"Envy," Steve finished. "I think the last one is Envy."

"Isn't that the same as Pride?" Trista wondered.

"I don't think so." Kat couldn't help but look around the room. Four people. Four sins. She knew her own sin. If being a cocaine addict wasn't gluttonous, she didn't know what was. She looked at the other three. Did they each represent a sin?

"This is absurd," Peyton snapped. "Are we really going to discuss theology? Shouldn't you be out there looking for that woman?"

"We couldn't find any sign of her. The screaming stopped. There was nothing left to follow. I think we have to wait until daylight. Unless you want to look yourself," Steve replied, extending the flashlight to Peyton.

"I'm not going out there. Why'd she go running into this hellish weather anyway?"

"Why was she screaming like that?" Trista asked, her voice still shaking.

"I've never heard anything like it," Kat agreed.

Steve only shook his head. "I don't understand what's going on here, but no one should be alone until we figure it out."

"You bet your ass," Trista replied, taking a step closer to Peyton.

"What about Gloria?" Kat asked.

"What do you mean?" Peyton retorted.

"We can't lock up the hotel with her out there. And I'm not sleeping with the door unlocked," Kat explained.

Trista's eyes grew wide.

Seeing the response, Peyton growled at Kat, "That is the stupidest thing I've ever heard. Maybe you've forgotten; we're trapped out here. Which means no one can get in, either. Unless you think they're sitting outside just waiting for us to leave the door unlocked."

Trista shook her head. "I'm with Kat; no way is that door staying unlocked. Screw Gloria, we need to be safe!"

"We can't lock her out," Kat said, hoping the others would disagree.

Peyton rolled his eyes. "My God! You two are ridiculous. It's one or the other. What else do you think we can do?"

"We can keep watch throughout the night in pairs," Steve suggested. "Two of us could start now while the other two sleep and then we could switch in the middle of the night."

Kat watched Peyton calculate and assess. Two things were clear – he wasn't buying any of this, but he knew he was outnumbered. Kat could have guessed his response even before he spoke. "Fine. Why don't Trista and I take the first shift? It's a little after ten now. We'll go until two. You can relieve us then. That should take us to dawn."

~ 55 ~

Steve followed Kat as they slogged upstairs, his soaked clothes clinging uncomfortably. They proceeded to Kat's room, but only after stopping to get dry clothes for him along the way.

It wasn't until they were both changed that Steve realized the implications of their situation.

"I guess I'll sleep out here on the couch," he suggested, unsure exactly what the appropriate sleeping arrangements were.

Kat seemed far less uncertain. "Not on your life. That bed is plenty big for both of us. You will not be more than five feet from me the rest of the time we're here."

Steve shifted uneasily. He didn't have to look at Kat to know that he wanted nothing more than to climb into bed with her. That was exactly the problem. Despite his desire, he knew what he needed to do. "I think we should focus on getting some sleep."

Kat held both hands up in a sign of peace. "I'm not suggesting anything but sleep. I swear. You can sleep on top of the covers if you want. On the floor next to the bed if you must. But you are sleeping within arm's reach of me. Things are much too crazy here."

Steve looked at Kat and then at the bed. The images that filled his mind had nothing to do with sleep. He took a deep breath and tried to think about anything else. "Okay. But don't you try anything," he joked.

Kat smiled the sweet grin he was growing so fond of. "I'll try to keep my hands to myself."

~ 56 ~

Trista was pacing the floor in the lobby. She was bored and aggravated to be standing watch. Who did that anyway? Stand watch? What was this, a bad war movie? Just lock the door and let the bitch fend for herself.

"I don't suppose we could just lock the door and pretend we guarded the entrance all night?" Trista suggested.

Peyton looked up from a magazine. "This was entirely your decision. Yours and Kat's. Don't come complaining to me now."

"Are you really clumping me with her? I would've let that lunatic rot out there. I just want to make sure we're locked in safely."

"We're completely isolated out here. That's the problem. It's also the reason it's utterly irrelevant if we lock the front door."

Trista stopped pacing and stared at the sophisticated man before her. Not a hair out of place. Not even the tiniest bit of fear behind his eyes.

Peyton leaned back and smiled when he saw she was watching him. "Is there something I can help you with?"

"You really aren't concerned about any of this," Trista observed.

"You wouldn't be either if you would calm down. We've seen a couple of dead people today. That, of course, is troubling, but you can't become paranoid."

"In a twenty-four hour period, two, possibly three, people have died. That's quick. Really quick. Even if the studio does send that helicopter, I'm worried it won't get here soon enough."

Peyton's slow, calm headshake did nothing to soothe Trista's nerves as she continued on her frightened tirade. "You admit yourself that Amy probably killed Waylan. Why wouldn't she go after the rest of us?"

Peyton laughed. "Why would she? It seems to me you two were friends. And as far as I can tell, she had a pretty good working relationship with Biff. I could see her being a little pissed off with Kat, but that sort of thing happens. And Steve swears he doesn't even know her."

"What about you?"

"What about me? I gave her the chance of a lifetime. None of us could have known Kat would overdose. If I ran into Amy tomorrow, I'm sure she'd thank me for the opportunity."

Trista just stared at him trying to decide if he really believed what he was saying.

He smiled at her. "Sit with me. Stop worrying."

She acquiesced, mostly because it was becoming embarrassing. This was her chance. Her moment with a rich, powerful man. This was all she'd ever wanted and she was pacing the floor talking about the Lichtenhoffs. It was lunacy.

She slipped under Peyton's arm and allowed him to play his fingers through her hair, massaging her scalp, sending tiny chills down her spine.

"Are you feeling better?" he asked.

Trista tucked in even closer and laid on the drawl for full effect. "I'm real sorry I was being such a loon. Thank God you kept your head."

"Keeping calm during crises is something I do well," Peyton replied, running his hand down her arm.

Trista looked up at him. "I think we should put our time to better use."

"Do you have any ideas?" Peyton asked, slipping his hand to her thigh.

She patted his arm and straightened up a little. "Oh, honey, that sounds good, too, but I was thinking we could talk a little business first." She shifted again, hoping to get a better view of his face.

Peyton's smile only broadened. She knew he found her scheming as sensual as anything else she could do for him. "What business did you have in mind?"

Trista considered beating around the bush, but decided more direct questions might catch him off guard. "You haven't explained why you've come such a long way to keep an eye on Kat."

He shifted uncomfortably. The flicker of hesitation behind his eyes told Trista she'd taken the right approach.

His answer was short and plainly incomplete. "We're preparing for the next movie. I need to be sure she's ready."

She went straight for the jugular. "Did you two have a relationship?"

"Me and Kat? No, no. It's nothing like that," he replied, a little too quickly.

Trista bit back a smile, certain she had him. "Why not?"

"What do you mean?" There was the slightest twitch at the corner of his eye. Peyton had recognized her trap, just in time to realize it was too late to escape.

She sat up even straighter, her head now slightly above Peyton's, her position of power becoming more apparent. "She's hot. You're hot. Why not? It's not like you're opposed to mixing business with pleasure."

"It just never came up." For the first time in the conversation, Peyton looked away.

She could smell blood now. "How many of your movies has she been in?"

This time he didn't even attempt to hold eye contact. "Four."

There was no way it hadn't come up. Trista wanted to believe that meant Peyton was only out for revenge, but she was smart enough to know he wouldn't have lied about that. Besides, it was a cardinal rule that men always wanted the thing they couldn't have. With time such desires became obsession. And obsession was the sort of thing that might derail her plans for Peyton.

Trista was not going to stand by and watch that vixen seduce her rich man. Playing coy might be working for the actress, but it needed to end. One way or the other.

~ 57 ~

Lying awake, staring up at the ceiling, Kat tried not to think of all the reasons Amy Light would want her dead. Steve was next to her, on his back with one arm under his head, breathing deeply and evenly. How he could sleep at a time like this was beyond her.

People were dying. And there was no logical explanation for why or how. There were only words carved in doors. Sins branding each victim with a scarlet letter of sorts – a proclamation of their failings.

Kat had never given much thought to the Seven Deadly Sins. Why would she? It wasn't her religion. Not her belief system. But there were people who took these things very seriously. As Kat laid there in the isolated hotel, she suddenly wished she'd been one of them.

She tried to force her mind to stop. Her analysis was absurd. It was an impossible riddle. And there was no way it mattered. Did she think she'd get some sort of prize for matching the sin with the correct guest? This wasn't some sick game show.

Yet her mind kept returning to the puzzle. When she realized her only other option was to stare at the ceiling and wonder if she would be the next to die, the decision was simple.

If the other three guests represented the sins carved on their doors, then logically the four remaining sins must apply to the four remaining guests. Kat believed her sin was the most obvious. Without Gluttony, only Lust, Pride, and Envy remained. She knew Peyton better than Steve or Trista, so she considered him first.

Peyton's sexual conquests were as renowned as they were notorious. So Lust was an easy fit. But somehow, it felt wrong. To call his serial womanizing lustful was inaccurate. It wasn't sex that drove Peyton; it was power, control, dominance. He was fixated on proving he was the best – at everything. Which Kat thought sounded a lot more like Pride.

The more she considered her assessment of Peyton, the more confident she became. Which left Trista and Steve. Kat didn't know how to deal with them, but for opposite reasons.

Based on what Gloria said earlier, Trista got around. And she had wasted no time climbing into bed with Peyton. But the question was – why? Yes, there was certainly sex involved, just as there was with Peyton. But was sex the goal, or was there more to it? Gloria had suggested that Trista couldn't stand for Amy to have something, or someone, she didn't. That sounded more like Envy than Lust. But, really, Kat didn't know Trista well enough to say.

Which left her with Steve. Kat looked at him, sleeping peacefully next to her like a man with a clear conscience. He'd been a perfect gentleman since she'd met him. Kind. Sweet. Respectful. Patient.

Lust? Envy? Kat hadn't seen even a glimmer of either. Unlike the rest of them, Steve appeared perfectly innocent. Yet, if the pattern were to fit, there must be something hiding behind those deep blue eyes.

Rejecting the notion, Kat was struck by an idea. Maybe their list of the Seven Deadly Sins was wrong. None of them were religious scholars. If they were wrong, it might explain why none of the sins seemed to fit Steve.

When she was in rehab, she'd asked Donnie to pick up a Bible for her. Though he clearly thought she'd gone completely off the deep end, he happily provided her with the most ornate one he could find.

The thing was monstrous, even for the Bible. It had multiple indexes, cross-referencing footnotes, and so many appendices it made her head spin. It was typical Donnie – only the best for "his girl." She'd laughed at his overkill at the time, but now she realized the book might provide her with exactly what she needed. Maybe the answers were tucked in the nightstand drawer where she'd placed the book only days before.

She slowly shifted in the bed and snapped on the light. She held her breath as she watched Steve roll on his side away from the light and mutter something incomprehensible.

Pleased she would be able to continue to explore her outrageous idea in private, Kat slowly and silently opened the drawer in the table next to the bed. The Holy Bible stared up at her. Even the sight of it brought a certain relief. The book had provided her with a good bit of guidance recently. She hoped it would help her again.

Kat quickly scanned the table of contents. "Old Testament." "New Testament." "Theology." "Seven Sacraments." "Gifts of the Holy Spirit." "Deadly Sins." There!

Quickly leafing to the appropriate pages, she began to read. In Catholic theological tradition, there were seven deadly sins. Popes and various religious scholars had added to the tradition over the years. The theology was detailed in numerous literary works, and most significantly expounded upon in Dante's *Divine Comedy.*

The list had expanded and contracted over the centuries and eventually evolved into seven – Pride, Wrath, Envy,

Greed, Sloth, Gluttony, and Lust. The appendix provided a subsection addressing each sin in turn, detailing both theological and literary interpretations.

The tradition of the Sins was nothing if not specific. They were ranked in order of severity. One being the most severe, seven the least. Kat leafed ahead to Gluttony, which ranked sixth. She took some solace in being that close to the bottom of the list.

In accordance with religious tradition, the gluttonous sinner would be punished throughout eternity by being force-fed rats, toads, and snakes. Kat wondered if the suggested punishment would have had any influence on her if she'd known about it before she'd done her first line of coke.

The punishments for Gluttony detailed in Dante's *Inferno* and *Purgatorio* were both very different. In Canto Six of the *Inferno*, the sinner was punished by constant and eternal rain that would fall cold and heavy upon the damned soul. Kat shivered at the descriptions, thinking of her earlier trudge through the driving rain.

The description found in *Purgatorio* was no more appealing. The punished soul wandered around endlessly in its purgatory weak and pale, emaciated from hunger.

Religion's view of her fate was too horrendous to be believed and she willed herself to close the book, let it go. What difference did it make? If she was destined for eternal torture, there wasn't anything she could do about it now.

Kat was about to give up when something caught her eye. The final part of the Gluttony description detailed miscellaneous facts, including colors and animals associated with the sin. If not for all she'd seen that day, the words would have made her scream. Gluttony: Color – Orange. Animal – Pig.

The lamp from the bedside table provided enough light to confirm what she already knew. The room was orange. A pretty pastel orange. The two pictures in the bedroom were both farm scenes. Though there were a couple of other animals in the pictures, the majority were pigs.

Kat slipped out of bed, gently closing the bedroom door behind her. In the sitting room, the same orange walls greeted her. Five paintings on the walls there. One of a mother pig and eight piglets. Three farm scenes. One had a farmer slopping the pigs. Another was an aerial perspective – chickens and roosters wandering, pigs in a pen, a farmer with an old dog. The third picture was almost identical to the second. The final painting was different. A family at dinner in a country-style home. There were eight at the table. It looked like grandparents and parents with some children. Kat scanned the image, not a pig to be seen. She was about to breathe a sigh of relief when she saw it. The father. Sitting at the head of the table. Carving a glazed ham.

~ 58 ~

Steve found Kat sitting in the living room muttering to herself, her eyes wild. Though she was sitting on the couch, it seemed she might spring to her feet without any warning.

"What's going on?" he asked groggily. "I woke up. You weren't there. You all right?"

"What color is your room?" she asked, in lieu of an answer.

"Blue. Why?" he asked, rubbing his eyes.

"Do you have pictures or paintings on the walls?"

Steve chuckled. "Yeah. Cows. Crazy, huh?" Noticing the paintings on her walls, he added, "Looks like you've got kind of a farm scene here, too. Tami must have an odd sense of humor."

His laughter stopped when he realized Kat was no longer listening. She was flipping through a thick book. She finally settled on a page, and then flipped ahead again. She paused a moment before her eyes grew wide.

"Hey," he said, sitting next to her. "What've you got there?"

"Do all the rooms have animal pictures?"

Steve stared at the desperation in her eyes. He considered questioning her, but thought better of it. "I think they all had something. Trista's was the first room I saw. She had dogs on her walls."

Kat's focus turned so completely to the book on her lap that she didn't respond. She flipped pages, stopping abruptly. Steve leaned in to figure out what she was looking at. He caught only a glimpse of a reference to dogs and something about the color green before Kat began firing more questions at him.

"Do you remember anything in particular about Gloria's room?" she asked.

Unable to hold his tongue any longer, Steve laid a heavy hand on the book. "What is this?"

Instead of answering, Kat simply held up the book for him to see. The Bible. Even as he read the words, he saw Kat was sinking lower into the couch. The urgency seemed to have passed now and she appeared almost resigned. She was muttering something about being a pig led to slaughter.

Steve grabbed her shoulders. "What the hell is wrong with you? So, it's the Bible. So what?"

Kat simply shook her head and leaned back against the couch, staring at the ceiling. As she did she handed the book over to him. The section heading on the page sent chills down his spine – "The Deadly Sins."

Before he could read anymore, Kat finally spoke, "Start with the sections on the specific sins. The first part's just background."

Obediently, he flipped ahead. Specific accounts contained very official-looking citations to sources both religious and literary. He considered asking where the hell she found a Bible that looked like this, but he knew there were more pressing issues.

Pride was described first. Panderers and seducers would be whipped by devils according to Dante's *Inferno*. Religious tradition claimed the prideful would be broken on a wheel. Other sources and other punishments were listed, but it was the final paragraph that caught Steve's eye. He immediately understood Kat's questions. The sin had a symbolic color listed. As well as an animal. Purple. Horses.

Had he seen a purple room? It took a moment, but it came to him. Peyton. Peyton's stupid royal purple room.

Suddenly, he felt a little sick. He flipped ahead. Envy was next. He skimmed through the punishments. Down to the last paragraph. Green. Dogs. Trista's room. He was sure.

Then Wrath. He began by skimming the punishments, but stopped short. The *Inferno* described men lashing out at each other. Tearing flesh with their teeth. The description was eerily similar to the scene in Suite One the previous morning, but that was not what made him pause. Dante's *Purgatorio* provided additional punishments, describing a thick smoke that burned the eyes.

They had completely forgotten what had originally brought them to the suite – Trista's cries that there was a fire. There had been smoke, but it dissipated quickly with no obvious source and at the sight of Waylan's body it had been completely forgotten.

Steve scanned down to the final paragraph and bit back bile as he read. Color – Red. Animal – Bear. How many times had he looked away from the body, trying to focus on anything else? The walls were red. He was certain, because it'd been hard to tell if there was any blood on them. There'd been one large black bear in a painting with blood splattered over its claws and face. He'd had to shake the notion that the bear had come out of the painting to maul the man lying on the floor.

He wasn't sure he wanted to read on, but there was one thing he had to confirm – a fear that had been lurking ever since the Deadly Sins discussion had begun hours before. Actually, he wondered if the fear had been there ever since they'd mentioned her name.

He flipped ahead, skipping Sloth, Greed, and Gluttony. The seventh sin lurked at the top of the page. He skipped the punishments.   He couldn't stand that.   The last paragraph was a description that could've been a decorator's guide to his room.

Dear God, he knew who Amy was.

~ 59 ~

Before Kat's eyes, the color drained from Steve's face, confirming her worst fears. He was as culpable as they all were. And that meant only one thing.

"It was all planned from the beginning," she said.

Steve dropped the Bible on the couch between them, the weight of its message clearly too much, but he didn't respond.

She put a hand on Steve's shoulder. He turned and looked at her, his eyes oddly pale and blank.

"You need to focus," she said simply. "We both do. Running away isn't an option."

Kat watched as he ran a hand over his rough chin. He blinked repeatedly as if to try to clear something from his mind.

"Okay. I'm focused," he said finally, clearly lying.

Despite an almost overwhelming desire to ask him what sin he'd recognized as his own, Kat pressed forward. "The rooms were designed for us. Specifically. What do you know about the owner?"

"Tami? Nothing."

"Seriously Steve, anything at all would be helpful. She gave you a job, didn't she? You had to have talked to her."

Steve met her eyes when he responded. The message was clear – he was serious. He just didn't have anything helpful to offer. "She called. Said we knew each other from one of my old jobs. I didn't remember her, but I didn't want to be rude. I thought I'd figure it out with time. I didn't."

"Nothing?" Though she tried to hide it, Kat could hear the frustration in her own voice.

Steve leaned back and ran his fingers through his rumpled hair. "How about you? How did you get here?"

"Donnie, my agent, he found the place. I don't really remember how he said he found out about it…" Kat's voice trailed off, as she silently cursed herself for not really listening when he'd been talking earlier. "Actually, I think he said he found out about it from a former client…" Again she paused as she dug back for the memory. "I think he said she was on my last movie."

"The one Amy was on?"

"Oh God, Amy. I hadn't even thought of that. It could have been Amy. And Peyton is just here following me. Which means four of us were brought here either directly or indirectly by Amy."

"And the other three brought here by Tami Ghyl."

"Tami the mystery woman." Though she hated to face Peyton or Trista right now, Kat knew she had to suggest it. "Do you think Trista knows who she is?"

Steve sighed deeply. "I sure hope so, because I think asking Biff is out of the question."

~ 60 ~

Trista was on the couch, nuzzling with Peyton when she heard them coming. Steve was leading the way with Kat not far behind. He was armed with the biggest Bible she'd ever seen, and a look of determination. She pulled Peyton a little closer before letting him go and facing the other two. Best Steve saw what he was missing.

Though she'd been ready with her best aloof expression, the story that Steve told had her captivated. It made sense. A lot of sense. And more importantly, it felt right. Her gut was telling her this was the truth of the matter, just the same way it had been telling her to ignore Peyton's reassurances. The Bible stuff was just weird enough to fit.

Peyton quickly made it clear that he was far less interested in their story. "You expect us to believe someone lured us here to kill us?"

Though Peyton was clearly hoping to get a rise out of Steve, the cowboy showed nothing but disdain. "Honestly Peyton, I don't care what you believe. Here are the facts. Our rooms match these descriptions. And Waylan was killed the way described."

"Give me that," Peyton ordered, snatching the Bible away from Steve. Trista read over his shoulder as he flipped through pages. He stopped abruptly at the section describing the punishments for Wrath. "It says here that religious tradition states the punishment is dismemberment. The smoke and the tearing of flesh are from Dante. Seems to me, if this person really wanted to follow the Good Book, they would've gone with dismemberment. It's probably an easier way to kill a person. Besides, are you suggesting the killer had a bunch of people gnaw on the big guy? Please."

Kat glared at Peyton. "You can believe whatever you want. We thought you should know what we found."

Peyton now flipped to the section on Greed defiantly. "Dante's *Inferno* says the punishment for Greed is pushing rocks around for an eternity. Tradition says they'll be thrown in a cauldron of boiling oil. Where are your snakebites?"

Steve pointed. "Scan down a little further. In the Greed description, they add a section from the *Inferno* that says the punishment for thieves is being thrown in a snake pit."

Peyton laughed. "This is like palm reading and fortune telling. You two are grasping at straws. Doesn't the little message on Biff's door say Greed? Then why would he get the thieves' punishment? Besides, it was snakebites. Not a snake pit."

"You're being hypertechnical," Kat responded.

"You're being paranoid. Are you really suggesting someone threw a bunch of snakes on Biff to kill him? We've already discussed this. That's absurd."

"What does it say for Sloth?" Trista asked. The theory made sense in her gut, but as usual, Peyton made a good argument.

"Oh, look, snake pits again," Peyton snorted smugly. "Religious tradition has them thrown into a snake pit. The *Inferno* has them festering in the mud of the River Styx. Do you think the river is close by? Maybe that's where Gloria went."

Steve shook his head. "Believe what you want. We really came down here to ask Trista about Tami."

"Who's Tami?" Peyton asked.

"The owner," Trista explained. "What do you guys want to know?"

"Anything you know about her," Steve replied.

Trista crossed her arms and looked at Steve skeptically. "I don't know anything. She called me. She told me about the hotel. Asked if I wanted the job."

"Why you?"

Trista shifted uncomfortably. "I worked at a diner back home. It was a busy place. She said she'd seen me working and thought I did a great job."

"Really?" Steve asked.

She saw the question in his eyes – who hired someone to be the cleaning staff for a start-up hotel after watching her wait tables? She hated the question, in part because she found it degrading, but more because she'd wondered the same thing. But she wasn't going to let any of them know that.

"I was an awesome waitress," she assured him.

"So you don't know anything about her?" Kat repeated.

"Not even a tiny little thing," Trista sneered.

"You know," Peyton began, looking at his watch, "it's one-thirty. And since you two are wide-awake and just dying to talk, why don't Trista and I go to bed? You can start the second watch now. Make sure you wake me if you find the River Styx," he mocked.

~ 61 ~

It was a little after five A.M. and Kat was dozing off. The lure of sleep was almost too much, and that – as usual – was a problem. She thought of the press junkets, red carpets, and opening night parties. She would never make it. Hell, if dead bodies couldn't keep her awake, nothing would.

She rose from the couch and stretched. She needed to stand. Maybe that would help.

Steve was at the window staring out into the black night. She walked up behind him and put her arms around him. It felt good to touch someone. To be near him. She leaned her head against his back and felt his heartbeat. The rhythmic sound reminded her they were both still there. Both still alive. Both worth fighting for.

He turned to face her, the shadow of his hat concealing his face. Though she knew it was selfish, she was glad she couldn't see the unspoken words that were undoubtedly written all over his face. She just wanted to escape. She wanted to pretend. He hugged her tightly and she allowed her face to be swallowed up in his strong chest.

As much as she wanted to block the tapping of the rain from her mind, it was all she could hear. The unceasing attack was extraordinary, almost supernatural. It was a lot like a man eaten alive by coyotes, bitten by a hundred snakes, or mysterious carvings on doors appearing from nowhere.

The question came out of Kat's mouth before she could censor herself. "When is it going to stop?"

Steve gave her a squeeze and then tilted her head up to look at him. "I'm sure it'll stop soon."

Clinging to the lie, Kat smiled back and agreed. That was when she heard the voices from behind them.

"Well, aren't you two just the picture?" Peyton mocked. "Kat, that was very much like the look you used in *An American Dream*. Actually, you've put a nice spin on it, a little less of a smile, more dreamy. It's nice. Good to see you used your rehab time wisely. Did you see the movie, Steve? Really, you two could have been running the scene, it looked so familiar."

Kat saw the twinge of skepticism on Steve's face, but pretended not to.

She spoke before Steve got the chance. She was proud of the strength in her voice when she replied, "Peyton, you're an ass. Shouldn't you two be sleeping or whatever it is you do?"

Trista was standing next to Peyton with a grin. She'd clearly seen the same twinge that Kat had, and she was obviously pleased with the victory.

"It's almost dawn. We wanted coffee before we embarked on the search for Gloria." Peyton gave Steve a look that said: *why don't you take care of that coffee-boy?*

"I'll help you get it," Trista volunteered.

Kat saw the setup, but was helpless to stop it. Trista was headed toward the kitchen before Kat could offer to help. Unless she wanted to make a big deal out of nothing, she was going to be alone with Peyton, just the way he'd planned.

Clearly recognizing the same thing, Steve gave her hand a supportive squeeze before he dutifully followed Trista, leaving Kat alone to face the inevitable.

Peyton sat on the couch and motioned for Kat to join him. Hoping to avoid active conflict, she sat on the chair opposite him instead.

"Why do you do that?" he asked, his voice thick with cunning charm.

Kat's heart lurched. Conflict, apparently, was not going to be that easily avoided. "I'm sorry, do what?"

"Make such a show about keeping space between us. It's as if you're concerned I'll cause you physical harm."

It was the mental and emotional harm she was worried about, but Kat didn't volunteer that information. "I have no idea what you're talking about."

"Sit with me. Please," he replied in his kindest voice.

Though Kat knew it was likely a mistake, she joined him on the couch. It felt like a stupid thing to fight about. She regretted it almost immediately.

Peyton slid closer and put his arm over the back of the couch. His one hand was less than an inch from her shoulder. The other just as close to her knee.

"Now, see, this is better. Don't you think?"

Kat tried to move away, but the arm of the couch was at her back already. Nowhere to go. "It's fine," she agreed.

He smiled supportively, but Kat suspected the smile was only joy at her discomfort. "We haven't really had a chance to talk. You know, not really talk, since that awful day. You scared the life out of me. When I saw you on the floor," he closed his eyes dramatically at the memory. "I thought you were dead," he added, sadly shaking his head.

"I'm sorry to have put you through that." Kat tried to keep her voice flat. She didn't want to care what he thought, but the embarrassment and the shame came rushing back.

Peyton put his hand on her knee. "Don't worry about it. I'm pleased you've gotten help. How are you doing?"

Kat breathed deeply. As her boss, he had every right to ask her these questions. She had no right to complain. "That day was the last time I used. I hope it will always be. I'll do everything in my power to make sure it doesn't affect a movie again."

Peyton smiled again. "Kat, I like you. Always have. You're a sweet girl. Probably too sweet for the monsters in this industry. I want you to know you can lean on me. I'll do whatever is needed to get you back on the front page." As he spoke, he began to run his hand slowly up and down the inside of her thigh.

Again, she felt her back against the proverbial wall. This was exactly what he'd done last time. Moving in slowly, in tiny increments, none seeming much more than what came before. All putting the onus on her to stop the interaction. She cursed herself for having no more strength now than she did then.

"Did Donnie tell you I was the one that pushed for you on the movie?"

It was exactly the opposite of what Donnie had told her. "No, he didn't," she replied, trying to steel herself for what was to come.

"The rest were skeptical you'd be ready so fast. And the director, I really have to warn you about him. He said some horrible things. There's no reason for me to repeat them, but I suspect you can imagine."

"Yeah, I can imagine." Kat knew he was probably lying, but the words cut. She'd worked with the director before. She'd always considered him something of a friend.

"That's why I came here. I'll bring a good report back; that'll ease their minds." He leaned in a little closer, his fingers trailing lightly through her hair. "It can be us against them, Kat. I can make the path easier for you. I'll make sure they don't push you too hard. Make sure your costar helps with promotion. I know how stressful you find the talk show circuit."

He was very close now. He'd just brushed his teeth; she could smell the mint on his breath.

He wasn't unattractive. Actually, many would consider him handsome. And he would keep the promises he made, at least most of them. Worse, he was not making idle threats. He could make sure the press before the opening was deadly. He could purposely delay shoots so she'd have extended days, hold back script changes so she'd have less time with her lines.

All she had to do was let him have her. Was it really that awful?

She didn't know what her decision would have been if Steve and Trista hadn't returned at that moment. The searing hatred coming from Trista was not surprising, but the look from Steve was devastating. In that instant, he'd made a decision about her, and it was not a good one.

Peyton squeezed her thigh and whispered, "We'll finish our conversation later." Then looking at the other two, he said more loudly, "Is that coffee? Exactly what I've been waiting for."

The moment Peyton's focus turned to the others, Kat jumped off the couch. The move likely made her look all the more guilty, but she couldn't resist the compulsion to escape.

~ 62 ~

Steve couldn't believe what they'd walked in on. Kat
had been so vehement about her hatred of Peyton, she even
seemed afraid of him. But the exchange they'd interrupted
couldn't have looked any less like fear. Kat's face had been
blocked by Peyton, but their body language spoke volumes.
When you were sitting that close there was only one thing
that happened.

Steve did see her face when she jumped to her feet.
Guilt. Embarrassment.

He felt a little jealous. But mostly, he felt hurt and
surprised, not only by her duplicity, but also by his gullibility.

They drank their coffee in relative silence, Trista glaring,
Steve avoiding Kat's eyes.

Finally Peyton finished his coffee and rose. "If you aren't
going to talk like civilized people, then we may as well go out
and see if we can find the crazy lady."

Trista was quick to agree. Plainly, she wanted to control
how they paired off this time. "Peyton and I should start
out back. You two can start up front."

Peyton smiled easily. "Perfect. Come on, Trista. Shockingly, I did not bring an umbrella to the desert with me, but I did bring a coat. You might want one too," he pointed out, leading Trista upstairs.

The instant they disappeared from sight, Kat spoke, "I swear to you that was not what it looked like."

Steve wanted to believe her. It would've been easier on his ego if he did. "It's no big deal one way or the other. It's none of my business."

"There is nothing going on. I told you about things between us."

"Well, yes, that was obvious when we came in. I mean, there must be bruises on your legs from where he was holding you down." His voice carried more anger than he'd expected.

"Steve, please, it's not like that. I swear to you. He's my boss. He could ruin me. It's complicated."

"I'm sure it is," Steve replied. He could hear the sarcasm in his voice, but he made no effort to control it. "Like I said, it's your business, not mine. Who am I to judge?"

She was looking up at him with those big brown eyes, chewing on her lower lip, as if to stop it from trembling. Pleading. The look might have brought him to his knees a half hour ago, but now it just looked like an Oscar-worthy performance.

"Do you want to get a coat, or go out like this?" he asked, placing his cowboy hat firmly on his head.

She shook her head. "I'm fine. Let's just go."

~ 63 ~

Trista wished she'd brought some kind of hat to protect her face. The rain seemed to have a life of its own, angrily pouring from the sky in an all-out assault. It was easy to see why the road had flooded. The pool was so overfilled that the water was flush with the patio.

The remaining grounds were no better. The previously dry terrain was muddy and riddled with puddles and streams. The dirt squished menacingly as she walked. It pulled at her sandals, trying to consume them and possibly Trista as well.

It didn't take long to realize how pointless a search was. The grounds were completely flat, with very few bushes and shrubs. There was simply nowhere Gloria could be hiding.

Plainly seeing the same thing, Peyton asked, "Should we look around the side of the hotel, too?"

Trista shrugged. "May as well. I'm drenched. More time out here won't make any difference."

There was shrubbery around the outside wall of the hotel. Peyton peered behind it as they walked.

"Where do you think she went?" Trista wondered, surveying the landscape.

"God only knows. The woman's a lunatic. I have no clue why we're doing this at all. You don't run out into a storm in the middle of the night without suicidal intentions. If she wanted to kill herself, that's her business. I don't see why I have to walk around in the rain looking for her."

"I agree, but we both know the Boy Scout wasn't going to let it go."

Peyton scowled. "It's all an act. Nobody's that kind and generous. You women fall for games like his all the time. You'd think you'd learn."

"Oh, and you don't play games," Trista snipped, embarrassed that he saw through her sarcasm.

His scowl turned into a sly smile. "Yes, but I can give you the world. All he can give you is a mediocre sandwich."

Trista knew exactly what Peyton could give her. She just wanted the sandwich, too. And it certainly wasn't fair that someone else might get it just because she'd opted not to take it.

"Speaking of games, how did your conversation with Steve go?" Peyton asked. It had been their plan earlier to split up the two lovebirds. Divide and conquer.

Trista purposely looked away as she responded. "My conversation didn't go anywhere near as well as your conversation with Kat."

He laughed. "There is no reason to be jealous. Kat owes a little debt. Once we take care of that, you'll have my full attention. So, what did Steve say?"

Trista considered pushing the point further, but she was afraid it would make her appear insecure. "He didn't say anything. He was very tight-lipped."

Peyton stopped mid-stride. "Really? Suspiciously so?"

Trista smiled. If Peyton thought Kat was using again, the game would be over. She'd be too risky for the project. A lie would free Trista from her adversary. It would also ruin Kat's career. The decision was simple. "Yes. It sounded like he was covering for her."

Peyton's smile grew broader. He gave Trista a big kiss. "Perfect. We need to keep at this then. Get something more concrete. If you help me take her down..." his voice trailed off. "Well, let's just say the rewards will be great."

Trista returned the kiss and his smile. She was confident Peyton would pay her well for her services. And, once she convinced Kat it was Steve who sold her out to Peyton, then Trista would have Steve too. A man jilted by a Hollywood starlet would be looking for a nice down home girl. Someone with a hot body and a playful smile. Maybe a little Texas drawl.

~ 64 ~

Searching the grounds with Steve was even worse than it had been the night before. The rain was still pummeling, the fog still surrounded them, but now she felt alone in it all. Completely isolated.

It was stupid. She knew that. He was just mad. She just needed to give him some time to calm down. But these days, time felt like a luxury she just didn't have.

She pushed the negative thought from her mind and willed herself to focus on the task at hand. She was staring out at a mostly open expanse that surrounded the hotel. And Gloria was nowhere to be seen. At least it was looking like it would be a quick search.

About a quarter mile away, the grounds and the driveway rose sharply. From what Steve and Biff had told them, the road was washed out just over that rise.

She scanned the saturated earth, and looked up the driveway toward the hill. "I guess we need to look out there?"

Steve shrugged and avoided her eyes. "I can't think of anywhere else she could be."

She plodded after him, only stopping short when they reached the top of the hill.

Less than a hundred feet away was an enormous rush of floodwater. It was so deep and flowing so quickly she almost didn't believe this was the driveway she'd come down just days before. The raging water was nothing less than a river, surreal as it sliced through the gravel driveway.

Steve's voice jarred her out of her transfixed stare. "There she is!"

As Steve rushed towards the water, Kat saw the small body, half on the muddy bank with her upper body and face floating in the water. Though neither of them had any doubt the woman was dead, they both hurried to her side.

Kat couldn't tell if it was Gloria, but the corpse looked about the right size. As Steve attempted to drag the body to the shore, Kat forced herself to look away from the face. The saturated, stringy hair and hideous bloating were more than she could stand. Instead, she stared at the woman's small feet. Skinny ankles. Tiny sneakers.

It was only then that she realized what she was seeing. There were roots wrapped tightly around Gloria's ankles. Slender roots that seemed to have shot out of the ground and grabbed their prey. As Steve moved the body, all of the roots snapped loose from her right ankle.

"Stop! Don't move her!" Kat exclaimed.

Steve looked up, straining to hold onto Gloria, water rushing over his feet.

"Her ankles. Look at the left one. It's as if she was tied down."

Kat reluctantly looked up the rest of the woman's body. Similar roots were wrapped around her calves and knees. Some of them had snapped off, but a few remained tightly wound around her.

Steve cautiously lowered the body. Kat could tell that he wasn't comfortable placing her back into the water, but it was more than obvious that Gloria was long past feeling any pain.

With water still rushing over his ankles, Steve leaned closer to examine the roots. As he did, Kat felt an odd relief that he could see them too. She had half expected that the whole thing was a hallucination.

"How the hell would they wrap around like that? I mean, she might trip over a root or something, but not this. They're wrapped against her skin, like ropes," Steve observed.

Before Kat could attempt to answer the unanswerable, Trista and Peyton appeared by her side.

"Idiot," Peyton muttered.

Trista hit him on the arm. "It's bad luck to speak ill of the dead."

"Bad luck?" he snarled. "Bad luck is getting stuck here in the fucking rain. Running out into a storm in the middle of the night is lunacy. It has nothing to do with luck. Though I'm sure one of you has a theory why we should still be worried someone's out to kill us."

Kat thought of the Bible and the section on Sloth. Hadn't there been a mention of souls buried in the mud?

As if he was reading her mind, Steve replied, "I don't know, Peyton, maybe we just found the River Styx."

Peyton's glare said that he remembered the conversation, but he was no more convinced now than he'd been hours earlier. "The woman threw herself into flood waters. Not really an odd thing to happen to someone running around in the dark screaming like a banshee."

"There're roots wrapped around her legs. It looks like she was tied down and left to drown."

Peyton squinted at the muddy body and then looked back at Steve. "Has Kat been sharing her stash?"

"They're right there. Are you blind?" Kat snapped.

As she spoke the words, she looked back at Gloria's ankle. There were red marks, but nothing else. No roots. In fact, no roots near either of her ankles. Or around her legs. She looked at Steve desperately. The confusion on his face told her he didn't have any idea what was going on either.

Trista laughed at their looks. "Steve, she's a bad influence on you."

"We both saw them. They were there," Kat insisted.

"I guess whatever evil force is out to murder us all can make roots disappear. Right?" Trista mocked.

Peyton shook his head, sending streams of water down his face. "This is asinine. In case no one else has noticed, it's raining. We found her. She's dead. Big surprise. Now can we go inside and dry off?"

Peyton was plainly not happy when Steve lifted the body to bring it inside, but he did nothing more than shoot him a look of disgust and march back to the hotel. Trista slipped her hand into his and without even a backward glance, they returned to the hotel.

By the time Kat and Steve made it back inside, the two of them were nowhere to be found. Kat locked the front door of the hotel and followed Steve to Gloria's wing. It was now the exclusive resting place of the dead. She couldn't help but think it was only a matter of time before the rest of them followed suit.

Steve gently laid Gloria's body on the canopy bed. Though he tried to place her as peacefully as possible, the gesture was pointless. She was dripping, her body rigid and coated in a rust-colored mud. Her eyes were still open. Staring wide. Blankly, yet desperately.

She averted her eyes from the ghastly image. "What do we do now?" she asked in a soft voice.

Steve shook his head and looked away. He looked as pained as Kat felt. She considered persisting, but knew it would be unfair. He didn't know any more than she did.

Instead, they left Gloria in her room and headed to the wing where the living still resided. Habitually they entered Kat's suite and sat together on the couch. Kat leaned her head against his chest in exhaustion.

"I'm sorry about what happened this morning with Peyton," she said after a moment. "I need to stand up to him. I know."

Steve nuzzled into her soaking hair, and kissed the top of her head. "It's okay. He's a slick guy."

Kat looked up and was again taken in by the kindness in his eyes. They held a mixture of innocence and sincerity, the likes of which she hadn't really seen since childhood. It was the reason she'd been attracted to him initially. The reason she still felt so drawn to him.

He leaned in and gave her a deep kiss, running his fingers through her dripping hair. Kat ran her hand down the T-shirt that adhered to his chest. She closed her eyes and enjoyed the strength of his embrace, the intensity of having him this close. It made her feel alive. It made her forget she was a woman marked to die a horrible death for her sins.

As suddenly as the kiss began, Steve pulled away, leaving Kat feeling disoriented. Even more perplexing was the sharp look in his eyes.

"You must be cold," he said, stiffly.

Kat squinted at the comment. She was sure she felt the opposite of cold. "I'm okay," she replied cautiously. "Are you?"

"You're soaked," he continued, ignoring her question. "You must want to change into some dry clothes. Maybe catch a shower."

"I guess," Kat responded, still trying to figure out what had just happened.

"Why don't you get some fresh clothes and I'll turn on the water for you? I'll sit out here and keep an eye on things."

Kat nodded in agreement, mostly because she didn't know what else to do. She'd been with some strange guys over the years, but Steve was proving one of the strangest.

~ 65 ~

Steve closed the door to the bathroom with a sense of guilt and waited for the water to switch from the tub to the shower. The moment it did, he grabbed a pad and pen. He knew his timing was terrible, but the realization that had just struck him simply couldn't wait.

He couldn't believe he hadn't thought of it before. The room numbers. That was the key to the whole thing. It had to be.

The first murder had occurred in Suite One. The second in Suite Two. The third didn't happen in Suite Three, but its occupant had died. The only problem was, Waylan was never supposed to be in Suite One. He'd been assigned Suite Three with Gloria. It didn't fit right.

As he stared at the pad in front of him, Steve thought of the descriptions they'd found in Kat's Bible. Despite the fact that Waylan was not assigned to Suite One, the suite had clearly been designed for him. The red walls. The bear paintings. The message on the door – WRATH.

Could it possibly be so simple? Were they being killed in order? If that was true, then they were up to Suite Four.

Trista's room. Steve thought of the décor. Green walls. Dogs. He flipped through the Bible to confirm. Green. Dogs. Envy. It sounded like Trista.

Before him was a list of seven names: 1. Waylan, 2. Biff, 3. Gloria, 4. Trista, 5. Peyton, 6. Steve, 7. Kat. He thought of the colors of the rooms. They matched their occupants' weaknesses. It didn't seem the rest of them would be switching rooms the way Waylan had.

Steve was staring at the list when he heard the shower stop. He briefly considered keeping this from Kat, but he knew he couldn't. She was last. She deserved the chance to decide if that was a blessing or a curse.

When Kat rejoined him she was wearing clean, dry clothes and she was still towel-drying her hair. It took her only a moment to read the expression on his face.

"What's happened?"

Handing her a pad, he said, "I think I've figured something out, something big."

She dropped the damp towel on the chair and joined him on the couch.

"Those are all of our names listed after our respective suite numbers," he explained.

He could tell by her expression that he didn't need to say much more than that.

"Does three make a pattern?" she asked.

"Would you rather wait until we have four?"

She looked between him and the list. He wondered what she was thinking. Did she see the advantage to being last? Or did she only see the curse?

"So, what do we do?" he asked.

She took a deep breath. "We have to protect Trista. She's next."

"And how the hell are we going to do that?"

~ 66 ~

Trista disentangled herself from Peyton. He stirred for a moment, and then settled back into sleep. He looked less handsome when he was sleeping, she realized. No sharp gaze, no confident demeanor. When he was asleep, his hair looked grayer, the lines on his face looked deeper, and the slight sagging in neck and cheeks more apparent.

That, however, was irrelevant. He had power. He had success. He was her means to fortune, maybe even fame. The key to a new life, the likes of which she'd dreamed of since she was a little girl.

If she could have him, she would be able to show them all that she was better than her insignificant hometown.

Sure, she wished he looked more like Steve and less like an old man, but you couldn't get everything you wanted in life. Well, at least not all at once.

There was only one problem. Kat. The desperation in Peyton's eyes when he looked at her was unnerving. His hunger for the actress was becoming obvious, his excuses more flimsy. She couldn't know how far he'd go to fill that need. And the risk was just becoming too great.

She had to make sure the actress lost her job. Without the job, they wouldn't be working together. And then Peyton's interest would wane, and he could focus exclusively on Trista's future.

Unfortunately, innuendos were only going to get her so far. She had to get Kat using again. And the only place Trista knew she'd find drugs was Biff's room. As unappealing as it was to be that close to a dead body again, she refused to risk losing her dream.

Trista looked at Peyton one more time as she slipped out. He'd be sound asleep for a while. He'd never have time to miss her.

She moved silently down the hall, her footsteps disguised by the incessant tapping of the rain. She crept quickly past her own room and into the other wing, trying not to look at the writing on Biff's door, not to think about what it meant.

Inside, Biff's untimely demise hung heavily in the air. From the doorway, Trista could see his suitcase at the foot of the bed, open and inviting.

She slunk inside, unsure if she was more afraid of snakes or the dead body staring at the ceiling. She watched Biff out of the corner of her eye while she dug into the suitcase. Somehow the idea that his corpse might rise up and attack seemed almost reasonable.

The suitcase was filled with wild shirts and tacky shorts. Underneath the clothes she found more porn than she'd ever cared to see. And tucked away in one corner was a small cardboard box. Inside was an assortment of cylinders and packets. Pills. Powders. Weed.

She considered taking the whole box with her, but thought better of it. She only needed a cylinder for Kat. If her plans worked, she wouldn't need to sell drugs to keep herself in the style she craved.

~ 67 ~

Even as they discussed how to proceed, Steve's mind raced ahead. If this was the schedule, if he'd really cracked the pattern, then he needed to focus on how he could use this information to protect Kat. If they could protect Trista and Peyton, Kat would be safe. They just needed to wait out the storm. Once the rain stopped, they could get the hell out of this mad house.

Steve was drawn to the window. It was pouring. A bright flash of lightning was followed immediately by a clap of thunder. He winced at the sound, feeling as if the storm was somehow intentionally working to trap them.

"It has to stop soon," he said, as much to himself as to Kat.

In a flat tone, Kat didn't even try to console him. "It should have stopped by now. Three people should still be alive. But, somehow, neither of those things is true. This is unnatural. Evil."

Steve wouldn't let himself think about the weird logic in her statement. If this was some force beyond them all, there was no reason to even try to fight.

After a long moment of silence, Kat said, "Of all the people in the entire world to be murdered for their sins, we don't deserve this."

Steve turned to face Kat. She was sitting on the couch, her hands in her hair. He couldn't tell if she was calculating or just collapsing under the weight of her guilt.

"What are you getting at?" he asked.

When she looked up, there was a surprising clarity in her eyes. "The Bible. The rooms. Somebody wants us here because we committed certain sins."

Steve nodded, but he had no clue what she was getting at.

It didn't look like she even noticed his response as she charged on. "I'm a rotten person." Steve started to interrupt, but she stopped him. "I am. But that's not the point. There are lots of people worse than me. Drug addicts that'll kill their mother for a dime bag. Yet it's me here. Why?"

Steve sunk back onto the couch. She made an excellent point.

She continued, "Waylan Lichtenhoff was a child abuser and a wife beater. An angry, violent man, certainly, but the worst of the worst? No. There are serial killers. Terrorists. Why him? Any one of us, you can say the same thing. None of us are saints, but none of us are the devil incarnate either."

"This has to be personal," he muttered.

Even as he said the words, the link jumped in his mind. The one thing they all had in common – Amy Lichtenhoff. Their eyes met for a second, and a silent agreement was reached.

Kat nodded slowly. "I'd want to kill me, too."

"You couldn't help it," Steve replied somewhat absently. His mind was on his own sin. It was easy to understand why Amy would want him dead.

He tried not to see the questions in Kat's eyes, but he could feel her gaze. Of course she was trying to read his mind, who wouldn't?

He knew that a real man would confess, but he would rather die than admit the truth. It was funny really, because death was quickly becoming a likely result.

It broke his heart when she finally spoke, her voice gentle and understanding. "No one here is blameless. I was selfish and stupid. I let myself hide in drugs. I knew I was hurting myself. I knew it was wrong. But I deluded myself into thinking I wasn't hurting anyone else. I was wrong – obviously. You and I," she paused, as if waiting for some response from him. Getting none, she continued, "We're friends, right?"

Steve wished he could believe that was something that wouldn't be affected by his secret. He glanced up for a second, then looked quickly away, the earnest glow of her eyes more than he could take. She didn't know what she was asking. She couldn't possibly.

"Do you hate me for what I did to her?" Kat asked, suddenly and sharply.

Steve's head snapped up. "No. Of course not. It was a mistake."

Kat caught his chin before he could look away again. "I won't hate you either."

But the truth was so much worse than she could imagine. "You don't know that."

"Yes, I do," she insisted.

Steve felt the tears in his eyes, and the shame was crushing.

Kat's eyes locked on his. Gentle, sweet, beautiful. She ran her hand across his cheek. Through his hair. "Please." The word came out so softly Steve wasn't sure she'd even said it.

He leaned in almost on instinct. He needed to be closer to her. Be near her. He wanted to trust her. He wanted to tell her. He just…

Before he realized he was doing it, he was kissing her, running his fingers through her silky hair and down her arms.

It felt like a promise, her way to show that he could trust her, that she believed in him. But it could never be. Eventually he would tell her and he would lose her forever – there was no way to avoid it.

But he pulled her desperately close. He needed her, just this once. He'd deal with the rest later.

~ 68 ~

Trista wanted desperately to run back to Peyton. The silent isolation of the hallway was quickly becoming more than she could take. But her pants had no pockets, and she needed somewhere to conceal Kat's gift until she had the right opportunity. She had to make one more stop.

Her room didn't look so beautiful now. The bright paint seemed dark and lifeless without the sunbeams pouring in the windows. It was pure fear that had her hurrying into the bedroom for a change of clothes. Suddenly it felt a little suicidal to be this completely alone.

"Yet somehow the little sheep keep wandering from the flock." The voice came from the sitting room behind her. Trista knew immediately who it was. Leaving Peyton's side for even a few minutes was about to be the worst mistake of her life.

She wanted to run, but it would be pointless. If Amy had thought there was any escape, she wouldn't have revealed herself so passively.

Swallowing her panic, Trista turned. Amy was sitting in a stuffed high-backed chair, legs crossed, looking perfectly at ease. Normal in every way but one – she was soaking wet.

"Have you been here all along?" Trista asked, taking a seat on the couch opposite her.

Amy nodded. "How are you, old friend? Enjoying my little game?"

Trista crossed her legs, mirroring her foe. "Eh, it'd be better if there was a bit more sun, but who can complain?"

Amy stared intensely before she said, "I always thought your cool demeanor was real, that you genuinely never worried about anything. The truth is, you worry about just about everything, don't you? Always worried someone has something better than you, something more than you, something that should be yours. I pity you a little. It must be exhausting."

Trista paid the words little heed. There was something different about Amy. It wasn't just the water; it wasn't just the passage of time. She looked strange, somehow wrong.

Amy continued, "I have to say, it's a different experience to be here with you now. Just you and me. And this time, I hold all the cards."

Trista shrugged. "So, how'd you do it? How'd you convince this Tami to let you use her hotel to kill all your enemies?"

A laugh lit Amy's face. "Oh, Amy Light and Tami Ghyl get along just swimmingly. It was really quite easy to set things up."

"I assume you're planning on killing me next?"

"You *are* in room number four."

Trista's laugh was just a little too shrill. She was beginning to realize all the things she'd missed. "It's so simple. I never would have thought of it."

"No need to make things unnecessarily complicated."

Trista leaned in, curious in spite of herself. "You killed them all?"

Amy shook her head. "I'm not sure exactly how you all are missing the connections here. They seem obvious to me. But somehow, I keep getting my chance."

"Honey, I've gotta say, I don't understand. Waylan, well sure, who could blame you for knocking the life out of him? What a piece of shit he was. Biff, I mean I was amused by him, but I can see how you might have problems with him. Gloria wasn't any better than Waylan, really. But me? Why me?"

"Why you? You're kidding, right?"

"No. We were friends. What did I ever do to you?" Even as she asked the question, Trista already knew the answer. It seemed Gloria's accusations had been far more accurate than Peyton's reassurances.

"Bobby Mitchell, Ray Peters, Tony Alonzo. Do I really need to go on?"

"You're really upset because I slept with some guys you liked? That is *so* ridiculous! It was high school. That's what happens!"

"You knew what my life was like at home. Knew I had nothing. My abusive father killed my mother. My stepmother didn't look up from the TV long enough to make sure I was still breathing when he finished hitting me. I had nothing. You were as poor as the rest of us, but at least your mom gave a shit. You could have dated any guy you wanted. Yet anytime a guy paid more attention to me than to you, you got so jealous you couldn't see straight. The guy didn't stand a chance, and neither did I."

"It wasn't like that."

"It was exactly like that. You were so obsessed with having everything that you were jealous of my pitiful life."

Trista sunk back into the couch under the weight of Amy's accusations. "Men find me attractive. I can't help that. What did you want me to do?"

"You could have started by not leading them on, not luring them away. The sex meant nothing to you. It was all about having what someone else had. Taking what somebody else wanted. I lived my childhood in a dark room without windows, and you took every flashlight that was handed to me."

Trista shook her head vehemently. "No. That's not true. I was your friend. I was there to cheer you up, there to help you with your books when you were on crutches. I found you a date for the prom."

"And then fucked him in the bathroom."

The shame of being caught washed over her. "You knew about that?"

"I do now. I know everything now. You've done the same stuff since you got here. You've done everything you can to keep Kat and Steve apart and everything you can to make sure you keep the upper hand with Peyton. I mean, why are you even here right now?"

"Are you defending them?" Trista shouted.

"No, not at all. I'm glad you've done it. It'll help me in the long run. Now, though, it's time to finish things." Amy rose from the chair.

Trista jumped off the couch. "What are you going to do?"

"I think you already know the answer to that question."

"I'll scream. The others are just down the hall. They'll come to help. Then what'll you do?"

"Go ahead. It won't make any difference. They won't be able to hear you."

Of course they'd hear her. They had to. Taking a deep breath, Trista let out a howl.

~ 69 ~

Kat was lying on top of Steve, her face buried in his muscular chest, one arm over the back of the couch. She couldn't move. She could barely breathe. She wanted to lie there forever, inhaling his scent, feeling his strength.

She was slowly drifting off to sleep when she heard something that caused her to sit straight up.

Steve had also been drifting off; Kat's sudden movement brought him quickly back. "What is it?"

"Did you hear that?" Kat asked, her eyes darting around the room.

"Hear what?"

Kat opened her mouth to explain, but then shut it just as quickly. What had she heard? It couldn't have been a scream. The volume was wrong – not muffled, but muted, as if someone had turned the volume down on the TV. Almost as if the sound had been entirely in her head. "I thought I heard a scream."

Steve smoothed her hair. "You were probably dreaming already. God knows we all have more than a thousand reasons to hear screams after the days we've had here."

Kat nodded. He was probably right. How many times had she woken up in the middle of the night unsure if she had heard something, or if it had only been a part of a dream? It had sounded so real at first, but the more she thought about it the more she decided it was one of those phantom sounds. The type where you realize that it really had no volume, no real sound, only the illusion created in your mind.

Still, Kat wondered if it was her subconscious reminding her of Trista. Things had gotten so distracting with Steve that she'd forgotten – Trista and Peyton needed to be warned about the pattern.

Steve ran his fingers through her hair. "What are you thinking?"

"Maybe we should go tell Peyton and Trista what we found."

His eyes ran down the length of her naked body. "Do you really think you can sit here in front of me looking like that and expect me to want to talk about Peyton?"

Kat couldn't help but return the look he had given her. His lean, muscular body was too tempting.

Seeing the hungry look in her eyes, he smiled. "Good, I see I've talked some sense into you. Now, I was thinking we should find our way to that big old bed you've got."

~ 70 ~

Trista's throat was raw and her abdomen sore, as she gasped for more air. They hadn't heard her. They were never going to hear her.

When she finally stopped screaming, the silence was deafening. Defeated, Trista sank to the couch.

"Are you done?" Amy asked, her lips curled in a confident smirk.

Trista stared at the pale, glassy-eyed woman who stood over her, hair still dripping with water. Weird how wet she still was. The water continued its constant stream, almost as if it was coming from inside her.

And that was when it all came together. Dear God, this was an even bigger nightmare than she'd originally thought.

"Is that salt water I smell?" Trista prayed she was wrong.

Amy winked. "Welcome to the game."

"Biff was right about you committing suicide?" Trista rubbed her arms, wishing she didn't understand.

Amy stood by silently, clearly waiting for Trista to finish.

"If you're dead, then what is all this about?"

"This is about you getting what you deserve."

"You kill yourself and they let you come back and take your revenge on the seven of us?" Who was running the cosmos if that was the way things went in the afterlife?

Amy sat down, crossing her legs casually, clearly enjoying the questions. "It's actually a little wager I made. Things will be a bit less unpleasant for me if I hand over the seven of you."

"Since you have the ability to make your father look like he was run over by a lawn mower, it can't be much of a challenge."

Amy chuckled. "There's actually a little catch. You each have to prove you deserve your punishment. Prove you are a sinner. That's the tricky part. Fortunately for me, you all are nothing if not predictable."

Trista thought of Peyton's Latin translation earlier. She was beginning to wonder if they did have the right translation for the hotel's name.

"I have sinned," she murmured under her breath.

Amy's smile broadened. "Was it Peyton? With a name like O'Neil, he's gotta be Catholic, right? And Catholics know their Latin." Amy stood abruptly and tossed a coarse bundle of material onto Trista's lap. "I'm done with the chitchat. Put the dress on."

Trista held the material out in front of her. It was nothing more than a burlap sack. "Cutting holes for my head and arms does not make this a dress."

Amy was not amused. Her glare was vicious enough that Trista almost reconsidered her sarcasm. But one look at the sack was enough to keep her focus. She'd been resigned to just about anything, but this was not going to happen. "You can kill me, but you can't force me to put this on."

"This is your last chance," Amy glowered.

"No," Trista snapped, throwing the bag back.

The sack flew through the air, floating more than it should have and ultimately stopping before it hit the floor. The only things more frightening than the levitating garment were Amy's eyes, which glowed black. Their rage pinned Trista to the seat.

Suddenly, there was a rush of icy air and Trista's clothes evaporated off her body. Before she could react, the sack rose up again and simply merged onto her, becoming one with her skin.

And then it was done.

Trista forced a laugh, pushing away the fear. "Are you going to kill me with bad fashion?"

Amy's eyes didn't look so dark now. They looked vague and almost dismissive as she walked away, wandering to the window.

From the couch, Trista wondered if it was possible to make it to the door and escape. Amy was on the other side of the room, the door was closer than she was. She was supernatural, yes, but Trista had to try.

Trista was sprinting for the door the instant she was on her feet. She hadn't taken more than three steps when she fell forward, face first into the ground. From behind, someone grabbed her hair and yanked her to her knees.

"Thanks, this is going to be a lot easier with you on the floor," Amy explained.

Amazingly, Amy was standing in front of her. Yet someone, or something, still clutched her hair.

"It will only hurt for a minute, old friend," Amy promised.

Squatting on the floor next to her, Amy leaned forward, raising her hand toward Trista's face. Her pinky and pointer finger were extended and her middle and ring finger were tucked away.

The two fingers went straight for Trista's eyes, as Amy made sure that she was the last thing that Trista ever saw.

~ 71 ~

Peyton was dreaming about Kat. They were on the set of the movie. The picture was going perfectly, and Kat was eager to show him how happy he'd made her. That gorgeous body men everywhere lusted after was finally his for the taking.

He rolled over, half-awake now, realizing Kat was next door with another man, but knowing Trista would provide a nice substitute for the time being. He was surprised to find the sheets next to him icy cold.

"Trista," he called into the other room. "Come back to bed."

Only silence answered his call.

"Come on. I promise I'll make it worth your while."

Still nothing.

Now Peyton was getting annoyed. The more he woke up, the more he lost the lovely images of sex with America's hottest actress.

He grumbled to himself as he grabbed a pair of slacks and a T-shirt off the floor. His fantasy quickly turning darker. The damn hick needed to learn to listen.

"Trista, answer me," he muttered as he wandered into the sitting room.

He'd expected she would be sitting there, watching television, maybe staring at the rain, but the room was empty. The bathroom door was wide open, revealing that it too was vacant, but Peyton still hurried inside, looking behind the frosted glass of the shower before the panic really set in. Trista had left him completely alone in this crazy hotel!

He rushed out of the room and to the door of Kat's suite. He knocked lightly at first, but when he didn't get an immediate response, he started pounding.

Steve answered the door in only a pair of jeans, the button of which was undone. Kat stood half a step behind him in a plush white robe.

Again, Peyton was taken aback. Trista had to be with them. But they had clearly been alone. And even as he processed the thought, Peyton's fear gave way to anger. Little Miss Prim and Proper was fucking the damn cook? He was sleeping in his room alone, having damned fantasies, and the hired help was getting the real thing?

Peyton was about to grab her by that slutty robe and show her exactly who was in charge when Steve stepped closer and growled, "What the hell do you want?"

Controlling his rage, Peyton pushed by Steve and into the room. He needed to gather himself.

"Excuse me," Kat said, grabbing his arm. "I don't remember anyone inviting you in."

The sitting room was somewhat askew, clothes tossed about. One cushion was falling off the couch. Peyton couldn't help but notice the bed looked even more tousled.

"Is Trista in here?" Peyton asked, trying desperately to calm down and focus on the reason he was there.

"Are you kidding?" Steve almost shouted. "No. She's not. Get out, you moron."

Peyton spun around to face them. Though he saw only rage on Steve's face, Kat's face was much more concerned. "Isn't she with you?" she asked.

"I woke up and she was gone," Peyton admitted.

A shadow crossed Steve's face. "What? Well, where is she?"

"I thought she might be with you two."

Steve shook his head. "What did you do to her?"

Peyton held up his hands. "I fell asleep. I woke up. She was gone."

Kat shuddered. "We have to go look for her."

Steve looked at Peyton and then at Kat. "I'll go look for her. You two stay here."

"Hell no," Kat said quickly. "I'm going wherever you're going."

Peyton shook his head in resignation. The woman was an idiot. "Whatever you want. Somebody needs to start looking."

~ 72 ~

Steve was furious that Kat wasn't safe in her room. Nothing good could come of all of them wandering the halls. Things were going badly. Very badly.

Kat had said she'd heard something earlier and he'd dismissed her, but now his panic was rising. Had it really been something? Had they ignored a cry for help?

He'd been so damned distracted. He, of all people, knew better than that.

He shook off the thought. Trista could still be alive. He wanted to believe it, but there was a fear in the air, thick as a choking smoke.

No one even took a moment to put on something more appropriate before heading out. Kat simply tightened the belt of the robe.

Steve called Trista's name as they went, but only the patter of the rain answered. Oddly, the rain seemed less clawing now, more cheerful, like it was amused.

They stopped short at the door to Trista's room. They had every reason to believe she was in there, and every reason to believe they wouldn't want to find her. Steve ignored the constricting fear in his throat. He needed to be strong. Brave. He needed to protect Kat. He needed not to screw it up this time.

Peyton scowled and pushed him aside. Causally, he knocked on the door. "Trista, are you in there?" His tone of voice was that of a gentleman picking up his dinner date.

Steve couldn't think of a time that he more wanted to slap the man.

No response.

Peyton knocked again, harder this time. "Trista? Is everything all right?" Steve thought he heard fear in the producer's voice.

Kat pointed at the door. "We can't just stand here. There's no writing yet. Steve, do you have the master key? Maybe we aren't too late."

Peyton scowled. "You can't just break into the woman's bedroom."

But Steve barely heard him. He hadn't thought of the writing. Kat was right, they might still have time. He shoved Peyton aside without a word, unlocking the door. He pushed it open slowly, petrified about what he might find. Snakes? Coyotes? Something worse?

Nothing could have prepared him for what they found. Trista was entirely alone, kneeling on the floor in the plush sitting area, dressed in what looked like a burlap sack. Her arms were drawn tightly behind her back, held there by some unseen force.

Her long blonde hair was pulled up in a ponytail. Almost as if it was purposely done to provide a better view. Though her head was slumped slightly forward, the blood was as unmistakable as its source.

Like a fountain of tears, two streams of blood ran down her cheeks, rolled off her chin. So much blood that the sack she was wearing was quickly changing color.

Peyton took a step back from the door. Steve rushed past him with Kat following quickly behind.

With all the blood, Steve had no idea how Trista was still kneeling. Yet somehow she maintained the strength to keep her balance. He took it as a hopeful sign she was still alive, at least for now.

When Steve placed a hand on Trista's shoulder she flinched, and cringed away.

"Trista," he said softly. "We're here to help."

When she turned her head in his direction Steve saw why she hadn't known it was them. Her eye sockets appeared concave – as if there was nothing behind her eyelids. And the lids themselves were sewn shut with thick black wire that wove four distinct stitches through each eyelid, permanently fastening them to her cheeks. Her tears of blood were flowing from beneath the fastened lids.

Trista collapsed against Steve's bare chest. She made a sound that might have been speech, but was more likely weeping.

Steve desperately wanted to help her, but he knew she was going to bleed to death. It was a miracle she hadn't already. The only thing left was to find out what had happened.

"Can you talk?"

At first there was only a squeak, but then, plainly reaching to the depths of her remaining strength, Trista found a voice. "Yes."

Steve could barely hear her. "Who did this to you? How did this happen?"

Trista lifted her head off Steve's chest. If it was possible, it seemed the blood was flowing more freely now. The motion threw Trista off balance. If he hadn't caught her, she would have landed face first on the ground.

"You need to tell us what happened. Trista, please."

Trista mumbled something inaudible and Steve could feel her body start to fall forward again.

He was about to ask for her help again when Trista spoke. "Revenge," she said in a hoarse whisper.

"What was that?" Peyton asked.

Steve waved him off. "Honey, whose revenge? Who did this?"

Her last word wasn't much more than a breath, but Steve was certain he heard it correctly.

"Amy."

~ 73 ~

The flow of blood from Trista's eyes had stopped. Kat didn't want to believe it, but there was no mistaking it. She was gone. Her labored breathing had stopped. Her body was no longer shaking with trauma.

Steve cast her a look of utter helplessness before he gently lowered Trista's body to the floor.

Only three of them remained. The only living souls left in the hotel. Except for Amy, that is, who seemed to move about freely.

Kat could feel the tears gathering in her eyes. She didn't know if it was sorrow or fear, maybe a little of both. "Is she…" Her voice trailed off.

Steve nodded and walked to the bathroom with heavy feet. The sound of the running water told her that he was trying to clean up the blood that now clung to his arms and chest.

Peyton took a small step closer to the body. "What the hell happened to her?"

Steve returned still drying his hands with a towel that had at one time been white.

Kat looked between Steve and Peyton. The questions streamed through her mind, *What could have gouged that poor girl's eyes out? Who would be so vicious? How would anyone – how could anyone – sew eyelids shut with metal wire?*

The look on Steve's face told her that he was thinking the same thing.

To her surprise, Kat didn't feel anything. No fear. No sadness. No anger. Just a great black hole of nothing. With half an ear, she listened to Peyton and Steve snipe at one another, while another part of her brain tried to calculate how to get out of all of this.

"How did you let this happen?" Steve snapped at Peyton.

Peyton only glared back. "Let it happen? I was sleeping. And besides, Trista was afraid to wander around the hotel alone. One of you must have lured her away."

"You're the one who was by himself when this happened. How do we know you didn't kill her?" Steve accused.

Peyton's eyes narrowed and for an instant it seemed he didn't view Steve as his primary enemy. "Trista told us what happened – it was Amy. That bitch is in this hotel somewhere. We need to find her."

Steve crossed his arms defiantly. "We already tried that. What we need to do is hole up somewhere until this rain stops. We stick together and we're gonna be fine."

"Your plan is to sit? Sit and wait to be picked off one by one? No thank you. We need to attack this aggressively." Peyton took a step toward Steve, daring him to challenge.

Steve held his ground. "Aggression will get us killed."

"We've been sitting around ever since we found the body yesterday morning. And by my count, three more people are dead. We need to change tactics."

Kat wasn't concerned about tactics or strategies or even Amy. She was focused on only one thing – cocaine. Why was she even trying to stay sober? Her career was over. There was no doubt at this point. She was going to die. And even if she didn't die, she was going to be in the tabloids again. And this time in a story about a mass murder. Any way it went, it was all over now.

"Excuse me," she said over the shouts. "I don't care if you want to argue about this until we're all dead, but could we do it somewhere else? I've got to get away from her," she added with a shiver.

Steve put a strong arm around her shoulders. "You're right. We should get out of here."

Because the bickering continued as they walked into the hallway, neither man saw what Kat did as they walked out the door. On the table just inside the doorway was a small, perfect cylinder. Inside was a beautiful white powder that was pure heaven.

The package was in Kat's hand and tucked safely into her bulky robe pocket before she even realized she'd decided to take it. Taking it didn't mean she was going to use it, she assured herself. And she almost believed it.

~ 74 ~

Kat pulled the glass doors closed and drew the blinds. Steve and Peyton were still arguing in the sitting room, but the closed doors muted the sounds.

She was alone now, in her bedroom. They thought it was safe enough for her to be on her own while she changed – an assumption that would have been significantly less reasonable if they knew she'd snatched enough coke to knock her ass firmly off the wagon. But she was not about to share that little piece of information.

She delicately placed the smooth glass cylinder on the edge of the dressing table. It was only an emergency stash. Something to dig into if things became unbearable.

Though the way her hand was shaking, Kat couldn't help but wonder if things weren't already unbearable.

As she dressed, her eyes kept returning to the powder. When she sat in the antique chair at the dressing table to brush her hair, she had to force herself to look away.

Instead, she focused on the tangles in her hair. The brush pulled sharply against the knots bringing bright jolts of pain. It almost felt good. Real. Normal. The pain reminded her of the simple aspects of life. Life without murders, mayhem, and bizarre supernatural occurrences.

For a shining moment, it felt like the fog of her dependency was beginning to lift, and rational thoughts had a chance to overcome blind addiction. That was until she placed her brush on the tabletop. She hadn't noticed it before, but the silver brush set that had been left for her on the dressing table was lying on top of an antique silver tray with a large mirrored bottom. The corners of the mirror were discolored, revealing their true age, but the center still presented a perfect reflection of her pale skin and dark, puffy eyes.

But Kat didn't see the reflection, only its potential. The mirror was a perfect surface. In fact, she'd had a mirror very much like this in her dressing room on the set of her last movie. She'd chosen a mirrored tray because it seemed less obvious. It looked like a simple antique dressing table set, but it was the perfect clean, strong surface to cut the cocaine.

Without a thought, Kat placed the brush on the table. The mirrored tray held only a thick sterling comb. In the good old days, there'd been an identical comb, underneath which she stored a razor blade. Her heart beating with anticipation, Kat lifted the comb.

The perfect rectangle that lay alone on the mirror didn't seem odd. Not like a trap, more like an engraved invitation.

In a blur, the blade was in her hand, fingers adeptly snatching it off the mirrored glass. In one fluid motion, she placed the dull end between her lips, as had become her habit over the years. The sensation of the blade was almost erotic. The familiar metallic taste made her longing all the worse. She could feel the sinus passages under her cheekbones begin to throb with need.

Without a thought, the tiny bottle was in her hand. Breathless, she was about to open it, when she heard it.

A voice. A whisper. In her distraction, she hadn't even noticed it, but an excited spike in the pitch brought Kat out of her addicted haze. There was a person in the room with her.   Behind her.   She spun around and for less than a second she was there. A woman. Blurry. Transparent.

The specter erupted into a flash of light and a great rush of air. The air blew right through her, and as it did, the voice became more clear.

"You're going to die."

~ 75 ~

Kat's scream brought them running. Steve made it through the door first. His fists were raised for a fight, but the door opened to reveal only Kat, standing alone on the far side of the room, near the dressing table. The chair had been tipped over. Otherwise, the room itself revealed no sign of trouble.

Yet there she stood, no longer screaming, but her breathing remained labored. Her hair had fallen in front of her face and concealed what Steve imagined could only be terror. Her fists were shoved deeply into her jeans pockets, her shoulders set squarely as if she was braced for a vicious blow.

"What the hell is the matter with you?" Peyton snapped. "Are you testing our response time?"

Steve watched as Kat slowly forced her muscles to relax. When she finally ran her fingers through her hair and revealed her face, the mask was firmly in place. She looked carefully at the two men in her doorway, clearly trying to judge the damage that had already been done.

"I'm sorry. I thought I heard something. I guess I'm jumpier than I thought," she said with a false chuckle.

Steve was caught between his concern for Kat and the knowledge that she couldn't and shouldn't confess any weakness in front of Peyton. The logical side of his brain urged silence. There would be time for questions later. In private. But he was unable to go without a word.

"What did you hear?" he asked.

Kat shrugged and slipped her hands more deeply into her front pockets. "I don't know. Nothing, obviously. It's just the three of us."

Steve's eyes darted around the room. "Are you sure it was nothing?"

Kat smiled sheepishly this time. The expression was designed to give her credibility, but Steve saw right through it. "I heard something behind me. It was probably the rain on the window. The strain of this is starting to get to me a little. I'm sorry to bring you guys in here."

Steve was staring into Kat's eyes, trying to read her mind, when Peyton spoke with a now-familiar disdain. "If you are done, maybe you can come join us in the sitting room."

Kat nodded vigorously, ushering them both out of the room and slipping the door closed behind them. "Steve, you're a total mess. I should have let you get a shower before I changed. I'm so sorry."

He looked skeptically between Kat and Peyton. He didn't like the idea of leaving the two of them alone together. The notion that he would have left them alone while Kat was still wearing nothing other than a robe was absurd.

Peyton chuckled at Steve's hesitation. "I assure you, she will be perfectly safe."

Steve knew it was anything but safe to leave Kat alone with Peyton, but the idea of Trista's blood slowly drying on his skin was becoming too much to take. He looked at Kat cautiously.

"You need to shower," Kat repeated. "I'll be fine."

The damp jeans Steve had worn earlier in the rain were folded over a chair. They hadn't had enough time to dry yet, but they were a lot better than the pair he was currently wearing.

Steve grabbed Kat by the shoulders and gave her a hard look. The color was completely gone from her cheeks. Tiny crow's feet at the corners of her eyes revealed how much the past few days had aged her. But the worst was the distant look in her eyes. She was slipping away from him.

He'd worried before that she was only acting, that her feelings weren't real. That somehow an actress could use her skills to play a part in real life. He could see now it wasn't true, at least not with Kat. She hadn't been acting before. It was obvious, because she was acting now. It was a subtle difference. She was adept at the art. But there was a difference.

She smiled broadly and gave him a kiss on the cheek. "Go shower. I'm fine."

He knew it was a lie, and he knew there was nothing he could do about it. He nodded and turned to Peyton. "If you hassle her, I swear, you won't have to worry that Amy's out to kill you. I'll take care of it myself."

Peyton rolled his eyes. "Could you cut the drama and take your damn shower? My God, she's a big girl. She'll be fine."

Steve scowled, gave Kat a kiss, and headed into the bathroom. He fully intended this to be the quickest shower he'd ever taken.

~ 76 ~

Alone with Peyton, Kat considered what to do next. He'd taken a seat on the couch. Since that game was far too familiar to be played again, she chose to stand, taking a position at the large window, staring out into the pouring rain, at the growing rivers cutting deep lines into the desert landscape.

Having her back to her nemesis didn't make it any easier. It was like being watched by a boa constrictor. He could slide up at any moment, wrap himself around her, and ever so slowly squeeze the life right out of her.

But he was the least of her worries. There was no mistaking what she'd seen in her room. She was certain. This wasn't some weird side effect of being off cocaine. It was something supernatural. Evil. And it was dead set against her.

Kat rolled her fingers over the cylinder she'd managed to slip in her pocket. At least she had an old friend to look out for her.

It was the good news and the bad news, really. The drugs would protect her, yes, but she couldn't have them and

Steve. He would see. He would know. She was pretty sure he already did. He was certain she was hiding something and it was only a matter of time before he asked her about it directly. Kat wondered if she'd tell the truth when he did.

As she should have expected, Peyton soon joined her, interrupting her thoughts. "Am I so terrible you can't even sit in my vicinity?"

Kat didn't even turn to look at him. "I think we answered that question this morning."

"What? What are you talking about? I didn't do anything. We were talking. I was offering to help with the movie. Is offering help to a colleague harassment these days?"

Kat spun around to face him. "Do you really think of yourself as savior of the world, or is it part of the act?"

Peyton crossed his arms defiantly. Though he tried to hide it, Kat could see the surprise on his face. "You know, one of the problems with cocaine is it can make you paranoid."

"If I have a problem, it's not being paranoid enough with you," Kat muttered.

Peyton winced dramatically at the retort. "Do you really see me as that kind of a bad guy? I want you to succeed. I need you to succeed. If nothing else, it's good business."

Kat ignored his response, choosing instead to turn back to the window. She knew her watch would tell her it was close to one in the afternoon. The sun should be high in the sky, burning through the dense black clouds that enveloped them. Kat was becoming more and more certain the voice had been right – she was going to die in this hotel.

"You're impossible," Peyton said in disgust. "I am not the enemy here."

He began to pace the room, like a caged tiger, ready to strike at anyone and anything that got in his way. He was still pacing restlessly when Steve rejoined them.

"I assume you two figured a way out of all of this mess while I was in the shower," Steve joked.

Kat wanted to smile at his attempt to lighten the mood, but she lacked the strength. Steve seemed to get the picture immediately.

"Let's sit down and discuss what we know and what we can do about it," Steve offered.

"If you two are done primping, I think that'd be a superb idea," Peyton snapped.

Kat turned from the window and joined Steve and Peyton in the sitting area. Avoiding Peyton on the couch, she sat on the floor at Steve's feet, leaning her head slightly against his knee. She felt overwhelmingly tired. It was all she could do not to curl up and go to sleep.

Peyton got right down to business. "Do think you can explain why we should stay locked up in a room until the rain stops?"

Steve answered patiently. "I just think before we go off half-cocked we should run through what we know."

"We know there were seven living people in this hotel and now there are only three." Clearly bored to be stating the obvious, Peyton continued, "We know Trista said Amy killed her. We need to find Amy and contain her. It's that simple. Amy is a petite woman. There is no reason we couldn't take her down once we find her."

To his credit, Steve's calm tone didn't falter. "I'm not sure it's that simple. We already searched the hotel once and didn't find her. I don't know how that was possible then; I'm not sure it's a good idea to risk it again now."

"Risk what? Jesus, Steve, she's half your size. What do you think she could do to you if you found her?"

Kat lifted her head at the question. It was oddly comforting to feel anger at the disdain in Peyton's voice. "You agree it's Amy who's done all this?"

"That's what Trista said. I see no reason she would lie about it."

"Actually, Trista said Amy attacked her. She didn't tell us anything about the others. And, to be honest, she barely got Amy's name out. Maybe she was saying something else."

Peyton frowned at her suggestion. "That's crazy. This all has to be connected."

"You're the one who keeps insisting it isn't," Kat pointed out.

Peyton opened his mouth to respond, but then quickly snapped it shut. Kat could see the wheels spinning in his head. In all of the commotion he'd clearly forgotten the reasonable explanations he'd been spouting for days. It told Kat two things – part of him never really believed them, and Trista's death caused him more fear than he was admitting. Otherwise he would never have allowed such a slip.

Kat felt a little bad for him. "I agree with Steve. We have to run through what we know, point by point. Then we can try and figure out what to do next."

Peyton nodded mutely.

Steve immediately took advantage of the silence. "Four people are dead. Four sins were carved in their doors after they died."

"There was nothing on Trista's door when we got there. Was there something on the way out?" Kat asked. She'd been too busy with old habits to notice.

"The door was carved like the others – Envy," Steve answered. "It was there when I locked the door behind us."

"Which leaves Gluttony, Pride, and Lust," Kat commented.

"It fits the colors," Steve agreed.

Again Kat watched the realization spread over Peyton's face. He was remembering the conversation they'd had that morning. He was realizing that it was possible he'd dismissed them too quickly. "Did the color of Trista's room match the sin carved on her door?" he asked.

Kat was surprised to feel her strength coming back. She took the Bible from the coffee table and flipped to the section on the Sins. "Envy. Color – Green. Animal – the dog."

Peyton nodded, plainly calculating. "I think that's right. What was the punishment listed?"

"A couple are listed in here. The traditional punishment is to be placed in freezing water. But there are references from Dante's *Purgatorio* about people in haircloth cloaks that blend with the rocks around them. They are bent over in remorse, clinging to each other because they cannot see. They weep because their eyes have been sewn shut." Kat felt a chill crawl up her spine. It was like reading an obituary. Not even Trista deserved this.

"What are the colors associated with the remaining sins?" Peyton asked.

Kat knew the answer without even reading the entries. "Purple is associated with Pride. Blue with Lust. Orange with Gluttony."

Without a flicker of guilt or concern, Peyton calculated. "So, Steve is Lust. Kat, Gluttony. And myself, Pride."

Kat only nodded and looked up at Steve. It still didn't make sense. What the hell wasn't he telling her?

"The other major thing," Steve pointed out, changing the subject, "is people seem to be dying in numerical order."

Peyton's brow furrowed in confusion. "Numerical order? Since when are any of us numbers?"

"Numerical order by our room numbers," Kat clarified.

And then Kat really saw the fear. Plain as day. Peyton had been in control until that moment. It was then that he truly snapped. In his eyes she saw him run through each of the murders. Watched as the pieces fell into place the only way they could. *Suite One – Waylan. Suite Two – Biff. Suite Three – Gloria. Suite Four - Trista. Suite Five….* She had to wonder what was worse, knowing you were next or knowing you were last.

~ 77 ~

Peyton's heart stopped at the suggestion. He wanted to scream out a denial. Assure them – and himself – that Steve's theory was asinine. Yet the more he considered it, the more queasy his stomach became.

Was he next? He couldn't be. He couldn't possibly be. He was an important man. A man of power. Success. Wealth. Respect. He controlled things. He overcame obstacles. He wasn't going to be the next victim of a murderous rampage. It couldn't happen that way. It wouldn't.

As his resolve grew, Peyton realized there were two idiots staring at him. And suddenly the only things worse than the gamut of emotions plaguing him were the looks of sympathy he was receiving.

"I know you want to sit in this god-awful claustrophobic room until the fucking rain stops, but I need some food," Peyton growled. "Besides, everything bad that's happened here has happened in our rooms. We need to get the hell out of the death suites."

Kat nodded. "I could use some coffee."

He saw the hesitation in Steve's eyes and Peyton almost begged him to disagree. The cowboy looked tough, but Peyton was sure that he could take him. In fact, the idea of a sucker punch right in that earnest face was very tempting.

Unfortunately, Steve quickly acquiesced. Peyton assured himself it was because he was smart enough not to want any trouble.

"Okay," Steve agreed, "but we have to stick together. No one is ever out of sight of the other two. Ever."

~ 78 ~

Steve cast a wary glance over his sandwich at Peyton. It was difficult to think of them as a team, but he had to. It was the only way they were going to make it out of this alive.

Even now, as they all were sitting casually eating lunch, there was a tension, an undercurrent of animosity between them. Steve just hoped that Peyton would focus his attacks on him instead of Kat, but somehow he knew that would never be the case.

As if to prove his point, Peyton sneered at the thick Italian hoagie that Kat had chosen for lunch. "Are you sure you should be eating that?"

Steve was both relieved and proud to see Kat dab some extra mayonnaise on the sandwich before she spoke. "If I were to die in the next few days I'd be angry with myself for eating a salad instead of a sandwich. God willing, we'll make it out of here. I'll go back on the diet when we do."

The remark, though intended to be funny, only darkened the cloud over the group. Steve couldn't help but consider his own regrets, most far more serious than an uneaten sandwich.

Peyton spoke finally, seeming compelled to end the silence. "Did you hear that Rob has been in contact with the Electric House?" he asked Kat. "It's looking like they'll be on board for the special effects."

Steve had no idea what they were talking about, but the way Kat's face lit up was information enough for him.

"Really? That's fantastic!" she gushed. Then, seeming to realize that Steve was more than a little lost, she explained, "Rob is the director of the new movie. Electric House is one of the biggest shops in L.A. for special effects. The movie itself doesn't call for a lot, but from what I understand the final scene is really going to need some awesome effects to make it work. It's a huge deal that Electric is considering signing on."

Steve nodded. The topic couldn't have been of less interest to him. But the smile on her face and the gleam in her eyes were fascinating. It was clear she loved her job, which explained why the risk of losing it was making her so crazy.

"What's the movie about?" he asked.

Kat looked to Peyton for the answer to the question, reminding Steve yet again of the power he held over her. He was her boss. The man with the money. She was just the actress.

In an instant, Peyton slipped into his role as producer. His voice polished, even slicker than usual. "It's the story of a deep-cover CIA agent living in Moscow. She meets and falls in love with a Russian-born physicist, only to find herself trapped between her loyalty to her country and her love of this Russian man."

Steve smiled at the description; it sounded terrible. "Sounds great," he lied, looking at Kat.

"You don't like it?" she asked. He could see she was a little disappointed.

"No, really, honestly, I think it sounds very interesting." He hoped that sounded more convincing.

"It's a chick flick. It's fine," Kat smiled at his discomfort. "It's nice to see you'll humor me, though."

Steve smiled back, wishing he could be more enthused. "I'm sure it will be a great movie. I told you before; I'm not a huge movie fan. I'm sorry."

Kat reached across the table to take his hand. "Really, no problem."

The moment was quickly interrupted. "Do you have a problem with the story?" Peyton snapped.

Though he should have held his tongue, Steve snarled back without thinking. "I barely know anything about the story. Like Kat said, it's probably more a movie for women."

Peyton turned his anger on Kat. "You need to review your press materials. We're trying to sell this as a movie that crosses gender lines. That's why we're bringing in the special effects guys."

"If you blow things up then guys will automatically like it?" Steve asked.

Peyton rolled his eyes. "You don't even have the first idea of how this process works. We pay a lot of people a lot of money to know exactly who will 'automatically like it' – as you say. I think we know what to expect."

Steve shook his head. "You said the word love like eight times in your little sound bite. That's not going to bring the guys in."

"Some men like love stories," Kat offered.

Steve sighed and tried to hold his temper. This was a stupid conversation. Attacking Peyton over something that didn't matter wasn't going to reduce tension. "I'm sorry, you're right. What do I know? Maybe if I heard a different pitch it would appeal to me more."

Kat laughed. "Since you've never seen any of my movies, I suspect that isn't true."

For reasons that Steve didn't understand, Peyton was intrigued by the revelation. "None of her movies?"

Steve shook his head. "Honestly, I don't really go to the movies."

"What was the last movie you saw?" Peyton challenged.

"I really don't remember," Steve replied cautiously, trying to figure out why Peyton cared.

"Come on. You have been to a theater, haven't you?"

The producer was baiting him – Steve could tell that, but he couldn't figure out why. Either way, he'd just finished telling himself to stop picking stupid fights. And this was a stupid fight.

"I've been to the movies." He strained to remember when. The image of his last movie sprang to mind and he blurted it out before he realized he should have censored it. "I took a date to the movies about fifteen years ago. We saw some romantic comedy."

"See, those chick flicks come in handy for dates," Kat teased.

Peyton's eyes narrowed. "You've gone fifteen years without seeing a movie?"

But Steve barely heard the question. Lucy. How could he have forgotten that? They used to go to the movies all the time. It was safe there. Had she really been the last woman he'd taken to a movie? Was that even possible?

"Steve," Kat began, squeezing his hand gently, "are you okay?"

He looked up quickly, meeting her eyes and hoping his distraction wasn't obvious. "I was just trying to remember what the movie was. I'm getting nothing."

Kat's brown eyes darkened with questions they both knew she'd never ask with Peyton in the room.

"She must have been something else, this date of yours," Peyton chided. "Look at you all caught up in the memory of love lost, and with a beautiful lady sitting right here."

"Peyton, don't be an ass," Kat snapped.

Peyton shrugged off the hostility. "Though I am fascinated by Steve's trip down memory lane, I wonder if we could discuss more pressing matters.   Like the issue of searching the hotel."

Though he wanted nothing less, Steve knew this was a battle he was certain to lose.

"You still think that's the best approach?" Steve asked, resigned to the answer.

"It's the only prudent thing to do," Peyton insisted.

Without a word, Steve walked over to the cabinets. If they were going to do this, they would have to be armed. He pulled a butcher's knife and a large bread knife from the drawer. He kept one of the knives for himself and gave the other to Peyton.

Peyton balked at the prospect. "What exactly do you expect me to do with this?"

"I'm hoping you figure it out when the time comes."

Kat looked between Peyton and Steve. "Um, I don't want to be pushy, but what about me?"

Steve smiled at her spunk. "I was thinking you might be better off with a bat or something. With your size, if you got close enough for the knife to do you any good, you would likely be in big trouble."

"Unfortunately, I don't think we have a baseball bat lying around."

Steve nodded.   That was exactly the problem.   He scanned the kitchen, but couldn't come up with anything more menacing than a rolling pin, until his eyes fell upon the stools next to the counter. He wasn't sure he could break them in any useful way, but it was worth a try. In a minute he'd either look like a genius or a destructive moron.

In one swift motion, he brought the seat of the chair sharply down on the counter, snapping it from the legs. From there it was relatively easy to separate an individual leg from the other three. The result was a three-foot T-shaped stick that resembled a warped wooden sword.

Kat smiled at the weapon. "My hero," she joked.

"Hey, you mock, but remember who gave you that stick if you are ever in the situation to use it," he replied with a wink.

Peyton rolled his eyes in disgust. "If you're done with all the drama, do you think we can finish our lunch so we can start searching the hotel?"

~ 79 ~

Kat was standing with Peyton and Steve in one of the chillingly empty employee rooms. It was odd, really. No one could stay in these rooms – no beds, no chairs. The owner was completely unprepared for any future guests. Almost like she was never planning on future guests.

And that was when it struck her. The owner. What was Amy's connection to the owner? Plainly the rooms had been designed for each of them – employees included. How could a girl of such limited means convince someone to design a hotel like this? To fashion these rooms? These personalized tombs that seemed to be waiting for a long-term occupant?

"We never figured out who the owner was, did we?" Kat finally said aloud, her voice echoing eerily in the vacant room.

Peyton scowled. "What are you talking about?"

"The owner. You know, the person who designed this place," Kat clarified.

Steve nodded as she spoke. "The person who left the instructions regarding what room everyone was to have."

"There were instructions regarding the room assignments?" Kat asked.

"Yeah. There was a book that Tami left in the office. Biff and Trista were reading it when I got here."

"Do you think it'd provide any insight into who Tami really is?" Kat wondered.

"It seems like a good place to look," Steve agreed, leading the way back to the office.

"Steve, I don't understand," Peyton chimed in, following behind Kat. "This woman is your boss and you have no clue who she is?"

"She called me. Said we worked together a while back. I haven't a clue if that's true or not. Until recently I didn't have any reason to believe it wasn't."

"What was it that Trista said about Tami?" Kat asked, trying to remember the conversation.

"I think she said Tami told her she had seen her working at her old job. Some diner in her hometown," Steve replied.

"Do you think there is some connection between Amy and Tami? Business partners? Friends? Would someone do something like this for a friend?" The stream of endless questions tumbled out of Kat's mouth as they entered the office.

Peyton held up a leather-bound journal. "Is this the book?"

Without waiting for an answer he began flipping through the journal. Kat peered over his shoulder, wondering how it was that Peyton – the one who hadn't seemed to have any interest in even looking at the journal – ended up taking custody of it.

A note to Biff on a loose sheet of white paper was tucked in the front of the journal. Nothing interesting – pleasantries, wishing him well and good luck, telling him to expect Steve and Trista. Nothing they didn't already know. It was signed simply: All the Best, Tami Ghyl. Peyton handed the paper to Kat to get it out of his way. And then flipped to the first page of the journal.

There was a hand-drawn map of the second floor of the hotel, which indicated where each room was. Listed below that were the room numbers for the four guests. Underneath that was the note indicating the staff could help themselves to the other suites, and specifying which suite went to which staff member. Nothing else.

The next page detailed the process for housekeeping – cycles for washing, vacuuming, dusting, making up the rooms. Followed by two pages on the process for the kitchen – ordering food, storage, the menus. The book seemed to be exactly what it purported to be: a user's guide to running the hotel. Nothing more, nothing less. It went on for about thirty pages.

"Well, that couldn't have been less helpful," Peyton pointed out as he snapped the book shut. "You two are just full of great ideas, aren't you?"

"It was worth checking, don't you think?" Steve growled, taking the book for himself and flipping through it again.

Kat still held the note from Tami. Something about it bothered her, something she couldn't quite put her finger on. She was considering it when she realized Steve and Peyton were staring at her, plainly waiting for some kind of answer.

"You think we can finish searching the hotel now?" Peyton obviously repeated, when her eyes focused on him.

Seeing the disdain on his face, Kat apologized. "I guess my mind wandered off. Sure, I'm ready."

Steve looked at her suspiciously. Unlike Peyton, he didn't look annoyed, just curious.

Peyton shook his head. "Dear God, they're going to have a hell of a time keeping you focused when shooting starts. You did a number on that head of yours."

Kat didn't even consider arguing the point. He was probably right. "Why don't we finish up the tour?"

Peyton led the way, giving Steve an opportunity to fall into step next to Kat. He put an arm around her waist and pulled the cowboy hat off his head. Leaning in he whispered, "Are you okay?"

Kat showed him Tami's letter. Then she folded it and slipped it in her back pocket. She spoke quietly so Peyton wouldn't hear. "There's something about the letter. It's nagging at me. I can't place it. I'll figure it out though. I just need some time."

"Time is at a premium these days."

"Tell me about it. I'll get it. First, we finish Peyton's ridiculous search. Then we can focus on things that might actually be helpful."

~ 80 ~

Kat quickly discovered that the walking tour through the rooms of the damned was even worse than the examination of the rooms on the lower level. There was nothing in the hotel. Just the three of them and four very dead bodies. The murderer was either hiding among them or something supernatural was lying in wait. She wasn't sure which option was more unappealing.

The search finished in Kat's suite, back where they started. Thunder rumbled and the lights flickered as they settled in the sitting room.

Steve let out a slow whistle. "All we need is to lose the lights."

"Is it really the plan to sit here and make small talk until the next person dies?" Peyton grumbled.

"What do you prefer we do?" Kat snapped. "I'm certainly open to other possibilities."

Peyton glared at her. "I've been coming up with the ideas all along. Why don't the two of you come up with something?"

Kat rolled her eyes. It was funny how the situation was changing things for her. For the first time in a long time, she didn't feel afraid of Peyton. In this world of hauntings and murders, he wasn't any better than the rest of them.

But the circumstances clearly didn't make Peyton feel that way. "Look, Bitch, it's your fault I'm in this mess!"

Kat was in no mood to back down. "How do you figure that?"

"How do you not? If you could have managed to stay sober on the set, we could've finished the movie. If we'd finished the movie, Amy would've gotten her break. I didn't do anything wrong here!"

"Bullshit!" Kat hissed. "You never intended to keep your promises to that girl. Never. I've seen you do that exact thing to some young actress during every movie I've ever been on. You'd have given her as little as you could and then just moved on to the next naïve fool."

Peyton's eyes narrowed and Kat could almost see him decide to change tactics. With a sneer in his voice, he said, "I take care of my girls. I took care of you, didn't I?"

He all but winked as he said it, telegraphing his message very clearly: *Kat hadn't been above putting out for a part.* Of course, it was a lie, but Peyton had never been held back by the truth.

"That's not true!" Kat said, as much to Steve as to Peyton. "Nothing ever went on between us."

Peyton chuckled. "Oh, yeah, you got your roles based on your talent. All the great ones do."

Kat met Steve's eyes with a pleading look. "I got my break in a supporting role in a movie. I got the part by auditioning like everyone else."

Peyton snorted at her defense, clearly believing he was winning. "Please, Kat, do you really want to risk going to your grave with a lie on your conscience?"

Steve looked at Peyton and then back at Kat. For a second, Kat worried that he was buying it, but the fear didn't last long.

"Don't be a jackass, Peyton," Steve said evenly.

Peyton stepped back as if struck. "Do you think you know her? Do you really think you understand what she's like? You know nothing. And you," he continued, looking at Kat, "do you really think you know him? Huh? If your little Seven Deadly Sins theory works, then Mr. Perfect over here is guilty of something also. Something he's afraid to admit to the rest of us. He's the only one who hasn't admitted what he did. The only one who didn't stand up like a man and explain why Amy brought him to this awful place."

The retort was hard to ignore, especially since his words so closely echoed her own concerns. In spite of that, the answer was obvious. There was only one person in this room she could rely on, and it wasn't Peyton.

"I trust him," she said simply, wishing the words sounded more sincere.

Peyton's face went red with rage. "Are you kidding me? You just met him! I've known you for years. I pay your salary. I need you for my movie. How can you possibly think I could want anything but the best for you?"

The tension had been building, the pressure increasing. Too many hard questions that could only have bad answers. But Peyton's indignation was so absurd she couldn't help but laugh. And once she started, she felt like she might never stop. Tears were running down her cheeks when she realized her mistake.

The veins stood out in Peyton's neck as he growled his response. "You ungrateful, insignificant piece of trash."

Kat's heart stopped at his rage. In her most sincere voice, she tried to fix it, knowing she would certainly fail. "Peyton, look, I'm sorry. I shouldn't have laughed. It's just that you don't really look out for my interests. It's okay. That's not your job."

Peyton only shook his head; words seemed to fail him. "I don't have to sit here and put up with this," he sputtered as he stormed out of the room.

He was in the hallway between the two suites when Steve jumped to his feet. "Come on now. Kat didn't mean it. Really, man, we need to stick together."

"Do you think I need you two? I don't need you! I'll be fine on my own."

Kat rose cautiously. "I'm sorry. Genuinely," she said. "Please. Don't be crazy."

"Oh, now I'm crazy? We just checked the whole hotel. There is nobody here. I'm going to my room. I need a break from you people." And with that he turned on his heel and retreated to his own room, slamming the door behind him.

~ 81 ~

Kat and Steve stood in stunned amazement, Peyton's overreaction still echoing in the room. They were supposed to stay together. They had to stay together. It was a matter of life and death.

It was Kat who finally broke the silence. "Do we go after him?"

Steve shook his head. "What the hell happened here? One minute he's being his usual obnoxious self, the next he's storming off."

"He has a vicious temper. He's known for it. I was stupid for reacting like I did. I should have known."

"Known he'd go on some suicidal rampage? I think that would have been pretty hard to anticipate," he snorted.

Kat ran a hand through her hair. "Actually, not all that hard. Peyton would never just sit here while someone like me laughs at him."

Steve considered Kat and then the closed door across the hall. "What do we do?"

"I don't know. He's not going to let us into his room. He probably won't even acknowledge we knocked on the door."

"We have a key," he suggested. "We could let ourselves in."

"Then what? He'll just leave the room. We'll spend the rest of our lives chasing him around the hotel. We need to wait at least a little while before we can apologize and kiss his pompous little ass. It seems better he's next door, don't you think?"

"We can leave the door to your suite open. Then we can keep an eye on his door. We can see if anyone comes or goes." *Assuming we can really see the threat*, Steve considered adding, but thought better of it. Unfortunately, it seemed to be their only option, short of tying Peyton to a chair.

Kat nodded reluctantly in agreement. She didn't say it, but she plainly had the same concerns about invisible enemies.

Steve stared for a moment at the number five on Peyton's door. If anything happened to him... Steve shuddered at the thought. He felt as if there was a giant number six tattooed on his forehead. He couldn't let anything happen to Peyton. The result was too horrible to even consider.

"Can you see into the hallway from the couch?" Steve asked, unwilling to move until he was certain someone was watching the room.

Kat shifted in her seat and then nodded. "We're all set."

Though Steve hoped they were, he had a suspicion they were anything but.

The seconds passed like hours as Steve sat with Kat staring at Peyton's door. Like the air before a twister, the room was still, but there was nothing peaceful about it.

In frustration, Steve started pacing. "He's going to get us all killed."

What Steve didn't want to say, what he didn't want to admit even to himself, was that Peyton's absence was only part of the reason for the tension in the room. The truth was, Peyton's angry threats carried a certain truth. A truth that Steve didn't want to talk about. A truth that he understood Kat needed to hear. And Steve hated Peyton for bringing it up almost as much as he hated him for putting their lives at risk.

Kat continued to sit silently, staring at the door. She was thinking what he was thinking. She had to be. No one stared that intently at nothing unless they were deep in thought.

As he paced, his eyes were drawn to the constantly pounding rain. This was hell, he was almost certain.

Out of the corner of his eye, he could see her. Her arms were firmly crossed in front of her. Her right foot was tapping impatiently. And if he'd learned anything about her in the time they'd spent together, then he'd bet she was clenching and unclenching her jaw in frustration.

"You know, you're going to ruin your teeth grinding them like that," he said, trying to lighten the mood.

Kat slowly relaxed her jaw, and even more slowly turned. "How do you know so much about me?" she asked, her voice wistful and a little sad. The unspoken words hung heavily in the air – *when I know so little about you?*

Steve held his breath and waited. Their eyes locked.

She spoke quietly, with no anger or accusation. "How did you know her?"

~ 82 ~

Steve didn't even consider evasion this time. It wouldn't have been fair. He knew it was going to ruin everything they had, but at this point continuing to conceal it was worse.

He looked away before he answered. He had to.

"About fifteen years ago, I got a job in Texas. It was a summer thing. My uncle and I had been getting on each other's last nerve and I needed to get off the ranch for a bit. He got me a job working as a waiter at a resort. I spent my time waiting tables, helping out in the kitchen any chance they gave me. I wasn't making much money, so when I got a chance to work at a nearby town fair, I jumped at it.

"You know that game where you shoot the water guns into the clown's mouth to blow up the balloon? The first one to pop the balloon wins." Steve didn't wait for a reply. The game didn't matter, he knew that, but the details delayed the confession. "The person who normally ran the booth had to be out of town for a week, so they brought me in. I was working the booth when the fair was in this little town – Ashton." The name hung in the air for a moment. Though

Kat didn't know the name of the town where Amy grew up, Steve assumed she knew where this was going.

"One afternoon, this mom and her little girl came to my booth. So you understand, nobody in that town was what you might call rich. At least not as far as I could tell. But these two really stood out. Old-looking clothes. A little greasy. Disheveled. The girl was tiny. Really skinny. Her arm was in a bright pink cast. I would have guessed her age at about six. That was, until she spoke. Then it became clear she was older than she'd appeared. Probably close to ten. But God, her eyes, she had the eyes of an adult. A miserably sad adult."

Steve swallowed deeply with the memory. He could still see the little one. The only image that stood out more vividly in his mind was the picture of her mother. "The woman holding her hand was the prettiest thing I'd ever seen. Very petite. Thin, like her daughter. Long, straight black hair in a braid down her back. Blue, blue eyes. Like pools of sadness. From the second I looked into her eyes I wanted to take her away. Take away all the pain I saw. It was one of those Romeo and Juliet love at first sight moments," he said with bitterness.

He allowed himself a glance in her direction. Kat's eyes were locked on him. They were full of sadness and what looked like sympathy. It should have helped, but it only made the truth harder to confess.

"The woman gave me a crinkled dollar to play the game. I refused to take it. Told her if she'd tell me her name, I'd let her play for free. There wasn't anybody else at the booth at the time, which made the whole thing pretty stupid. The point of the game was to race somebody else. There was nobody there to race. The woman cringed when I refused the dollar, and if I hadn't handed the water gun to the little girl, I think she would've left right away. But the girl was intrigued with the idea of the game. Very excited," Steve's voice trailed off, lost in the memory.

He could still see her, the memory as vivid as the reality, maybe more. The beautiful raven-haired woman, hidden beneath the layers of grit and subjugation, playing that foolish game with her mistreated daughter. Steve would never forget the small smile on her face when the girl won, or the giggle of laughter that bubbled up before she had a chance to suppress it. They were people who longed for simple happiness. People who, for that instant, had found it, but knew not to try to hold on to it for too long.

He took a deep breath and continued on. "Her name was Lucy. She wouldn't give me her last name. And the little girl was Amy. I saw Lucy's wedding ring, knew she was taken, but I couldn't resist. I was so young. I was so certain I could help them. Certain I could save them both from whatever it was that was haunting them.

"We started spending a lot of time together, the three of us. Lots of movies. Meetings in coffee shops outside of town. Any place where we wouldn't be noticed. It soon became clear the troubles were with her husband. I could tell from her stories he was vicious. Amazingly, she wasn't afraid for herself, she worried only about Amy. She was worried he would ruin the little girl. I found her information about some shelters. Places they could run away to. Homes that would help them make a fresh start. She'd settled on a place. It was in Kentucky."

Steve remembered the disagreements they'd had over the shelters. Over the locations. He wanted her as far away from her bullying husband as possible, but he wanted to go with her. He wanted to help her start that new life. But Lucy would have none of it. Originally she'd insisted she wouldn't tell Steve her final choice. She thought it was best if she took the information he'd provided and made her choice in secret. She wanted him to leave town the same night. To head back home to Montana. Then there would be no way for her husband to track either of them down.

But Steve had been adamant. He wanted to go. Wanted to be with her. There was nothing for him in Montana. No reason to go home. His uncle would barely even miss him. Besides, Steve was certain she needed him. It wasn't until Lucy pointed out that both of them traveling together might be easier to track that Steve finally backed down. She was running. Running from a terrible man. Steve knew he needed to let her do that, and despite his feelings for her, he had to let her go. Lucy finally agreed to tell him where she was heading and promised to send an unsigned note from Kentucky. Nothing that could be traced. But enough that he'd know she made it.

Looking back now, Steve couldn't believe he'd thought it would be that simple. "I'd even managed to find her a car. The thing was a heap. Needed fresh water in the radiator almost constantly. We were all worried the car might not make it that far, but it was the best I could do with what I had."

Steve paused and looked desperately at the woman sitting in front of him. He wished he could just stop the story there. God, if only that was where it ended. *And Lucy and Amy rode off and they lived happily ever after....* If that were true, none of this would have ever happened. Instead, Steve was responsible for starting the cycle of destruction that had led them all here today.

But the story went on, and Steve found himself unable to stop telling it. "Lucy and Amy met me in a crappy little motel outside of town. The plan was they would leave the husband's car there, take the car I was giving them, and disappear. But I was twenty years old. I had needs. I was in love with this woman. I thought I deserved a night. Just one. Just the two of us. So, I borrowed some cash from a buddy and I got two adjoining hotel rooms. We hid her old car in a dark corner of the lot and I convinced her to stay with me. Reluctantly, she agreed. She wanted to stay as much as I did, I know that, but she was worried. You see, she knew him. She was wise enough to know my little plan wasn't as foolproof as I thought."

Steve didn't realize he was crying until Kat handed him a tissue. He took the offering, but couldn't meet her eyes. He had to finish. "Around two A.M. she woke me. She told me she had to go. She wanted me to help her carry Amy to the car. I protested, of course, but, after a few minutes, she wore me down. I was putting on my jeans when the door crashed in. The shots were immediate. Rapid fire. Six I think. The first one took out the lamp. The rest hit her. In the dark, I ran to her, but it was too late. The guy was big. Really big. With one gloved hand he grabbed me around the neck, and with the other, he forced the gun into my hand. He slammed me up against a wall, and then he vanished, as quickly as he'd appeared.

"I checked Amy's room, but she was gone. He must have taken her. And that was when I heard the sirens approaching. I didn't know what to do. Lucy was dead. I was covered in blood. I was with another man's wife. The gun had my fingerprints on it. I wiped off the gun and I ran. I didn't know Lucy and Amy's last name until I got here. I'm the reason that girl lost her mother."

When the story finished, Steve simply felt empty. He sank onto the couch, lacking the strength to do anything else. It was the first time he'd told anyone what had happened that night. It was oddly cathartic to talk about it, but the guilt still felt staggeringly fresh. And absolutely unbearable. Here he was, alone in a room with a magnificent woman. Possibly the only woman he'd had a chance to love since that night. And he knew he'd ruined things again. Worse yet, he'd started this whole process with Amy. So, indirectly, once again, he was responsible for putting a woman he cared about in mortal danger.

Steve's hands were clasped tightly on his lap. He couldn't raise his eyes to look at anything but his knuckles, watching them grow white and then pink as he clenched and unclenched them. They were remaining white for longer with each passing moment, until Kat's perfectly manicured hand slid over his.   Gently she pressed her fingers in between his.

"You're going to hurt your hands," she said softly.

Her voice broke as she spoke. It took a moment for Steve to realize she was crying. He wanted to say something. Wanted to speak, but the words wouldn't come.

"I'm so sorry," she said, as she separated his hands, taking them into her own. "I'm so sorry you had to go through that. That horrible man."

He didn't believe what he was hearing. Maybe he'd told the story wrong.

"Honey," she continued, "you tried to save her. To save both of them."

Her hands looked so small in his, but there was strength in her grip, a firmness that told him she was capable of taking care of both of them if need be.

There was so much he wanted to say, though only three words came to his lips. "I don't understand."

"That's okay, I do," she said firmly.

~ 83 ~

Peyton had paced. He'd ranted. And when none of that worked, he snatched his briefcase off the table and sat firmly on the couch. In one motion, he snapped open the locks and pulled out a file of paperwork. Work was the answer. It would calm him down. Put his mind at ease. He would be back in control.

Peyton shuffled his papers back and forth around the coffee table. It was ridiculous, but he couldn't focus. His mind kept turning to the two next door. He couldn't believe they hadn't tried to follow him. They hadn't even knocked on the door. He had no intention of letting them in, but that wasn't the point.

How dare they disregard him? How dare they ignore him? They needed him. They were just too stupid to know it. He had half a mind to go over there and tell them how idiotic they were being, but he knew he needed to be cool. Give them a chance to come crawling. They would. He was certain.

"What I really can't believe is that you're still obsessing about her." Her tone was singsong, but there was an undeniable undercurrent of rage. "You're so determined to break her you'll wait your whole life to get the chance. You do know she doesn't give you anywhere near this much thought, don't you?"

The sound of the voice startled him, and the realization of who was speaking was paralyzing.

"Peyton, you disappoint me. I've never seen you at a loss for words."

The voice was closer this time. Behind him. She couldn't be more than ten feet away. She was going to murder him. Suddenly he wished he had paid more attention to the punishments listed in Kat's stupid book. Then at least he'd know what was coming.

Peyton's voice remained calm. "All I have to do is shout and they'll come running."

Amy shrugged. "Do what you need to. It won't matter. But if you must try, then you must."

He turned and stared in disbelief. "They're just next door. They'll hear," he repeated.

"My father, Biff, Gloria, Trista. Do you really think none of them screamed, shouted, or called out? But you heard nothing. Get a clue, Peyton."

"Are the rooms soundproof?"

"If that explanation makes you feel better about it, sure."

He stood, trying to capture control of the situation. "I want to know what's going on here."

"It's funny. I'd expected this to be one of my more interesting endeavors. I figured you would have a ton of indignant questions. You're the first one smart enough to understand what I'm doing. Hell, you're even Catholic. You should be familiar with the deadly sins. I thought this would be stimulating, Peyton. I think you owe me that. Don't you?"

Peyton's fear turned to anger in a flash. "Owe you? Owe you? What the hell are you talking about? What did I ever do to you other than give you a chance? Are you punishing me for that? This whole thing is absurd. Absurd! You want to kill your abusive father and his screwed-up wife? Fine. Whatever. You want to bump off a couple of old friends for stabbing you in the back? Well, that's a little extreme. But this? Really? I don't understand you. I honestly don't."

As he shouted at her, a slow, satisfied smile crept over Amy's face. "Actually, I think you do understand me. That's what's aggravating you. Leslie Beekman. Audrey Hillyard. Jessica Young. Are those names you're familiar with?"

His heart skipped a beat, but his voice remained calm. "Of course. They're former actresses."

Amy snickered. "Former? You say that so innocently. Leslie had an affair with her married costar while they were shooting one of your movies. The bad PR tanked the box office sales. The studio lost money. You lost face. She'd be lucky to shoot a dog food commercial now. You saw to that."

She leaned against the doorframe now, calm, casual, perfectly in control. "Then of course there was Audrey. She was up and coming, lined up to be in one of your big budget movies. You had your eye on her. She refused to sleep with you. You refused to back her. And suddenly, the studio started hearing some rumors that Audrey had a problem with pills. That little issue lost her the job. It was odd really – Audrey never used drugs, but those pills that appeared in her dressing room were her undoing."

Amy smiled. "And of course, Jessica. She challenged your authority in front of the director and one of the other producers. Ironically, she made herself look pretty stupid in the process, but you were so obsessed with the idea she'd made you look bad that you had to regain your control of things. A week later, a sex tape Jess had been foolish enough to keep ended up on the Internet."

Peyton's jaw dropped at the accusations. "I would never… I don't know where you heard that… Where the hell did you get that information?" he sputtered.

"Don't bother with the denials. A waste of breath, really. And, frankly darling, you don't have much breath to be wasting. My point is, you understand me very well. You and I really aren't that different. It's all about revenge, Peyton. You understand revenge."

For the first time, Peyton took a close look at the woman holding him hostage. She looked mostly the same as she had the last time he'd seen her. The obvious difference was she was dripping wet, but there was more. Her eyes had been blue, a pretty, dark blue. The casting people had loved it, because her waifish body, black hair and blue eyes contrasted so nicely with Kat.

As Peyton stared at her eyes, he realized they were now raven black. So dark you could hardly see the pupils. The woman standing in the room with him was Amy, yet she wasn't.

Answering the unspoken question, Amy continued, "I've changed a lot since we last saw each other. Diving off a boat into the Pacific will do that."

"You really killed yourself?" Peyton shook his head in disbelief. "You killed yourself to get revenge on us?"

Amy laughed. "No. I killed myself because my life was ruined. Because I had nowhere to go. Nothing to look forward to. It was over. So, I ended it. That simple. Things didn't get interesting until afterwards. That was when I realized what I could do. What I could accomplish. The opportunity was too fantastic to turn down."

"You expect me to believe you're dead? That you're a ghost?"

"Ghost is such a childish term. Brings to mind images of Casper and other silly things like that. I'm just dead, Peyton. A dead woman out to kick your ass. That's really all you need to understand."

"I don't suppose there's some way we could get around this. Some way we could make this end a little differently? I could help you get Kat and Steve? That'd be a fair trade, don't you think?"

"Sorry, Peyton, my deal is very clear. You guys slip up. I get my chance. You slipped, that's the end. I'm going to enjoy this. Of all of them, you held the most direct power over me. Now, it's my turn."

Amy looked deeply into Peyton's eyes. In the center of the blackness were flames, fire burning deeply inside her. "Any last requests?"

Amy paused long enough to give Peyton a chance to cower. He saw the joy she took in his fear, and knew that she wanted him to beg. But that was something Peyton would never give.

Though his heart pounded and his throat was so tight he could barely breathe, he raised his arms in surrender. As smugly as he could he said, "Well, then, let's do this. Finish it. I'm not going to sit here and grovel. You've won. Let's be done with it."

Amy nodded and smiled. "It won't be that easy, darling. Down on your knees."

~ 84 ~

It was a long time before they spoke, each absorbing what the other had said. For Kat it was the moment when it all came together. Until then, she'd held back as much as she could. She'd wanted to believe in Steve, wanted to trust him, but she'd known that there was still a secret, still a reason she couldn't completely engage in this thing that was between them, whatever it was.

Now that she knew, it was different. He was the man she'd always believed he was, possibly an even better man than she'd dreamed. He'd given so much and yet all he could see was his failure. She knew that being too hard on yourself was sometimes more devastating than never trying at all. It was a lesson she'd thought she'd learned, but now she realized she'd slowly been letting it slip away.

She was lost in her thoughts when Steve spoke. "I don't know that I can ever thank you enough for that. How is it that you really understand? Hell, I don't even understand."

"Let's promise we'll both keep being understanding for each other. Neither of us is very good at understanding ourself." Kat gave Steve a kiss on the cheek and hurried off to the bedroom.

The quick movement caught Steve off guard. "Where are you going?" he called after her.

Kat didn't even hear him. In her head, a screaming voice begged her to stop. To leave things the way they were. The voice pleaded. Cried.

The voice, she knew, was her weakness. Her fears. Her insecurities. The voice sounded like it was trying to protect her, but she knew better. The voice would kill her if she let it.

Her hands were shaking so badly by the time she reached the bedroom she could barely hold the cylinder she'd taken from its hiding place. But she clenched it tightly in one fist and hurried back into the living room. Steve was still sitting on the couch looking bewildered when she grabbed his hand and dragged him with her to the bathroom.

"I took this from Trista's room," she explained, holding up her nemesis for him to see. "I almost used it, but I didn't. I was going to keep it, in case I decided I needed it. We both know I need to dump it. That's what I'm going to do."

The declaration would have been more convincing if she could have willed her hands to move. Instead, they remained frozen. Cocaine held high in one hand, the other hand standing helplessly by, unable to put an end to the powder.

Images flashed through her mind. Dead bodies. Sins carved in doors. Spirits haunting her. Punishments. Horrible punishments. She couldn't take all of it. She wasn't that strong. She couldn't be asked to do this alone. She needed help. What harm would a line really do?

The question was still echoing in her mind when Steve took her free hand. He lowered her down to her knees next to the toilet and then took a spot next to her.

"You can do this," he whispered.

The words were trite, predictable, something anyone could have said. But somehow, they were exactly what she needed to hear. Before Kat even realized she was doing it, she had the cap off the bottle and the drugs and their container were sitting at the bottom of the toilet. She almost felt physical pain when she flushed, but she did.

Steve pulled her close. "I think this locks it up. Apart, the two of us are like a one-legged man trying to hobble through life. Together, by God, we're a whole two-legged person."

Kat laughed at the ridiculous analogy that was delivered in Steve's most humble Midwestern accent. "You may be on to something there, you one-legged freak."

They savored the moment before they acknowledged what they had to do next.

"It's time to convince Peyton to come out of his room," Kat said finally.

Steve nodded and took her hand to help her to her feet. "Let's promise not to let him get to us?"

Kat rolled her eyes. "Yeah, sure, no problem."

Steve knocked on the door first. "Peyton, come on, open up. We're sorry."

Only silence met the call.

Kat tried next. "Peyton. Seriously, please open the door. Really, we were both very rude before. I'm very sorry, and I know Steve is too. Please let us in."

Still nothing.

Steve knocked even harder. "Peyton! Open up! I'm going to use the key if you don't let us in."

In response came a familiar sound. It was soft at first. The sort of noise a mouse might make inside a wall. But as it grew louder, Kat recognized it. She stepped away from the door and looked down. As she watched, the D was being drawn. She grabbed Steve's arm as the E was formed.

PRIDE was scrawled boldly on the door. That could only mean one thing. They were too late.

Steve dropped the key once before his shaking hands were able to get it in the lock. As great as the fear of the unknown had been, what they found inside was so much worse.

A man. On his knees in the middle of the room. Bent forward, so his forehead touched the floor. Arms at his side. The body was unrecognizable. Clothes shredded. Blood pooled all around him. Soaking into the carpet. Its shining darkness reflecting the lamplight.

A black leather whip lay next to him. The whip fanned out at one end to four lines, at the end of each was a bloody metal spike.

Kat thought of the reference to Dante in the descriptions of the punishments for Pride – panderers and seducers would be whipped by devils.

For Steve, accepting his own mortality had been difficult, but accepting that his death was likely to occur in the next twenty-four hours was far worse. Amy had successfully isolated five individuals from a group of seven. She had gotten each to go to his or her predetermined room, and she had murdered them.

Now, only two people remained, trapped by an infinite and brutal storm. What chance did they have that the others hadn't?

"We know what's coming," Kat pointed out. "We know she has to separate us. We know she has to get you into your room and me into mine. That has to be an advantage."

"What if she just goes after both of us at the same time?" Steve had no interest in being objective. He'd just seen a man who had literally been torn to shreds.

But Kat would not be stopped. "Everyone has been alone. There has to be a pattern to that. We need to focus on things we can control. We can control this. We stick together. Forever if we have to."

"I don't know what the hell it is we are dealing with here, but Kat, it seems like some kind of supernatural power."

They had both seen the carvings and the roots that fastened Gloria to her muddy grave. Someone, or something, had gotten into Peyton's room unnoticed. Certainly someone might have slipped in while they were in the bathroom, but it seemed unlikely, if not ridiculous. Then, of course, there was the rainstorm. Days of rain in the desert. It was suicide not to acknowledge there was a great power at work here.

Despite it all, Kat was eerily composed.

"How can you sit there so calmly?" Steve exclaimed. "We're going to die!"

Her response was unexpected. A small smile tugged at her lips. Though she clearly tried to suppress it, it was there.

"What? What is it?" he asked, concerned she'd simply lost it.

Realizing she was caught, Kat allowed the smile to come through. "Don't you see? Looking back, it's obvious we've been as good as dead since the rain started. The only difference between then and now is now we know what's going on. We know the pattern. We know the motive."

"Is that really going to matter?"

Kat shrugged. "Maybe. But things are getting better, not worse. I'm ready to fight back now. We're going to start by breaking the pattern. Neither of us is alone, ever. Maybe we can wait her out. Maybe we can't. But I'm ready to try. How about you?"

There was a fire in Kat's eyes when she spoke. An aggression. An inner strength that Steve had only seen flickers of previously. It was hard not to be convinced they could win this. It was impossible not to want to try.

~ 86 ~

They spent the afternoon in the hotel's sprawling lobby, talking about their jobs, their lives, their dreams, their plans for the future. It seemed important to talk about life away from the hotel and try not to focus on their impending doom. They both tried to think of it like a normal rainy afternoon, even though nothing could have been further from the truth.

Though their conversations were breezy and light, Kat remained acutely aware of every creak, real and imagined. When they moved about, she never released Steve's hand, concerned some unseen force might attempt to separate them.

Outside, the rain continued, constantly pelting the windows with a frightening force. The grounds grew more and more flooded, causing her to wonder if they might drown long before Amy isolated them in their respective rooms.

She was lying on the couch, her feet stretched over Steve's lap, when the local weatherman gave the five-day forecast. Sunny and clear every day. A chance of clouds was a remote possibility for the weekend. She sighed deeply at the report.

Absentmindedly, Kat took the letter from Tami out of her back pocket. It was probably irrelevant at this point, but it still bothered her that they didn't know who this mysterious hotel owner was. Who exactly was giving Amy Light the run of her hotel? Did she know what Amy had planned? Was Tami in on it?

Kat stared at the page, hoping whatever it was that was nagging her would somehow suddenly become clear. It was a basic letter. Nothing strange. It was typed, but signed by Ms. Ghyl.

It was a weird name, actually. Ghyl. Creepy. Maybe that was what was bothering her about it. It sounded like something out of an Edgar Allen Poe story.

Maybe she was Transylvanian? Kat thought, chuckling to herself at the idea the hotel owner was a vampire. Vampires. Frankly, it wasn't the craziest explanation she could think of. Actually, things might be easier if Tami Ghyl was only a vampire.

And that was when it hit her. Suddenly it was so obvious she couldn't believe she hadn't realized it before. When was the first time she'd heard Tami's name? How many people were still alive then? How many people could still be alive if she'd really thought about it, instead of focusing on her addiction and her guilt over Amy's death? Damn it! It was so obvious. TAMIGHYL. It was all a game!

She swung her feet to the floor and stood over Steve, waving the paper. She wanted to speak, she wanted to explain, but the frustration was too much for words.

"Stupid. Stupid. Stupid," she growled to herself. "How could I be so stupid?"

He grabbed her arm and forced her to stop. He locked his eyes on hers and silently begged her to explain.

The gesture was enough to get the words flowing. "She's playing games with us! Fucking word games!" Kat took a deep breath and willed herself to calm down. Yet the pounding of her heart continued, her anger grew. To Amy this hell was just a gigantic fun park.

"Tami Ghyl is nothing more than an alias. An anagram. The letters of her name – when you rearrange them you get Amy Light. The owner, our host, was not Tami. There is no Tami! It was Amy. It was always Amy."

She watched as the recognition flooded over Steve's face. As it did, she broke free from his grasp and began pacing. They'd been lured here by Amy herself. The hotel was never meant to serve as anything but a tomb for the seven of them.

Resignation and fear were not enough to stop her words from tumbling forth now that they'd started. "It was a huge clue there for us the entire time! The entire time! If we'd realized earlier..." Her voice trailed off.

Steve grabbed her again. "Even if we'd realized, so what? What difference would it have made? We made the connection with Amy almost immediately, at least the rest of you did."

"We could have done something."

"Like?"

"We could have stuck together."

"We've been supposed to be sticking together for a while now. Yet somehow Trista and Peyton managed to wander off. Would knowing about Tami have changed anything? Wasn't it you saying earlier we shouldn't focus on things that are beyond our control?"

Kat bit her lower lip in frustration. With one hand she balled up Tami's letter and with a roar she threw the paper across the room. Tears of regret and anger ran down her cheeks as she fell into Steve's arms.

~ 87 ~

For Steve, there was only one thing that would always make the strain disappear – cooking. The trick was not thinking of it as their last meal. He promised himself he would whip up something so incredible that neither of them could focus on the negatives.

"Are you sure you want to go to so much trouble?" Kat asked.

He only laughed. "Well, I am terribly busy. I'm not sure I have the time for a real masterpiece, but I suppose I could try to squeeze some cooking into my hectic schedule."

Kat laughed along with him. "Even the thought of food has put us both in a better mood."

"See, it's magic, I tell you. Magic. If it's all right with you, I'd like to peruse the cabinets. See what brilliant ideas I can come up with."

"I think we can arrange that."

Steve snatched his hat off the coffee table, took her hand, and led Kat into the kitchen. She took her place at the table while he began scanning through the cabinets.

"You really don't have to go to all of this trouble," Kat repeated.

"Trouble? You really don't cook, do you?"

She chuckled. "Two, maybe three times, I managed to make my way through a recipe."

He paused in his search, and turned to face her. "Have you ever gotten so into a project everything else fades away?"

"You've pretty much just defined my job. Is that really what cooking's like for you?"

"It's like meditation," Steve replied, unable to keep the awe from his voice.

"Then what are you doing talking to me? Cook, boy, cook." Kat laughed.

The teasing tone and her warm smile brought its own comfort. And for the first time in years, it seemed his life's contentment might be found in something other than food preparation.

But the peaceful feeling didn't last long. Steve was dicing an onion and whistling softly to himself when he heard the voice. It was barely a sound at first, more like a breeze or a soft breath. Gradually, the volume rose.

It was the whisper of a child. There was a sadness to it. A heavy, crushing sadness that was clear, even though the words were not.

"What is it?" Kat asked.

Her voice sliced through the sound. Immediately the child was gone.

"Steve? Are you alright?"

He smiled casually. "Yeah, I'm sorry, I thought I heard something."

Kat looked skeptical. "What did you hear?"

"Obviously it was nothing. I guess it was the wind or something."

Even as the words came out of his mouth, Steve realized that Kat had said the same thing earlier that day. He couldn't help but wonder if she'd been lying then the same way he was now. Not only did he not want to confess to his own lie, Steve realized he didn't want to know if Kat had been hearing things too.

~ 88 ~

As Steve rustled through the cabinets, Kat stared absently at the single ring on her hand. It made her think of her mother. Her family.

Just one more reason to fight, she thought. Though the sentiment was strengthening, the thoughts of home were painful. She hated that this might be how things ended.

"Hey, are you okay?" Steve asked.

Blinking back tears, Kat looked up and offered a small smile, hoping he'd let it go.

He placed a bag of potatoes on the counter and sat in the chair next to her. "Talk to me."

His strong hand closed around hers, covering her fingers and the ring. It felt almost symbolic. Her mother had given her the ring to protect her, a promise she would always be with her. Though her mother was far away, Steve was close. She was not alone. And that was what her mother had always wanted for her.

She thought of the Bible quote that was lying on the table in her room, and the choices it promised. In all of this insanity, were there really any choices left? But in that moment she knew what choice she would make if she was given the option.

Steve's dinner was a culinary masterpiece that still managed to be comfortable, almost homey. Kat knew that the homey feeling had more to do with the company than the food, and she wished desperately that they could have met under different circumstances.

She was considering that when Steve took her hand.

"You may think I'm crazy," he began, "but I have to say this. In spite of everything, I think I'm very lucky to be sitting here with you."

Kat laughed. "I thought you were a unique guy from the first moment we met. Upbeat. Positive. But it's amazing that you can see a bright side, even in all of this."

"At least we got the chance to meet."

The reply only brought pain for Kat, despite Steve's intentions. "I'd have liked to do more than just meet." Kat could see in his eyes that he felt the same way. She adored him for trying to sound more positive.

He squeezed her hand tightly. "Theoretically, we still have that. Right?"

"I sure hope so." Kat wished her voice carried at least a small amount of optimism, but she couldn't quite manage it. She'd been so alone for so long. It wasn't fair that her chance was going to be stolen away.

She was bitterly considering her fate when she heard it. It was like a breath, barely a whisper. Completely inaudible, but it sounded like a few words, repeated over and over. It had to be the same message as before – *You're going to die*. It was hard to remember that it was only a threat, not a fact.

Steve didn't seem to hear it. He was focused on his food. But the more she looked, the more she wondered. Was he really that focused on his food? The way he picked at the plate, it almost seemed like he was listening to something, something far away and very troubling. Could it be that he was hearing the same thing as she was? It was impossible to say for sure.

She wished that she had the courage to ask him. She told herself that she was protecting him – if he wasn't hearing things, he didn't need the extra burden of knowing she was. But the truth was, she was afraid.

After dinner, they settled on the couch downstairs. It seemed like as good a place as any to rest their heads, since neither of them had any intention of going upstairs ever again.

Steve ran a gentle hand over the dark circles that had begun to gather under Kat's eyes. "You look exhausted. Why don't you try and get a little sleep? I'll wake you in a bit and we can switch. I'm not sure it's a great idea for us both to sleep at the same time."

He could see that she wanted to object, but also that she was too tired to give up the chance he was offering.

"Are you sure you'll be okay?" she asked instead.

Steve moved one of the pillows so Kat could rest her head against his leg. "Stretch out a little and rest. I'll watch some TV and I'll wake you in a few hours. Then I'll take a turn."

She obediently stretched out and grabbed his arm, pulling it across her body. She clenched his hand tightly as she threatened, "You are not to leave my side for even a second."

He laughed. "You have nothing to worry about. I'd have to be suicidal to wander off. And trust me, I have a very strong will to live."

Kat kissed his hand tenderly. "Then you won't mind if I hold this arm captive until I wake up? It'll make me feel better to know you're close."

"Your wish is my command."

In an odd way, he couldn't think of a better moment. Just the two of them, his arm wrapped protectively around her slender frame, her head leaning against him.

He'd been joking when he'd said he had a strong will to live, but now, as he felt her relaxing by his side, Steve realized his will to live was stronger than it had been in years. His whole life, it seemed, he'd been searching for meaning. Searching for a family. A place where he belonged. Now that he'd found it, he wasn't going to let it go without a fight.

~ 89 ~

Images of darkness and violence, blood and gore flashed through Kat's mind. A cacophony of screams and shouts for help – many of them her own – assaulted her and kept her from a peaceful rest. But sleep had come nonetheless; she'd been so exhausted it felt like she was being pulled into quicksand. Though her mind and spirit feared attack, her body demanded slumber; there was no fighting it.

When the visions became too horrifying, Kat struggled to regain consciousness, often bringing herself close enough to control the pictures in her mind, but sometimes she was so lost in sleep she was unable to escape the demons that chased her.

In a dream, she heard Amy's whispered threats of death. Torture. Pain. Isolation. Horrors beyond her wildest imaginings. Amy appeared before her in the same clothes she had worn in her movie role. In one hand was the whip that had been left at Peyton's side. Her eyes were wide with hatred as she laughed at Kat's fear.

Kat's eyes snapped open, fleeing the horrible laughter, pulling herself out of the dream. Her heart was pounding, a scream caught in her throat.

Nothing could have prepared her for what she saw.

She was alone. In her bed. In her suite. The orange walls assaulted her eyes. Paintings of playful pigs taunted her. She tried to flee, only to discover she couldn't move. Her hands were at her side, not bound, but somehow frozen in place. She tried to scream, but no sound came. She was trapped.

As she struggled against her paralysis, she heard a steady scraping noise – the sound of dragging feet approaching. The dead were coming – she'd seen enough monster movies to know that sound. Clomp. Swoosh. Clomp. Swoosh.

Slowly they came into her line of vision. Four of them. Tiny Gloria. Beautiful Trista. Stately Peyton. Wacky Biff. At first, they appeared perfectly normal, as they'd looked on the day they arrived at the hotel. But then, slowly, she saw the truth.

Biff was more pale than she remembered – his striking California tan replaced with a ghostly pallor. But not just pale, blotchy. The blotches stood out starkly on his skin, red welts that began to swell and ooze before her eyes. Snakebites. Covering him from head to foot, revealing the poison that had destroyed his body.

Kat averted her eyes, but, since she was unable to move her head, her vision only fell upon another of the four. Gloria, who also looked normal at first. Her thin face was worn by hard living. Yet as Kat stared, she realized there was mud caked around the woman's mouth. Inside her nose. Over her eyes. The mud-encrusted eyes were not a normal brown, but instead were covered by a thick glaze, a pasty cataract obstructing her vision.

Looking away, Kat saw Peyton. He was very close, only a few feet away. Maybe he could help her get out of here. She tried to plead for her life, but the words wouldn't come. Peyton only stared, his face remained stoic, until a trickle of red ran down his forehead, over his nose, dripping onto the floor. Another ran down his temple. A third dripped off his ear. That was when she noticed his suit. A dark red, almost black, substance was seeping across the fabric, spreading from back to front.

Kat watched as Trista ran her hand down Peyton's back. When she pulled it away, it was saturated with blood. Blood that she then ran over her own face, revealing to Kat hollowed eye sockets sewn shut. Peyton's blood blended with Trista's own as she slowly smiled.

She whispered in a voice that belonged to Amy, "You're going to die."

Kat's own scream was what finally woke her. She was in the hotel lobby, lying on the couch. Steve's hands were on her shoulders, trying desperately to wake her.

She was not in her suite. The dead were not coming for her. Or at least not the four from her dream. Unfortunately, Amy remained very likely dead and certainly out to get both of them.

"You're okay, it was a dream," Steve was repeating reassuringly.

There would be no more peace, Kat realized. Even sleep would provide no escape from the horrors of her waking nightmare.

"I haven't had a full night's sleep since we arrived. That was what, three days ago? A person cannot survive without sleep. It's impossible. It'll make you crazy eventually, I imagine. It would have to. And in a place like this it would be awfully easy to go stark raving mad."

Steve's voice was soothing, but Kat could see he shared her concern. "You can rest easy. I'm here. I won't let anything happen to you."

"All the Valium in the world couldn't make me rest easy. The images in my head… Jesus, there are people in padded cells that have more peaceful dreams!"

"Honey, we talked about this. She can't hurt us down here. We know the pattern. We can protect ourselves now."

Kat only shook her head. "It's too much. It's already too much."

She stood and began pacing. Flashes from her nightmares tormented her. She thought about the frivolous conversations about "normal" lives she and Steve had earlier. It was a joke. Even if they managed to survive this, nothing would ever be normal again.

"Do you want to talk about the dream?" Steve asked.

Kat laughed. The pitch was higher than it should have been, strained. Maybe a little crazy. "I don't think there's any reason to rehash it."

"Is there anything I can do?"

"Follow me into my dreams and fight off the bad guys?"

"In my role as the man of your dreams, I think it's the least I could do," he joked.

"Well, so long as you're trying to help." Kat smiled weakly. She had to keep fighting. If she was going to let the dreams get to her, then she might as well go upstairs, sit in her room, and wait for Amy to come.

"Come here," Steve said, patting the spot on the couch next to him. "Sit. Rest."

Kat shook her head. "There will be no resting. Not any time soon. I've seen enough for a while. But you should probably close your eyes. You need some sleep, too."

"I'm fine. Just sit down. I'll rub your head. You look exhausted."

"I am exhausted. But I'm not ready to brave nightmare-world quite yet. And since we can't sleep at the same time, you should take advantage."

Kat could see that part of him wanted to decline. He wanted to stay awake forever, protect her forever. But his need for sleep was too strong. "Are you positive you're okay?"

Kat smiled weakly, but genuinely as much for herself as for him. "I'll be all right. I promise. Sleep."

~ 90 ~

It was a dream, part of his mind understood that, but it didn't make it any less frightening. He was alone in the hotel, wandering through the hallways. He had to find Kat. He'd searched everywhere, but he couldn't find her. It was as if she'd vanished.

The vivid colors of each of the suites assaulted his eyes. Paintings of animals seemed to laugh at his failure to find the only thing that mattered.

He reached the top of the stairs and sitting on the couch in the lobby, with her back to him, was a woman. Kat! It had to be.

He ran to her and grabbed her in an embrace. But when he touched her he realized it wasn't Kat. The build was too slight, her hair too thin. Steve slowly pulled away and saw a woman from more than a decade's worth of nightmares.

Lucy. Even now, he couldn't think of her as Lucy Lichtenhoff. She'd always just be Lucy.

"Steve, my angel, what's wrong?" she asked in that familiar husky whisper. She had hardly ever spoken in more than a whisper. Now he understood why.

He knew he should answer, but he could only stare. She was too young to be gone. Too innocent and kind to have been treated so horribly.

She touched his cheek. "What is it, baby? You look so sad. We have each other. We don't need anything else."

Steve shook his head sadly. "Waylan?" he whispered.

Lucy shook her head violently. "I don't want to talk about him. Not ever. Don't ever say his name."

"This isn't real," Steve muttered to himself. "A dream. It's a dream."

"No, no," she said, stroking his cheek. "Not a dream. It's real. It's all real. We're going to be together. Just hold me."

Steve pulled away. "No. I can't. We can't. It's not safe."

As he spoke the words, he was catapulted back in time. The world around him was no longer a dream. It was real. They were in the dirty hotel room. The room where she had died. *This time*, his mind screamed, *this time you can save her!*

"You have to leave. You have to get out of here!" Steve shouted, pushing her towards the door. "You need to run. Get away from here. He's coming!"

Lucy was confused, concerned. "He doesn't know where we are. It's okay."

"He knows. He's coming," Steve continued urgently, still pushing her towards the door.

As Steve spoke, he could hear the footsteps. He could almost see the huge man coming. He grabbed Lucy's arm; he dragged her to the door. They had to run. He swung the door open and was face to face with *her* – not Waylan, but Amy. He turned and looked at the woman standing behind him. It wasn't Lucy. It was Kat.

"You couldn't save Lucy. Do you really think you can save me?" Kat taunted.

Amy laughed heartily at the accusation. "It seems your own subconscious frightens you more than any threats I can make."

Steve looked from Kat to Amy and back again. It was a dream. Only a dream. It couldn't hurt him.

"Oh, dreams can hurt you," Amy explained. "They can hurt you very deeply. Your subconscious is wrestling with all sorts of things right now. Guilt. Fear." Amy paused, and then added with a smile. "Maybe even love. God, I hadn't counted on that. That's pretty funny. You've fallen for her. I can see it now. It's almost a shame that I have to kill you first. It would have been so much better to have let you suffer through another murder. Hell, Steve, remember what happened to the last woman you claimed to love?"

"This is still only a dream. You can't hurt us," Steve insisted.

"Oh, right, sorry, I got a little sidetracked there. I was explaining. The subconscious. You need your sleep, you see, to work through all of these overwhelming feelings you're having. You're vulnerable when you sleep. Vulnerable to my manipulations. Even more so than when you're awake. As you wrestle with your feelings, I get to play a little. Twist things around. Mess with your memories. Put you in this hotel room – for example."

Steve looked around and saw the dirty walls. He smelled the musty curtains. Lucy was with him and Kat was with him. They were both in danger. There was nothing he could do to protect them. Nothing.

"You see," Amy continued. "Dreams are like a playground for me. First, you're here with my mother. Then you're here with the woman who destroyed my career. Now look in your hand. How'd that get there?"

Steve looked down. The hand that had been holding Kat's was now holding a heavy silver revolver. Black handle. He knew the gun. He'd seen it before.

"Wow, a gun," Amy teased. Though in an instant the jest vanished from her voice and her eyes blackened with rage. "You know what I think? I think you may as well have pulled the trigger yourself. I think you murdered her. I think you're the reason I lost my mother. You're the reason that man was able to destroy my life. Just like he destroyed hers. You may not have shot her, but you are a murderer."

Steve looked desperately between Kat and Amy. Between the future and the past. There was only one thing he could do. And the gun gave him the power to do it. He turned away from Kat and faced Amy directly. As she spoke, Steve could feel his arm rising. He was pointing the gun at Amy. "I won't let you kill Kat."

"Empty threats, lover boy. I have the power here. Not you."

"I'll stop you."

Amy laughed. "There's nothing you can do, murderer."

"There's plenty I can do."

He squeezed the trigger and fired off six shots in rapid succession. As he did, the vivid reality of the dream broke down. Images blurred into flashes. Memories of Lucy in the room that night. The man at the door. The gun. Shots fired. Blood. Death.

When the barrage of images ceased he was back in the dank hotel room. He was leaning against the wall, gun in his hand, just as he'd been years before. Waylan was gone. And there was a woman in the darkness at his feet. He slid down the wall to the floor and took the hand of the dead woman. It was then he realized things were different.

The lamp had not broken, so the room was still well lit. The door to the hotel room was closed. But the most horrible thing was the hand he was holding. A strong, smooth hand. With manicured nails. A simple, but very expensive white gold ring. Five tiny pearls surrounding a small yellow diamond.

His heart shattered with the realization. He turned her head to him. Her sweet brown eyes were closed forever. Her spirit gone. It was Kat's body that lay by his side. Not Lucy's. Not Amy's. And in that moment, he knew. He knew he couldn't change things. He knew it would end the same way. He'd kill her. Just like he'd killed Lucy.

As the weight of his failure sunk in, Kat's eyes snapped open. She whispered to him in Amy's voice, "You're mine now."

~ 91 ~

Steve woke with a start. Sweat was running down his face and his heart was pounding. Kat was sitting next to him, stroking his hair, and looking very concerned.

"Thank God you're awake. You wouldn't wake up. You were thrashing in your sleep. Are you okay?"

It was a dream. Only a dream. He needed to calm down. The fear in Kat's eyes was real enough though, and that was what he needed to focus on.

"I'm fine. A nightmare. I'm sorry I worried you."

Steve sat up on the couch and poured himself a cup of lukewarm coffee from the carafe. He took a long drink and then tried to focus on Kat. She was staring vacantly at a movie on television. She looked exhausted. She needed sleep. They both did. Yet Steve now knew that getting some was not going to be easy.

Kat spoke without looking away from the television. "I don't know if she was getting in my head during my dreams. With all that's been happening, it would be only natural to have nightmares. But my gut tells me it was her. She's going to torture us while we're awake and then terrify us while we sleep. Eventually the sleep deprivation will drive us crazy."

Steve couldn't help but think of Amy's own words – *dreams are like a playground for me.* Maybe Kat was right. This was how it was all going to end.

"I can't argue with you," he said with a sigh. "What do you want to do?"

Kat shrugged, but still avoided his eyes. "I've been thinking a lot about that. As far as I can tell we don't have too many options: suicide, or slowly being driven insane and eventually murdered."

"Have you decided the method of your choice?"

"Suicide is a cowardly alternative. I'd rather not die that way."

"It'd be comparably peaceful."

He could see Kat truly consider the alternatives for a moment. She knew as well as he that the punishments in her Bible were nothing to be trifled with. Her eyes drifted to the rain-spattered window and he was reminded of one of the punishments listed for Gluttony – souls battered and beaten, worn down by a constant pounding rain. His own heart shattered with the image. That was what was to come. They both knew it.

Yet she tore her eyes from the window and shook her head. "No. It's too much like the drug use. Too much like that woman who refuses to take what she has coming to her."

"You don't have this coming to you."

"That, I think, is actually up for debate. What do you want?"

Steve thought of the dream. He had no doubt that there were thousands more where that came from. Nonetheless, there was only one answer. "I have to fight this. You don't deserve this. Hell, I don't deserve this. I won't just lie down."

"He who doesn't lie down will most likely be pushed down," she replied, her voice sounding flat, almost dead.

Steve took Kat's hand and turned her face to meet his eyes. "I'm going to stand next to you and fight. We'll stick together. I won't leave you."

~ 92 ~

Morning came, though the sun didn't seem to rise. Each day the clouds had become more dense. Torrents of rain poured down, soaking the already saturated earth. They each slept on and off throughout the day, stealing moments of fitful sleep, hoping meager rest would soothe their weary bodies.

Around noon, Kat was pacing the lobby. Steve was enjoying what appeared to be a peaceful sleep. She could only stare with furious jealousy at the gentle rise and fall of his chest, the relaxed way his right arm hung over the couch.

It wasn't fair. She was so tired. So horribly, horribly tired. Her joints ached with exhaustion. Her chest was heavy with fatigue. Her mind weary with the knowledge that she'd likely never again have a peaceful night's sleep.

"Peace is there for the taking. It's your choice."

Kat didn't even flinch at the familiar voice. It haunted her dreams. Why not her waking moments too?

"None of this was my choice," Kat replied.

"Don't you just hate it when other people's choices make your life unbearable? I understand. Really, I do. People spread pain with their own bad choices. I lived with it. It's your turn now."

"I didn't intend to hurt you," Kat replied, not turning to face the voice, knowing she didn't want to see.

"I don't care what you intended. Why would I? You did hurt me. You ruined me. You were the reason things ended the way they did. That's why you're still here. The others played their part. They continued the cycle. But you and he are the bookends. He started it and you ended it."

Kat was surprised to realize Amy's words no longer carried any impact. She'd accepted her role in all this. She didn't know if it was the exhaustion or simply resignation, but she was no longer able to feel pain about it. No longer able to feel guilt. She was as good as dead; there was nothing left to be afraid of.

"Then why don't you just kill us?" Kat asked.

Amy hesitated, as if Kat had caught her off guard. "It doesn't work that way."

Kat smiled. Even as the grin spread across her face, she wondered if she'd lost it. Maybe this was what it felt like to be crazy. She was standing in the middle of a hotel lobby having a conversation with a ghost. If that wasn't crazy, she didn't know what was. Yet she smiled broadly at Amy's reply, mostly because of the truth it revealed.

"Then we're right about the rooms. We're right about the isolation. We're right about the order."

Only silence met the question, stillness that told Kat she was alone again. She wasn't sure she'd expected an answer, but it was disappointing not to get a reply.

Steve began to toss in his sleep, his peaceful rest stolen again. Amy had made her point. She'd be visiting. There was nowhere left to hide.

~ 93 ~

Around six they ate, but it was nothing like the previous night. They ate merely because food was necessary to sustain life. Kat was too tired to feel hungry. Actually, the thought of food made her nauseous. It was ironic, actually, that a woman who'd spent the better part of ten years dieting was spending her last hours forcing herself to eat. Calories meant energy, and energy, she hoped, would make it possible to function without sleep.

It was during dinner that the horrible became worse. With a flash of lightning and a thunderous clap, the lights snapped off. The black was enveloping and completely opaque. Even after a few moments to adjust her eyes, Kat could still only discern faint outlines.

Steve reached across the table and took her hand. It was a gesture of support, of strength. But she knew it was also an expression of fear.

"I guess we should've seen this coming." He'd clearly intended it to be a joke, but his voice revealed the strain.

Kat also tried to keep her voice light. "We probably should be surprised it's taken this long."

"There are more windows in the lobby and more comfortable seats. Shall we?"

"Sounds perfect. Though I insist you never again let go of my hand."

Steve slipped his arm around Kat's waist and they walked very closely as they felt their way back to the lobby. Somehow, the hotel seemed even more silent without the lights. Their footsteps echoed on the wood floors.

The only other sound was the rain on the windows, a million tiny monsters trying to claw their way inside.

Steve pulled her close to him on the couch. "I love you so much, Katherine Lincoln," he whispered. "I am so sorry you're here, and I promise I will keep you safe."

The promise was an empty one. They both knew that. But that didn't make Kat appreciate it any less.

~ 94 ~

Though he couldn't see her face in the dark, the sound of her breathing made Steve think Kat had fallen asleep. Even in her slumber, her hand was still wrapped tightly around his.

He desperately wanted to save her, to help her, but they were losing. That much was clear. He hoped it wouldn't be this dark during the day, but he knew it would be. Each day the sky only got darker. There was no way out.

"Now you're getting the picture," a voice whispered in his ear.

Steve shuddered at the sound. Amy.

"There's no way out. Time to stop fighting me. It's becoming tedious."

Instinctively, he pulled Kat closer to him, but she continued to sleep.

"She won't wake up. She's exhausted. It's just you and me," Amy hissed.

"I won't let you hurt her," Steve snapped.

"What are you going to do about it?"

"I'm going to sit down here until I die of old age. You can't hurt me unless I'm in that room."

"You think I'm going to let you two sit down here forever?"

Steve considered the question. This was a power that had the strength to murder five people more brutally than he would have imagined possible. Yet, here she was, vaguely threatening him. Why? It was that question that reminded him of Kat's Bible verse, the laminated yellow card that was most likely still on the coffee table in her sitting room. *When God, in the beginning, created man, he made him subject to his own free choice.... Before man are life and death, whichever he chooses shall be given him.*

"You can't force us, can you?" he asked, realizing the truth.

Though he couldn't see Amy, Steve could feel her anger.

"I do not have to negotiate with you!" she roared.

The rage didn't bring the fear Amy intended, instead it buoyed his confidence. "You really can't hurt us down here?"

"I am losing patience with you two." Her voice wasn't as loud this time; it was more of a growl.

"Then just go ahead and kill us, why don't you?"

A small part of Steve's brain was screaming at him to stop yelling at the woman who had the power to kill him. But he couldn't help it. It was as if something had snapped.

"Come on, Amy! I'm next, right? Hit me with your best shot."

Even as he spat the final words, Steve knew he'd overplayed his hand. A sudden flash of lightning brightened the room, revealing the woman standing over him. She appeared impossibly tall, her black hair dripping, her eyes ablaze with rage.

As the room returned to darkness, a deafening clap of thunder shook the walls. In the same instant, her hand slapped his face with such force it knocked him back against the couch. Though he fought to maintain consciousness,

Steve could feel his eyes rolling back in his head. And then the blackness became complete.

~ 95 ~

Steve didn't know if he blacked out. It felt like Amy was gone, seemed like time had passed. The throbbing pain around his jaw told him the altercation with Amy hadn't been a dream. He tried to look at his watch, but the blackness was too dense. He could barely see his own arm.

And then he panicked. His arm was free. His hand was free. Kat wasn't holding his hand. He felt the length of the couch and came up empty. She was gone. He felt his heart crack in half. Had they been wrong? Was there no order? No rules?

He called her name into the empty lobby, but his voice only echoed off the walls. He shouted over and over, until he was sure that even the dead bodies could hear him, but only silence met his calls.

He considered searching the lower level, but it seemed pointless. There was only one place she would be.

He made his way up the stairs past Trista's doorway. Walking up here, walking towards his suite, was nothing less than walking into his own tomb. Yet he knew couldn't play it safe. Not when there was the slightest chance they might be wrong. Decision made, Steve took a firm step into the hallway.

He ran his hand along the wall as he walked, feeling his way. His hand ran up against the doorjamb to his own suite. The door was wide open, beckoning him to enter.

He slid past the door and found the knob to Kat's suite. The door was closed. Locked. He fumbled the master key from his pocket and wrestled it into the keyhole. Though it fit as it should, it wouldn't turn.

Steve looked through the open door at his right. The message was clear. That was where he belonged. Just as it was clear that Kat's lock would never budge.

The message only served to encourage him. Kat was in her room. He was sure of it. The doors were thick, as were their frames. The concept was ridiculous. But Steve found himself taking six or seven long strides backward down the hallway. Then, lowering one shoulder, he broke into a sprint and hit the door with all his momentum and weight. He was met with a resounding thud and rockets of pain that shot through his shoulder and down his spine.

Unfazed, he repeated the process. The second time went just as poorly. The third time he thought he felt something tear in his shoulder. The fourth time was agony. His shoulder gave out completely on impact and he went headfirst into the door.

Flat on his back in the darkness, Steve began to cry softly. The pain was extraordinary. She was going to die and there was nothing at all he could do about it.

~ 96 ~

There was a pounding. A deep pounding. One, two, three times. After the third was a sort of strangled cry. Then a fourth, followed immediately by a fifth. It was the fifth thud that brought Kat around.

She blinked slowly awake. It was pitch black. Despite that, she could tell she was lying on the floor, which didn't make sense. The last thing she remembered was being on the couch with Steve. Nothing after that. Yet instinct told her where she was.

Cautiously, Kat rose to her feet and began to feel her way. A chair. Wooden back. Upholstered arms and seat. A couch. Soft and overstuffed. In front of it was a table. One of the suites, most likely hers. She was alone. In the dark. In her suite. Remembering the dream, Kat sharply pinched the flesh on her forearm. Pain shot through. She was awake. It was a nightmare all right, but she was awake.

The weird thing was – she was alone. Or she seemed to be. No sign of Amy. No sign of Steve. She had to get out of there and she had to find Steve. He was next. He couldn't be alone.

Walking cautiously, with one hand out in front of her, she began to feel her way to the door. She shuffled her feet as she went. That was why it was so surprising when she lost her balance.

Her toe caught on the rug. Just for an instant. It shouldn't have caused more than a minor stumble. But she careened forward, completely out of control. She might have gotten her arms in front of her quickly enough to stop the fall, but her head caught the edge of the end table. She was unconscious before she hit the floor.

~ 97 ~

"Jesus Christ. What did my mother see in you?"

From the corner of his eye, Steve could see the faint outline of Amy in the open doorway of his suite. He could feel a fire rising in his soul. Maybe he could beat her. He had to stand up. He had to fight. He had to try.

Slowly, using his good arm for leverage, Steve got to his knees and rose unsteadily. His bad arm hung limply at one side. It felt longer than it should have. Moving, even breathing, brought pain. Yet he needed to keep doing both if he was going to save Kat.

"I won't let you kill her," he said simply, wishing his words carried more conviction.

"This again? Really? Why can't you see that there isn't much you can do about it? I made a deal with someone. I promised the seven of you and I'm going to deliver. This isn't how I was planning on doing it, but this will do just fine."

Amy took two small steps back into the suite, in a transparent attempt to lure him inside.

"You don't think I'm that dumb, do you?" he asked. Though taunting her hadn't worked the last time, Steve couldn't think of a better plan.

"I was hoping you would join me. We'll sit. Talk. Maybe we can talk about making this as painless as possible."

"I want you to let Kat go."

"I wanted to have a normal, quiet life. We don't always get what we want."

"Look, I think you're missing the point here. I'm pretty sure you have to kill me before you can do anything to Kat. And we both know you need to kill me in that room. I'm staying out here unless we can negotiate some kind of agreement for Kat."

Amy laughed. "Negotiate? Are you kidding? I don't have to negotiate anything."

She reached out, and as she did, her arm became immeasurably long. She grabbed Steve by his bad arm and dragged him into the suite, slamming the door behind them.

Though Amy stood less than a foot away, Steve could only see the faintest outline of her features. The pungent smell of salt water radiated from her body.

"I'm sorry I won't be able to see your face, at least not at first. But I need the darkness to create the necessary chaos. Kneel down," Amy ordered.

Though arguing seemed pointless, Steve didn't have it in him to go peacefully. "Um, no," he replied.

"Kneel down, wise ass."

"Make me," he snapped.

Amy stepped forward. Her eyes were even with his, though he would have sworn she'd been almost ten inches shorter only a few moments before. Her eyes were faintly illuminated in the darkness, glowing with the blue light of a raging fire. All at once, he wished he'd done what she'd asked.

She raised one hand and placed her index finger on his forehead. She pushed him to his knees with the force of a falling anvil.

"Isn't it easier to cooperate with me?" she asked. "Now you are going to stay there. That's not a request, by the way, it's a fact."

As she spoke, he could feel a sudden tightness around his arms and legs. It felt like two ropes were wrapping around him. When he tried to move his arms he realized she was right, he wasn't going anywhere.

Amy roared, "Now we finish this!"

With a flourish, she raised both her arms and an explosion of light flashed all around them. The sudden brightness was blinding, but Steve could smell what had happened. Fire. His punishment would be from Dante – the lustful sinner would be left writhing in the eternal flames.

~ 98 ~

Kat was floating. Actually, it felt more like drowning. She had to fight this. Had to fight back. Steve needed her; he needed her help. She couldn't let him die. But her spirit was not enough to fight the enveloping darkness.

She could feel herself giving up. Giving in. Resigning herself to what she knew was a well-deserved punishment. She thought of her family. She thought of Steve. And all she could say was she was sorry. For herself, she had only one regret: that she would die like this, completely and absolutely alone.

And that was when it happened.

In a breath, she realized she wasn't alone.

A force surrounded her. It was nothing she could see. Nothing she could feel. But it was there. A peaceful presence. Soothing. Inspiring.

It was air. Light. Hope. Love.

She had died. She was certain. The oddest thing was, it seemed like heaven. Hell would never be this wonderful.

She had died and gone to heaven? Impossible.

Kat was wrestling with this question when she heard the voice. "Katherine. You need to wake up. This isn't the way it works."

The voice came from all around. It was booming, but only a whisper.

"Katherine," it continued, "you always have choice. Before you is the choice. She can't change that. Now get up."

Kat turned her neck to find the source of the sound and, as she did, everything changed. She could feel the rough fiber of the rug on her cheek. The pain in her wrist, which was twisted under her. She could taste the blood in her mouth. She was back in the room and she had to wonder if she'd ever left.

The voice seemed like a dream. An insane and bizarre dream. Yet the memory of it filled her with strength. It cleared her mind, despite the very nasty bump that stood out on her forehead. Gingerly, she rose to her feet and was happy to discover she was able to stand without difficulty.

Once she was standing, though, she realized something else was very wrong. Smoke. Dense smoke was filling the room. Though it was too dark to see, she could smell it. She forgot about her injuries and dashed for the door. Incredibly, the knob turned easily.

The smoke in the hallway was even more dense. Though she still couldn't see, it seemed the source was the room to her left. Steve's suite. A touch of the knob confirmed her fears. It was red hot.

Kat considered the predicament. Safety stood before her. Head towards the lobby, away from the fire. She would make it out. She might actually live through this. She didn't know where Steve was; he might not even be in the room. He wouldn't have taken a risk to come up to the second floor, even if she'd gone missing.

It was the final lie that stood out most. The idea that she might still escape wasn't a lie. Likely a false hope, but not a lie. But the idea that Steve wouldn't have risked everything to save her, that was a complete lie.

And it meant she was faced with a simple choice. Try to save Steve. Or try to save herself. The answer was obvious.

The wave of smoke that escaped the room when she opened the door almost sucked the oxygen from her lungs. She had to grip the doorframe to regain her balance.

Inside, things were even worse. Pillars of flame climbed the walls and licked at the ceiling. The smoke swallowed any light the flames provided.

Initially, there was no response when she called his name. But then she heard some coughing near the center of the room.

"Say something, Steve. I need to follow your voice."

A scratchy voice responded, barely choking out the words. "Get the hell out of here. Run away. Please run away."

The protest was enough to lead her to him. Her outstretched hands grazed his head. He was kneeling on the ground.

"Steve, come on," she said, reaching for his hand.

He seemed to hesitate, and then he grabbed her hand in response. She pulled him to his feet and they ran for the door. The smoke was lighter when they reached the top of the stairs and breathing was no longer a struggle in the lobby. Instinct had them out the door before they realized what they were running into.

At first the rain was soothing on their overheated skin. The air was gloriously fresh as they both gulped it in. It was actually brighter outside than inside. The light of the fire reflecting off the fog created a glow. Sounds of shattering glass told them it was spreading quickly. Minutes after they fled into the rainstorm, the fire broke through the roof.

Oblivious to the rain, Kat sank to her knees in the mud, exhaustion and pain threatening to overwhelm her. She could see her wrist was resting at an odd angle. A failed attempt to bend the joint confirmed it was probably broken.

Steve's arm looked even worse. It hung limply by his side. He looked oddly like Plasticman, one arm too long for the rest of his body.

"What happened to your arm?"

Steve smiled grimly and took a seat next to her. "I bumped into a door a couple of times." Noticing the confusion on her face, Steve dropped the joke. "It's my shoulder. I think it's probably dislocated. Come to think of it, it hurts like a son of a bitch."

Kat was about to smile at his humor, when a voice reminded her the nightmare was not over.

"You must think you're so fucking smart, slipping out like that. I don't know how you did it. That last knock on the head should have kept you down until I was ready, you prissy little pain in the ass."

Kat's head throbbed at the threat. She remembered waking up the first time. She remembered falling. And she remembered Amy's voice as her head hit the table, *Not until I'm ready for you, Bitch.*

Amy's tirade continued, without regard for Kat's memories. "And you, in your goddamn cowboy hat. I had you bound to that spot. You shouldn't have been able to move." She turned back to Kat. "How the hell did you get him out of that room?"

Rage radiated off Amy as she glared at the two of them, but then she seemed to shake it off. Amy continued, her voice calmer, quieter, "Well, no matter. This is the final punishment. Gluttony wasn't really your thing Steve, but I guess it'll have to do. An eternal round of cold, heavy rains, beating your body until it drives you insane. You see, Kat, this was the ending I'd planned for you all along. You will die in the mire. Fallen in the stinking mud. I think it would have been all the more dramatic if you'd had to endure it alone. But I guess I can live with a dual killing. I mean, why not?"

As Amy asked the rhetorical question, Kat remembered the beautiful voice that had called to her. She spoke without really understanding what she was saying. "Free will."

Amy rolled her eyes. "What the hell is your problem? It's over. Don't you see?"

"Oh, it's over, but not in the way you think," Kat countered. Her voice gained strength as she spoke. It was becoming clear in her mind. The voice that woke her. The reason she'd made it out of the hotel. "Free will. No matter what happened in that hotel, it was always our choice. You certainly put the temptations there. Taunted a little. Coaxed a bit. But we had the final decision. That all changed tonight. Steve and I never chose to be alone with you. It probably should have worked, I know. I was so close to using again. So close. A few times, my God, I could almost feel it. But Steve helped me. That's what you didn't count on. Our friendship. Our love."

Amy began to clap. "Clearly, being off drugs has improved your acting. Bravo!" She chuckled. "You don't actually believe that crap, do you?"

Kat smiled back. "Actually, I do believe that crap. I believe it because you admitted it to me yourself. You never had the power to just kill us. You only had the power to punish us. That's why we're still here." Kat thought of the Bible verse that had gotten her through rehab. She didn't need the laminated card any longer, she'd learned the lesson. "I choose life."

Amy shook her head. "Technicalities. You both deserve what you're getting. That's all that matters. Rules or not. This was never about choice. It was about blame."

Amy looked at the building crumbling behind her. They all knew the fire was so hot it would destroy everything. With a wave of her hand, a ball of flame erupted in the parking lot, consuming the cars.

"Philosophize all you want, Kat. It's done. You're too far away from any life to escape. The elements will kill you, one way or the other. Though it's been fun, I've gotta go.

I've got an eternity to spend, warmed with the memories of your collective downfall. You two may want to slide a little closer to the flames. I've gotta tell you, it's fucking cold where you're headed."

And in a blink, she was gone.

"Jesus Christ," Steve breathed. "What the hell was all that? Were you bluffing?"

Kat exhaled slowly. "You wouldn't believe me if I told you."

Steve smiled. "Honey, I think I'd believe just about anything at this point. But I'd like to call it divine intervention and go on with my life, if that's all right with you."

"That's fine, but I think Amy made a pretty good point." Kat looked up at the hotel. One wing already had partially collapsed. "Left to the elements, we don't have much of a chance."

Steve shook his head. "It seems pretty dire. But it looks like Amy's left us – for good this time. I think that's a positive step. Let's clean up that cut on your head. We'll worry about the rest later."

~ 99 ~

Slowly but surely the rain lightened. By six A.M., it had completely stopped, and the sun was rising in the east. The brilliant rays quickly burned the remaining clouds from the sky, and by seven it looked like a normal desert day.

The morning's light revealed only rubble. Anything that was more than ash continued to smolder. Gone was the hotel. Gone were five bodies. Which left them with no food, no shelter, a lot of mud, and the beating desert sun.

"Do you still think things look better?" Kat asked, as they surveyed the remains.

"Better than when Amy was standing over me and setting fire to the room? Yeah, this is an improvement. Not a big improvement, but an improvement."

Steve's arm was in a makeshift sling made out of the shirt he had been wearing the night before. His jaw was swollen and an ugly shade of purple. The way he moved, Kat could tell he was in a lot of pain.

"What exactly do we do now?" Kat asked. Her own wrist ached, her head throbbed.

"We wait for another miracle."

Kat couldn't help but smile. "Is that all?"

Steve put his good arm around her. "Care to sit in the mud with me and enjoy the sun?"

Kat leaned in in agreement and they both sat gingerly on the ground. The sky was beautiful, as was the sun. Days without any sunlight really did take a toll. Steve was right, it was an improvement.

"Do you think that someone'll come looking for us?" he asked eventually.

"I think my parents would give me a couple of weeks before they really started to worry. They might just figure I was busy or I needed space. You?"

Steve snorted at the prospect. "My uncle and I go months without talking. I'm no help."

"Should we try to walk? Should we try to do something? It isn't like help is just going to happen upon us out here."

Kat thought of the empty desert road from the drive in. Even when the flooded road became passable, she wondered what they were really heading toward. If they were one hundred percent healthy the odds would be poor. From the looks of the two of them, it seemed impossible.

That was when she heard it. It was distant at first, vague, almost like the threatening whispers that had haunted her in the hotel. But as it got closer it became more distinct. She leapt to her feet, squinting at the horizon.

She could sense that Steve had risen too. He heard it. She wasn't crazy.

It was coming from the east. The glare of the sun was too much for her to see what was coming, but the closer it got the more certain she became.

"What the hell is that?" Steve asked, as he squinted at the sky.

"That's the miracle you ordered," she grinned, kissing him hard on the lips.

From the sky came a bright orange helicopter. It was from the studio – Kat would have recognized it anywhere. Ernie, the pilot, was out of the chopper the moment it hit the ground. Kat and he were friends from the old days – pre-drugs, as she liked to think of them.

"Oh, my God! Kat!" he exclaimed, running towards her. "Are you okay?"

Kat simply smiled. *I am now.*

The lie came with amazing ease. There was nothing else she could do, really. No one would believe the truth. "Ernie! Thank God you're here. There was a fire. A terrible fire last night. We tried to get the others out, but it moved too quickly."

"What about Peyton?" he asked, though he looked far more concerned about her.

Kat only shook her head sadly.

Ernie looked at the remains of the hotel. Nothing left. Absolutely nothing. It only made the lie more believable. Then he noticed the man standing next to Kat.

Kat was quick with the introductions, "This is Steve. He was the chef here. Steve, this is Ernie. Who will now be known as my hero. How did you know to come?"

"I didn't. The studio needs Peyton for some paperwork and a couple meetings. He hasn't been returning their messages."

"No cell phone service out here," Kat explained.

She was about to come up with an excuse for the saturated ground when she realized she was standing on firm, dry soil. It was as if the days of rain had never occurred. It was over. It was all over. And somehow, someway, she was still breathing.

"Ernie, could you give us a lift? We need to get to a police station and tell them what happened. And I think we both need to get to a hospital."

Ernie nodded eagerly and hurried back to the helicopter.

Steve grabbed Kat's good arm before she could follow. "What do we do now?"

"I think we go home."

Steve looked back at the rubble. "That was home. Everything I had. Money. Clothes. Everything was in that hotel."

Kat ran her hand over his cheek. She leaned in and gave him a long, soft kiss. "I've got plenty to share. And, you know, I was thinking about investing in a restaurant. All the celebs do it. The problem is I've had trouble finding a good chef to partner with. You know anyone who might be interested?"

"You know, I think I may know just the person."

"Well, then, you have to come back to L.A. with me and introduce us."

"Sounds like a plan."

And though neither of them believed it was a very well thought-out plan, they knew it was exactly the right choice to make.

Keep Reading for a Preview of....

~ ~

Vendetta

By Elizabeth Flaherty

~ ~

Coming Spring of 2013

~ 1 ~

She could stand for hours watching, waiting. Alone in the silence. Alone in the darkness. Perfectly comfortable with both. Hatred boiled in her heart, driving her, as it always did.

In the dense vegetation just off the path, she stood as still as a statue, invisible in night's shadows. The only sign that she was still alive was the trickle of sweat that slid down her back.

Like he had done every night for the past week, the man passed her on his walk home. He was predictable, very predictable. She'd discovered over the years that most people were. Most had no idea they were watched, which made them very easy to catch. And once they were caught, their fear was a more effective weapon than any gun.

Fortunately for the world, most criminals were impulsive and stupid. They didn't stalk their victims. They didn't research, or plan, or wait for the right time.

She wished she believed this was evidence that she was more than just a criminal, but she knew the truth. Outlaws went out with the wild west. No matter how noble her quest, how righteous the goal, she was a criminal – nothing more, nothing less.

But tonight she thought little of any of that. She just watched him. It was the tenth day now, and every night the same pattern. Tomorrow, she decided. Tomorrow would be the night.

He was within only a few feet of her now. So close that she could smell the sharp cologne he practically bathed in. She rustled the bushes where she hid. As she'd expected, he didn't even glance her way. Like most predators, he was far too confident. That arrogance was about to catch up with him and she was going to enjoy it when it did.

~ 2 ~

Bethany Chase stood in the shadow of the grandstand, one of the few spots that offered a reprieve from the day's relentless heat. But it was the sounds of laughter that soothed her, more than the shade or the blasts from the industrial fans that cooled the event staff.

This was what she did. Who she was. She needed these events to remind her of that. They were all that kept her from floating into the ether like a child's abandoned balloon.

Next to her, folded into a small stack chair, was Geoffrey Quinn. His head was down, studying note cards, preparing for his big moment.

This was who he was, too. This was what they did. Together. Their engagement made sense. Marriage would make even more sense.

Geoffrey looked up and smiled at her. He tucked his note cards into his suit pocket and he stood, taking her hand.

"Almost time," he said.

She ran a hand over his always perfect hair, as if that could fix any hidden flaws. He straightened his jacket and the collar on his button-down shirt. He looked the part of the candidate – pressed, polished, but somehow casual, comfortable. He would be a good mayor, a very good mayor.

Twenty-five years ago, a six-year-old version of herself had been placed on a path that led her to this point, made her into the perfect person to be in this place at this time. Bethany wondered if that was why she still had doubts. How could she trust anything connected to that awful day? Frankly, it was a better excuse than most of the others she'd invented over the years.

The sound system squealed to life and a voice asked for the crowd's attention. The sounds of the carnival rides, squeals of children, buzz of adults, faded.

"Welcome to the seventh annual Family Day here in Central Park. As always, we're sponsored by the Chase Family Trust. I am happy to report we have broken an attendance record again this year and the park safety patrols are going to be able to expand their efforts even more than in years past! Thank you all so very much!"

The crowd roared in triumph and Bethany gave Geoffrey's hand a squeeze. "You ready for this?" she asked.

He winked at her. "I was born ready for this."

His tone was pure sarcasm, but Bethany knew the truth. He had known most of his life that this was his goal. Part of him did think this was some sort of birthright, something he was destined to do.

She gave him a kiss for luck before she approached the back stairs to the grandstand and prepared herself to do what she had been destined to do.

The voice of the M.C. spiked again, quieting the crowd. "It is my honor to introduce the reason you're all here today. The president of the Chase Family Trust – Bethany Chase."

The roar of the crowd was familiar, as were the flashing cameras. Bethany ascended the steps to the grandstand with the grace of a runway model. Sunglasses hid her eyes and a broad smile concealed the rest. She knew what the crowd saw and she played her part with finesse.

She scanned the crowd for the cameras. News crews were poised. Though her events always garnered at least a token cameraman from the network affiliates, this was different. Reporters were positioned by the cameramen, pads ready. And they weren't the people who did the fluff pieces. They were ready for the night's lead story. Clearly Geoffrey's campaign had leaked what was needed to the people who needed to know. She wondered if her staff had noticed the peculiarity yet; she wondered more why she'd chosen to keep it from them – from everyone.

She flashed one final broad smile to the audience and waved again before she approached the microphone. It was time. There was no delaying it any longer.

"Thank you all for coming out this afternoon. I know it's a little hot, but remember proceeds are all going to park safety. So, help yourself to as many ice cream cones as you can eat!"

She paused and allowed them to cheer, raise their ice cream, their children and generally behave like normal people. "I know you all believe, as I do, that it's very important to create a safe place for families to play together, to remove the fears and anxiety we have to endure in this city. You have all helped make that possible, but there is still more work ahead."

"Today," she continued. "Today I want to talk about the future. About what we can do going forward, what we as a community can join together and stand behind. We can't allow our view to become myopic. We have to look beyond the Park. Look to the city. The entire city!"

Bethany paused for the cheers, and looked off to the shadows behind the grandstand. In the glare of the sun it was hard to see Geoffrey, but she knew he was there waiting for her to invite him up on stage.

"I'm going to introduce you to the man who can make that happen, the man who can lead us to that place. I think most of you know him already. He's an assistant district attorney here in Manhattan, a graduate of Fordham and NYU. And most importantly, he's a New Yorker!"

Bethany smiled broadly at the roar from the crowd. "I've gotten the chance to get to know him pretty well over the past three years. I've come to discover he's a man who thinks big, who dreams big, and who is big enough to make those dreams come true. And that is why I admire him so very much. Today I would like to introduce him to you again. Not just as my fiancé, not just as a tireless prosecutor and servant of the people of the City of New York, but as a candidate to be the next mayor of this great city! Ladies and gentlemen – Geoffrey Quinn!"

Geoffrey bounded up on the stage with an energy Bethany had come to love. He waved to the roaring crowd and then gave her a tight hug.

"You are the best opening act ever," he whispered in her ear.

"Knock 'em dead," she whispered back.

Geoffrey gave her a big kiss, much more for the audience's benefit than hers, and greeted the crowd.

"Isn't she the most extraordinary woman in the world?" he asked, pausing to allow the applause to subside. "As you all know, I've worked hard for this city for my entire adult life. Many of you know me from my work in the D.A.'s Office, but I hope even more of you know me from my charitable endeavors. Like you, I love this city!"

Geoffrey glanced over at Bethany and then back to the crowd. "But unfortunately many of the people in this city are victims of violent crime. Many others live in fear. I know that many of you have been touched by that type of violence. I personally have seen the way that violence changes lives. I've seen it through my work and I see it every day when I look at the woman that I love."

As he spoke, Bethany could feel the humid air begin to close around her. The reference had been inevitable, even expected in light of his platform. But, as always, she felt her heart constrict at the reference to her mother.

As he spoke of the way violence ruined people and communities, she assured herself that he was speaking generally, speaking about the victims he knew from work as much as about her, but she heard the accusation in his voice, the judgment. Maybe he did think of her as ruined; maybe it was unrealistic that he would see her any other way.

She watched Geoffrey as he continued his speech, and she thought of Richard, her closest friend in the world and the only person who she knew loved her flaws as much as the rest of her. He was going to be furious that she'd kept this news from him. The fact that she hadn't told Annie either wouldn't help cushion the blow. She could only hope her two best friends could commiserate and find solace in numbers.

Applause brought her out of her thoughts. And Geoffrey's tone told her he was wrapping up. He stood tall and proud, beaming. "I'm going to keep this short. It's important you get out there and enjoy the activities that were planned. But I will leave you with this one thought – Vote Quinn for a Brighter Tomorrow!"

Geoffrey waved vigorously at the cheering crowd. Taking Bethany's hand, he raised it with his in victory. As she stood there, her hand in his, Bethany realized they were inextricably linked. She just wished she was sure it was what she wanted.

~ 3 ~

Richard Marshall was stretched on his couch with the baseball game playing silently on his television, trying to convince himself he wasn't waiting for her to return. Though he was on his feet at the sound of the elevator bell, he forced himself to walk casually to the door. Her apartment was directly across the hall. The only other one on the floor. There was no way she could avoid him.

At the sight of her chestnut hair in the peephole, he greeted his best friend. "Not so fast."

"Damn elevator bell," Bethany muttered to herself.

"Now don't blame the elevator. I would have heard your door open. I have ears like a bat."

Despite everything, he smiled when she turned to face him. She looked beautiful, as always, and her expression was not unlike when she was eight and had been caught trying to steal a pack of gum. "Ears like a bat?" she asked. "The last time the fire alarm went off in the middle of the night I had to pound on your door for almost five minutes to wake you up."

He scowled in response, his square jaw set tightly, promising himself he would not be charmed. "I'm a heavy sleeper. That doesn't mean I don't hear everything that's going on over here."

Bethany snorted at the suggestion. "I know you're going to let me have it, and you should, why don't you come in?"

He followed her inside and flopped onto his favorite side of the couch, propping his feet on the coffee table. He considered saying something to start the conversation, but he waited to hear what she would offer first.

"Geoffrey's running for mayor," she blurted out.

He almost laughed. "Really?" He glanced at his watch. "It's not as if I read that information on-line twenty minutes ago or anything. Is that why you told us to skip the fundraiser this year?"

He wanted to grill her a little, get the real story. Frankly, with her and Geoffrey there always seemed to be the need to pry information out of her. But she looked like a trapped animal. It was a look he'd seen in her eyes far too often recently.

His voice softened, in spite of himself. He patted the couch next to him. "How about you sit?"

She followed his direction and sunk on the couch next to him. "I should have told you. I don't know why I didn't," she said.

"I don't know why you didn't either," he said. "I imagine you were keeping this huge revelation from your father, and I can't say I blame you for that, but I can keep a secret. I've never told anyone you made out with Jack McKee at summer camp."

Bethany rolled her eyes. "Does it always have to come back to Jack?"

"Hey, I'm willing to tell the world about good old Jack if you want, tell them all about your attempt to convince very gay Jack that girls were better than boys."

"Fine, you've made your point. As you always do. You can keep a secret. I know that. I guess it's just a little weird talking about Geoffrey with you guys. I know you and Annie aren't exactly thrilled with him," Bethany replied.

Richard searched her face for any clue as to what was going on. "Annie and I both love you. We just want you to be happy."

"Geoffrey makes me happy. He's a good man. This will be a really good thing for him."

Richard considered giving her the speech again, reminding her that her near obsession with saving the world was not a basis upon which to build a relationship. But she looked too tired to listen and he had no interest in starting a fight.

"It's not just a big thing for him, Beth," he said. "It'll be huge for both of you. You'll have some power, too."

A buzzing from her purse distracted her. Without a word, she checked the caller ID and then dropped the phone on the coffee table.

"Reporter?" he asked.

She shook her head. "My father."

He ran a hand over her shoulder. "You know, ignoring problems doesn't make them go away."

She offered a weary smile. "But it does give them a little time to cool off."

Aston and Bethany Chase had legendary fights. They were Tyson and Holyfield without the ear biting. As a rule, Geoffrey did not bring out the best in them.

"Does Aston actually cool off? I'm not sure I've ever seen that side of him," Richard said.

His joke was rewarded with a more sincere smile. "I can hope, can't I?"

After a moment, she said, "I hate to cut this short, but I have a training session in about fifteen minutes, I need to start getting ready."

"Oh, so now you're lying to me and you're choosing time with your trainer over me? I'm pretty sure the Karate Kid was never this disciplined."

"Ah, yes, the Karate Kid – a role model of mine." She stood, laughing at his comparison. "It's healthy to have a hobby, you know."

"A hobby? This is not a hobby, it's an obsession." Richard didn't entirely know what went on in the martial arts studio a block from their apartment building. He was pretty sure he didn't want to.

He was heading for the door when he stopped. "I almost forgot. Annie called just after the announcement hit the news. She was thinking we should grab dinner tomorrow, significant others included. Then we can congratulate you and Geoffrey."

Bethany's green eyes sparkled. "Are you going to be bringing a significant other?"

"Whoa, there. No. I will be attending all on my own. There is no way I'm going to subject anyone to you and Annie."

"How is Trisha these days?"

"Tracey," he corrected.

"Whatever. If any of your girlfriends manages to stick around for more than a month, I'll make an effort to get to know her name."

He shrugged. "There's a lot of beautiful women out there. If I stick with anyone for too long, I could miss out on something."

Bethany gave him a kiss on the cheek. "Yeah, you'll miss out on something sooner or later, that's for sure."

Richard glared at her. "How did this suddenly get turned around on me? We were picking on you. Not me. So, dinner tomorrow night?"

"It sounds nice. I'll double check with Geoffrey and let you know."

"Perfect. I'll set it up," he replied, heading back to his apartment.

Richard left her to prepare to battle her demons, or whatever it was she really did over at the studio. He wished he felt better about the conversation, but she'd done nothing to put his mind at ease. There was something wrong and no matter how hard she tried to cover it up, Richard wouldn't rest until he figured it out.

~ 4 ~

She waited in the shadows, knowing tonight she would finally act. The cocky bastard thought he was untouchable, thought his connections to the Timminolo crime family could protect him from anything. He was about to find out that all the protection in the world wasn't worth anything if the right person wanted to get you.

She hated to work in such a public place, but she had looked at it from every angle. This was her best shot. And she had to admit, it seemed somehow poetic. Central Park had brought such pain to her life, it seemed only appropriate that it provide her safe harbor for her quest.

The soft sound of footfalls reached her ears, expensive leather shoes, bought with money from killers. Under the mask, she felt her cheeks flush with rage. She embraced the anger, pulled it close. And as he came into sight, she pounced.

Before he even realized he was being grabbed she had one arm around his throat, another pulling his briefcase out of reach. There would be a gun inside the case. It would be better if that was taken out of play completely. She tossed the briefcase into some bushes and pulled one of Manhattan's best criminal defense attorneys off the path into a secluded area.

Though he squirmed initially, his pudgy frame was now still enough that she eased off his throat. An unconscious Gary Nettle would not do her any good.

At the edge of a small pond, she threw him to his knees. She waited for him to take a deep breath, but before he could do anything more, she shoved his head under the water. Pulling his arms behind his back, she secured his hands with zip cuffs. With the plastic tight around his wrists, she allowed him to surface for some air.

He coughed and sputtered, gasping as his head broke the surface.

Before he could speak, before he could even think, she leaned close. Her voice was distorted electronically as she spoke through the mask. "Don't pass out on me there Gary, we need to have a little talk."

He turned his head to look at her, the awe and fear obvious. She knew he saw barely more than a shadow. Dressed entirely in black, with a hooded mask, she could scare the truth out of anyone. And that wasn't just an expression. She knew it for a fact.

"I don't want to hurt you, Gary. We can do this really easily. I have a couple of questions that need to be answered. Do you think you can handle that?"

Nettle nodded attentively, his flabby neck swaying. But he said nothing. Silence was good. Silence meant she had his attention.

"Good. That's what I like to see. Word is you've been running your mouth about the Rita Chase murder."

"Rita Chase's murder? What do you mean? That happened twenty-five years ago. Why are you asking me questions about that…"

She cut him off before he could say anything more, shoving his head back into the water, counting slowly to herself, holding him under just long enough that he would begin to feel the desperate need for air. Then she pulled him back to the surface, slamming his knees deep into the muddy earth.

"You answer questions Gary. It's simple. No comments. No expounding. Just answer the question you are asked. You're a lawyer, you should understand the concept."

Wet stringy hair dripped in his eyes. "Look man, I got it. Just cool off. I got it."

He was still too unconcerned for her taste, but his comment amused her. It was amazing really. They never knew she was a woman, never even considered it. Chauvinistic sons of bitches.

She knelt down behind him, shoving his face forward when he attempted to look at her. This was going to be a very satisfying conversation. One way or the other.

"You know Gary, I was just reading the other day about the complexities of the joints in the fingers. Fascinating stuff. The knuckles are kind of like a hinge. But like any hinge, you bend it the wrong way and it'll break."

As she spoke, she wrapped her fingers around his left pointer finger, slowly, methodically tightening her grip.

"Rita Chase's murder. What do you know about the guy that killed her?" she asked again.

"I don't know anything about the murder." His voice was high, almost shrill. He sounded scared now.

But apparently not scared enough.

"You see Gary, I'd like to believe that, but I've got a friend who told me you said you knew what happened. That means you're lying to one of us. You don't want to be lying to me."

"I can't tell you anything," he said without conviction.

She laughed at his assertion. Without a second's hesitation, she snapped his finger back, allowing the tip to touch the back of his hand, savoring the sensation of the snapping tendons. She quickly submerged his head, muting the inevitable scream.

When she let him up, he was choking back what sounded like a sob.

She let him look at her now. He would see only black eyes set deep in the black mask.

"I can't," he finally said.

"Don't be afraid of the mob Gary, be afraid of me." There was no threatening calm now, only vicious rage. She grabbed his middle finger and snapped it back.

Again, she muffled his cries with the water, but brought him back to the surface quickly enough that she was sure he wouldn't choke.

Despite her efforts, Gary's eyes looked unfocused when she pulled him up. A slap across the face brought him back. "It's not going to be that easy, you bastard. Look at me!" she ordered.

Gary shook his head, focusing.

"The right hand is next Gary. You're right handed, so that's going to make work more difficult."

"Who the hell are you?" he asked, seemingly unable to say anything else.

Stupid lawyers and their stupid questions. Grabbing the final two uninjured fingers on his left hand, she snapped them back, muffled his cries and then brought him back to the surface.

"I'm asking the questions Gary. And we're now officially onto the right hand. That is unless you want me to go for the thumbs next. I was going to save those for last."

Finally, there was some clarity in his eyes. "Rita Chase was killed in Central Park about twenty-five years ago," he began.

She wrapped her fingers around his second pointer finger.

"It was a hit," he added quickly. "A paid contract. The hitman waited for her and her kid in the park. The method was supposed to be a single shot to the head. And that's what happened."

"I know all that. Tell me who the hitman was."

There was a flash of something in his eyes. It almost looked like relief. That was not the look she wanted.

"Tony Niccolini did the hit," he said. "He was a client of mine at one point. He told me about it."

"What do you mean he told you about it?"

"He was a hitman. On trial for murder. We were talking strategy. I think he was bragging. He figured he could brag because of the attorney-client privilege."

"Who hired him?"

"I don't know anything else. I just know that Tony said he did it."

The rage flared again. There was more. There had to be more.

She leaned in closer, again pushing his finger back slowly. He should be feeling real pain in the joint now. With the memory of the other hand, he would want to tell her the truth. "I think there's more to the story," she said.

His eyes were desperate again, pleading. "There was nothing. He was bragging. Just bragging about the hit. He wanted to tell someone the details. How he stood there in the trees waiting for them. How he got the shot off clean. And he told me about the kid. How upset she was. He got off on it. That was all he talked about. He didn't say nothing about the business side. I'm not sure he even knew who he did the job for."

She could see it all and it didn't bring rage, it only brought pain. But she shook that off, focused on the task at hand. "Where's this hitman?"

Nettle's voice was soft when he spoke. "He's dead."

She acted without thought, without consideration, without conscious awareness. She snapped two fingers on his right hand back, barely feeling the crack of the bone, not hearing the snap of the joint. She shoved his face into the water, not really intending on ever letting him up.

But she did let him up. He was choking when he finally broke the surface, his nose and chin covered in black mud.

"You tell me a half-assed story about this hit; tell me you don't know anything useful; and then tell me the guy who was directly involved is dead? That's pretty fucking convenient," she said.

"It's true. I swear. Tony died in prison. Early nineties. Stabbed in a prison fight. The word was that he got knifed because he was talking to the feds to get his sentence lightened. The people he'd worked for, they didn't like that."

She ordered herself to calm down, to breathe. There might be something here. "Was there a particular Family he did most of his work for?"

"Tony was a freelancer. Worked for himself. No loyalties," Nettle said.

The answer was too simple for her taste. "But you defended him?"

"Yes," he said cautiously, "but that was years later."

That meant Niccolini had to be connected to the Timminolo family in some significant way. Otherwise the great Gary Nettle would not have been made available to him.

She wanted to ask more, but she knew that was the end of it. She wondered where she'd go from here. "Niccolini? Died in prison early nineties?" she repeated.

Nettle nodded.

She grabbed his throat, lifting him off the ground. "If you are lying to me, I'm going to shove your face in that water until the pond fills your lungs and you never breathe air again. You got it?"

She was rewarded with a look of pure fear. "Yeah. I got it."

She threw Nettle back to the ground. Before he could regain his balance, she shoved a sock into his mouth and slapped duct tape across his lips.

Pointing to a long sharp knife that she'd driven into the ground not far from him, she said, "That's how you get out of here. You cut the zip cuffs, then move on with your life.

Maybe you should get a doctor to look at those fing
will be back if you aren't telling me the truth."

Then, as quickly as she appeared, she vanished into
darkness.

~ 5 ~

Bethany's day began with a ringing phone. At barely eight a.m. she didn't need to wonder who was calling. She dreaded the call, but she knew she had to take it.

"Good morning, Dad," she said, trying to shake the sleep from her voice.

Aston Chase's voice carried even more fury than she'd expected. "Good? What exactly do you think is good about it?"

Bethany sat up in bed, pushing the sheets aside and steeling herself for the fight she'd avoided the night before. "Do you want to talk about this or do you want to yell?"

Not surprisingly, the question did nothing for his mood. "I'm just surprised you've finally decided to take my call."

"I saw your message last night," Bethany confessed. "It was just a busy night. I planned on calling you this morning."

"He uses the Chase name to launch his campaign and you don't think I deserve a call before the announcement?"

Bethany stood and started pacing, her frustration and anger growing, as it always did in moments like this with her

father. "I run the Trust. Not you. I decide what happe
the events. Not you. With his platform, the event yeste.
was a logical place to announce."

"Have I not made my position clear about him? Maybe
need to say it again?"

"I'm not a teenager, Dad. I don't have to break-up with
someone just because you don't approve."

Aston snorted at the suggestion. "He's using you. Using
your position. Your family. And by extension he's using *me*
to gain his political footing."

"I am not going to have this conversation with you again.
You know that isn't true. If you found even the tiniest bit of
evidence to suggest that you would have barraged me with it
years ago."

"What more evidence do you need? He's using your
event. The event sponsored by a charity that carries my
name! *You* are his platform for god's sake. And you still
think he isn't using you? You're smarter than this."

Bethany absorbed the words the same way she absorbed
punches during training sessions – muscles taut, teeth
clenched, breathing even. "Are you done?" she said with a
calmness that concealed her anger.

"I am not even close to done! I won't have this!"

"I don't think you have much choice in the matter,"
Bethany replied.

Bethany could almost hear a snap as Aston realized he'd
been manipulated. "You knew this conversation would go
like this. That's why you didn't tell me until after he
announced."

She made no effort to deny it. "And now it's done.
Don't you see? It's done. There's nothing you can do about
it."

"The hell I can't!" he roared. "If you really think there is
nothing I can do about this, then you, my dear, do not know
me very well."

"What are you going to do, oppose your future son-in-
law's campaign?" she countered.

law yet," Aston threatened.

"That's it. It's barely eight a.m. I _ work. I don't have time for this."

_ation is not over," he insisted.

_thany knew it was the truth, she said, "It is for _e disconnected the call.

_ in the t-shirt and shorts she'd worn to bed, Bethany _ed out of her apartment and across the hall to _ichard's. She pushed open the door without knocking. She knew it would be open. It always was.

Eyes half closed, wishing she could return to the sleepy state her father had so cruelly stolen from her, Bethany took a mug from the cabinet and poured some coffee.

She heard his voice before she saw him. "Ah, if it isn't my favorite coffee thief. You're a little late this morning."

Bethany shook her head as she drank down the rich blend. No one in the world made better coffee than Richard.

"One of these days you're going to try to barge into my apartment and discover the door is locked."

She only laughed and finally looked up at her old friend. "You start locking your door; I'll start locking mine. No free coffee for me and no free food for you. Nobody wins there."

Richard finished knotting his tie. "You look like hell this morning."

"Thanks for noticing. I feel like hell. Woke up to a phone call from my father. Not the best conversation ever."

One of the advantages of having a friend who'd known you since you were four was that you didn't have to explain much. She knew Richard would know immediately what she was talking about.

"He's going to warm up to him eventually," he assured her.

Bethany doubted that. She doubted that any of them would.

Richard poured his own cup of coffee and asked, [...] Geoffrey moves in, should I expect that he'll also be [...] looking for coffee?"

She hopped up on his counter. "We haven't even s[...] date. I don't think you need to worry about your precio[...] coffee just yet."

"You know, I find it very interesting that he doesn't stay at the casa de Bethany more often."

She rolled her eyes at the implied question. "Really? You're really asking me that at this hour of the morning?"

Behind Richard's cheerful grin was a glimmer of concern. "I figure you're so grumpy and disoriented before your coffee you might slip up and give me an honest answer about lover boy."

"I like my space. You know that."

"Isn't that going to make the whole marriage thing a little tricky?" Though Richard's tone was sarcastic, Bethany knew the question was a serious one. She also knew that Richard was the last person she could have this conversation with.

She laughed it off. "Look bud, I came here for coffee. I'm now heading back to my apartment where I am going to find some smashing ensemble and then I am going to go to work. I have a Board meeting this afternoon, which means I get to spend some time with dear old dad. It's going to be a rough day. There is no need to start it with a bad game of twenty questions."

Richard's expression quickly changed. "You have a meeting with the Board today? The timing really couldn't be worse on that."

Bethany tried to rub the sleep from her eyes. "Unfortunately, I don't set the dates for the board meetings and I'm not running the campaign. You know, now that I think of it that way, I can't help but notice just how powerless I really am."

Richard ignored the self-deprecation. "Aren't you scheduled to pitch that gun exchange program today. Aston is not going to like that idea."

his best mood."

 us coffee and then added, "He's
 ont of the whole Board, isn't he?"

 ne back of her neck in a fruitless effort
 of the tension that was already starting to
 m going to have to say, yes. It certainly looks

 ard topped off her cup. "Honey, you're going to
 that."

She ran her hand over Richard's arm appreciatively. "What I'm really going to need is a drink at the end of the day. You said the reservation was for Alfelini at eight?"

"That's Geoffrey's favorite, right? I figure that's appropriate, since it's his big celebration."

"That's great. Geoffrey's excited. He really appreciates you guys doing this for him."

Richard shrugged off the thanks. "It's the least we can do. But first, off to work with you. The sooner you start, the sooner it'll be over."

Bethany nodded and plodded back to her own apartment, wishing she could climb back into bed and pull the covers over her head. It was hard to say what was stressing her out more, the impending Board meeting or Richard's unwelcome grilling about Geoffrey. With Richard, there was a fine line that always had to be walked. That had been the case for years now, ever since the day he'd kissed her.

Of course there'd been alcohol consumed – quite a lot of it – before the incident. And of course Richard had blamed the whole thing on the drinking. But Bethany knew better. It had been college. Drinking was a big part of what they did most weekends. And despite that, it had only happened the one time.

Richard moved on. He hadn't seemed bothered by the rejection. He'd almost shrugged it off. Bethany often wondered what had hurt more – turning him away or the fact that he hadn't seemed to care.

But she pushed such thoughts from her mind. She and Richard could never be. That was the way it was. The way it needed to be.

She had to forget how perfect the moment had been, had to forget the way everything else had faded away, because it was only that – a moment. And she knew all about moments. She'd experienced more than a lifetime's worth of loss in a moment. The haunting memory of her mother's blood on her hands was enough to remind her of that.